SHEILA BRANDON OMNIBUS

Children's Ward
The Lonely One
The Private Wing

BY THE SAME AUTHOR

The Meddlers
A Time to Heal
The Burning Summer
Sisters
Reprise
The Running Years
Family Chorus
The Virus Man
Lunching at Laura's
Maddie

The Performers
1 Gower Street
2 The Haymarket
3 Paddington Green
4 Soho Square
5 Bedford Row
6 Long Acre
7 Charing Cross
8 The Strand
9 Chelsea Reach
10 Shaftesbury Avenue
11 Piccadilly
12 Seven Dials

The Poppy Chronicles
1 Jubilee
2 Flanders
3 Flapper

SHEILA BRANDON OMNIBUS

Children's Ward

The Lonely One

The Private Wing

BY CLAIRE RAYNER
Writing as Sheila Brandon

WEIDENFELD AND NICOLSON
LONDON

CHILDREN'S WARD
Copyright © 1964 by Sheila Brandon

THE LONELY ONE
Copyright © 1965 by Sheila Brandon

THE PRIVATE WING
Copyright © 1971 by Sheila Brandon

Introduction
Copyright © 1989 by Claire Rayner

Published in Great Britain in 1989 by
George Weidenfeld & Nicolson Limited
91 Clapham High Street, London SW4 7TA

All rights reserved. No part of this publication
may be reproduced, stored in a retrieval system,
or transmitted in any form or by any means,
electronic, mechanical, photocopying, recording
or otherwise, without the prior permission of the
copyright owner.

ISBN 0–297–79529–5

Photoset by Deltatype Ltd, Ellesmere Port

Printed in Great Britain by
Butler & Tanner Ltd, Frome and London

CONTENTS

Introduction   vii
1 Children's Ward   1
2 The Lonely One   119
3 The Private Wing   251

INTRODUCTION
By Claire Rayner

Twenty-five or more years ago, I was a young would-be writer, trying to learn how to make my way in the world of books. I was writing for magazines and newspapers and I'd produced a couple of non-fiction books, but story-telling . . . that was a mystery to me. I knew I liked stories, of course; I've been an avid reader since before I was four years old and to this day I'm a pushover for a well-told tale. But how to tell a tale well – *that* was the mystery.

So much so that it simply did not occur to me that I might be able to write fiction. But I was persuaded to try my hand. And because I knew that it is a basic rule of the learner writer always to write what you know, I opted to write about hospital life. After twelve years of sweat, starch, tears and bedpans as a nurse and then a sister in a series of London hospitals, I had an intimate knowledge of how such establishments work. I also knew that a great many people love peering behind closed doors into worlds they don't usually get the chance to experience.

So, I had a go. I started to tell myself stories of hospital life – rather romantic, but none the worse for that – only instead of keeping them in my own head as I had when I'd been a day-dreaming youngster, I struggled to put them on paper. And to my surprise and delight I found that publishers were willing to have a go, and gamble on me. They put my words into books – and I was delighted.

But also a bit embarrassed. I know it isn't an attractive trait to admit to, but there it is – I was a bit of a snob in those days. Not a social snob, you understand, but an intellectual snob. I had the notion that stories like these were a bit 'ordinary', that what really mattered was Literature with a capital 'L' and I knew perfectly well I wasn't writing that! So instead of using my own name on my first published attempts at story-telling, I borrowed my sister's first name and a surname from elsewhere in my family. And Sheila Brandon was born.

Now I am no longer a literary snob. I know that any story-telling that gives pleasure and interest to readers is nothing to be ashamed of and has a right to exist. It may not be Literature, but then what is? Dickens was just a story-teller in his own time, the equivalent of the writers of 'Eastenders' and 'Coronation Street'. Today he is revered as a Classic. Well, these stories of mine are never going to be classics, but I don't think, now I re-read them, that I need blush too much for them. So, here they are, the first efforts of my young writing years, under my own name at last. I hope you enjoy them. Let me know, either way!

Children's Ward

1

From her desk in the glass-walled office, Harriet could see the long ward stretching dimly into the shadows, each small bed and cot humped with the figure of a sleeping child. The little boy in the third cot had both his blue pyjamaed legs stuck out through the bars, and for a moment Harriet wondered whether it would be better to leave him in the hope he would wriggle back under the covers later in the night, or whether to risk waking him by moving him now. And then she remembered wryly just how loudly he could shriek when he was disturbed, and decided to leave him in peace.

The senior night nurse moved silently through the ward, checking on each child, comforting the odd ones who were still awake and restless. There was a subdued rattle of dishes from the kitchen where one of the juniors was laying the trolleys ready for breakfast the next morning, and there was a distant heavy thumping of traffic from the main road five floors below. With a soft sigh, Harriet looked down at her desk, at the neat piles of charts, the completed day reports and lists for the next morning, and slowly reached for her white cuffs to slip them over the dark blue sleeves of her dress.

It was half past eight, and clearly there was no further excuse she could find for staying on duty any longer. Another day, she thought, another full day of activity, but without a sight of him.

I'm worse than the silliest schoolgirl, she told herself bitterly, hanging around in the hope he'll come to the ward for some reason or other – and even if he did, it probably wouldn't make any difference –

The big double doors of the ward swung open with a soft swish, and with a moment's wild hope, she peered through the glass partition to see if perhaps it had been worth hanging about after all, but the dim gleam of a white cap sent the hope stillborn back to the pit of her stomach.

Sally, soft footed, came into the office, dropping her blue cape onto the only armchair with a grunt of fatigue before sprawling long-leggedly on top of it.

'You busy too? We've been like Paddy's market today – three lists and a blasted ectopic at half past seven. At this rate I'll die of exhaustion before I'm thirty. Why I ever opted to be a theatre sister I'll never know – ' She rubbed her snub nose wearily, and peered up at Harriet. 'Aren't you finished yet? We're supposed to be meeting them at nine, remember – '

Harriet made a face. 'I hadn't forgotten,' she said, a little shamefacedly. 'I was just finishing off a few odds and ends. I'll be ready – '

'You've been hanging around waiting to see if Weston would come,' Sally said accusingly. 'Honestly, Harriet, you are a nit! Quite apart from the fact that he was in theatre till seven o'clock and probably won't do any ward rounds tonight, what's the point? It's not as though he ever paid any attention to you – and there's Paul – '

Harriet looked at her, an almost comically guilty expression on her face. 'I know, Sal. I'm an ass, I'm an idiot, I'm everything you ever care to call me, but I can't help it – he just has that effect on me.'

Sally got to her feet and came to stand beside Harriet at her desk looking down at the bent head with a sort of annoyed sympathy on her round face.

'Harriet love. Listen to me. You've got yourself into a stupid state over this man. You say yourself he never seems to notice you as a person – just treats you with a sort of remote courtesy. As far as he's concerned, you're just Sister Brett, Children's Ward. And for a whole year, you've been mooning around after him as though he were – were Adonis and the Boy David and James Bond all rolled up into one! What's the use? Forget it, lovey. Here you are with Paul ready to lie down and die for you, and all you do is take him for granted! And he's much better looking, and more fun than ten Gregory Westons! Grow up, Harriet, for God's sake – '

And Harriet couldn't argue with her. Everything Sally said was perfectly true, but no matter how often Sally said it – which was very often indeed – Harriet couldn't, or wouldn't listen to her.

From the first time Gregory Weston had come to the Royal, as surgical registrar, a year before, he had seemed to Harriet all she ever wanted in a man. Certainly he wasn't as good looking as Paul Martin, the medical registrar, with whom she had, until Gregory Weston turned up, thought herself mildly in love. Paul had fair classic good looks, a cleft chin, the physique of an athlete, a personality that made every girl on the nursing staff shiver delightedly whenever he spoke to them. And Gregory? What was it about him that made Harriet's knees turn to water at the sight of him, made her pulse beat thickly in her throat till she thought she would choke? Lean, not particularly tall – a bare three inches more than Harriet's own compact five foot five – a saturnine face under crisp dark hair grizzled with white. Perhaps it was the fact that he was a good deal older than most of his contemporaries, obviously nearer forty than thirty, perhaps it was the closed face that rarely relaxed into a smile, perhaps the low deep voice with its precise accent – but whatever it was, Harriet loved him.

And in all the year she had been cherishing this ever growing feeling for him he had never made the least sign of regarding her as any more than an efficient ward sister. Harriet's only comfort – and it was a cold one – was that he never paid any attention to anyone else at the Royal either. Most of the other men on the staff had their special friends among the nurses; over the years many of them had married girls they had met around the wards of the big London hospital, but Gregory Weston went his own self-contained way, aloof, solitary, seeming to have no need of any human contact outside his work.

Once, when Harriet had managed to ask Paul a few casual questions about him, when she was at the hospital's annual Christmas dance with him, Paul had said disgustedly, 'Old Weston? That man's got ice water in his veins instead of blood. He never joins in any of the mess affairs – pays up like a lamb whenever we whip round for a party, mind you, but goes off and spends the evening in his own room. Look, there're the others – they're making for the bar. Come and get a bit sloshed, and then we'll go and neck somewhere like civilised people – '

And Harriet had gone to have just one drink, and then pleading a fictitious headache, had slipped away, much to Paul's disgust.

Quite what she was to do about Paul, Harriet didn't know. At the beginning, before she had first seen Gregory, she had enjoyed his company, liked his casual love-making after their frequent evenings out together, had even thought seriously about accepting the proposal that her woman's intuition told her would one day come. But all that had gone, melting like snow in the sunshine, and for the past months, she had avoided Paul whenever she could, staving off the inevitable proposal as best she could. Not that her coolness had made any difference to Paul. Indeed, in a way it had made him more ardent. Paul Martin wasn't used to girls who cooled off before he did, and Harriet's arm's length attitude intrigued and piqued him. So he persisted, nagging her till she was forced to accept his invitations. Her only defence had been Sally, Sally and Stephen, the senior pathologist who regarded Sally as his personal property. They were an easy going pair, and didn't seem to mind when Harriet insisted that they made up a foursome with Paul and herself, didn't seem to notice how often Paul was irritated by their presence, sublimely ignoring his attempts to get Harriet away on her own.

Harriet pulled herself out of her reverie, and looked up into Sally's troubled face. 'I'm sorry, Sal' she said wearily. 'We'd better get changed, I suppose – or Stephen'll think you're not coming – '

'He knows me better than that,' Sally said, her face melting into a smile as she thought of her Stephen's rangy body and unruly brown hair. 'To tell you the truth, I'm more bothered about old Paul. He's awfully miserable about you, Harriet – and he's a nice chap, really, you know. You could do worse. And to be completely practical, if not romantic, you'd be more than an idiot to let him go for the sake of a starry eyed dream about a man who doesn't know whether you're alive or dead.'

Harriet grimaced. 'Come off it, Sal. I mayn't be a pocket Venus, but I hardly have to hang on to a man I don't care about just as a – a sort of insurance. There's more to life than just getting married for the sake of it – '

'I'm not so sure.' For all her soft round face and pretty ways, there was a strongly practical streak in Sally. 'Do you want to spend all your life looking after other people's sick kids? I can't see you settling down into a career for ever and a day. You ought to be married, with kids of your own – and Paul would make a very good husband. And as for not caring for him – piffle. You cared about him before you went all moony and schoolgirlish over Weston. You're just peeved because he takes no notice of you. I'll bet my all that if he once took you out, and you could really get to know him, you'd come running back to Paul with your tail between your legs – '

'Drop it, Sally,' Harriet said sharply. 'Just drop it. I may be stupid, but that doesn't give you the right to be damned rude – '

'Sorry.' Sally said penitently. 'It's just that you make me so *mad*. And I like Paul. He's too nice to be a doormat – '

'Come on,' Harriet said shortly, reaching for her own blue cape. 'Enough of talking – we'd better change.'

And Sally, who had known Harriet long enough and well enough to know when to give up, picked up her own cape, and followed her friend out of the office.

Harriet stopped by the kitchen door, and put her head round it to say 'Goodnight' to the night nurse, and the two Sisters padded softly along the dimly lit corridor towards the lift gate. Sally pressed the button, and then leaned against the iron gates, rubbing her face again with a tired gesture.

'I don't suppose we'll be going anywhere at all special – Stephen's broke again, and Paul usually is – do you suppose it'll be all right if I just put on slacks and a sweater? That'll do, won't it? And if *you* wear slacks too, it won't matter.'

Harriet nodded, peering down the lift shaft to where the cage was grinding its noisy way upwards. 'Slacks it is then – ' she said, and stood back as the lift arrived and the gates rattled open.

There was a trolley in the lift, with a small shape bundled under the red blankets, and in the corner, a young woman with her face drawn and frightened huddled against the wall, clutching miserably at a little parcel of child's clothes. And next to the trolley, one hand under the blankets to hold onto the invisible wrist of the small patient on it, stood Gregory Weston, his narrow mouth in a grim line.

'Sister!' He seemed a little surprised to see her. 'I thought you'd have gone off duty by now – is the cubicle ready?'

'Cubicle?' Harriet stared at him. 'What cubicle? I'm sorry – is this patient for my ward?'

He looked angry for a moment. 'Didn't Casualty 'phone up?' Harriet shook her head, and stood back as the porter manoeuvred the trolley out of the lift.

'I'm afraid not,' she said crisply. 'But not to worry. I'll have a cubicle ready immediately.' She looked across at Sally, who had gone into the lift and stood ready with her hand over the button. 'Sorry, Sally. I'll have to stay. The senior night nurse is new on tonight – it wouldn't be fair to lumber her – explain for me, will you?' and putting a friendly hand on the arm of the young mother who was standing looking unhappily down at the trolley, Harriet crisply shut the lift gates on Sally's exasperated face, and followed the trolley into the darkened ward.

She dropped her cape at the kitchen door, and sent the junior nurse scurrying off to prepare an isolation cubicle at the end of the ward, sent the other junior nurse to settle the young mother in the office with a cup of tea, and hurried down the ward after the trolley and Gregory Weston's lean shape.

'Boy of three,' Gregory said succinctly. 'Pulled a kettle of boiling water over himself. They're busy in Cas. so I said I'd examine him in the ward – it's cleaner here, anyway. Cas. is full of drunks. Have you a dressing trolley I can use?'

Harriet nodded, and led the way into the far cubicle, where the nurse had just pulled the cot coverings back, and put the heater on to warm the small glass walled room.

'Bring the emergency dressing trolley from the sterilising room please, Nurse Hughes,' she said, 'and set up a barrier nursing table outside this cublicle. There's a mask by the wash-basin, Mr Weston.'

Rapidly, she and Gregory masked and scrubbed their hands, ready to put on the gowns the junior brought with the trolley, and then they stood back as the nurse, at a sign from Gregory, carefully lifted the covers from the child on the trolley, before coming close enough to look down on the small figure that lay there.

He was sleeping the shallow restless sleep of shock, his small arms thrust out to each side of him, red and shiny skin swelling painfully against the sopping wet sleeves of a grubby sweater. By some miracle, his face had escaped any injury, and Harriet crouched beside the trolley, laying her face against one tear blotched cheek to murmur reassurance, as, with the delicacy of a prowling cat, Gregory began to clip the clothing away from the injured area.

The boy whimpered, and stirred, trying to pull his arm away from Gregory's gentle but firm hold, and Harriet crooned softly into the child's ear, watching Gregory's fingers as they manipulated scissors and forceps, easing the fabric away from the swollen flesh and angry red skin.

8

It took twenty minutes of careful work before the sweater and small vest, cut beyond any hope of repair, were lying on the floor beside the trolley. Gregory straightened his back, and looked down at the child who had drifted off to sleep again as soon as Gregory had finished cleaning the angry reddened scalds. 'Mmm.' He looked consideringly at the small chest and arms. 'Not too bad at all. Lucky little devil. I'll leave the blisters, Sister, for tonight. Just nurse him in the open, and tomorrow we'll have another look and see what's what. I'll put up a drip now – glucose saline, please – and he can have some nepenthe if he needs it. I'll write it up when I've got the drip going – '

By half past nine, the child was settled in bed, a special nurse sitting gowned and masked beside him to watch the slow drip of fluid into the vein in his ankle. The young mother, reassured as much as possible, had been sent home with the promise that a message would be sent if the child's condition seemed bad enough to warrant it.

In the office Gregory watched her go, and sighed impatiently, turning to where Harriet was completing the chart, to reach for the prescription sheet.

'Silly creature,' he said with cold anger. 'All this because she hadn't the wit to make sure he couldn't get at a kettle of boiling water. Some of these women don't deserve to have children.'

Harriet, chilled by his attitude, said sharply. 'It was probably less her fault than the fault of the way she has to live.' She thrust the chart at him, and pointed to the address on the cover. 'Fontana Street. That's a road of houses that should have been condemned years ago – and she told me she only has one room, and a very small room at that. It can't be easy to look after a child properly in those sort of conditions – she hasn't even got a proper cooker. She has to do all her cooking on an oil stove. With a lively three year told to look after, and pregnant again into the bargain, is it any wonder this happened?'

He signed the prescription sheet, and looked up at her under drawn brows. 'You managed to discover a lot about her?'

Embarrassed, she shrugged slightly. 'It's part of my job, isn't it? To know about patients' backgrounds, I mean. It makes a lot of difference to the sort of care they need. This boy, for instance, if he came of well-off parents, the chances are he would be well fed, and in good condition to cope with this accident. As it is, he probably eats poorly – because his mother can't afford to feed him as he should be fed, even if she really understood much about nutrition – and doesn't get enough sleep or fresh air, so he'll need extra vitamins and so on while he's in here – and a long convalescence in the country after he's better – ' She faltered. 'I'm sorry. You must be tired. I shouldn't waste your time nattering like this.'

'You're tired too, I imagine.' He made no attempt to go, sitting perched on the corner of her desk, looking down at her where she sat in her usual chair. 'I'm sorry too. I shouldn't have been so quick to criticise, I suppose. I – get angry when I see children with unnecessary injuries.'

'Don't we all!' Harriet said, and smiled up at him a little shyly. 'I didn't mean to sound so sharp – but so often doctors don't seem to know about the sort of lives their patients live outside hospital. It *does* matter.'

He nodded, still looking at her considering. 'I'm not arguing with you – you had every right to tell me off. How did you know what – ' he peered down at the chart 'what Fontana Street was like? Is your home around here? I thought all you sisters lived in the hospital.'

'We do.' Harriet said, 'And my home's in Devonshire – but when I got this post, after I finished my training, I thought I ought to know something about the district – so I went around looking.'

'Just like that?' he asked curiously. 'Just went walking around?'

Harriet nodded. 'I suppose it sounds a bit silly, really. But I like walking, and I wanted to know – '

He was silent for a moment, and then he said, with an odd diffidence, 'You make me feel a little ashamed. I ought to know more about the district too, I suppose. As you say, it helps when you come to think about patients and their diagnoses and treatment. I just never got around to looking at much outside the hospital – '

Without thinking, Harriet said, 'But how could you? You never go out.'

'How do you know that?' he asked, his voice suddenly rough.

Harriet's face flamed a hot red in embarrassment. 'I – I beg your pardon,' she stammered. 'I didn't mean to be rude – but – well, you don't, do you? I mean – well, you never go to any of the parties in the doctors' common room, and someone once said you never go out either – '

He stood up, and turned to stare through the glass partition at the darkened ward stretching into the shadows.

'No, I don't go out very much – ' he said slowly. 'It's a sort of – habit, I suppose. I never seem to get around to much at all outside my job.' He turned and looked at her, at the fading red in her face and even white teeth biting her soft lower lip in ashamed embarrassment. 'Does that sound – silly?'

'I suppose not.' Harriet managed to smooth her face into a semblance of calmness. 'If that's the sort of life you really want. But there's so much more to living than just one's job, however interesting that job may be. Anyway – ' she took a deep breath, and looked straight at him, her pulse thickening in her throat. 'I think you do a better job if you take a rest from it sometimes. Unless you really want to live like a hermit, of course – '

Any minute now, part of her mind jeered, you'll be asking him to go out with you. How silly can you get about this man, for God's sake?

'Perhaps I do – ' For a moment, his habitual grimness returned, banishing the few moments of relaxation that had been the first sign of humanity Harriet had ever really seen in him. But then, he sat down on the corner of her desk and looked at her again.

'Sister – Brett – Harriet, isn't it?' She nodded wordlessly. 'As you say, I really ought to know a bit more about the district this hospital is serving. And as you seem to know it pretty well, perhaps you'd spare some time to show me around it? If you aren't too busy – '

'I'd like to,' she said, a little breathlessly. 'I can always find time to walk – I enjoy walking – it's more fun in the country, at home, but even here, in streets and in all the traffic it's quite pleasant – ' she was gabbling a little, so full was she of delighted surprise. 'Just let me know when you can manage it, and I'll arrange my off duty accordingly – '

He nodded gravely. 'I have a half day this Friday. Will that be suitable?'

She nodded too, and smiled brilliantly. 'Fine. I'll be off about two o'clock.'

'That's settled then.' He got to his feet, and went to the door. 'And I'll be up in the morning to see this child again. He may need to go to theatre to have those blisters snipped. I'll decide tomorrow. Goodnight, Sister Brett.'

'Goodnight, Mr Weston.' Harriet said, and sat in a bemused silence long after the double doors had stopped their swishing behind his departure, guiltily blessing the child whose scald with a kettle of boiling water had made her so happy.

2

Harriet was perched on top of a ladder sorting through the top shelf of the linen cupboard when Sally put her head round the door.

'Hello,' Harriet said absently. 'Fifteen nightgowns – five bibs – honestly, I think those babies must eat them. We've lost nineteen since the last inventory.'

'The nurses probably use 'em as dusters, if your lot are anything like mine. I've lost six dressing towels since the last count. But at least I've finished my inventory. Why are you so late with yours?'

'We do work here sometimes.' Harriet said. 'I've had three babies with pneumonia this last week, on top of all the usual surgical stuff – I haven't had time.' She put the last pile of clothes back on the shelf, and came down the ladder to make a note in the linen book. 'Now, what can I do for you? I haven't had a chance to get the list for tomorrow straight yet, so if that's what you're after you'll have to wait. I'll do it after lunch.'

'No – ' Sally grinned. 'I'm off tomorrow, so the list'll be Staff Nurse Baker's headache. I want to know what's happening tonight – if you don't mind my asking,' she finished sarcastically.

'Oh – tonight.' Harriet led the way out of the linen cupboard, and Sally followed her into the ward. They picked their way over the small groups of children playing on the floor, dodging an active game of tag played by two small boys both of whom had one eye covered with a bandage, an affliction that seemed to hamper them not one whit. Harriet scooped a diminutive child up from an absorbed game of scribbling on the floor and with a pat on his pyjamaed behind sent him off to the lavatory, correctly interpreting his wriggling as an urgent need to visit there. 'If I don't watch that one, we get puddles all over the place,' Harriet said, watching the child trot off obediently. 'I don't think his mother ever got around to explaining to him what lavatories are for.'

'Harriet,' Sally said with exaggerated patience. 'Will you please concentrate on me for a moment? I want to know what is to happen tonight. Are you coming with us, or aren't you?'

Together, they went into the office, and Harriet sat down at her desk and swung her chair round to look at her friend where she sprawled in the armchair.

'I don't want to,' she said. 'You know I don't. But what can I do? Paul just won't take no for an answer.'

'Then you *are* coming?' Sally said.

'I suppose so. I wish Paul wouldn't nag so – '

'What it is to be Harriet Brett!' Sally said theatrically. 'Two men on a string! How do you do it? What have you got that I haven't? Just the same, if a little less of it – ' and she looked down at her round shape with a sigh. 'How goes things on the Weston front?'

Harriet grimaced at the pun, and said 'I don't know what you mean – ' avoiding Sally's eye as she said it.

'Come off it! You know damned well what I mean! You've been going around with him for nearly two months now. Are you any nearer getting to know him than you were before?'

Harriet sighed. 'Not really,' she said unwillingly. 'We walk a lot and talk a lot, but that's about all.' She leaned back in her chair, and stared down the ward absently. 'It's odd, you know. I've told him all about myself – about the family, that sort of thing, and he seems interested – asks about them, asks about me – what I like, what I don't like. But somehow we never get around to talking about him. For all I know, he just happened – like Topsy. He never says anything at all about his own background, or where he comes from – '

'Have you asked him – outright, I mean?' Sally said curiously. 'I would.'

Harriet smiled. 'I know you would. If I didn't tell you everything you want to know about my private life you'd only nag me skinny till I did – '

'Why not? If you don't ask, you never know – and I like to know. *Have* you asked him about himself?'

Harriet shook her head.

'He's not that sort of man. I don't deny I've – fished a bit. But he always clams up, and I'm not the sort to persist when someone isn't willing to talk. So there it is – '

'Has he ever kissed you?' Sally asked baldly.

'Sally, really!' Harriet said crossly. 'You go too far sometimes – '

'Has he?' Sally ignored the protest.

'No,' Harriet said shortly. For a moment, she remembered the way he always seemed not to notice her upturned face whenever he brought her back to the nurses' home, the way her whole body ached to feel his hands over hers when they sat side by side in a theatre or cinema, the way he got out of the car as soon as they got back to the hospital, never once lingering as other men did after a date – as Paul always did.

'I suppose he's all right.' Sally said, a question in her voice.

'All right?' Harriet echoed, and stared at Sally, 'What do you mean?'

Sally shrugged, embarrassed for once. 'You know what I mean. Some men just – never make passes at women.'

Harriet reddened with a mixture of embarrassment and anger. 'If you are suggesting he's at all queer, you're wrong,' she said shortly. 'I've been around long enough to recognise a man when I meet one. He's perfectly "all right" as you put it. I'm sure of that. No – it's something else – '

What she didn't tell Sally about and didn't intend to yet, if she could help it – though she knew quite well that Sally would get it out of her eventually – was the conversation they had had the last time they had been out together. They had been sitting over the remains of dinner at a small restaurant Gregory had taken her to once before, and he had said suddenly, without looking at her, 'Harriet – I want to talk to you.'

She had looked up from the glass of amber wine she had been twisting between her fingers, and said softly, her heart lifting with a wild hope for a moment, 'Yes? What is it, Gregory?'

He had leaned back in his seat, so that his face was hidden in the shadows of the dimly lit restaurant.

'You – do you enjoy these evenings we spend together? The afternoons when we walk around the streets? Or do you just come because you're sorry for me? Think I'm lonely, and that you can help me to be less of a hermit?'

Harriet had smiled then. 'Of course I enjoy them, Gregory. I wouldn't come otherwise. I'm not the sort to go in for pity, you know. Not like that. Any pity I've got I use in my job. Outside of that, I live like anyone else – doing what I want to do, because I want to do it. I don't see you as a pitiful object anyway.'

'I'm glad of that,' he had said gravely. 'I'd hate to think you were just – mothering me. I don't like motherly women.' He had paused then, and after a moment went on with an oddly painful note in his voice. 'I enjoy these times we spend together, too, Harriet. They – they've come to mean a lot to me. Are you a patient woman, Harriet?'

She had stared at him then, surprised by the sudden shift.

'Patient? I don't know. It depends. I can be, I think. If I *must* wait to get what I want, then I *can* wait – is that what you mean?'

He had leaned forward then, so that she could see his face, see the red lamplight glinting on his cheekbones, deepening the fine lines round his mouth.

'I can't explain now – not really. But it's just this. Would you be willing to go on as we are – going out like this, seeing each other whenever we're off duty together, and leave it at that – just for a while? It's a lot to ask, I know. You're a – popular girl, aren't you? I mayn't spend much time in the mess, but I'm there often enough to know that Martin regards you rather highly – '

Harriet reddened. 'Paul is – is an old friend,' she said a little brusquely. 'I've known him a long time.'

'Yes – I gathered that. Harriet – would it be asking a lot of you to go on seeing me? And then, in eighteen months' time, perhaps – perhaps we can talk about the future.' His voice died away, and for a long moment, Harriet stared at him.

'Eighteen months?' she asked at length. 'Eighteen months? I – I don't understand.'

'I can't explain – not now,' he had said miserably. 'I will be able to – then. But not now. Are you patient, Harriet? Can you accept that and understand enough not to ask questions?'

She had sat and looked at him, at the face she had come to love so much, the deep set eyes, the glint of white in his dark hair, and thought confusedly, Wait? What for? For you to love me? Will you ever love me? Are you trying to tell me that you do care for me now? And if you do, why must you wait for so long to 'talk of the future'?

He had seemed to interpret her silence as refusal, for he had leaned back, and said in a flat voice, 'I'm sorry, Harriet. I had no right to suggest it. It's a lot to ask a woman to take on trust.'

She had put her hand out impulsively, and said softly, 'You had all the right in the world, Gregory. I can't pretend to understand – but that doesn't matter. I – ' she picked her words with care. 'I enjoy your company a great deal, Gregory. I would be very unhappy if we couldn't see each other as we do. And if you want to go on as we are, that's fine with me.'

He had stared at her then, his face lifting into a rare smile. 'Thank you, Harriet. Thank you. I – my God, I wish I could explain – but I can't – not yet – '

'Then don't try. If you don't want to talk about anything, you don't have to. I'm not a baby, Gregory. I'm a grown woman – and I hope I'm intelligent enough to accept a situation I can't understand yet in the promise that I will understand it eventually. Gregory – ' she had looked down at her hands, loosely clasped on the table-cloth, and with a steady voice that surprised her, she said, 'Gregory – you know, don't you? Know I – I care a good deal for you?' She lifted her eyes to look at him. 'I'm not good at pretending, Gregory. And there it is.'

'I know,' he had said in a low voice. 'That's why I – why I had to ask you to wait for me. I – I care for you too, Harriet. More than you might suspect. Just give me time, Harriet. Just time.'

And that had been all. They had gone back to the hospital in silence, not a strained one, but a silence full of thought on both their parts, though Harriet couldn't even begin to try to imagine just what form Gregory's thinking was taking. He had said goodnight with his usual formality, only saying 'thank you' in a low voice before driving back to the main courtyard from the Nurses' Home, leaving Harriet staring after the winking tail lights of his car, her mind whirling.

Even now, two days later, she couldn't assess her own feelings. Part of her was full of relief, relief that this man she loved with all her heart cared for her. But the rest of her mind seethed with questions. Why eighteen months? Why hadn't he made any attempt to kiss her? He must know – she was sure he knew – how much she wanted to feel his touch. And she knew, too, with all the woman in her, that he wanted to hold her close. Why didn't he? Why?

Sally's voice pulled her out of her abstraction.

'Here's Paul,' she said hurriedly. 'I'm going.'

Harriet looked across the ward to the big double doors where Paul Martin's tall figure was standing with a small girl clutching at his white coat. He looked up and saw her at the same moment, and disentangling the child he made his way with an oddly purposeful tread towards the office.

'Don't go, Sally,' Harriet said urgently. 'Stay – '

'Not on your life, ducky,' Sally said. 'I'm sick of playing gooseberry to you two. You settle this on your own. 'Bye!' and she slipped out of the office, to stop and say a few words to Paul before disappearing through the doors.

He came in to stand beside the desk, where she immediately busied herself over a chart, trying to present a calm façade.

'Hello, Harriet,' he said, putting a hand on her shoulder to pull her round so that she had to look at him.

'Hello, Paul,' she said with a brightness that rang false even in her own ears.

'Have you come to see that child with the Still's disease? He's doing very well on steroids – '

'No I haven't,' he said flatly. 'I've come to see you.'

'Paul, really, I can't stop now just for social visits. I've far too much to do – the ward's pretty busy – '

'You're always too busy to see me. And you've broken more dates than I care to count. The way you go on, you'd think no one else worked on this ward. You can't be kept late on duty *every* night – and you know damned well you're avoiding me. What is it, Harriet? What have I done?'

She rubbed her face wearily. 'I'm sorry, Paul – truly I am. But – I have been busy, really I have.'

'You didn't used to be,' he said softly. 'Not at first. Remember?'

'That was a long time ago, Paul. Things change – ' she looked at him miserably. 'Please, Paul, don't force me to say hurtful things. I've tried to show you – but you keep persisting – '

'What else can I do?' he said roughly. 'I *need* you, Harriet – and all you do is slip away all the time – I can't *get* at you. You hide behind Stephen and Sally whenever we're together – you never give us a chance to be on our own – what's the matter, for Christ's sake? I thought – I thought you cared for me once.'

'I thought so too, Paul,' Harriet said unhappily. 'But I – I was wrong, I suppose. Can't we just – just be friends? Please, Paul – try to understand.'

He looked at her, his face full of misery. 'Friends? Is that the best you can do, Harriet? I love you – you know that, don't you? I want – I want to marry you, Harriet – '

'Don't – please, Paul, don't!' She couldn't bear the misery on his face, the look of a slapped child that filled his eyes.

'It's no use bleating "Don't!" at me,' he said, anger suddenly flaring at him. 'It's a bit late for that now. At the beginning you weren't like this. If you hadn't been so affectionate then, do you suppose I'd have got myself into this state over you? What do you think I am, for God's sake? A bloody idiot? You can't just act as though you love me one minute and drop me like a piece of garbage the next! Is that all you are – one of those women who like to get a man into a state and then stand back and watch him squirm while you giggle?'

She closed her eyes in sick distress for a moment.

'I suppose I deserved that,' she said at length. 'But it isn't true, Paul. I don't deny I thought I cared for you at first – but I was wrong. And that's that. I've been trying to avoid this – this sort of scene. I thought if I avoided *you* you'd understand and we could end an episode with – with dignity and still be friends. I was wrong. I should have told you outright.'

He thrust his hands deep into the pockets of his white coat and turned to stare down the ward.

'I'm sorry, I shouldn't have said that,' he said at last. 'I should have known better than to think I could salvage anything out of this by being – unpleasant. I've been trying to persuade myself it wasn't true, I suppose. About you and Weston.'

'Weston?' she said awkwardly.

'This is a hospital, remember? You don't suppose you can go around with someone here without everyone knowing about it, do you?'

'I hadn't thought of that,' she said slowly. 'I'm sorry, Paul. But at least you know now.'

'I can't think what you see in him,' Paul turned from the window to look at her. 'Look, Harriet – this isn't just me being a – a bad loser. But he's an odd bloke – secretive. No one knows anything about him. At his age – well, he's a bit of an oddity. Most men at his stage are married. For all you know he *is* – had you thought of that?'

She stared at him, her chin lifting. 'I'm not going to discuss him with you, Paul. It's none of your concern.'

'No – I suppose not. The fact that I love you and I'm stupid enough to go on loving you even when you don't want me to gives me no right to be interested in what happens to you,' he said bitterly. 'I'm sorry to be a nuisance.'

'Please, Paul – don't be so angry,' she said impulsively. 'It's – it's very kind of you to be concerned. But this is my affair. And whatever Gregory is or isn't, I – care for him. Please, try to accept that, will you?'

'I've no choice, have I?' He went to the door, and pushed it open. 'Forget tonight's date, then, Harriet. Let me break this one for once, hmm? It'll make a change,' and he pushed his way out of the ward, ignoring the children who looked up at him in surprise, missing the sweets he usually carried in his pockets for them.

She stood and stared after him, sick with misery, yet at the same time oddly relieved that the whole thing had happened. At least he knew now, at least he would stop following her around, forcing her to think up ever more excuses for not going out with him. But –

A nurse put her head round the office door.

'The lunch trolley is up, Sister,' she said. 'Are you ready to serve them?'

'Mmm? Oh, yes. I'm just coming – '

She served the children's meals abstractedly, filling plates with minced beef and vegetables, making sure that all the toddlers were fed, checking the special diets automatically. And all the time, Paul's voice rang over and over in her mind.

'Most men at his stage are married. For all you know he *is* – had you thought of that?'

And it was this that surprised her. Because she hadn't. In all the long hours she had spent thinking about Gregory, about his need for time, his promise that after eighteen months they could 'talk about the future' it had never occurred to her that he might be married, that it might be this that stood between them.

She sent the nurses to their own lunch, and settled the children in their cots for their afternoon naps, pulling blinds so that the thin winter sunshine was blotted out, walking round the ward softly, promising the unhappy ones that their mothers would soon be coming to visit them, wiping lunch-smeared faces clean, giving chocolate to those who could have it. And all the time, her thoughts whirled with a sick persistence. Why? Was he married? Wasn't he?

For the rest of that long afternoon, as she went through the usual routine that was the day's work she thought about it. And at half past six, when she went off duty for the evening, she had at last come to a decision. She would ask him. He had asked for patience, but she would ask him for this one explanation. She had to know.

3

There was a bitter wind blowing, whipping her apron high, tugging at her cap, as she hurried across the courtyard through the early darkness of the winter evening. But cold as it was, she paused for a moment at the gate that opened on to the Nurses Home path, and looked back across the wide courtyard at the hospital.

The main ward block loomed blackly into the wintry sky, pierced at regular intervals with the oblong yellow patches that were the ward windows. She could see the shapes of nurses flitting past each window as they hurried round the wards, preparing the patients for supper, see high on the fifth floor the dimmer red oblongs that were the windows of her own ward, where the children were already asleep. There was a faint white patch out on the balcony, and automatically she thought – Nurse Jenkins – she's forgotten to bring those bits of washing in again. It's no wonder we lose linen. Those nightgowns'll blow away any minute. I'll give her a rocket in the morning –

It's odd, she thought. This place is full of misery for so many people. Everything about it is alarming. The huge impersonal mass of it, the faint smell of antiseptic and anaesthetics that could be recognised even out here, in the windy courtyard. Visitors, patients -- they can't get away from the place quickly enough. But for me, this is home, this is security. For a brief moment, she let her mind run off into fantasy, imagining herself working here for the rest of her life, giving all of herself to the illnesses of other people, gaining peace of mind and security while she did it. Wouldn't that be better – infinitely better – than this aching yearning inside her, this longing for one person's presence, this need for one man's touch? She felt as though she were poised on the edge of a huge pool of water. She could choose – still choose,

choose whether to turn back from the edge to the safety of dry land that stood behind, or whether to take a big breath and leap into the water in front of her, the water that symbolised in her fantasy the relationship she was trying to build with Gregory, the relationship that she was trying to end with Paul.

And then, her intellect took over, and with a wry grin in the darkness she remembered her psychology lectures. Water, in dreams and fantasies – water was the recognised symbol of sex. The psychologists are right, she told herself. Why else would I see myself as standing on the edge of a pool, why else do I see my situation as that of a swimmer battling against huge waves, being buffeted by the sheer weight of blue water? I wish I were less of a woman, that I didn't have this need for Gregory. But there was no escaping it. She had already jumped into her pool, was already committed to building her future with Gregory, and no matter how much she wanted to turn back, avoid the uncertainty that the future seemed to hold, she could not. She loved him. There was nothing else to be done but go on loving him.

Shivering a little, she turned and hurried on. I'll phone him, she thought, see if he's off duty tonight, and suggest we go out for a drink somewhere. And then I'll ask him. I must. If he is married, I must know. Quite what she would do if he admitted he was, she didn't allow herself to consider. That hazard must be dealt with as it arose. No amount of thought now could guide her. As she got to the Home, and stood in the brightly lit hall, blinking a little as she shook the creases out of her apron, the receptionist who sat all day in the little cubby hole that held the small Home switchboard put her head out of the door, and called, 'Sister Brett!'

'Letter for me?' Harriet asked. There should be a letter from Sybil, her sister. She hadn't written for a week or more, though Harriet had learned to accept her sister's spasmodic letters as normal; a busy Vicar's wife, with three small children of her own, a couple of foster children, as well as all the parish work to do and a huge rambling house to look after, had little time for the luxury of letter writing.

'Yes, Sister.' The receptionist smirked at her with elephantine roguishness. 'A special one – internal mail, you could call it. Brought it himself, he did. It's here – ' She fumbled beneath the cluttered shelf in front of the switchboard, and brought out a small parcel, wrapped in white tissue paper, with a square white envelope stuck to it with a piece of transparent sticky tape.

Surprised, Harriet took it. The envelope had 'Sister Brett' written on it in a strong slanting handwriting, and for a moment she stared at it in mystification.

The receptionist giggled, and said again, 'Brought it in himself he did. Isn't that nice?'

'Who brought it?' Harriet asked stupidly.

'Why, that nice looking doctor did – I don't know his name, mind you – I don't get to see the doctors very often. Know their voices on the 'phone, like, but not their faces. Very distinguished he looks, doesn't he? I like a man as *looks* like a man myself. And that grey in his hair – very distinguished looking, isn't it, Sister?'

'Yes – ' Harriet said absently, 'Very distinguished. Thank you, Miss Chester – '

She took the parcel and the letter up to her room to open them, much to the disappointment of Miss Chester, who liked to share in as much of the nursing staff's life as she could. Even watching someone open a letter gave her a vicarious thrill, a sense of sharing in a busy life, for her own was notable only for its lack of incident.

Harriet sat on the edge of her bed, her cape in a heap on the floor at her feet, and put the little white parcel down beside her. Slowly, she pulled her cap off, and ran her fingers through her hair, staring at the writing on the envelope like a woman in a trance.

Why on earth should he write to me? Has he had second thoughts? Is he regretting saying what he did – the promise of 'talk about the future' in eighteen months time? I won't open it – panic rose in her – I won't.

But she shook her head in impatience at her own stupidity, and pulling her scissors from her belt, slit the thick white envelope.

'My dear Harriet' – the strong slanting writing began – 'you will no doubt think me quite absurd to be writing to you in this way when I am so near to you, when I could come to the ward to talk to you, could arrange for us to go out somewhere where we could talk face to face. But I find it a great deal easier to talk to you like this, with a pen and paper. I've lost the habit – if I ever had it, which I begin to doubt – of being able to say all I would like to say in the usual way. So, a letter.

I want to thank you, Harriet, for your promise of patience, your calm acceptance of what must seem to you an unpleasant secretiveness on my part. I have learned to care a great deal for your opinion of me – long before that scalded child gave me an opportunity to take you out of the hospital somewhere, to have your company away from a ward full of children and nurses, I wanted to do just that. And I was right in what I had first seen in you. You have a serenity, an adult maturity of understanding that I would not have expected in someone as young as you are. I'm thirty eight, you know – and you're just twenty five. But even though I have thirteen years on you, you make me feel that in some ways you are infinitely older than I am with that maturity that is so wonderful a part of you.

It is that maturity in you that makes me so happy now. I know I need not fear what I would certainly have to fear in any other woman – a probing, a nagging if you like, an inability to accept without questions. Because I could not bear to be questioned. Believe me, if I could explain to you now why I cannot say to you all that I would like to say, why I cannot yet give you all I would like to give you, I would. But with you, I need not be afraid, need I? Thank you for that, Harriet.

But even if I cannot yet give what I want to give, I can offer you one concrete object as a small token of my appreciation and esteem. Please accept it.

And please, don't let us talk of this letter when we meet to go to the theatre next Friday. I'm so very bad at talking.
Gregory.'

She let the letter drop onto her lap, and stared out of her window at the few stars that shone steadily in the dark panes, at her reflection, a little twisted by the distortion in the glass, and felt again that odd mixture of joy and frustration that she was coming to recognise as an inevitable part of her feeling for Gregory.

So that's that. I can't ask him now. How could I? Not now. For a moment she hated Paul, Paul whose hurt anger had made him suggest that Gregory was a married man, that he was too secretive to be otherwise. Until Paul had said so, it had never occurred to her that this might be the case. But then her anger subsided, for she realised quite well that the same thought would have come to her eventually, even if Paul had never said anything.

Her hand slid off her lap, and with a start, she looked down at the little parcel that it had touched. Slowly, she picked it up, and began to peel off the layers of tissue paper.

It was a tiny piece of French porcelain, a model of a girl sitting on a bench, her lap full of flowers. It was barely three inches high, yet every detail of the tiny face was perfect, each petal of every flower breathtakingly beautiful in its minute detail. The colour was exquisite, the girl's dress falling to her delicate feet in folds of cerulean blue, the flowers in tints of pale lemon and pink, with shimmering green leaves. And the girl herself had hair that was the colour of sherry, a soft amber tinted brown, each carefully modelled strand of hair curling with a reality that made it look as though it could be curled round a finger, if there were a finger small enough to do it. Her eyes, eyes that looked into the distance with a melancholy that seemed to transmit itself to the beholder, were the same colour, with minute flecks of lighter amber in them.

Harriet stared at the lovely thing, and then, without stopping to think, took it across the room to her dressing table. She switched on the light in front of the mirror, and bent to look into the glass, holding the little figure against her face. The hair was exactly the same colour as her own, the eyes that looked so remotely into the mirror seemed to sparkle a little, seemed to recognise the same amber flecks in the depths of Harriet's own eyes.

She put it down in front of the light, and sank slowly into the chair in front of the dressing table. The little figure threw its shadow in front of itself, the girl's face seeming to droop sadly in the flood of light above it, the tiny mouth looking as though it would tremble into life at any moment.

And then, Harriet wept, drooping her head into her hands and giving herself up to an agony of sobbing that seemed as though it would shake her to pieces.

So lost was she in her weeping, so isolated in her distress, she didn't hear the door open behind her, didn't realise that she wasn't alone until she felt Sally's hands on her shoulders.

'Harriet – Harriet, honey, what is it? What's the matter? Is something wrong at home? What is it, love?' Sally dropped to her knees beside Harriet, and pulled her round till she was weeping against her friend's shoulder, patting the heaving back in an effort to stop the tearing gulping sobs.

Gradually, Harriet regained control of herself, managed to sit up again, groping for a handkerchief to mop at her red eyes.

'I'm sorry, Sally – I didn't mean – I'm sorry – ' she said huskily, scrubbing at her face, blowing her nose, trying to control the painful breathing that still tugged unevenly at her chest.

Sally, practical as always, thrust her hand into her pocket, and pulled out a crumpled pack of cigarettes. Gently, she put one between Harriet's shaking lips, and lit it.

'I'll be right back,' she said crisply, and went purposefully from the room to return a few seconds later with a toothglass in her hand.

'Here you are, lovey. Whisky,' she said. 'I keep it for Stephen, but he can spare this one.'

Harriet took it, and coughed a little as the raw spirit pulled at her throat, then relaxed slowly as the warmth of it began to spread through her chilled body.

Sally sat down on the bed, and looked at Harriet where she slumped in the dressing table chair.

'Now, lovey. Tell me what's upset you.' Then, as Harriet began to shake her head, she said, a little roughly, 'You'd be much better if you did – I'm not just prying, Harriet, believe me, but talking about whatever it is'll help. Come on, now.'

Harriet stubbed out the cigarette and stood up, going to stand at the window, to stare out at the winter darkness, the deep shadows under the trees of the Nurses' Home garden, breathing deeply of the rich wet smell of rotting leaves that came up through the slightly opened window.

'It's all such a mess, Sally,' she said at length, her voice heavy with reaction. 'Such a mess.'

'Gregory? Or Paul?' Sally asked from behind her.

'Both, I suppose.' Almost in surprise, Harriet realised that her storm of tears owed as much to her distress at the scene with Paul that morning as to her feeling about Gregory. 'He – Paul – we had an argument, if you can call it that, this morning. But he knows now. I won't be going out with him any more – and he won't ask me to again either.'

She turned to look at Sally then, came to sit beside her.

'I want it that way, believe me, Sal. But – well, it's been a long time, hasn't it? And even if I don't love him now, I did once – a little. It hurts when things die, even if you want them to. And I hate making Paul so miserable. He's a – a bit like a child, in some ways. I feel as though I've abandoned him. Or does that sound arrogant? I don't know – '

'No, you aren't being arrogant, Harriet. He does need you, I think. And he is a bit – immature, I suppose. He needs people all the time – needs their admiration to bolster himself in his own estimation,' Sally said. 'But that immaturity'll be his salvation, in a way. He'll – what's the word? – he'll rationalise his way out of this. Does he know about Gregory?'

Harriet nodded.

'It's just as well,' Sally went on. 'I mean, he'll be less hurt, in a way. It would have been much worse for him if you'd rejected him just because you found you didn't care for him. This way, he'll see himself as a sort of – honourable loser. Do you know what I mean?'

Harriet managed a smile, and put her hand out to touch Sally's. 'Bless you, Sal. You make me mad sometimes, but you know how to say the sort of things that'll help me when I need help. I think you're probably right. Paul will get over this. I'm not the end of his world, and I needn't persuade myself that I am. It's a comfort.'

'But it wasn't only Paul you were crying about, was it?' Sally said shrewdly. 'What else, Harriet?'

And Harriet, lost as she was in the conflicting state of her feelings about Gregory, told her. About his need for time, his request for patience on her part, the letter, the gift of the porcelain girl and her lapful of flowers.

'What can I do, Sally?' she asked piteously. 'What can I do? I love him – it's as though I never felt anything in my life before I felt this. He's everything to me – if he didn't exist, I think I wouldn't – not properly. I'd just be a shell without this feeling. I'm lost, Sal – lost,' and for a moment, tears rose in her again, threatening to swamp her in a luxury of bitter weeping.

Sally put a strong warm hand on Harriet's cold one, and said with brisk practicality. 'Then you'll have to learn to live *with* it, Harriet. I can't pretend to understand properly – I guess I'm just not made for the grand passion. But you – you're different. All you can do is hold on to things as they are. If he loves you – and you think he does – '

For a moment Harriet stopped to think, and then relaxed. She didn't need to think.

'Yes,' she said softly. 'He loves me. I know that, if I know nothing else. He hasn't said so in so many words, but he loves me. It's odd, really. I know it as surely as I know I love him – '

'Well, then, it's all right, isn't it? People like me and Stephen –

well, if things don't pan out for us, it's because we're not made as people like you and Gregory are. But they'll come right for you, Harriet. They'll have to, won't they? God knows how, but it'll *have* to come right. If he's anything like you are – and I suppose he must be, or you wouldn't love him as you do – then it's inevitable. Whatever happens in between, somehow it'll come right.' Sally grinned a little shyly. 'I'm not explaining this well, Harriet, I suppose. It's just something I feel. Like algebra.'

Diverted for a moment, Harriet stared at her.

'You know – you can't understand exactly, you struggle with all those ghastly figures and a's and b's and x's and y's, and you think none of it can possibly make sense – but all the time you know it does, really. That there's an answer there somewhere, a logical obvious answer if only you can find it.' Sally groped a little. 'That's how it is with you. You're lost in a mess of numbers and letters, and you can't see the way out. But it's there – somehow, it *is* there – '

And suddenly, Harriet knew she was right. No matter what misery she felt now, no matter what happened, somehow it would one day be right. She and Gregory. Together, one day, they would find the obvious logical perfect answer to everything they had ever needed.

4

Harriet was more than usually grateful for Christmas this year. As she sat at breakfast the next morning, a little abstracted over her coffee and toast, the voices of the other Sisters, discussing with varying degrees of anticipation the preparations they would be making for the holiday in their own wards, she pulled her thoughts away from her private problems, and forced herself to think about what would be happening on the children's ward. Sally grinned at her approvingly as Harriet turned to the Sister from the Maternity block and asked her whether she could share her Crib fittings this year. The Sister from the Maternity block immediately assured Harriet that she hadn't as much as an Ox or an Ass to spare, so many pieces of her Crib had been broken the year before, and Sally laughed at Harriet's chagrined face as the other Sister swept huffily from the dining room.

'Attagirl!' she said softly. 'Much better for you to get peeved with old Misery-Chops than think about Gregory or Paul. I must say – I'm damned grateful I'm on Theatres come Christmas. We may have a hell of a life all the year round, but at least we don't have to spend hours filling stockings and decorating wards – '

'Oh, I don't know,' Harriet said, ignoring the reference to her problems with the men in her life. 'It wouldn't be Christmas for me if I didn't have a ward full of children to think about – I enjoy the rush – and the stockings are fun. And since you aren't busy yourself, you can come and help me with them. I'll have thirty to fill, and that means hours of shopping. I'll see how much money the office have for me to spend this year, and let you know when we're going to get the stuff – and you aren't getting out of helping, I promise you – '

'Why can't I keep my big mouth shut?' Sally groaned. 'I swear I'll be too busy – '

'Nuts!' said Harriet, firmly. 'You can come shopping with me – and if you're good, I might even let you wrap the sweets for the stockings. You'll love that – you can eat yourself sick on jelly babies – '

The next three weeks went by in a rush of normal ward work complicated by Christmas preparations. Each afternoon, the children who were well enough collected around the big table in the middle of the ward, dressing gown sleeves rolled up, piles of coloured strips of paper in front of them, a glue pot apiece and a brush clutched in each small hand, to manufacture strings of rather grubby and wobbly paper chains. Harriet loved these afternoons. The children were so happy, so absorbed in their paper work, and she would look at the small concentrating faces shining under the big lights, pink tongues held between teeth, happy to see them so involved. It's a wonderful thing to be so young, she would think sometimes, so utterly wrapped up in the present. When you are five, tomorrow has little meaning – only today – this very minute – counts, and Harriet watched the children, and learned to be like them, thinking only of the moment and its work, thinking nothing about tomorrow and its problems.

The day before Christmas Eve, she and her nurses set to work to decorate the ward. The children were full of excitement, squealing joyfully as the nurses dragged the big boxes of prepared paper chains and tree trimmings into the ward, jumping excitedly on their beds and cots as Harriet began to blow up balloons. For the children Christmas had already begun, and Harriet laughed a little ruefully as she listened to the noise they made, the shrieks of joy whenever a balloon, blown too enthusiastically, burst loudly into shreds of coloured rubber.

'They'll all need tranquillisers tonight,' she told her staff nurse above the hubbub. 'At this rate, they'll all be dead from excitement before tomorrow – '

But she caught their excitement, too, as several of the doctors arrived in the ward to join in the fun of decorating. However busy the rest of the hospital was, most of the staff tried to come to the children's ward for a while to help – it was the warmest and happiest place in the building at Christmas. In the other wards, patients tended to be depressed and miserable, sad to be spending Christmas in hospital instead of at home, but here, the children were just plain happy, even the homesick ones joining in the laughter and the oohs and ahs of delight as each gay string of paper snaked across the ward.

By six o'clock, the decorating was finished. Bright loops of paper chains covering the ceiling, crisscrossing round the lights in a fretwork of red and blue and yellow and green, balloons hung in fat bunches over each bed, and the huge Christmas Tree in the middle of the ward shimmered with tinsel and the fairy lights, strings of fluffy white popcorn gleaming gently against the deep green of the branches, translucent baubles swaying and turning in every breath of a draught that moved across the big room. Harriet turned the main lights off when the tree was finished, and stood at the end of the ward looking at the children perched on their beds as they stared at the tree with flushed faces, eyes sparkling in the reflection of light from the strings of winking fairy bulbs, gazing up at the big twinkling star that Harriet had fixed firmly to the topmost branch.

The ward slid into a breathless silence as the children stared, open-mouthed and absorbed, and the adults stood in the shadows and looked sympathetically at them. Harriet's heart twisted sharply with pity as she looked at them, sad that their very youth was so transient. Soon, very soon, she thought sombrely, they'll grow up and the world won't be a sparkling place any more, a place of gay Christmas trees and tinsel and balloons. And then she shook herself impatiently and began to tuck the children in for the night, quietly shooing out the doctors and nurses from other wards, so that the children could be soothed into a restful state of mind, ready for sleep.

The following day was full of activity, as Harriet and her nurses tried to fit the business of stocking filling into the day's routine. The children were all excited, as parents brought mysterious parcels to stack on each bedside locker, as more parcels piled up under the Tree, ready to be distributed next day by Santa Claus. There was an hilarious half hour for the nurses in the kitchen when Dr Bennett, the senior consultant, came to be fitted for the Santa Claus suit, and stood awkward and self conscious as Harriet draped the red suit round his lean frame, and showed him how to hook the fluffy white beard over his ears.

It was long past six when the stockings were ready to be distributed, lying in piles on the floor of Harriet's office, and then Harriet and the nurses set about the solemn ritual of hanging empty stockings on each bed and cot. Harriet was nothing if not thorough, and she had collected thirty empty stockings, huge white operating ones, to be hung on each bed, as well as preparing thirty full of toys and sweets and fruit.

She went from bed to bed, cot to cot, tucking each small body under the covers, carefully helping each child hook his white stocking on the end of his bed, promising them all that Santa Claus would come. One small boy, a five year old wearing a big bandage over the head injury he had got in a traffic accident asked her anxiously how Santa Claus would know where he was?

'Last year, I was at home,' he explained worriedly. 'An' he knows where I live. I haven't told him I'm here now – how will he know?'

'I 'phoned him,' Harriet assured him gravely. 'This morning. I 'phoned him specially, to tell him who was here this year, and he said that would be all right – '

'Oh – ' the little boy thought for a minute, 'Well, that's all right then. Mummy said he's bringing a puppy this year, you see, so it's important. It'd be awful if he took the puppy and put him in the wrong stocking, wouldn't it?' and he snuggled happily down under the covers, peering trustfully up at Harriet.

'Ah – well, now, the puppy,' Harriet said, thinking fast. 'He did mention that – and asked me to give you a message. He said would you mind if he sent the puppy to your house? He's got some other things to bring for your stocking here, but he thought it would be better if he took the puppy to your house – he's a shy puppy, you see, and Santa Claus thought he might be a bit upset with all these people around – '

The little boy bit his lip, and tears brimmed in his eyes for a moment, and hurriedly, Harriet said. 'I'll tell you what. I'll 'phone your Mummy and Daddy, and ask them to bring the puppy to see you tomorrow – will that be all right? Then you'll know he's arrived safely.'

The little boy sighed, and then nodded. 'I s'pose so. Poor old puppy – do you think he'll mind my bandage when he sees it?'

'Not a bit,' Harriet assured him, tucking the bedclothes round the slender neck. 'You'll see – '

And as soon as she had finished her round of all the children, she spent ten minutes on the 'phone explaining to the little boy's parents what she had promised their son, and they assured her gratefully that the puppy had indeed been bought, and would be brought to the hospital the next afternoon.

She went off duty at eight, weary, but happy, too involved with the preparations for the next day to think much of anything at all. Indeed, she was so absorbed, that when a hand fell on her shoulder as she hurried along the lower corridor towards the nurses' home, where the staff were collecting to set off on their carol singing tour of the wards, she nearly jumped out of her skin.

'Merry Christmas, Harriet.'

It was Gregory, and she whirled to look up at him, to feel the familiar lurch of pleasure at the sight of his thin face and tired eyes, the drumming of her pulses in her ears at the nearness of him.

'Merry – merry Christmas, Gregory,' she said, smiling up at him.

'I've bought a present for you. I was going to put it under the tree in the ward, but – well, I'd like to give it to you now,' and he pushed a small parcel into her hand, and stood smiling a little diffidently at her.

She looked up at him in the dimly lit corridor, and said breathlessly, 'You – you shouldn't – really – '

'Why not? I want to. I – I haven't many people to give presents to. Let me have the pleasure of giving one to you – '

And Harriet laughed a little shyly. 'You – you'll find a parcel under the tree in the doctors' common room,' she said softly. 'I hope you'll like it – '

Three of the other Sisters came bustling along the corridor towards them. 'Come on, Brett!' One of them called, pulling at her arm as they went by. 'You'll be late for the carols – ' And Harriet let herself be hurried away, smiling back to Gregory over her shoulder as she went, clutching her little parcel under her cape.

All through the carol singing, as the little procession of nurses wound its way through the hospital's wards and corridors, their capes turned inside out to show the bright red linings, she could feel the weight of the parcel in her pocket bumping softly against her leg as she walked. The wards were dimly lit, only the tree in the middle of each one sparkling with its fairy lights, as the nurses padded softly past each bed, their voices high and clear as they sang the familiar melodies. And, as every year, Harriet felt sympathetic tears pricking her own eyes as she saw women lying against the white pillows wipe tears from their cheeks as they listened, saw men sniff loudly and bury their chins in their pyjama jackets so that the nurses wouldn't see the bright gleam of tears in their eyes. Only on the maternity ward, where they sang the traditional 'Unto us a son is born' did the sense of sadness, of the loneliness of people forced to be ill in hospital instead of happily at home, leave her. They stood in the middle of the maternity ward, singing lustily, smiling a little when one or two of the babies, lying in cots next to their mothers' beds, joined in with thin wails, crumpled fists waving furiously as they cried.

And later, when the carolling was finished, and Harriet returned to her own ward, to creep softly from bed to bed, replacing the limp empty stockings with bulging ones, she felt again the sense of certainty that somehow, no matter what, all would come out well for her in the end. She felt, obscurely, that whatever happened with Gregory and Paul, however sad she may be in the future because of Gregory, some things would always be the same, some sources of happiness and contentment would always remain to her. There would always be work, always be Christmas, and in these things, there was a sort of happiness to be found. 'Even if I never do find a life with Gregory,' she told herself as she walked across the courtyard towards the nurses' home, and the traditional sherry party in the Sisters' sitting room, 'There will always be something to enjoy.'

And when, last thing that night, before she went to bed, she opened her parcel from Gregory, to find another tiny porcelain figure, this time of a dark haired boy leaning over a stile, a cap on the back of his curly head, his tiny legs crossed nonchalantly, his brown eyes looking cheerfully out at the world, she smiled. There were no tears in her this time, no feeling of misery as she looked at the pair of little figures where she set them on her dressing table. For there were two of them; and despising herself a little for her own lapse into superstition, she saw them as a happy omen.

5

Christmas Day at the Royal followed its time-honoured pattern. Those adult patients who were well enough came in their pyjamas and dressing gowns to the children's ward to watch the excited opening of stockings; nurses snatched minutes from their own wards to trail happily round the hospital admiring the decorations other nurses had put up; the Theatres were full of hilarious doctors stuffing themselves with mince pies and coffee long before ten o'clock; the local Mayor and various dignitaries came to make their usual pompous tour of the wards, and in the kitchens, cooks and dieticians sweated hectically over the dozens of colossal turkeys and plum puddings, working against the clock to have the patients' Christmas dinner ready by noon.

Harriet, trying against all odds to get the usual dressings and treatments done on the children's ward, in a welter of paper wrappings, dealt with those children who managed to eat themselves sick soon after breakfast, and turned a blind eye to those of her nurses who left the ward more often than they should have done on visits to other wards. Christmas Day was one day when a Sister expected to carry the main burden of the ward work, and she didn't really mind having to work so hard – this was one of the nicest parts of being a children's ward sister, and she was happy.

At three o'clock, when the parents filled the ward, and as many of the staff as could had arrived to watch the fun, Dr Bennett, sweating uncomfortably in his red suit, jumped through the fire escape door with many loud 'Ho-Ho's!' and a deep 'Hello Children!' to distribute the presents from the tree, accompanied as usual by the brawniest medical student who could be found, tastefully dressed in a fairy costume from beneath which hairy legs adorned with football socks and boots capered cheerfully from bed to bed, hugging the children, and kissing every nurse he could catch. Harriet, in her place beside the tree, ready to hand the parcels to Dr Bennett, was just about to begin the job, when the 'phone made itself heard, ringing shrilly above the shrieks of the children, and the giggles of nurses busy dodging the enthusiastic attentions of the fairy. The Staff nurse answered it, and came picking her way through the crowd to whisper in Harriet's ear.

'There's a child with virus pneumonia on her way up, Sister. Dr Weston's bringing her – ' and with a sigh, Harriet relinquished her place beside the tree to her staff nurse, and hurried out to a cubicle to prepare for the admission. She always hoped nothing of this sort would happen on Christmas Day, but all too often, it did. Illness was no respecter of occasions.

As she finished opening the cot, setting the electric blanket to warm the sheets, Gregory appeared at the door of the cubicle, a small child held in his arms, an anxious man behind him.

'Acute virus pneumonia,' he said shortly, carefully laying the child into the cot. She was very small – barely a year old, and her face, an olive skinned pointed one, with the liquid brown eyes and curling black eyelashes of the Greek Cypriot, was waxy, with tinges of blue round the pinched nostrils, which flared with each struggling inhalation as the child fought to breathe. Her curly black hair was sticking in tendrils to her broad forehead, and she whimpered miserably, struggling weakly against Harriet's gentle hands, as she began to take her clothes off, putting a small gown on the narrow olive-brown body.

'She'll need oxygen – ' Gregory was saying, 'and some antibiotic – can you get a tent up while I fix a jab for her?'

Harriet nodded, and with rapid movements, pulled an oxygen cylinder towards the bed. Gregory disappeared towards the sterilising room, while carefully, Harriet fixed the small mask from the cylinder over the child's face, and turned to the man hovering anxiously beside the cot.

'You are her father?'

'Huh? Father – yes, father – speak – no English – ' the man said, crouching beside the cot to peer with frightened eyes at the small girl tossing a little on the white pillows. 'Anna – my Anna – you make well?'

'We'll try – ' Harriet said gently. 'Please – hold this. I must get a tent up – ' and carefully, she put the man's hand on the mask, showing him how to hold it in place, before hurrying to fetch the big polythene oxygen tent, the ice and spare cylinder that would be needed to surround the child with the oxygen she needed so desperately.

She had the tent up round the cot before Gregory returned with an injection ready on a tray, and together, with their arms carefully pushed through the special apertures at the side of the tent, they thrust the fine needle into the small buttock, and as the child squirmed feebly and whimpered, sent the plunger into the barrel, to fill the blood stream with a million units of penicillin.

Beyond the glass-walled cubicle, Harried could hear the shouts and laughter of the children, the deep voice of Dr Bennett calling names, the squeals of joy as the beefy fairy capered from bed to bed, bringing each child to Santa Claus to get his parcels. Above the tent, inside which small Anna lay breathing agonisingly quickly and shallowly, a bunch of balloons swung with incongruous gaiety, and the head of the silent father, now hovering with piteous anxiety against the wall, was outlined with a loop of gaudy paper chains.

Gregory and Harriet stood silently, looking down on the child in the tent, at the half closed eyes beneath which a rim of blue-white could be seen, making her look sickeningly like a half-dead creature – as indeed she was. And as they watched, her face seemed to get bluer, her neck stretched backwards in an agonising effort to breathe, and her mouth opened in a grimace of pain.

Swiftly, Gregory thrust a hand through the tent to feel for her pulse, as the child suddenly lay quite still, not breathing at all.

'She's in collapse – ' he said, and pushed the tent back with impatient fingers.

'Start artificial respiration,' he said shortly. 'She'll need a direct heart stimulant – where're the other nurses? We'll need help – '

'They're in the ward with Santa Claus – ' Harriet said, as she began a rhythmic movement of her hands on the child's thin chest, trying to inflate the small lungs again.

'Bloody Christmas – ' Gregory said with a flare of anger, 'I'll get someone – '

As he turned to hurry from the cubicle, the medical student appeared at the door, to peer round it with elephantine coyness, 'I'm looking for Sister Brett!' he chirped, in a falsetto voice.

'Santa Clause wants Sister Brett – ' and then, as he saw the tableau of now weeping father, angry Gregory, and desperately working Harriet, he dropped his voice and said quickly, 'Need any help?'

'Yes,' Gregory said roughly, 'Take over here, while we get a heart jab organised – jump to it, man!'

The medical student pulled his frizzy blonde wig from his head, and ran over to the cot, to take Harriet's place at artificial respiration, and she moved away gratefully, already feeling the strain in her shoulders and back from the even movements she had been making. Still the child didn't breathe alone, and the medical student, his frilly tu-tu spread absurdly over the sheets, his face, under its comic plastering of make-up, stern and worried, moved his heavy shoulders gently as he tried to pump air into the still body.

Harriet's fingers shook as she prepared the special syringe in the sterilising room, fixing the long needle in place on the barrel, handing it to Gregory to draw up the colourless stimulant from the small ampoule he had brought from the poison cupboard. 'Don't let her die – don't let her die,' she prayed silently, as together they hurried back to the cubicle. 'Don't let her die – '

Gregory pushed the medical student away from the cot side, as Harriet quickly replaced the mask from the single oxygen cylinder over the blue face, and then held the shoulders straight for Gregory.

With an unusual tact for a medical student the boy in the tu-tu put a friendly arm across the shoulders of the man standing weeping helplessly against the wall, and tried to lead him out, but the man refused to go, holding on to the cot head with one desperate hand, watching Gregory's fingers as he ran his fingertips over the framework of ribs, seeking the place to make the heart injection.

They all held their breath, as they watched him, cocooned in a brilliantly lit glass cubicle while the sounds of singing of 'Jingle Bells' came discordantly from the ward beyond, and the glass walls rattled slightly as some of the children in the ward began to bounce on the floor in a gay dance.

The syringe barrel flashed a little as Gregory found the spot he was seeking, and eased the long needle through the fine skin, deep into the chest. Slowly, his eyes never leaving the child's face, he pushed the plunger home, while Harriet held the bird-frail wrist seeking eagerly for the leaping of a pulse.

But it made no difference, Gregory withdrew his needle, and they stayed very still, watching the tiny body with all their will for her to live in their eyes. But she didn't move, her eyes still half open above the dark green rubber of the mask, the oxygen hissing gently, the respiration bag on the cylinder limp and still.

Gregory moved at last, and leaned forward to take the mask from the little face with steady fingers. He pulled his stethoscope from his pocket, and began to move the bell across the still chest, his eyes abstracted as he listened for signs of life. Then he pulled the earpieces away from his head and stood up.

'I'm sorry,' he said to the man, with a brusqueness born of distress. 'Sorry. Nothing we can do. We did our best. I'm sorry.'

The man stared at him with uncomprehending eyes, as Harriet and the medical student stood in helpless pity. 'My Anna?' he said huskily. 'You make her well? My Anna? She well soon?'

Harriet moved, walked round the cot to put her hands on his shoulders.

'I'm sorry,' she said softly. 'So sorry, my dear. But she is dead. We did all we could – '

'No! No – ' The man pulled away from her, his eyes blazing with sudden anger. 'No – ' and he bent to the bed, to pick up the frail body, clutching her close, shaking her, shouting at her in Greek as he tried to make her move, breathe again.

Gregory, with a sudden angry shrug, turned away from him, going to the door.

'We aren't God, man – we aren't God!' he said, his voice loud and harsh. 'We did all we could – all we could – for Christ's sake – ' And then, he came back, his eyes deep and shadowed in his face, to take the dead child from her weeping father.

'Come,' he said, laying the child down again on the cot, leaving Harriet to gently pull a sheet up across her small still face. 'Come – ' And he led the man from the cubicle.

Harriet watched them walk through the ward, past the gay children and laughing parents, all of whom seemed unaware of any crisis going on, saw the man stumble as the little boy with the bandaged head chased his frisking puppy across the ward, saw them go into her office. There was some brandy there, and she could see Gregory pour a drink out for the man who slumped in the chair and stared out at the noisy ward with blank eyes.

The medical student said with a rough voice that barely disguised the tears that were hovering very near the surface.

'Why? Why do kids have to die? Bad enough when old men do – but why kids? I'll never do paediatrics when I qualify – so help me God, I won't – '

Harriet, with a steady movement that belied her own distress began to pull the curtains around the glass walls, ready for the last task of preparing the child to be removed to the mortuary.

'That's stupid,' she said huskily. 'Stupid. Of course we all feel like that when a child dies – it's tragic waste, bitterly hurtful. But not so long ago, a death like this was commonplace. Children died of pneumonia all the time. But because people who were distressed by their deaths went on caring about children, trying to find ways to stop such deaths, tragedies like this are rare now. That's why it hurts more, in a way. When it was common, doctors – people – everyone really, even parents, took it for granted – it was one of those things. When it happens now, we feel – lost, diminished. If you are really upset as you seem, then you *will* go on to do paediatrics. There's more to caring about children than providing fun – ' she looked into the ward again before drawing the last curtain, at the happy faces, the laughing parents, the warm gay busy safety of it all, and with a crisp rattle of curtain rings, shut the sight out, and turned back to the boy standing in ridiculous finery behind her. 'And do you know what you're going to do now?' she said to him, putting a hand over one of his cold ones. 'You're going to put that absurd wig on again, and you are going to go out into that ward and giggle and caper for all you're worth. Those children and parents there – they don't have to be punished because of your sense of inadequacy, because one child slipped through our fingers. We aren't God – Dr Weston was right – we aren't, and we have no right to make others suffer because we don't always manage to be like Gods, and save lives. So go and make those children laugh – go on, now.'

He stared at her, his face angry for a moment, as though he would argue. Then he managed a small grin, and nodded, reaching for his frizzy wig to thrust it over his own crew cut head.

'OK Sister. Thanks a lot,' he said, and went. She followed him, and watched as he took a deep breath before leaping into the ward with a squeal, sending the children into renewed gales of mocking laughter.

And then, she too, pulling her stiff face into a semblance of a smile, followed him out, to make her way through the ward to the kitchen, to see that the children's special Christmas Tea was ready.

As she passed the office, Gregory and the man came out, Gregory's arm over his shoulders, and she took his other hand, and led him to the door.

'So sorry,' she said, looking into the face now blank and limp with reaction. 'So sad' – and the man looked at her, and nodded heavily.

'I'll drive him home,' Gregory said crisply, and Harriet saw them both into the lift, watching the cage rattle downwards with a sense of despair that she knew would remain with her for a long time, as it always did after those rare occasions when a child died.

As she went back to the kitchen, to check on the teas, and then later, as she went back to the cubicle, alone, to look after the last offices for the dead baby, she thought confusedly about Gregory. This episode had somehow increased his stature in her eyes. He had none of the obvious, almost facile, distress that the medical student had shown, a distress that showed itself in a tendency to want to run away from such happenings. His pity was real, real enough in spite of his brusque speech and unsmiling face, showing itself in care for the bereaved father, in providing a drink, and making sure the man got home. And that, she told herself, as she looked down at the body of the child when she had finished her job, that was the essence of working in a hospital. You did what you could for each patient, and when you had done that, you turned to care for someone else. And as she later settled the exhausted and over-excited children in their beds for the night, and tidied away the drift of paper wrappings from parcels, the already broken toys, the mess of fallen pine needles from the Christmas tree, she said a confused prayer for the dead child, mixed up with a sort of thanksgiving for being able to find other people to help, even though the help she had offered to Anna had been useless.

6

The year drifted gently on its inevitable way, the hospital reflecting the changes of season that happened in the world outside its self-contained life. The pneumonias of the winter months gave way to the increased surgical lists of children who had been waiting for beds to have their operations, and Harriet was busy all day with the rush of admissions, preparations, post-surgical nursing and discharges and the increased activity brought with it.

As Spring slowly and reluctantly made way for the warmth of summer, the balcony outside the ward echoed with the shouts of those children well enough to be up and playing about, and the sunshine lit the ward itself into bright patches of light that showed the shabbiness of the old paintwork all too clearly.

But Harriet hardly noticed the passage of time, so thoroughly had she managed to convince herself of the need to live only a day at a time. Her mind refused, now, to think of the future. Each day was sufficient to itself, each day with its work, each evening with Gregory.

And as their relationship ripened, as she came gradually to know him more and more, so she came to respect and lean on his judgement. He still never offered any information about himself, never made any mention of his family if he had one, never talked of any part of his life before he had come to the Royal, and Harriet resolutely never asked him, never questioned his past even remotely. She never even asked him if he had been to a particular restaurant before, if he took her to a new one, meticulously avoiding any line of conversation that might lead logically to reminiscence.

Sometimes, in the deep of the night when she couldn't sleep, when her pillow knotted itself into hard lumps under her restless head, some of her fears would surge upwards, some of her distress about his lack of demonstrativeness would lift its head, and resolutely, she would push it down again. For he still made no attempt to touch her, except in the most impersonal way, handing her into the car, helping her into her coat so that their hands brushed against each other in what was, for Harriet, an electric moment. Yet despite this, she knew that he loved her, knew that he wanted to touch her, to hold her, to kiss her as much as she wanted to respond. She was always aware of the iron control he exercised over himself, the strength of his intention to avoid the physical contact she knew they both needed so much.

Paul, much to her relief, had seemed to accept her loss – if that was how he regarded it – with equanimity. Although he had made no regular attachment with another girl, he was as socially active as ever, appearing at the doctors' mess parties with a different nurse or sister each time, racketing around the hospital in his old insouciant way, greeting Harriet when they met with a casual friendliness that deceived everyone, including Harriet. Only Sally and Stephen knew that his hurt was still there, still very real, though Sally, with unusual taciturnity, said nothing to Harriet about this; she felt, wisely, that it would do no good for Harriet to know of the occasions when Paul burst out bitterly against Gregory to Sally and Stephen, that Harriet had enough to cope with without having to worry about Paul.

Harriet spent a fortnight's holiday in Devonshire, early in April, with her sister and brother-in-law and their delightful children, grateful for the respite in one way, impatient to return to the hospital and Gregory in another.

Sybil, at thirty three already very matronly, was a little worried at the change in Harriet, perturbed by the way she had seemed to fine down, the way her skin had developed the translucence of thinness, even though the change suited her. Harriet, as Sybil told her husband privately one night, must be in love – really in love. She had become more than just the pretty girl she had always been, had developed a remote beauty that was startling in its delicacy.

But in spite of the closeness of the sisters, a closeness that had developed since the death of their parents many years earlier, Sybil couldn't discover with whom Harriet might be in love, and she had the good sense not to probe.

On the last day of Harriet's holiday, however, as they packed her bags in the middle of the hubbub five children under six can raise when they really try, she did tell Harriet to remember that the Vicarage was her home, and would be as long as she wanted it to be.

'We'll always be here, Hattie,' Sybil said, using the childish nickname. 'If ever you need us, or you've got any problems, remember that, won't you? And it isn't only me – Edward is as attached to you as I am. So if you need us, or if you've got any – difficulties – give a shout. We'll be listening for it.'

Harriet hugged Sybil's plump figure, and clung to her for a moment before thanking her, and promising to remember.

'I don't know myself how things are going to be with me, Sybil, but as soon as I do know, I'll tell you. Bless you for being so understanding. Not one question – and I know you've got lots!' and they laughed together, and Harriet went back to London and the Royal with a warm feeling inside that whatever else happened, Sybil and Edward and their fat babies would always be around to be loved and to love in return.

Gregory met her at the station, his eyes kindling with pleasure at the sight of her head thrust out of the carriage window as the train ground into the huge terminus. And she, in her turn, felt the familiar lurch inside at the first sight of his lean body and grizzled head, a feeling complicated a little by a sudden rush of tenderness. He looked so lonely, standing there against the garish colours of an advertisement hoarding, his rather shabby overcoat hunched round his thin shoulders.

'I've missed you,' he said, as he picked up her two cases, and walked beside her to the barrier.

'And I you,' she replied, looking up at him, smiling, love in her eyes as naked as a child's. And that was all they did say on a personal level, talking desultorily of hospital doings as they drove back to the hospital, though beneath their casual chatter both were almost painfully aware of the other's physical proximity.

She went on duty next morning with real pleasure, looking forward to the rush of work that was the only thing that really kept her going. It had been the lack of mental preoccupation that had been the hardest thing to bear about her holiday, though she had benefited in a physical way from it, looking more rested than she had for months. Her uniform felt stiff and strange, even after only two weeks out of it, and she stretched her neck against the grip of her starched collar with a sort of masochistic pleasure in the stiffness of it.

Later, at ten o'clock, she was tube feeding a baby in the far isolation cubicle, a two week old scrap of a creature whose hold on life was pathetically precarious. As she manipulated the fine red tube, watched the milk formula drip through the glass connection, all that made her a children's ward sister came bubbling up in her. Nothing she felt, could ever be as rewarding as this, this struggle to care for these children. If they survived – and she was grimly determined that this one certainly would – they would grow up never knowing anything about the woman who had helped to make their lives possible, and for Harriet, this was one of the joys of nursing children. She had always found the gratitude of adult patients she had nursed somehow distasteful. She did her job because she loved it, and to be treated by a patient as though she were a sort of angel of mercy, as many adults did, embarrassed her, took some of the bloom from her pleasure in her job.

As she finished the task, and checked the incubator for temperature and oxygen flow, one of the nurses tapped on the glass partition, and nodded. Harriet came out, leaving the baby to digest its feed and go on with the slow process of healing. She hung her gown outside and as she washed her hands in the basin on the barrier nursing table, the nurse told her of a new admission on his way up.

'It's a bit of an oddity, Sister,' the nurse said. 'Casualty sister said the police brought him in. He's about five or so, she thinks, but he won't talk – so they don't even know his name. She says the police have no idea who he is – found him wandering around somewhere, and brought him here.'

Harriet dried her hands, and sighed a little. 'These police really are a bit much,' she said crossly. 'They treat this hospital as a clearing house for all their problems – '

The nurse grinned. 'It's a true bill this time, Sister. I mean, there *is* something wrong with the child,' she peered at the scrap of paper in her hand on which she had made a few notes as she had spoken to Casualty sister on the telephone. 'He's got some injuries – a few abrasions, a huge bruise on one hip, and query a fracture of a bone in his foot – they're waiting for an X-ray report on that. Sister says she thinks he might have been hurt in a road accident or something – '

'Hmm,' Harriet made her way through the ward. 'All right, nurse. Put him in bed seven, will you? At five, he's a bit big for a cot, I imagine. I've got to take Casey's stitches out, and then I'll come and see our little mystery. Not that he'll be a mystery for long. They never are. There'll be an agitated parent rushing in any minute, I daresay.'

When she brought the little Jamaican boy back from the dressing cubicle, his appendix wound now minus its stitches, and tucked him back into his cot, a piece of chocolate in his hand because he had 'been such a good boy and hadn't made a fuss,' Harriet turned to bed seven.

At the sight of the child who sat on it, pressed against the white painted iron bars at the head, his knees drawn up, his head down in a classically defensive pose, Harriet's heart twisted with pity. He looked so bereft, so lost, so utterly bewildered in this strange huge room full of oddly dressed people and rows of beds and cots. She picked up a toy from the bottom of Casey's cot, which didn't disturb that small brown child in the least, so plentifully did his adoring parents supply him with toys, and went to sit at the edge of bed seven.

He was small, with fine bones only lightly covered with flesh, and the delicate blueish skin of the very fair. His hair was the colour of spun barley sugar, and lay on his head in a smooth cap that was grimy now with dust and a patch of oil. He had huge blue eyes, the pale china blue that so often goes with very fair hair, and startlingly dark brown lashes, lashes that curled at the edge to a fringe of gold, glinting in the morning sunlight. His face was pointed, the chin held rigid now in an effort to keep his soft mouth firmly closed, and he stared at Harriet with suspicious eyes, trying to shrink into an even smaller ball, pulling back against the bars at the head of the bed as though he would have gone right through them if he could.

'Hello,' Harriet said softly.

He sat quite still, never taking his unwinking eyes from her face, making no sign that he had heard her at all.

Gently, Harriet put the little toy engine she was holding in front of him, and for a moment, he looked down at it. Then, seeming to dismiss it as an irrelevance, he raised his eyes to her face again and ignored the engine.

'What's your name, lovey?' Harriet asked softly. Still no response, just that unwinking stare. He might be deaf, Harriet thought. I've seen just this look on the face of a deaf child before now. Surreptitiously, she dropped her hand below the level of the side of the bed, and watching him carefully, snapped her fingers with a sharp crack. The child's eyes shifted briefly towards the sound, then returned to her face. Not deaf then.

She tried another ploy. From her top pocket she pulled a small chocolate bar – for she always carried some, knowing how few children could resist sweet things. She held it out to him, but after a brief glance at it, he ignored it. She took the silver paper off, holding it out again, invitingly, but though he looked longer at the rich brown of the chocolate, he refused to be tempted. So Harriet dropped it onto the bed, and with a smile, stood up. She crossed the ward to stand at the table in the centre, ostensibly busying herself with an injection tray, but watching him covertly from under her lashes. After a while the child stirred a little, looked sharply at her bent and apparently absorbed head, and then picked up the chocolate. For a moment he peered around with the cunning suspicion of a marauding cat, and when he was sure no one was looking at him wolfed the chocolate with a voracious hunger that wrung Harriet's heart with pity. He's starving, poor little devil, she thought. Who on earth could let a child get as hungry as that?

With apparent casualness, she returned to him, sitting again on the edge of the bed, saddened by his immediate shrinking into his corner again.

'Let's play a game, shall we?' she said. 'I'll try to guess your name, and if I get it right, you shall have lots and lots of chocolate – piles and piles of it, all you can eat. Shall we?'

Still he made no response, but Harriet persisted.

'Andrew? Adam? Barry? Billy? Charles? Craig? – ' Working through the alphabet, she said name after name, trying desperately to remember the sort of names that had been fashionable to give little boys about five years ago, the sort of name he might be expected to have. But it was useless. He showed no sign of recognition at any name, not for a moment giving that faint flicker that Harriet was watching for so closely, that slight movement of muscle that she knew would show his recognition of familiar syllables.

From behind her, a voice said, 'Hello, Sister. Trying to solve our little mystery, are you?'

She got to her feet. 'Good morning, Dr Bennett,' she said

formally, and the senior paediatrician smiled down at her from his considerable height, and said, 'Glad to see you back. Had a good holiday?'

'Very pleasant, thank you sir,' she said, and they moved away to the centre of the ward, where Dr Bennett perched himself against the table, and swung a long leg idly as he looked across at the child in bed seven. 'Casualty told me about this child. Very odd altogether.'

'The police brought him in?'

'Mmm. But not before they had tried very hard to find his people. I don't know the details – apparently there's a policewoman on her way up from Casualty to see me about him. I told them I'd be here in a few minutes, so they said – '

The double doors swung, and a fair girl in the neat blue uniform of a woman police constable came down the ward, her heavy shoes clacking noisily on the wooden floor.

Dr Bennett stood up, and nodded at her, and the policewoman smiled back, pulling her notebook from her pocket.

'They told me you were the best person to talk to about this child, sir,' she said. 'We picked him up at six o'clock last night, down at the market – '

'The market?' Dr Bennett interrupted.

'Street market, sir, at the corner of High Road and Jefferson Street.'

'Not far from the underground station,' Harriet said. 'I know it. Mostly fruit and vegetables, and a couple of gimcrack stalls and old clothes stalls – '

'That's it, Sister. Well, we got a call. This child had taken some fruit from one of the stalls, and the stall-holder had caught him. And when he couldn't get any sense out of him, he called us – it's as well he did. Well, we couldn't find out who he was, and the station sergeant said seeing no one had reported a missing child, and he looked a bit small just to be wandering on his own, we'd better put out a search for his people. We tried all evening, put him in a bed at the station, and waited for someone to claim him. Well, sir, no one did – and that's really odd. We've never had a child of this age so long without *someone* reporting him missing.'

'Quite.' Dr Bennett frowned. 'Six o'clock last night, you say? Hasn't he said anything at all since then?'

'Not a word, sir. Wouldn't eat, either, though we tried all we could to make him – anyway, he slept all right, and this morning we put out an all stations call to check on missing kids. He's not been reported anywhere, it seems, and we've covered the area very carefully. They're checking outside London now. Well, sir, this morning, I thought the kid ought to – ' she blushed suddenly. 'Well, sir, he hadn't been to the lavatory since we got him to the station, sir, and we haven't any kids' clothes if there's any accident, so I took him. He fought like a mad thing – ' and she held out a scratched hand ruefully. 'But I managed to get his pants off, sir, and sit him on the lav – the toilet. And then I saw the bruise. So we thought we'd better bring him here.'

'Hmm,' Dr Bennett nodded. 'As well you did, constable. He's got several abrasions, and a badly bruised foot. They had some trouble trying to X-ray him, I gather, so I don't suppose the films'll show much – but it seems possible he's fractured a metatarsal. We'll get the orthopods to have a look at that. In the meantime, we'll keep him in, and try our best to get him to talk to us. If you hear from his people, you'll notify us, of course – '

The policewoman, clearly relieved at being rid of her burden, took herself off, and Harriet and Dr Bennett returned to the child's bedside.

He had made no move at all, still sitting crouched against the head of the bed, his eyes staring around him with a lack lustre look that was pathetic in its emptiness. Dr Bennett tried to persuade the child to talk, but after ten minutes of gentle urging, he sighed and stood up.

'Completely withdrawn, Sister,' he said. 'No contact at all, is there? Look, treat those abrasions in the usual way, watch him for any signs of other disease – it's possible he was in an accident and those abrasions certainly look as though they were the result of a bad tumble which might have inflicted some internal injury, and I'll get the orthopods to see his foot. He's all yours, Sister. Perhaps when he's been here a while you'll be able to make some contact with him. Offer him some loving – you know the sort of thing I mean – and try to get him to talk. And see the night staff observe him carefully. Children who refuse to talk while they're awake sometimes talk in their sleep. Right?'

Harriet nodded, then suddenly she said, 'We'll have to call him something, sir. We can't just say "you" all the time, can we? Not very loving – '

Dr Bennett looked down at the silent child, and sighed sharply. 'Yes – ' then he smiled a little grimly. 'He's come to us out of the blue, Sister – a gift from the gods, if you like. Call him Theodore, hmm? The gift of God.'

Harriet smiled too. 'A shade – stiff sir?' she ventured. 'Could we shorten that perhaps? Tod, say?'

Dr Bennett laughed, and nodded. 'You are quite right, my dear. Tod it is. Nice and simple. It'll do till we find out what it really should be. I hope it won't be long before we do – '

And after he had gone, Harriet stood at the door, looking down the ward at the slight little boy in bed seven, and silently agreed with him. No one should be as unhappy, as lost, as abandoned, as this pale fair scrap of a child. Tod, she thought. An anonymous sounding syllable for an anonymous child. I hope someone claims him, soon.

7

But no one did. The police checked with every station in the country, but Tod fitted none of the descriptions of such children as were missing. The aid of newspapers and television was sought and Tod's thin little face stared out from front pages, from television screens, and still no one came to say they knew him, let alone claim him.

A special court was convened in the hospital, and Tod was solemnly described as an infant in need of care and protection, and put under the impersonal guardianship of the State.

'It's all we can do, Sister.' Dr Bennett told Harriet, afterwards. 'This way, we can at least treat him properly – if he needs surgery for example – which he doesn't as it happens – we'll be able to perform an operation with the Court's consent. But it's an odd business. I'd have thought someone somewhere would have recognised his photograph – '

'What will happen to him?' Harriet asked practically.

Dr Bennett shrugged. 'We'll get him physically fit, first, of course. Then I suppose we'll have to get the trick-cyclist on to his mental condition.' Dr Bennett had all the old fashioned physician's fine scorn of psychiatrists. 'This refusal to speak could be the result of a traumatic experience – the accident, whatever it was, that gave him those injuries – or it could be a form of juvenile amnesia. I'm not much up on this sort of thing, quite honestly.'

'Then we'll keep him here?' Harriet persisted.

'Not for long, Sister. I suppose they'll find a vacancy in some institution for him – one for the mentally handicapped perhaps – '

'Oh, no!' Harriet said. 'Surely not! He mayn't talk, but he's not lacking in intelligence – I'm sure of that.'

Dr Bennett looked at her shrewdly. 'Don't get too attached to him, my dear,' he said gently. 'He's a pathetic little creature, I know, but we can't keep him here indefinitely. This is an acute hospital, you know – not a depository for unwanted children.'

Harriet, forced to agree, watched Dr Bennett go, and went back to Tod's bed, to sit beside him and look with a frustrated sympathy at his silent face. They had made some progress with him, and little as it was, Harriet felt a little cheered as she thought about it.

With infinite patience on her part, she had managed to coax him to eat, putting all the most tempting things she could think of in front of him. Once he had tried something – and Harriet had given him a paper packet of potato crisps, knowing how most children adored them – and had reassured himself that the food she gave him was really meant for him, that he wouldn't be punished for eating it, he ate hungrily, refusing nothing, drinking hugely, filling his small frame as full as he could.

But that was all. He refused to play, ignoring every toy they gave him, looking at the brightly coloured books or playthings on his bed as though they were objects he had never seen in his life before. All day, he would sit in the corner of his bed, his legs drawn up, just sitting, making no response to any overtures, even from the other children. Some of them would come and stand by his bed, talking to him, but his refusal to respond chilled them, and they would drift away, back to their toys and other friends, shunning the silent boy in bed seven.

Harriet had tried to get him to walk, but when she lifted him out of bed, putting a dressing gown on to him, fitting slippers on to his little feet, he just stood there, making no effort either to return to bed, or move away from it. He had let the orthopaedic surgeon examine his feet (and fortunately, there was no fracture to be found) had allowed Harriet to put a supportive bandage on the swelling without fighting, but that had been all.

There was one good sign, Harriet thought, leaning forward to move a toy near to him, in the forlorn hope that this time he would respond. He had some control over his body, still had some social ability. She had put a potty beside his bed, and gone away, watching him from out of his line of vision, and been glad to see him use it. Whatever had happened to him, it hadn't had the all too common effect of making him incontinent.

She leaned forward suddenly, and with an impulsive but gentle grasp, lifted the child out of his corner, and held him on her lap. He did not resist her, but sat there, his legs held stiffly in front of him, his back rigid, staring ahead of him in silence.

Slowly, Harriet began to rock to and fro, her arms about the slender little body, and under her breath at first, then more audibly, she began to croon a song at him. Quite why she chose the song she did, she never knew, but she found herself singing an old popular song called the *Umbrella Man*. 'Any umbrellas, any umbrellas to mend today – he'll mend your umbrellas and go on his way singing – any umbrellas, any umbrellas – '

The child on her lap shuddered slightly, then, to Harriet's intense joy, his body began to relax. She made no sign that she had noticed, just crooned on, rocking at the same rhythm.

And gradually, Tod softened, gradually his head dropped towards her till his fair smooth hair was just beneath her chin, nestling against the starch of her apron. His legs came up under him, and he thrust the two middle fingers of one hand into his mouth, until he was curled on her lap, sucking at his hand like a child of half his apparent age.

And soon he slept, but Harriet crooned on until she was sure he was fast asleep. When her staff nurse came over at a sign from Harriet, she looked a little surprised.

'Look Staff!' Harriet whispered. 'This is the first time this child has shown any appreciation of any human contact. And I don't want to spoil it. I'll have to sit here till he wakes up. Maybe he'll talk to me then. Can you manage to finish off and get the children settled? There's the tube feed for the baby in the end cubicle and the skin prep for tomorrow's orthopaedic list – ' rapidly she gave her instructions, and sent the nurses scurrying round the ward on the evening's tasks, and still Tod sat on her lap, his head under her chin, and slept on.

She called one of the nurses to tuck a blanket over Tod's small body, and watched the nurses settle the children into bed, watched the light diminish as each window blind was pulled down, saw the familiar evening face of the ward appear as the red shaded central lights were put on, and the children were tucked in for the long night's sleep ahead of them.

She listened to them all, carefully flexing her stiff legs and arms, doing her best not to wake the sleeping child on her lap, listened to the odd snufflings and little moans that sleeping children always seem to produce, and smiled a little as she listened. It was almost like a room full of small snuffling furry animals, she thought. Warm, baby ones.

And then, just a little while before the night nurses were due to come on duty, Gregory's white coated shape came through the big double doors. He looked round with the characteristic swift appraising look she knew so well, and came over to her as soon as he could make out where she was in the dim light.

He leaned on the foot of the bed, smiling a little at the sight of her, sitting there in a low bedside chair, a blanketed child on her lap.

'It suits you,' he said in a low voice. 'You both look – right, somehow. Did you know it suited you to have a child on your lap? Is that why you work with sick kids?' and his dark eyes glinted at her with rare humour.

She gave a soft snort of laughter. 'Of course. And I always choose blonde children to sit with,' she said. 'They suit me best of all.'

'Couldn't you just put him to bed now? He's flat out. And we're supposed to be going out to dinner tonight. Had you forgotten?'

Harriet smiled up at him. 'I haven't forgotten. But I'm hoping he'll wake up before long, and maybe talk to me.'

'Talk to you?' he sounded puzzled.

'Haven't you heard about our small mystery?' Harriet asked. 'This is the child the police brought us – '

He came round the bed to perch on the edge and peer into the sleeping child's face.

'I did hear something – what's it all about? I haven't had many patients on this ward this week, so I haven't been around much – '

Briefly, she told him, about how Tod was found, the way no one had come to claim him, and Gregory's face softened as he listened. 'Poor little monkey,' he murmured. 'I can't imagine how people can be so cruel. Someone somewhere must belong to him. To abandon him so – '

Harriet looked down at the child, and nodded. 'I know,' she said softly. 'I couldn't do it, no matter what happened – I couldn't do it – '

'He's fast asleep, Harriet,' Gregory said, after a long pause. 'Are you going to sit with him all night? Because I shouldn't think he'd wake before morning now – '

'I suppose not – ' she stirred experimentally, and very carefully stood up, still holding Tod gently, but he didn't wake. Gregory pulled the blankets back, and she put the child into bed, tucking him into the covers with a careful touch. Tod moved a little, snuffled softly, and slept on.

They stood together for a moment, looking down on the fair head, the golden edged fringe of long lashes that shaded the thin cheeks, and then Harriet stretched a little.

'I did so hope he would wake,' she said regretfully. 'I thought perhaps that I could talk to him while he was still half asleep, and get him to say something. Anything. I'm sure if I can once get him started on speech, we'll be able to find out about him – he just needs to start – '

Gregory looked at her in the half light, and said softly, 'You're getting very fond of him?'

'He's so alone,' Harriet said defensively. 'So lost. I can't bear the thought of him going to an institution somewhere. Oh, I know they're good places, that they do their best, but – '

'I know,' Gregory looked down at Tod's sleeping face. 'I can understand how you must feel about him. But it isn't much use, is it? You can't adopt him – '

All through their dinner that evening, Harriet was abstracted, somehow unable to keep her thoughts away from the child sleeping in bed seven, for once less concerned with Gregory than with her job. Gregory, with the swift understanding she was coming to value in him, didn't seem to mind her abstraction, only saying, as he said goodnight, 'I hope your Tod is claimed soon, Harriet. As much for your sake as his. It's not much fun being as miserable about a patient as you are about him.'

And Harriet had smiled up at him gratefully, and on an impulse put her hand up to touch his face, more from gratitude for his understanding than because of her ever-present need to touch him, to have some physical contact with him. But he had made a tiny movement, an almost instinctive rearing back, and a little chilled, she had dropped her hand, and said 'Thank you, Gregory. Good night,' and gone to bed, unhappy and bewildered again, the ache in her heart sharpened by his lack of response.

If she had thought about it at all, she had certainly never thought that anything Gregory could do or say could make her any more bewildered and unhappy about him than she was. Until the next morning.

A child with a suspected intussusception was sent up from Casualty as an emergency at half past nine, and as Gregory was the surgical registrar on call, Harriet sent a message to the mess for him.

He came promptly, and with all the gentle skill that Harriet found one of the most wonderful things about him, examined the child, and managed to soothe the frightened parents with a few words, arranging to operate later that afternoon. It was when they had finished with the child, while Harriet and Gregory were walking down the ward towards the office, that it happened.

The ward was unusually quiet for once, many of the children being out on the sunny balcony, listening to the hospital school teacher read a story to them. The few children still in bed in the ward were sleeping, or just lying quietly staring at the ceiling thinking the imponderable thoughts of the very young.

Then, above the crisp fall of their footsteps, a voice said 'Greg – Greg.'

Puzzled, Harriet turned, and looked back down the ward.

Tod was sitting bolt upright, his thin face unusually flushed, his chin up, staring at Gregory with an intensity that made his blue eyes seem to blaze. And then, never taking his eyes from Gregory, who had himself turned to stare at the child, Tod moved forwards, sliding his thin legs over the side of the bed, to stand swaying a little beside it.

He looked oddly adult somehow, despite the way his gaily coloured pyjamas hung on his thin frame, the way the trouser legs creased themselves over his narrow feet. He stood still for a moment, and then started to walk, a little wobbly on his legs, legs that had not moved of their own volition in all the three days he had been in the ward, and came pattering barefooted over the polished wooden floor towards them.

For Harriet, time seemed to stand still. In the quiet sunny stillness she watched Tod come towards them, watched his hair blaze and fade alternately as he went past each bright window, watched his eyes, their intensely blue gaze never faltering from the face of the man who stood as still as herself beside her.

Tod came to stand in front of Gregory, staring up at him and put a hand out tentatively.

'Greg?' he said again, his voice high and thin, the voice of a frightened bird. 'Greg?'

Gregory looked down at the child, his face closed and

expressionless. Then he moved, stepped back, and said in a voice that sounded strangely thick to Harriet, 'What? What did you say?'

Tod's hand dropped and he stood quite still, watchful and suddenly on guard again.

'Greg,' he said again. 'Greg. Greg. Greg.'

Harriet, her head feeling empty and suddenly light, managed to move, to drop on her knees beside Tod, to put an arm round his narrow shoulders, managed to turn her head so that she could look up at Gregory, suddenly seeming to tower above her like a giant.

'What is it – who – you know him, Gregory?' her voice came huskily, forcing its way past the constriction in her throat.

Gregory never took his eyes from the child's face. For a long moment there was silence, then he said roughly. 'Know him? Of course I don't. I never saw him before in my life.'

In the circle of her arm the child never moved, even though she tightened her grasp on him, ignoring her as if she were no more than a fly that had alighted on his shoulder.

'But – ' Harriet felt as though she were lost, groping in a huge dark room, a room with neither walls nor ceiling, just an infinity of blackness. 'But – he said your name – he knows you.'

Gregory thrust his hands deep into the pockets of his white coat, and with a voice devoid of any expression said again, 'I never saw him before in my life. Never.'

'Greg,' Tod said again, in the same flat monotone, no question in his voice now. 'Greg. Greg. Greg.'

'I tell you he knows *you*,' Harriet cried, her voice high and shrill. 'It's the first time he's spoken – and all he says is your name! He knows you, Gregory – *he knows you!*'

Gregory looked at her now, his eyes deeply shadowed, so that she could read nothing in their sombre depths.

'I tell you I never saw him before in my life. I'll tell theatre about that intussusception, Sister. Have him ready for two o'clock, will you?' and without looking at Tod again, he turned, and walked from the ward, his footsteps loud in the silence.

Together, Tod and Harriet watched him go, both of them seeming frozen into immobility, both staying quite still long after the double doors had stopped their slow diminishing swing behind Gregory's figure, long after they heard the lift gates clatter open and closed, heard the lift whine away to the ground floor of the hospital.

8

In a way, Harriet was grateful for the afternoon's rush of work. In addition to the child who was to go to theatre at two o'clock, three children were admitted from Casualty just after lunch suffering from coal gas poisoning. A fractured gas main near their home had sent them, together with their mother, into the Royal in a state of collapse that was ominous.

Paul, as the medical registrar on emergency call for the week, came to the ward with them, together with his junior houseman, and the three children, the oldest of whom was just five, the youngest under a year, kept them and Harriet extended at full pitch until long after seven o'clock.

By then, when Harriet could at last relax a little, she was too exhausted to think very much about Gregory and Tod – indeed, the long struggle to keep the youngest child, who had suffered most from the gas fumes, just breathing, had wrung her dry of any feeling.

She followed Paul from the big cubicle where the three children were being nursed together, trailing wearily behind him through the darkened ward, past each shadowed bed, past Tod's humped shape in bed seven, her head spinning with fatigue, the faint sickly smell of gas still seeming to linger in her nostrils.

Paul subsided into the armchair in her office, while she sat down at her desk and began to write the ward report ready for the night staff. He watched her in silence, only stirring to grab gratefully at the coffee a sympathetic junior nurse brought to them both, watching Harriet above the rim of his cup as she sat with bent head, scribbling away at her report.

'I think they'll do,' he said at length, when she had finished, dropping her pen to flex cramped fingers. 'That baby had me more than a little worried for a while. It must have been a hell of a leak – '

'It was,' Harriet told him. 'The ambulance man who brought them in told Casualty sister that their house was next to that new development up by the rope factory – you know where I mean? He said it couldn't have been more than half an hour the house was full of gas – seems they knew what had happened on the building site – they'd used a charge of explosive to shift a main wall they were demolishing, and it cracked a main supply pipe. And for these kids to get enough to have this effect on them, it must have been a hell of a big pipe – '

Paul reached for the 'phone. 'Phillips was looking after the mother. I'd better see how she is – '

The report from Women's medical was fortunately a good one; the mother had been deeply unconscious for some hours, but now she too was out of the wood, and beginning to regain consciousness, and Harriet smiled a little tremulously at Paul when he hung up the 'phone, and passed the information on to her.

'Thank God for that,' she said wearily. 'It would have been too awful if the three of them had lost their mother – '

'Mmm,' Paul yawned widely, cracking his jaws and stretching luxuriously. 'Bad enough to have one apparent orphan in the ward, without three more – how *are* things with your mystery child? Have they found his people yet?'

All Harriet's misery came flooding back at his question. She sat still, her head bent, looking down at her desk, trying to get her thoughts into some sort of order. She knew what she ought to do; Tod had spoken for the first time, and she should tell Dr Bennett about it, so that the police could be told, so that Gregory could be officially questioned about him. She had the first clue to the child's identity, and she ought to see that this important clue was properly followed up. But Gregory – unconsciously, she straightened, and raised her head to look directly at Paul.

'No,' she said evenly. 'He's still a mystery. They haven't found his people yet.'

'It's a problem,' Paul said. 'What'll happen to him? Will they send him to a home somewhere?'

'I don't know,' Harriet said. 'He's still not ready to be discharged from the ward – those abrasions aren't quite healed yet. I – suppose Dr Bennett will decide what to do when he *is* ready.'

He got to his feet, and stood for a moment looking down at her. 'Harriet – ' he began. 'Harriet – '

She looked up at him, at the familiar face she had once found so exciting, and thought vaguely, he's a nice man. I wish – I wish I could have cared for him –

'How are things, Harriet?' Paul said awkwardly. 'I'm not prying – really I'm not. But I'm fond of you, you know. A friend. I just wondered – you're looking a bit peaky.'

'Just fatigued,' Harriet smiled at him a little shyly. 'Just a bit tired, that's all. Occupational hazard with nurses, isn't it? But I'm fine – '

'I suppose it is,' he said soberly. 'Though it isn't like you to look quite so – bothered. Look, Harriet – ' He stopped, and then said with shyness that sat oddly on his handsome face, 'Don't forget that I *am* your friend, will you? I'm interested in you, and if I can ever be of any help – well, just ask.'

She managed a bright smile that stretched her stiff lips a little painfully. 'Help? What sort of help would I need, Paul? I'm fine – really I am – '

'Oh, I don't know. You look so – hagridden. As though you've got to carry the world and his wife on your back. It doesn't suit you. So if you ever need a shoulder to cry on, I've got a pair of the most absorbent shoulders in the business – '

'Thank you, Paul,' she said softly. 'I'll remember,' and with a curt nod, he turned and went, disappearing through the double doors with a flick of his white coat.

For a moment, she wanted to run after him, to accept his offer, to rest her tired head on his broad shoulder and tell him of her misery, of what had happened that morning with Tod and Gregory, to throw all her worries on to him, to relax in the sure comfort of his affection for her.

And then she shook herself a little impatiently. It's no good, she told herself. Gregory is my problem, and no one else can help me but Gregory himself.

For a while, she sat with her chin propped on her fists staring unseeingly at her reflection in the glass wall of her office, trying to decide what to do. But her thoughts went round in circles, persistently coming back to the same point. I'll have to talk to Gregory about it – ask him – *make* him tell me how Tod knew his name, force him to explain. I can put up with just so much secretiveness and no more. He'll have to explain.

She pulled her eyes down, to look at the 'phone beside her elbow, sitting black and mute waiting for her to pick it up. With a conscious physical effort she reached out her hand, and started to dial the mess number, then stopped. I don't want to have to ask someone to get him for me, she thought. If I have to sit here and hold on while they get him, I'll hang up – I won't have the courage to wait. Instead, she dialled the switchboard, and asked the impersonal voice at the other end to put Gregory's call lights on, and then hung up, to sit staring at the panel above the ward door as it started to flick a red light on and off, the red light that would tell Gregory to contact switchboard.

After a long moment, the light stopped, and then the 'phone rang, shrilly, beside her. She looked at it, and with her heart beating with a sick thumping that made her want to run away, she picked up the receiver.

'You wanted me?' Even with the distortion of the 'phone, his voice carried deep tones that made her shiver with pleasure.

'Yes – yes,' she managed. 'Gregory – I want to see you.'

'Is something wrong with that intussusception child?' His voice was distant, a little unfriendly.

'No. He's fine. Round from his anaesthetic and sleeping quietly. This – this is something else. I must see you.'

There was a long silence, so long that she said, 'Gregory?' a little uncertainly.

'I'll meet you by the gate to the Nurses' Home garden. In ten minutes. Will that do?' he said.

'Half an hour would be better,' she said. 'I'll have to give the report to the night staff – '

'Very well,' he said shortly, and hung up, leaving her listening stupidly to the high buzz of the dialling tone.

She waited for the night staff, giving them the report, telling them what to do about the post-operative child and the gassed children with her usual efficiency, while a heavy lump of fear pressed thickly in her chest. The coldness of Gregory's voice, the chill that had come through the 'phone at her, made her feel icy herself. He will tell me to mind my own business, she thought miserably, tell me that I have no right to question him. And that will be the end of everything. All he wants from me is patience, an unquestioning patience, and now I'm nagging him, and he won't ever want to take me out again, and the future will be empty. That will be the end.

And then her basic common sense asserted itself, made her feel strong again. I have every right to question him, she told herself firmly. Whatever the explanation is, I have a right to ask for it. Quite apart from our relationship, there's Tod to consider. And right now, he matters more than my feelings.

So it was with a strong step that she made her way towards the Nurses' Home, her cape pulled closely round her against the cold night air. No high emotion, she promised herself. No accusations. I'll just ask him, calmly, to explain.

He was leaning against the gate as she got there, his face lit with the glow of a cigarette. He dropped it as she arrived, to grind it out under his foot, and after a momentary pause, followed her through the gate.

The garden was empty, the faint rattle of dry branches in the trees making the only movement there was. Harriet led the way to one of the wooden benches that a grateful patient had donated to the hospital, and sat down in a corner, to huddle herself even deeper into her cape. He sat down at the other end of it and she could feel his eyes on her in the darkness.

'We won't be interrupted here,' she said, her voice high and thin. 'And I must talk to you.'

'Well.' There was no question in his voice, no apparent awareness of her tension, her anxiety.

She bit her lip, putting out her hand towards him for a moment. Then, when he made no attempt to move, no sign that he had seen her gesture, she dropped it, and said evenly, 'It's about Tod.'

'Well,' he said again.

'Gregory, not so very long ago, you told me – asked me to be patient with you. You – you gave me some reason to believe that you felt a little about me as I do about you, but you made it clear that I would have to wait for some time before – before you could talk to me, either about your own feelings, or mine. And I accepted that.' She stopped, and looked across at him, at the faint glimmer of his white coat in the darkness, the dull gleam of the stethoscope that was sticking out of his pocket. He made no move, sitting there still and silent, his eyes still on her.

Painfully, she began to speak again. 'Well, that was all right. I – I care enough for you to wait. But now – now it would seem that other factors are involved. When it was just a matter of you and me – just my own unhappiness, I could cope, could manage not to question you. No one suffered but me. Now – it's different.' She leaned forwards, trying to see some flicker of response in his dark face. 'Don't you see, Gregory? This child *knows you*. He's a lost child – no one seems to care about what happens to him. And if he knows you, it's obvious you know him. And however much you may deny it, it's pretty obvious to *me* that this – acquaintanceship between you has some bearing on the situation as it stands between us.'

Still he made no answer, no movement.

'Gregory – help me!' she let her unhappiness show in her voice, despite her promise to herself that there would be no high emotion in this conversation. 'Give me credit for some understanding, Gregory! Don't shut yourself away from me! Tell me what it is – tell me who this child *is*, what he is to you, *who* he is! I'm not just asking you for my own satisfaction, Gregory, believe me I'm not. If you don't want to tell me about whatever it is that makes you so secretive, I don't want to know. But this child – he matters, Gregory! I've got to know who he is, where his mother is, find out why he's been abandoned. He's not just a – a cipher. He's a person – and a bitterly lost person at that. In all decency, Gregory, you've got to tell me!'

In the silence that followed, she seemed to be able to hear every tiny movement in the dark garden, the faint chatter of dry branches, the soft whisper as the wind moved the leaves of the flowers in the dark beds lining the lawn, and beyond, the ever present muted thunder of traffic on the main road that flanked the hospital. Then, he moved.

'I told you this morning that I had never seen this child in my life before, Harriet. You don't believe that.' It was a statement, not a question.

'How can I?' she asked miserably. 'How can I? It can't be mere coincidence. If yours was a common name, perhaps – perhaps it could be. But Gregory isn't a common name – and he said "Greg" as clearly as it could be said. And his recognition of you was the first sign of any – any real response he had made. That, and your name – obviously he knew you! You must see that. And how could he know you if you never saw him before?'

'I don't know,' his voice was still flat, still cold. 'I'm as mystified as you are.'

'Oh for Christ's sake!' she was angry now, bitterly angry. 'Do you take me for a complete idiot, man? Do you think I'm the sort of besotted creature that will accept *everything* without question? I may have made myself look a fool, may have grovelled in front of you – but I haven't lost every vestige of intelligence just because I'm stupid enough to love you – '

He moved then, leaned towards her, 'Don't, Harriet, don't – please.'

But she was too angry now to heed the sudden note of pain in his voice. 'You – you, a doctor! You're supposed to care for people, you're supposed to be giving your life to caring for the sick. And all you care about is your own self centred need! Never mind what happens to other people – as long as Gregory Weston can live his life safely wrapped up away from other people, the rest can go to hell! What you're doing to *me* is bad enough – but I'm damned if I'll let you get away with treating this child as you are. And I'm warning you, Gregory. Either you tell me right now who this child is, or I find out myself – somehow. I'll find out – and I don't care if you do get hurt in the process – '

Suddenly he was close beside her, his hands on her shoulders, gripping her through the thick fabric of her cape so hard that she winced.

'Listen to me – listen to me, Harriet! You must believe me! *I don't know who this child is.* He's a complete stranger to me. Selfish I may be – but even I couldn't lie about this. I have – I haven't ever seen him before – '

She looked up at him, at his face so close to her own, closer than it had ever been.

'But – but you must have some idea – ' she said a little uncertain now, convinced almost against her will by the urgency of his tone, the note of truth that burned in his words.

He dropped his hands then, and said, 'Perhaps – but the idea I have won't help. I – even if I knew his mother once, it's been a long time. I had thought – oh, what's the use.' He turned his head away from her, to stare up at the trees. 'It's over now. Finished. Whatever happens now, it's finished. I can't see you again, Harriet. I'll have to leave here, now. I couldn't bear to go on seeing you about the hospital, and not be able to – ever see you outside it. And I can't – not now.'

Her heart twisted sharply at the sense of loss he transmitted in his voice, and without thinking, she put her arms round him, pulling him close to her, so that his head came down to rest on her shoulder.

For a moment he resisted, and then, almost as though against his will, his own arms went round her, and his cold lips were on hers, kissing her with a hunger, a need, that seemed to cry aloud in the silence.

For a long moment, they clung together, locked in an embrace that carried Harriet away, made her whole body seem to melt in a rush of sensations she had never felt before.

He raised his head then, to pull her roughly against him, to murmur brokenly into her ear words she couldn't hear, words that didn't matter. All she knew was that she loved him, that she needed him.

And then, with a suddenness that left her gasping, he stood up.

'It's no good, Harriet,' his voice was harsh again. 'No good. It won't work – '

She stared up at him, and said softly. 'But it will. It must. I love you, Gregory. And you love me. You can't escape that – '

'Yes – I love you,' he said hopelessly. 'But I'll have to get over that – somehow. I'm sorry, Harriet.'

She shook her head. 'No,' she said. 'No. Whatever it is that makes you so – so unhappy, you'll have to tell me. And you might as well tell me now. Nothing is as bad as it seems if it's put into words – '

But she was talking to empty air. He had turned and gone, his lean body melting into the shadows of the garden, leaving her alone on the wooden bench, her mouth still feeling his kiss, still hurting from the roughness of the urgent passion she had felt in him.

For a long time, she sat there. And all she could think was 'Tod. He still hasn't told me. What do I do about Tod?'

9

She spent a miserable sleepless night, tossing and turning through the long hours, grateful when the Sisters' maid arrived with her early tea, one of the few extra privileges the Sisters at the Royal enjoyed. She was still undecided, still not sure what she should do about Tod, as she pinned her apron round her, fixed her cap on her head with unsteady fingers. As she dusted powder on her face, trying to cover the blue shadows under her eyes, the little porcelain girl on the dressing table looked out into the room, her delicate face seeming to hold an aloofness that suddenly made Harriet angry. With a childishness she recognised in herself, a childishness that somehow made her even angrier, she thrust the pretty thing and its laughing-eyed companion into the top drawer, hiding them under her handkerchiefs. Gregory's gifts seemed to mock her now, and she couldn't bear even to look at them.

On an impulse, she decided to call in at the theatres as she went on duty. With luck, Sally would have a few moments to talk to her, and Harriet felt a very definite need of some of Sally's calm good sense.

The theatres were humming with activity as she came through the swinging double doors, nurses already in the tight caps and light cotton dresses and white socks and plimsolls they would wear through the day's operations. As Harriet took in the atmosphere of the place, the gleaming green tiles, the huge instrument cupboards glowing with the cold chrome of equipment, the bubbling of the sterilisers in the annexe, she wished for a moment that she, like Sally, had decided to work in the theatres. No patients to get involved with, she thought bleakly. Just things – and no one can get unhappy about things. People are more complicated.

Sally was checking a tray of instruments, chivvying a rather scared junior as she counted them.

'You'll need twelve haemostats of this size, Nurse. Do you suppose Mr Best will wait about for you to boil up more in the middle of the operation? And for heaven's sake, girl, what size clamp do you call this? We're removing an appendix, not a horse's guts – ' The junior flushed miserably under her mask, and scuttled off to correct her errors, as Sally caught sight of Harriet standing at the door, and came over to her.

'I don't know where Matron finds these girls, really I don't,' she grumbled. 'Nurses today haven't the wit they were born with. When we were in training – '

'Bully,' Harriet said, smiling at Sally's cross face in spite of herself. 'You were just as dumb as they are now – and you know it.'

Sally grinned back. 'I suppose so. Now, ducky. To what do I owe the honour of your presence? If you want to borrow the sucker again, we're using it till ten – '

'No – ' Harriet followed her into the anaesthetic room, and watched Sally as she began to check the machines, sending gas hissing through the connections as she expertly turned each cylinder on and off. 'I need a bit of advice.'

'Ask away – ' Sally said, and stumbling a little over her words. Harriet told her of what had happened, of Gregory's flat denial that he knew anything about Tod, despite Tod's obvious recognition of him. Told her everything except of Gregory's kiss the night before, his statement that he would have to leave the Royal. That episode was too personal, and its implications too confused even to think about, let alone talk about, even to Sally.

Sally listened in silence, and when Harriet's voice died away, she looked up at her friend shrewdly and smiled at her. 'You don't really want my advice, Harriet. What you want is for me to listen while you tell me what you're going to do about this business. So tell me. I'm listening.'

Unwillingly, Harriet said, 'I don't want to start anything I can't control, Sal. I mean – suppose I do tell Dr Bennett what Tod said – and he puts the police on to Gregory? However I felt about him – if he was no more to me than just a member of the staff, I'd hate to do that when he so obviously doesn't want me to.'

'It would be a bit – sneaky,' Sally admitted. 'But aren't you being a bit schoolgirlish about this? What matters most? Tod, or an old fashioned notion of honour that if you follow it will leave Tod just where he is – unknown and unwanted? That's the real crux.'

Harriet nodded unhappily, and began to walk towards the door. 'I'd better get on duty,' she said. 'I suppose you're right, Sal. I just wish there was another way to find out – on my own, without going running to Dr Bennett and through him to the police.'

Behind her, Sally said with a diffidence that Harriet could almost feel. 'I – I suppose you've realised what this could mean, Harriet? You know so little about Gregory, don't you? He – Tod could be – related to him,' she finished awkwardly.

Without turning, Harriet said evenly, 'You mean Tod could be his child? Yes, I've thought about that. It's that that makes it – worse, somehow.'

'I imagine it would,' Sally said dryly. 'If I were you, I'd want to cut your precious Gregory's throat for him. But as I've said before, you and me – we just don't function in the same way.'

And as she made her way up to her own ward, Harriet thought bleakly, I wish I were as uncomplicated as Sally. But I'm not. And the possibility that Tod is Gregory's child makes me care even more about what happens. I love Gregory enough to love his child – even another woman's child – But she pushed the thought away, sickened suddenly by the vision that came unsought to her mind, a vision of a happy, gay Gregory, loving another woman, loving her more than Harriet, loving her enough to –

The ward was buzzing with activity as she came through the door, children bumbling about in their usual way, nurses feeding toddlers with plates of porridge and scrambled eggs, the ward maid lackadaisically pushing cots about as she started the day's cleaning. Harriet took the report from the tired night nurses, before sending them off to their breakfast and well earned sleep, and started her morning's round of her patients. The gassed children were lively this morning, showing little evidence of the state they had been in the night before, and the oldest asked her eagerly if she could see her Mummy. Harriet 'phoned the women's medical ward, and asked if the children could see their mother, and was told that the woman was much better this morning, and would be better still for the sight of her family. So the three children were wrapped in blankets, piled into one big wheelchair, and sent with a nurse to see their mother, bouncing joyously as they went, in imminent danger of tipping the chair and themselves down into a pile of kicking arms and legs.

Harriet smiled as she saw them on their way, relieved for them that they had survived their experience so well, and turned back to the ward to see the rest of the children. The child who had had his operation the day before was doing well, though feeling a little weepy and irritable, and Harriet promised him that his parents would be coming to see him very soon. As she tucked the miserable little creature more comfortably into his blankets, she could see Tod across the ward, sitting as usual in the corner of his bed, watching the children in the ward with his usual disinterested stare. Almost furtively, almost against her will, she watched him, trying to see some resemblance to Gregory in him. Was that how Gregory held his head? How his eyes were set in his face? But even with her now firm belief that this child was Gregory's son, she could see nothing of him in the small fair head, the wide blue eyes, and narrow face with its pointed chin.

There was a squeal from some of the older children as old Nickie, the hospital's elderly postman, came padding into the ward, his hands full of envelopes and parcels. The children clung to his knees, chattering excitedly, trying to pull the things from his gnarled old hands, and with his usual friendly grumbles, Nickie began to distribute his mail. Those children who could read grabbed their envelopes, and hurried off into corners to open their letters, and those who couldn't tore open theirs as nurses came to read the contents to them. When all the children had at last accepted that there were no more for them, and those without letters at all had been comforted by the sweets the old man always carried for the disappointed ones, he came over to Harriet, where she was rearranging a bandage on the ear of a child who was doing his best to remove it, a large parcel still under his arm.

'There's one here I'm not sure about, Sister,' he said, wheezing a little. 'Delivered by hand and addressed to this ward clear enough, but it just says "Tod" on it. No last name. Who would that be, now?'

Harriet, puzzled, put her hand out for the parcel, and Nickie gave it to her. It was neatly wrapped, and the label bore the sign of a big shop Harriet knew well, a shop in the main road near the hospital. It read 'Tod, c/o Sister, Children's Ward, Royal Hospital.' And Harriet took it over to Tod's bed, to sit with it beside him.

'This is for you, Tod,' she said gently. 'Would you like to open it?' but Tod just looked at it, and made no move.

With a sigh, Harriet opened the parcel, and slowly began to pull out the contents.

There was a pair of brown corduroy trousers, a neat red sweater, a woollen vest and underpants, and a pair of long brown socks. Under this, there was a brown duffle coat, and a yellow woollen cap with matching mittens, and a pair of red slippers, with cowboy hats embroidered all over them. A pair of red wellington boots completed the clothes, and tucked into one of them was a small blue toy car.

There was nothing else. No letter, no card, nothing. Just the things, and the label on the wrapping. Harriet slowly began to dress Tod in the clothes, pulling the straps of the trousers up with a pin, for they were too long for the frail child, sending a nurse to get a needle and thread to make a more permanent alteration. Tod seemed uninterested, making no effort to stop her, but also not helping her to put them on. The slippers fitted well, and when she had dressed him, putting the coat, cap, mittens and boots in his empty locker, Harriet carried him to the pile of toys in the middle of the floor, sitting him down with the other children in the hope he would start playing with them. But he just sat, his legs thrust out in front of him, his face watchful.

They suit him, she thought, these clothes. And they're good ones. That's an expensive shop – but who? –

With a sudden thought, she left Tod, and tearing the label from the wrappings of the parcel, hurried to her office. With crisp movements, she dialled the number of the shop, and when they answered, asked for the manageress.

Lying with a smooth facility that surprised her, she said glibly, 'I'm so sorry to bother you – but there seems to have been some sort of mistake. A parcel arrived here this morning – ' she described the contents, and said then, 'And this little boy doesn't know who sent them! He's the only one we have called Tod, but we wondered if there had been a mistake. May I ask if you can remember who bought them? The little boy's family would like to know if they were meant for him so that they can say thank you – '

The manageress seemed to be unsurprised, and went off to find the saleswoman who had arranged the sale, leaving Harriet clutching the 'phone with a cold hand. Maybe it was a relative, she thought with wild hope. Maybe someone does know he's here, and just doesn't want to claim him – but still wants to see he's properly equipped –

The voice of the saleswoman came clacking tinnily through the 'phone.

'Hello, Madam? You were asking about some clothes that I sold?'

Again Harriet described them, told the same lie about the child's parents, and the saleswoman seemed to accept her lies.

'Yes, I remember the sale quite well. Yesterday it was, just before we closed – it was a man bought them. He didn't seem to know the size – said the boy was about five or thereabouts. I hope the things fit all right?'

'They fit,' Harriet said quickly. 'Look, could you describe this man – then I can tell the child's parents – ' And with a great deal of careful attention to detail, the voice described Gregory, faithfully, even remembering his voice.

'A very nice man, he was,' she said cheerfully. 'Money no object, you know – wanted the best. Nice of him, wasn't it? I hope the parents like the things – '

'Yes – thank you,' Harriet said mechanically, and put the 'phone down as the saleswoman burbled on. She had known, really, she told herself dully. It had been mad to hope that it had been otherwise. Gregory had bought these clothes for Tod, had gone out at the end of a long day's work expressly to equip a child he swore he had never seen before in his life –

'Dr Bennett's here, Sister,' a nurse's voice brought her up sharply and Harriet hurried out of her office, pulling her cuffs straight on her sleeves as she went.

Dr Bennett was standing beside the group of children in the middle of the floor, a tall man beside him, both of them looking down at Tod's still little body, an oasis of silence in the middle of the noisy group of children.

'Good morning, Sister.' He greeted her with a cheerful smile. 'This is Dr Jeffcoate, Psychiatrist, you know. He's come from the University to see our little mystery. I thought perhaps he'd succeed where we failed – '

The tall man nodded at Harriet, and said, 'I'd like to examine this child – ' and Harriet picked the unresisting Tod up, and led the way back to her office. She sat Tod on her desk, and the two men stood and looked at him, while Tod looked silently back.

Crisply, Dr Jeffcoate began to ask questions of Harriet, about Tod's behaviour, the way he ate, moved, slept, and with equal crispness, Harriet answered him. She described the one occasion when Tod had seemed to respond to her, when he had slept on her lap after she had sung to him, described it in some detail. But she said nothing of what had happened the previous day.

'And he has never spoken,' Dr Jeffcoate said, watching Tod.

'No,' Harriet said in a low voice, almost sickened by her own lie. But she couldn't do it – couldn't possibly tell them of Gregory and Tod's recognition of him. That was something she would still have to work out for herself.

Swiftly, Dr Jeffcoate began to make a detailed neurological examination of Tod, pushing the things on Harriet's desk out of the way, and pillowing the child's head on the cushion from her chair, brusquely refusing her offer of the dressing cubicle.

'I can manage here,' he said, and put out an imperious hand for an ophthalmoscope, bending to peer intently through it at Tod's blue eyes, while Tod just lay on the desk, unresponsive as ever.

Dr Bennett and Harriet watched in silence, and at last, the psychiatrist straightened, and stood looking down at Tod.

'This may be a long job,' he said at length. 'Whatever has happened to this child has been clearly catastrophic as far as he is concerned. It will take considerable testing and observation before I could hazard a guess at his condition or prognosis.'

Dr Bennett said quickly, 'We can't keep him here for much longer, Jeffcoate. Quite apart from anything else, this is a general hospital – we haven't the facilities – '

'I realise that,' Dr Jeffcoate said. 'I could perhaps get him a place at one of the homes I visit. And as he's a ward of court, there'll be no problems about parental consent, of course – '

'Sir,' Harriet's voice sounded a little cracked as she moved forwards to stand protectively beside Tod. 'Sir – may I make a suggestion?'

Dr Jeffcoate peered sharply at her under bushy eyebrows, and Dr Bennett, one eyebrow raised interrogatively, looked at her with a trace of irritation in his face.

'Well, Sister? I've told you already we can't keep him here, however attached you may have become to him – '

Beseechingly, Harriet said. 'But – look, sir. The police found him near this hospital. He's too small to have wandered all that far from wherever he lived. Couldn't – couldn't I try to find his home? Just give me a little time, sir, before you move him to somewhere else. Please?'

'How do you propose to find his home?' Dr Jeffcoate asked dryly. 'I gather the police have failed – how do you think you can succeed if they can't? Or have you some information we and they haven't?'

Harriet pushed her guilty memory of Tod's behaviour yesterday away, and said eagerly, 'But even so, sir, no one's tried to use *Tod* to find out. Suppose – suppose he actually *saw* his home? Wouldn't he recognise it?' Of course he will, her mind said. He recognised Gregory –

'It's possible,' Dr Jeffcoate said. 'Remotely possible – '

'Let me try, sir,' Harriet said. 'Let me take him out – let me just walk him around the district and watch what happens. I know the area very well sir – I've made a point of getting to know it – and perhaps, if I'm lucky enough, I'll find a place he knows. Then – then perhaps we'll be able to discover who he belongs to – '

There was a long silence, Dr Bennett standing still, his face showing nothing, Dr Jeffcoate thinking carefully.

Then, Dr Jeffcoate said, 'It will be a couple of weeks before I can arrange a vacancy in a home anyway. If you're happy about the idea, Bennett, I see no harm in it. It'll get the child out of the ward and that won't do him any harm, and there's always the possibility that Sister here is right. He could perhaps be made to respond in an environment he remembers. And once he does, of course, the problem is solved. These acute conditions rarely require intensive psychiatric treatment once the initial block is broken down.'

Harriet turned and looked at Dr Bennett, her eyes pleading with him. 'Please?' she breathed. 'Please, sir?'

Dr Bennett cleared his throat harshly, and said, 'Oh, all right, Sister. If you can find the time, and Jeffcoate is sure it will do no harm, what can I say? We can block a bed for a couple of weeks, I suppose. As it's summer, and we don't get quite so many emergency demands for beds this time of the year. But just two weeks, mind.'

'Thank you, Dr Bennett,' Harriet smiled brilliantly at him, and picking Tod up, held the small body close, looking at the two men over the narrow shoulders. 'If I can just *try* – '

Dr Jeffcoate smiled suddenly, his face lifting out of its grim lines. 'He's a lucky child, Sister. At least he's got someone to care for him. And he needs that.'

And Harriet held Tod close, and said, 'Yes. I care for him.' She rubbed her cheeks against his smooth fair head. 'I care for him.'

10

Harriet spread the map on her bedroom floor, and fixed the corners firmly with books. Then she sat back on her heels, and looked at it.

'See, Sally? If I use the hospital as a central point, and draw circles out from it, then I can map out exactly which areas to cover each time we go out. And if I really study it, then there'll be no danger of missing a single street.'

Sally, lying on her front on Harriet's bed, her fair hair flopping over her face as she twisted her head to see the map the right way up, sighed, and said, 'I still think it's crazy. This hospital's in the middle of one of the most tightly packed areas of London, and you think you can cover on foot every possible place this kid could have come from. And anyway, you've no proof he even lived anywhere near hear.'

Patiently, Harriet went over her reasoning, point by point. 'He's too small to have travelled far on foot. It is more than unlikely that any bus conductor would have let him ride on a bus by himself – even if he'd had the fare, which is equally unlikely. If he even managed to travel on the underground, why should he have chosen to come to this particular area? I know he was found near the underground station, but that was just a coincidence – '

'Hasn't it occurred to you that it's a pretty wild coincidence that he should have turned up here in the first place? I mean, if Gregory is related to him – '

'I know,' Harriet said brusquely. 'But maybe it isn't such a coincidence after all. I mean, if Gregory – knows – the child's mother, there'd be every reason for – for her to live near where he works – '

'Poor old Harriet,' Sally said softly. 'This is cutting you to ribbons, isn't it?'

'Can't be helped,' Harriet said, and bent her head to her map again.

And indeed, every way she turned, the situation seemed loaded with pain for her. Convinced as she was that Tod was Gregory's son, she had been forced to face the fact that somewhere there was a girl who belonged to Gregory, belonged to him in a way she longed to belong herself. Bleakly she felt that whatever happened, even if by some miracle she and Gregory ever did build together the life she wanted, it would always be shadowed for her by the memory of this other girl. Not that it looked as though there would ever be a future now.

'He's leaving, you know,' Harriet said suddenly.

Sally raised her head sharply. 'Leaving? Gregory?'

'So he said,' Harriet still didn't look up.

'But – he can't be,' Sally said. 'He's been offered the junior consultancy in urology – '

'What?' Harriet did look up now, her face blank with surprise.

'They were talking in theatre this morning,' Sally explained. 'Old Peter Leeman is retiring this autumn – and Sir David told him that Gregory had been accepted by the Board to replace him. He didn't tell you?'

Harriet shook her head. 'When did this happen?'

'Yesterday, as far as I know. Look, it's quite possible Gregory doesn't know himself yet. The Board only met last week, and you know how long it takes them to publish their mighty ponderings. I shouldn't have heard it myself – but I always eavesdrop on the surgeons' room. I can hear every word from my office, and I make sure I always do! It could be that they won't announce their decision till Founder's Day, next month – old Sir David likes to bring a bit of pomp and circumstance into things, and it'd be just like him to announce the new appointment then.'

'Maybe he won't leave, then,' Harriet said slowly. 'It's quite a thing to get an appointment like that – not even Gregory could turn it down – just because of me.'

'Who knows? If he's as mixed up with his private life as he seems to be, maybe he'll be forced to give the job a miss. Face it, Harriet, for God's sake! He's supposed to be in love with you, yet it seems he's got a family of some sort already – in a mess like that, the only thing to do *is* cut and run. Quite honestly, love, it'd be best for you if he *did* leave. Give you a chance to get over him, hmm?' but Sally didn't sound too hopeful, and was forced to reply with a grin to Harriet's own rueful grimace.

'Sure,' Harriet said wryly. 'Gregory goes away and whoosh! All gone nasty miseries! Harriet's the same old Harriet again! I wish it were as easy as that.'

Sally wisely left it there. There was little point in trying again to change Harriet's point of view. And as Sally herself had realised, the day she had found Harriet weeping so bitterly over the little porcelain girl, somehow this love affair was meant to be. For all her practicality, Sally was aware of the inevitableness of it, the very real mutual attraction that pulled these two people together so powerfully.

So she made a pot of coffee, and sat quietly drinking hers while Harriet made a rough drawing of the area she meant to cover with Tod the next day, the first half day she had been able to arrange since Dr Bennett had given her permission to take Tod looking for a place he might remember.

She hadn't seen Gregory since that evening in the garden, when he had kissed her, a kiss she could still feel bruising her mouth if she let her thoughts take her back three days. The patients he had on her ward were either seen by his house-surgeon, or a message would come up from outpatients where Gregory would be holding a clinic, asking her to send those children he needed to see down there. There was no doubt in Harriet's mind that he was avoiding her, and much as she ached for a sight of him, to have him near enough to remind herself of the way his arms had felt about her that night that now seemed so long ago, she was obscurely grateful for his absence. In a way, she had transposed some of her feeling for Gregory to Tod, and there was one thought now that persisted above all others. She must find Tod's home. Somehow, she must find it.

It was with an absurdly optimistic lift in her heart that she got Tod dressed in his new duffle coat the next afternoon. The shoes he had been wearing the day he was admitted were polished carefully, and didn't show their shabbiness quite so badly, and she pulled the little woollen cap over his fair head, and put the mittens on his hands, even though it was summer now; he looked too fragile to be warmed even by the fitful sunshine of a typical May afternoon – typically blowy, as only an English May can be.

She had managed to beg the use of an elderly pushchair from the physiotherapy department, and she tucked Tod into it at the main gate of the hospital, and looked deeply into his eyes as she crouched in front of him, strapping his narrow body in.

'I'm going to take you for a walk, Tod, my love,' she told his silent face. 'Just for a walk. And if you want to go anywhere special, just show me, hmm?' But he made no movement in reply.

In later years, Harriet was to remember that first afternoon when she walked with Tod through the narrow clamorous streets of the close packed corner of London that she knew so well, remember that first afternoon in detail. She trudged up street after street, past high narrow fronted houses with flights of steps in front of them, past the blocks of flats that reared their massive bulk over the bare patches that had once been bomb-damaged during the war, threading her way through pavements filled with chattering groups of women, dodging screeching children, passing small shops, big shops, edging past patient bus queues, waiting wearily for traffic lights to change green so that they could cross the wider traffic-roaring roads.

The passing scene blurred a little, seeming to bob up and down with her own movement, and Tod's brown coated form sat slumped in the pushchair in front of her, his yellow hat bobbing too, as the pushchair went on its creaking way, the wheels squeaking their lack of oil at her.

And gradually, the circle she had planned to cover round the hospital on that first afternoon was covered. Street after street passed by them, mile after mile of grey pavement slid away under her weary feet. Three hours after she had left the hospital she began to work her way back towards it, passing along ever new roads, past rows and rows of anonymous houses. And still Tod sat still, not moving, no sign of the stiffening of the shoulders that Harriet was watching for, the sign of some sort of tension that would show her she was near his home ground.

And for a whole week, it went on. She arranged for her own off duty to be every afternoon, much to the joy of her nurses, who thus had more free evenings than they were accustomed to get. Harriet's days became a weary trek, each morning occupied with the rush of ward work, each long evening on duty ending with an exhausted bath and restless sleep, with the eternal trudging through the streets every afternoon, with Tod in his pushchair in front of her, a Tod as apparently unaware of his surroundings as he seemed to be in the ward.

Most evenings, Sally would call in at the ward on her own way off duty to ask with a mute look for news, and each time, Harriet would shake her head silently. Sally could have wept for Harriet, at the way her eyes seemed to grow larger in her face as she lost weight almost visibly, at the violet shadows that stained the hollows of her cheeks, painting the skin under her eyes with the ugly badge of fatigue. Even Paul, on his visits to patients in the ward, was worried, asking Sally privately what was the matter with Harriet – was she ill? And Sally, almost impatient at her own loyalty to what she considered Harriet's idiotic behaviour, didn't tell him, passing it off as 'just one of those things'.

Paul asked Harriet one evening what was the trouble, and the concern on his friendly and familiar face made the weary Harriet want to cry, to throw herself onto him, to hold onto his strength. But she had laughed with a lightness she had to fight to dissimulate, and changed the subject to a discussion of one of the children in the ward.

On each of the long afternoons when they walked through diesel smelling streets, Harriet would stop the chair for a while, would lift Tod out, and put his mittened fist on to the side of the pushchair, closing his unresisting fingers round it, so that he held on. Then, slowly she would walk on, and Tod, pulled by the chair, walked too. This at least, Harriet felt, was something. By the end of the week, he was walking more strongly, and for longer periods, before showing signs of being tired, would even begin to trot beside her if she did not make him hold on to the chair. And even as her own physical health seemed to suffer from the long and agonising programme she had set herself, so Tod seemed to improve. The food he was eating so voraciously began to show on his thin frame; he filled out, his legs losing the pathetic skinny spaghetti look, his cheeks beginning to flush with the faint rose that other children had even in these crowded city streets.

As they walked, Harriet dividing her attention between the route they were taking and Tod's face, always watching for some sign that he recognised the street they were in, her thoughts would take their own way, and she was too bone tired to be able to control them.

She wondered about this girl – Tod's mother – the girl she felt sure she would find soon, one of these afternoons. For there was no doubt in her mind now that Tod had a mother, somewhere. She knew enough about children to realise that whatever had broken the bond between his mother and himself – whether it had been a street accident, or what it had been – Tod had had a close relationship with her, and it was the loss of this closeness that had driven him to the silent misery she felt in him.

She found herself weaving fantasies about the girl, fantasies that could explain her silence, explain why she had not come to find this little boy who trotted so quietly at Harriet's side. And as she grew tireder, so her fantasies became wilder, filled with melodramatic ideas of abduction, even murder. But when this happened, she forced herself to stop, telling herself with heavy common sense that the girl had probably just run off somewhere, sick of caring for her child, sick of Gregory's silence. For Harriet now believed that Gregory had wilfully abandoned the girl, the girl and her child, and had left them without a backward glance.

And so her attitude to Gregory changed, sick loathing of him fighting the love that still filled her whenever she thought of his lean body and grizzled head, until her head spun wildly, till she hardly knew what she felt or what she was doing. Only a dumb determination to find the answer for Tod's sake kept her going.

And then, so suddenly that she was caught unawares, the very thing she had been hoping would happen did at last happen; and so tired was she that she had almost forgotten why she was walking these dreary streets with Tod.

They had just turned into a narrow alley-way of a street, a street lined on both sides with small houses whose chipped and peeling front doors opened directly onto the greasy pavements. There was no sign of any green anywhere, no front gardens to hold the dusty privet hedges that helped to liven some of the roads in the district. Only patches of gay curtains in one or two of the windows lifted the general greyness, and these were few; most of the houses were as dirty and ill kept as they were ugly.

Tod stopped short, and Harriet had walked on a few paces before she realised that the yellow hat was no longer bobbing at her side. She turned, and stared back at Tod, where he stood stock still in the middle of the pavement.

His head was up, his chin pointing straight ahead of him, his whole body rigid as his blue eyes slowly moved along the street, staring at a tiny grimy shop window full of empty packets of cigarettes and dusty models of boxes of chocolates, at the rubbish filled gutters, the narrow houses.

Almost too tense to breathe, Harriet watched him, making no sound. Then slowly, Tod began to move, to walk first, and then to run, his thin legs gathering momentum. He ran past her, without looking at her, and abandoning the pushchair, Harriet ran after him.

He stopped at the last house in the street, to stand at the front door, a door that had once been green but now bore only traces of paint on its blistered woodwork. His face had lost its stillness, the emptiness that Harriet had come to accept as part of him, was crumpled in an agonising grimace. Then, suddenly, he pushed on the door, pushed hard, and the door clicked and opened.

He stood poised in the dark opening, and Harriet stood behind him to look into the narrow hallway beyond, hardly seeing the dirty wallpaper, the unscrubbed bare wooden boards, the broken bicycle leaning against one wall.

From beyond a tattered curtain that screened the far end of the dingy hallway, a voice called "Oo is it? That you, Joe? – 'Oo is it?' and the curtain parted. An old woman in a dirty overall, her thin hair pulled into metal curlers, a smudge of grime across her forehead, came slouching towards them, a frown appearing on her wrinkled face.

'Oo – ' Then she saw Tod, and with a look of pure surprise she cried 'Davey – Davey! Where you come from, Davey?'

And the child at Harriet's side screamed a loud inhuman scream, and turned to Harriet to bury his head in her skirt, to weep the first tears she had seen him weep since she had first known him.

11

He clung to Harriet, held on to her with all the strength he had, and Harriet held him close, picking him up to croon gently to him, rocking him in an attempt to soothe the bitter weeping that threatened to tear him apart.

The old woman in curlers, clucking a sympathetic counterpoint to the child's noisy weeping, pulled them both into the house, leading them into the kitchen at the end of the hallway. Even in the midst of her distress for the child who was clinging so tightly to her, Harriet was repulsed by the smell of the cluttered room, the mixture of cats, of meals long ago cooked, eaten and forgotten, of sheer dirt. The woman shoved a pile of newspapers off a shabby broken armchair, and pushed Harriet into it, and she sat and rocked monotonously, until the shaking body in her arms gradually relaxed, till the tears that stained the swollen eyes and ravaged the smooth young cheeks had stopped.

'Well, I never,' the woman said, moving heavily about the tiny room, making ineffectual attempts to tidy it into some semblance of order. 'What's up with him? Why's he crying so? Poor little feller – takin' it hard, is he? Well, it's no wonder, is it? Always was a quiet one, was Davey, and these quiet ones – well, they do run deep, don't they, like people always say? Quiet ones run deep.'

'Look,' Harriet said. 'I must talk to you – but it's a bit difficult with Tod – Davey here. Is – can I 'phone from anywhere? I'll try to get him back, and then I can talk to you – '

The old woman looked dubious, and peered suspiciously at her. 'Well, I don't know, I'm sure – I mean, why should you want to talk to me? From the Council are you?' She looked at the scrap of dress that showed beneath Harriet's coat, her uniform dress.

'No, I'm not from the Council. I work at the Royal – and Tod – Davey's a patient there. And I must get him back before I talk to you – '

'There's a 'phone over at the shop,' the woman said unwillingly. 'But I – ' Awkwardly, because of the way the child was clinging to her, Harriet fumbled in her pocket, and pulled a crumpled ten shilling note out. The woman brightened, and said with senile briskness, 'Well, I suppose I could go for you. 'Oo do I 'phone?'

'The Royal – and ask for Sister Andrews on the theatres. Tell her, will you, that Sister Brett needs her at once. Tell her what the address is, and tell her to take a taxi – say it's urgent.'

Mutttering the message under her breath, and repeating the number to herself the old woman slouched off, and Harriet was left sitting in the dim and dirty kitchen, the child on her lap still snuffling softly as he clung to her.

Gently, Harriet disentangled his grasp, pulled him up till she could look at him. 'Davey?' she said gently. 'Davey?'

The child lifted his head, looked at her and repeated, 'Davey,' in a voice thick with tears.

'Did you live in this house, Davey, love?' Harriet asked softly. 'Was this your house?'

The child nodded jerkily, and then he said, 'Mummy – Mummy –'

'With Mummy?'

His face crumpled again, and tears filled the blue eyes. 'Mummy – ' he said, choking through his misery. 'Mummy won't wake up – Mummy – '

And Harriet, unable to bear the look on his thin face held him close, letting her pity and love pour over him, too upset herself to question the pitiful little boy any more.

The woman came back very soon, and told her that she had spoken to Sally, that 'She's comin' right over, she says. Says not to worry – she'll be here soon as may be. Must be well off, you hospital people, takin' taxis all over the place – '

Harriet answered absently, still holding Davey close in her arms, her head full of the questions she must ask this woman, but feeling instinctively that she could not ask them in the child's hearing. Whatever had happened here was too raw, too agonising to be talked about in front of him.

The fifteen minutes that it took Sally to arrive seemed to

Harriet an eternity, and her relief when she heard the door rattle, heard Sally's clear voice calling out her name was so great it almost overcame her.

She hurried to the door, carrying Davey with her, and very quickly, told Sally what had happened.

'His name is Davey – and he's desperately upset, Sally. Look, I must talk to this woman, but I can't – not till Davey's settled. Please, Sal, take him back for me, will you? Get him to bed, and get Staff Nurse to give him some nepenthe – it's written up for him and I think he needs it. I'll get on to Dr Bennett myself as soon as I get back – '

Sally nodded, and climbed back into the taxi that still sat at the curb, its engine ticking over quietly. Davey resisted at first, as Harriet gently put him onto Sally's lap.

'It's all right, love. This is Sally and she's my friend. She'll take you back to bed, and then I'll come soon. I must talk first – I won't be long – ' and the child was suddenly too weary, too emotionally exhausted by his distress, to argue. Harriet watched his white face at the window as the taxi disappeared round the corner on its way back to the Royal, and then she turned, and stopping to salvage the pushchair, made her way back to the house where the slatternly woman was standing leaning against the door, chattering busily to the few women who had emerged from their own houses to watch what was going on.

'I'm sorry there was so much noise,' Harriet began, feeling she must propitiate this rather horrible woman if she was to get anything out of her. 'But now, if you could spare the time, perhaps we could talk?'

The woman peered at her and said with a cunning sideways look at Harriet's coat pocket, 'Well, time's money you know – ' and obediently Harriet reached for her purse, and found another ten shilling note.

'Well, now Sister – Brett wasn't it?' The old woman led the way back to the dingy kitchen and settled herself in the armchair. She looked up at Harriet and grinned. 'I'm Mrs Ross – owns this house I does. What can I do for you?'

'You know that little boy?' Harriet asked crisply.

'Know 'im? Know 'im? Course I do! Lived in my house two years he did! Course I know him!' Mrs Ross looked suddenly suspicious. 'Any reason why I shouldn't?'

'I'd better explain – ' Harriet said wearily, and as simply as she could told Mrs Ross the whole story of Tod – Davey – she would find it difficult to use his real name for some time –and the mystery that surrounded him. The woman listened enthralled, her mouth half open. 'I thought I'd find somewhere he'd recognise if I tried hard enough,' Harriet finished. 'And he recognised this house – and that's all I know. The rest I've got to find out from you.'

'Well, I never.' Mrs Ross was clearly delighted. 'There's a thing! Just like a film, 'nt it? Poor little sod – '

'Please,' Harriet said, sickened by the look of senile pleasure in Mrs Ross's eyes. 'Who is he? Where's his mother?'

'Well, that's it, you see! He's lost her – dead she is! Poor little thing!'

Slowly, Harriet got the story out of her, patiently questioning, leading the garrulous old woman back to the point every time she strayed off it, which was very often.

Davey's mother had been a girl called Susan Brooks, and she and Davey had come to Mrs Ross's house two years before. She had told Mrs Ross that her husband was dead – though Mrs Ross, with all the painfully acquired wisdom of her London background, didn't believe for one moment that she ever had a husband. Mrs Ross had let her the two top front rooms 'at a shockin' low rent, mind you, but I was sorry for the poor cow – ' and they had moved in. She had made her living as a dressmaker, taking in work from a small wholesale dress factory round the corner, and a very poor living it had been.

'Hardly set foot outside the place she didn't, except to fetch and carry her work. And wouldn't let the boy out neither. She wouldn't let her Davey play out in the street, not her! – kids down here not good enough, I suppose – but I'd let him play out in my back yard sometimes. She'd take him walks around the streets now and again, but not too often. And she never talked to no one, nor got a letter or anything. I told her – only a few weeks before she died, poor thing, told her she'd have to let the boy go soon. Couldn't keep him at her apron ends always, I told her. He'd have to go to school, one day – five he is, and the truant people'll be after you, I told her. But there – she just smiled the way she did, all secret, and never argued or said anything – '

'So that's why no one came forward – ' Harriet said slowly.

'Eh?'

'His picture was put in the papers, and on television, but no one seemed to recognise it. If she never let him go out, no one but you really knew him well enough to recognise him – '

'In the papers, was it? Well, there! If only I'd 'a' known! But I don't take a paper – can't be bothered to read much, like – not at my age, and people like me, we can't afford no television sets – ' and she leered up at Harriet greedily.

Harriet ignored the hint, and asked, 'What – happened when she died?'

'Well!' Mrs Ross settled herself more comfortably in her chair, and began to talk, taking a morbid delight in her story, a delight that made Harriet's flesh creep.

Late one afternoon, Mrs Ross had gone panting upstairs to get something from the back room she used as a general junk room – she rarely climbed the stairs otherwise – and had seen Susan Brooks's door open. The other door – their bedroom door – was closed, and Mrs Ross had looked into the room they used as a living room 'to say hello, like. I'm friendly, always was – ' and seen the girl in a heap on the floor. In a great flurry of excitement, she had shrieked from the window to call a neighbour, and an ambulance had been called. Susan Brooks had been taken off to hospital – not the Royal, but the smaller hospital on the other side of this particular part of London, but she had been dead when she arrived there.

'Just collapsed, they said,' Mrs Ross said ghoulishly, 'Just up and died, the doctor reckoned. Didn't feed herself properly, he said, and then went and got this virus pneumonia. I daresay you'll understand better'n I would – '

Harriet nodded. A girl in a poor state of health could well die quite suddenly from a virus pneumonia, even after a very short illness.

'But what about Davey?' Harriet was puzzled, 'Why didn't you tell anyone about him?'

Mrs Ross looked a little furtive, and glanced sideways at Harriet with hooded eyes. 'Well, I never thought to, like. I mean, I wasn't to know was I? I thought as how she'd maybe sent him off to visit someone or something – I wasn't to know.'

'You said she had no friends,' Harriet said, cold with anger.

'Well, I wasn't to know! He wasn't here, that's all I knew. And it wasn't none of my concern. I had enough to put up with, what with her dying here like that – I wasn't going running around after a kid that's got nothing to do with me – '

'He must have found her,' Harriet said, remembering the pinched little face, the way he had said, 'Mummy – won't wake up – ' and she felt sick. 'He must have found her, and tried to rouse her, and when he couldn't, just ran out of the house in fright. No wonder he got into such a state – he must have been hurt in a traffic accident as well, and in the state of mind he was in, I'm not surprised – How could you just *do* nothing – not tell someone – the police – anyone, about him?'

'I don't go tangling with no police,' the old woman said belligerently. 'I told you, it was none of my concern. He wasn't my kid, was he?'

And Harriet was forced to leave it at that. How anyone could be so indolent as to do nothing in such a situation, she could not for the life of her understand. But so it had been and she had to accept it.

'They gave me the death certificate,' Mrs Ross seemed herself to understand Harriet's anger, and began to offer more information without waiting for questions. 'I couldn't do nothing about a funeral, of course – cost money, they do – but the hospital said they'd take care of that, as there was no relatives or nothing, so there you are! But I kept all her bits – well, all except for those I had to sell to get my rent – entitled to that, I was, in law – '

Harriet didn't argue, and in a cold angry silence, took the paper carrier bag the woman pulled out of a cluttered cupboard and turned to go.

'I hope you got enough rent money,' she said bitterly. 'It would never do if you *lost* money, would it?'

'Don't you be so high and mighty, you!' Mrs Ross flared in sudden rage. 'What do you know about it? You with your taxis and your tenshillingses? You never went without in your life, did you? Well, I did, and I ain't going to again, not if I can help it. I had to clear those rooms, had to get another lodger for them – and I had every right to sell those bits. She had no one, had she? And I reckoned if the boy had run off, it'd be best for him. If I'd have gone and told, they'd just have copped him and shoved him in a home somewhere – some rotten home. I reckoned he'd be better running off if that was what he'd done – better running the streets than locked up in some lousy home, poor little bastard – '

And for a moment, Harriet could understand, feel with this woman, see the reality of her dingy existence and what it had done to her. And in all fairness, her silence about Davey could have been rooted in a misguided kindness of heart. When this woman had been a child, orphans had a pretty tough time of it, she reminded herself, looking down on the dirty face peering bitterly up at her in the dull hallway. Perhaps she really meant well.

Impulsively, she put her hand out, and took Mrs Ross's gnarled one.

'I'm sorry,' she said. 'I think I understand. I was – upset. I've become fond of the boy, you see. Thank you for your help.'

'That's all right,' the woman mumbled, suddenly shy. 'You wasn't to know. But like I said, when you're old, and on your own, like me, you got to take care of yourself – look after number one. No one else won't will they? I did my best for that poor cow and her bastard – and *I* like him too. He'll be all right now, won't he? You'll see after him, won't you?'

'I will,' Harriet said, and left Mrs Ross standing in the door of her dirty little house, watching her as she hurried down the street towards the main road and the hospital.

Harriet turned and looked back once more, before she finally turned the corner, at the ugly little house that had been Davey's home as long as he could remember, probably, at the narrow street that had been the only place he had known. Then, with a brief wave of her hand at the distant shape of Mrs Ross, she hurried away, clutching under her arm a paper carrier bag, a bag which held all that Davey owned in the world, his inheritance from the girl who had been his mother.

12

She took the paper carrier bag on duty with her, hiding it under her cape, for she had no time when she got back to the hospital to do more than put on her cap and apron and hurry on duty. And she felt that she couldn't wait till the end of the evening to look at the contents of the bag.

Tod – Davey, she reminded herself again – was sleeping the exhausted sleep of the very young when she got to the ward, and a note from Sally was waiting on her desk.

'I had to get back on duty,' she had scribbled, 'ran out in the middle of a list when that ghastly old woman 'phoned, so I daren't hang about. He didn't need the nepenthe, poor little scrap – he was flat out before we got back. I'll try to come to the ward as soon as I'm straight in theatre to find out what happened and apologise. I never thought it would work! If I can't get to the ward I'll see you over in the Home – '

Mechanically, Harriet worked through the evening, and when the last baby had been fed, the last visitor had left and the children were settled for the night, she almost fell into the chair at her desk. Her staff nurse, a quiet girl for whom Harriet was grateful at this moment, silently brought a tray of tea and toast, and insisted she finished all of it before consenting to go off duty.

'You look bushed, Sister,' she said with some severity, 'and you'll be ill if you don't eat something – you've missed your lunch every day this week,' and Harriet didn't argue, drinking the tea with thirsty gratitude under the staff nurse's watchful eye.

She went eventually, leaving a junior to move quietly round the ward finishing off odd jobs before the night staff came on duty, and Harriet at last could examine the carrier bag and its contents.

She sat and looked at it for a moment, and her mind dredged up a memory of something she had read somewhere, about the death of a woman. 'And all those things she didn't want seen, and all those things she didn't want touched, they were seen and touched by strangers – ' and the infinite tragedy of these inanimate objects in their shabby torn container washed over her almost unbearably. And then she looked through the glass partition down the ward to where she could see bed seven with its crumpled pillow hiding Davey's fair head, and reminded herself that this was his, this bag of oddments, and that she must investigate them for him. With shaking fingers, she pulled the bag towards her, and began to pull the things out.

There were pitifully few. A cardboard box with a few pieces of cheap costume jewellery, too cheap even to have been worth Mrs Ross's attention, a needle book, a box of pins, several reels of sewing thread, a tape measure, a thimble. A writing pad and a ball point pen, a child's picture book, and a pile of photographs in an envelope completed the collection.

Harriet slowly picked up the envelope, a big brown one, and shook its contents out on to the desk. Most of them were snapshots, fuzzy blurred pictures of a fair haired girl, some taken in a garden, some on a long forgotten seaside holiday. There were a few of a child, a solemn fair baby, and peering at them, Harriet could recognise Davey's face as it had been in his infancy; even then he must have been an unhappy child, for none of the pictures showed him smiling, just staring at the camera.

And at the bottom of the pile, there was one other picture in a cheap plastic frame. Harriet turned it over, and stared at the face that looked up at her from behind the distorted clear plastic covering. It was Gregory's face, a younger Gregory, with his dark hair free of any hint of white, his face less lined than she knew it, but Gregory just the same.

She stared at it for a long time, her mind numb. So this was how Davey had recognised Gregory. This picture. The corners of the frame were scuffed with long standing on a hard surface, and Harriet thought dimly – it must have been kept where he could see it, on a table perhaps – fantasy took over again.

'Who is that, Mummy?' she seemed to hear the child's high voice asking. 'That? Gregory, Davey, That's Greg.' but she couldn't imagine the voice that made the answer, couldn't really visualise the girl in the photograph alive and talking to her child.

She put the picture down, and as she did, the pile of photographs slid to the floor. She bent to pick them up, and a piece of paper she had not noticed before fell out of the pile. Carefully she smoothed its grimy folds.

It was a birth certificate. David Weston Brooks, the firm handwriting in the section marked 'Name' read. Born in the Borough of Marylebone, date of birth August seventh. Mother Susan Weston, Dressmaker. Father Timothy Brooks, Medical practitioner.

Harriet stared at it, her thought whirling. He's nearly six then, she thought vaguely. Too small for his age – much too small. Timothy Brooks? Who was he? And then suddenly, the full implication of the child's name hit her. David Weston Brooks. Weston. And her heart lurched sickeningly.

There was a movement behind her, and she raised eyes blurred with sudden tears to see the night nurses at the door, looking at her with faint surprise on their faces, the newly awakened look that is a night nurse's badge at the end of everyone else's day making her suddenly aware of her own deep fatigue.

With cold fingers she thrust the certificate and the photographs back into their bag, and stumbling a little over her words, gave the night nurses the report, before taking her cape and, hugging the bag close to her, slipped silently from the sleeping ward.

She stopped outside the double doors, to look stupidly at the lift waiting to take her down to the ground floor, at the porter with the pile of drums to be sterilised waiting to close the gates after her.

'I'm going down with this lot, Sister,' he said cheefully. 'But there's still room for you – '

But almost without thinking, she shook her head at him, and he clashed the gates shut and rattled the lift away. Her feet seemed to move of their own volition, carrying her down one flight of stairs, along a quiet corridor, towards the doctors' quarters.

The door to the common room was half open, and she could hear a burst of laughter from the men who were sitting there over their after dinner coffee, smell the tobacco smoke that came curling through the door out into the dimly lit corridor. A maid came out of the common room, balancing a tray on one hip as she closed the door. She peered up at Harriet with some surprise, and Harriet said unevenly, 'I – I was looking for Mr Weston. Is he in the common room?'

The maid looked knowingly at her, and grinned. 'No, Sister.

He's in his room. Always has his coffee on his own, he does. Down the end,' with a jerk of her head she indicated a row of doors that ran into the shadows along the corridor, and grinned again as Harriet thanked her, and began to walk down the corridor towards the end room. Harriet could feel the girl's eyes on her back, could almost hear the unpleasant thoughts she was obviously relishing, wanted to turn and shout at her – I'm not what you think – I'm not – but she ignored her, and with a resolution she hardly knew she had, raised her hand and tapped on the wooden panels.

There was silence for a second, then his voice, a little surprised, called 'Yes?'

Slowly, she turned the knob, and pushed the door open. He was sitting in an armchair, a book on his lap, the light from the small table lamp beside him throwing deep shadows on to his face. He stared at her for a long moment, then got to his feet, letting the book fall to the floor to lie ignored in a tangle of flopping pages at his feet. Slowly, she closed the door behind her, and leaned against it, her heart thumping thickly under her ribs.

'Gregory – ' her voice sounded harsh, croaking, and she swallowed in an effort to clear it. 'Gregory – ' she said again, and then went dumb, standing there, swaying a little, her eyes on his face.

He seemed to Harriet to be standing in a nimbus of light, as the lamp behind him threw his body into sharp silhouette, and when he moved sharply towards her, the whole room seemed to blur, the light suddenly shimmering redly before her eyes. It had not occurred to her that she looked anything but her usual self to Gregory, and the sudden look of anxiety that she saw on his face startled her. But to Gregory, she looked dreadful, her face devoid of any colour, her cheeks muddy, her eyes looking huge in her pinched face.

Swiftly, he pulled her forwards, leading her to the chair, taking her cape from her, and she sat still for a moment trying to push away the sudden sensation of giddiness that was making her head swim. Then, her vision cleared, and she looked at him where he sat on the edge of his bed, his hands lying loosely clasped between his knees.

'I'm – I'm sorry to come here like this,' she began huskily. 'I had to show you something.'

She dropped her head before his steady gaze, and began to

fumble in the bag she was still clutching. The big brown envelope with its pictures and Davey's birth certificate stuck for a moment almost as though it had a will of its own and didn't want to be brought out, but she managed to extricate it, and wordlessly, held it out to Gregory.

There was a shadow of a frown on his face as he put out a hand to take it from her.

'Open it,' she said. 'Open it. It – I think it concerns you.'

Slowly, he turned the envelope upside down, letting the contents fall onto the counterpane beside him, and with steady fingers, picked up the pictures one by one. She couldn't watch him, couldn't bear to see how he would react, and she closed her eyes sharply, leaning back against her chair, listening to the faint rustle of paper as he picked up the birth certificate.

The silence seemed to stretch into eternity. Slowly, she opened her eyes, blinking a little against the sharp onslaught of light.

He was sitting quite still, staring ahead of him, Davey's birth certificate in one lax hand. And then, to her sick horror, she saw the glint of tears on his lined cheeks, saw the empty misery in his dark eyes, and without thinking, she threw herself from her chair, came to crouch on the floor at his feet. He looked down at her, making no attempt to hide his tears from her, and his face crumpled at the sight of her own anxious face so close to his.

Gently, she put her arms round him, pulled his head down to rest on her breast, held him as she would a child, and he shook in her arms, trembling like a frightened baby.

How long they sat like that she didn't know. All she could think was that she had done something quite dreadful, and hurt this man she loved as no one had ever hurt him before. And then he moved, pulled himself away from her, and walked across the room to the window to stand staring out of it into the darkness.

Then his voice, thick, shaking a little with an effort to control it, came quietly across the silence.

'You had to do it, didn't you, Harriet? Had to know?'

'Yes,' she said gently, suddenly feeling strong again, the weariness and misery that had beset her for so long seeming to change into a strength and a compassion she must give him. 'I had to know. Not for my own sake, Gregory – not entirely. But he's so small, so lost. I have to know for him – whatever it did to you.'

'Seven years ago I married Susan. Susan.' His voice seemed

remote, as though he were talking of someone else's marriage, not his own.

'She was twenty – eleven years younger than me. And I loved her. I'd never loved anyone before. Not till I saw her. But she – she was young, and a little spoiled, and I thought she needed me. So I married her.'

'Please – don't, Gregory. Don't tell me if you don't want to. I – all that I wanted to find out was about Tod – Davey. I – '

She didn't want to listen to him, didn't want him to strip himself before her like this. It was almost indecent, as though she was an evil minded creature, as though she were sitting watching a man suffer for her own pleasure. 'Don't tell me – '

'I'm going to tell you!' He whirled from the window, came to stand above her, staring at her angrily, his face harsh and ugly. 'I'm going to tell you! You've done this yourself – you've made me grovel, and by God, you're going to sit there and bloody well listen – and I hope you enjoy it!'

'No – ' she said. 'No – '

But he stood there, towering above her, making her look at him, fixing his eyes on hers.

'I loved her – but I couldn't love her as she wanted. Do you know what I mean? Do you? She wanted physical love – needed it as no woman ever needed anything – and I couldn't satisfy her. She laughed at me – taunted me. I worshipped her – wanted to cherish her, but she threw my love back at me. I wasn't a man, she said, wasn't a man. I couldn't satisfy her.' He laughed suddenly, a bitter laugh. 'Oh, don't look so sick! It wasn't a complete frost – I consummated our marriage, if that's what you're wondering. But I couldn't – couldn't – satisfy her. She was – voracious. She didn't want my sort of love – gentle love. She wanted – '

Harriet, her hands shaking, dropped her head into them, tried to cover her ears, 'I don't want to know – don't – ' but he pulled her hands away, made her listen, made her hear him.

'And then she found other people who could satisfy her – not just one – others. And when – when I tried to make love to her, she told me about them, described them – can you understand that? What it was like? Can you?'

She was crying now, tears running down her face as she shook her head at him piteously, begging him with her eyes to stop, aching at the agony in his face.

But he was remorseless. 'And then she got pregnant. And the

man who gave her that baby was a friend of mine – a friend. And when I told her I would go on loving her, that she would have her baby, that I would care for it, she laughed again, and told me she was sick of me, that she didn't intend to live a life with a man who couldn't please her – and she went. Just went – '

And then he stopped, sat down suddenly beside her and stared at her bleakly. Trembling, she rubbed her wet face, and looked back at him, at the brooding eyes, the tight mouth. She wanted to run, to turn and run from him, from this room, run till she could run no further. But instead, she put her hand out tentatively, closed her hand on his, and said simply. 'I love you, Gregory. I love you.'

It was as though a blow had come from nowhere and sent him reeling, as though an explosion had happened inside him. He seemed to crumple, to lose the bitterness that had filled his words, and his face blurred suddenly as though he would weep again.

'I know, Harriet – I know. And I love you, my own Harriet – I love you, but what can I do? How can I – what can I do?'

'Whatever happened in the past, Gregory – it doesn't matter any more. Nothing matters any more. I – I'm not as – she was. And I love you – '

He slipped back into memory, his eyes going blank as he spoke.

'I looked for her, you know, Harriet. Whatever she had done to me, she was my wife, and I looked for her. But I couldn't find her. And Brooks went away, and didn't even bother to tell me he was going. I never saw either of them again. And I looked for a long time – '

'She – she's dead, Gregory.' Harriet said gently. 'Dead.'

He looked at her then, and his face twisted suddenly into a sick grin. 'Dead? Susan? Dead?'

'Yes – ' and then he began to laugh, a horrible shrill laugh, so that she shook him, put her hands on his shoulders and shook him, forcing him to stop.

'My God!' he gasped. 'My God – that's funny – funny – ' and he shook his head as the laughter seemed to bubble up again. 'Do you know why it's funny? Shall I tell you? She left me five years ago – and in a year or so from now, it will be seven years. And do you know what that means? It means I'll be free. That I can presume her dead – that I'll be free – that I can think about you, you and me – ' and he threw back his head and laughed again, laughed till tears ran down his face, till the tears began to be sobs, till he was crying in earnest, his whole body shaking with the agony of his distress.

But this last burst of feeling seemed to wring him dry. Slowly, he relaxed, relaxed in the arms Harriet had put round him again, till he was almost himself again, only the red eyes and lined face showing any sign of the storm he had gone through.

It was a long time that they sat there, she holding him close, he just lying against her, seeming to absorb strength from her. Then he moved, and sat up, running his hands through his hair, rubbing his face with still slightly shaking hands.

He stood up, and went back to stand at the window.

'Thank you, Harriet. I had no right to explode like that,' he said at length, the words coming painfully.

'It's all right, my love,' she said gently, and came to stand beside him. 'It's all right, you know. I love you. And I'm going to marry you. Do you know that?'

But he shook his head. 'No, Harriet – no. Not now. I had thought – but not now. It's – ruined. I would have told you about her when the seven years had gone – but I wouldn't have told you why – why she left me. I thought – I thought I could marry again, marry you, but I can't – not now. I couldn't let it happen again – '

'But it won't happen again – ' Harriet cried. 'It won't! I'm not like she was – it won't.'

'But I'm the same man, Harriet. The same man who couldn't make one woman happy. And I couldn't – couldn't make you happy either – it's ruined now – '

'No – no,' she began, but he shook his head at her, touched her face gently.

'I can't my love. I can't. Don't ask me to – please. I can't try again – not take a risk like that again. Don't you see? I love you – and I can't marry you. Not possibly. I can't marry you.'

13

How she got back to her room, she never knew. She had stared at his face, at his reddened eyes, and then turned and run, unable to face things any longer. It had been too much for her.

Sally had been waiting for her in her room, and at the sight of her face, had said nothing, only helping her undress, making her drink hot milk, putting her to bed as though she were a child, giving her a sleeping pill so that she drifted off into an exhausted sleep.

She went on duty the next morning with a head heavy with reaction, her face bleak and somehow old in the morning light. Her nurses looked at her in surprise, but said nothing, only working through the morning's routine with an efficiency that meant she could at least not worry about the ward, could leave things to them, and for this she was grateful. She could not have worked properly for the life of her.

The paper carrier bag with the photographs and the birth certificate was waiting on her desk for her, with a note from Gregory on top of it.

'You'll need this,' he had written, in a scrawled uneven script, 'They belong to Davey. I'm sorry, Harriet. I can't say more than that. I'm sorry.'

She sat at her desk staring at the note for a long time. It was Dr Bennett's step behind her that pulled her back from her painful thoughts, her agonising memory of the previous evening.

He looked sharply at her drawn face, and said, 'You're overdoing it, Sister. Not good. Not good.'

She ignored his concern, reaching into the paper bag for the birth certificate.

'I've found out,' she said baldly, and gave it to him, and he took it, and read it silently.

'Well done, Sister! I must confess, I thought you'd set yourself an impossible task – but well done – '

With a voice devoid of any emotion, she told him what had happened, what Mrs Ross had told her, and he listened with a grave face.

'Poor little devil – poor little devil,' he murmured, and looked through the glass partition down the ward at bed seven, where Davey was sitting a little hunched up, staring round him at the other children, at the bustling nurses, with a flat look on his face, but at least with some apparent understanding of what was going on.

'Quite what we'll do with him now, I'm not sure,' he sighed heavily. 'There'll be no need to get him into a special home, not if he's managed to make some contact with us. He's more of a social problem now than a psychiatric one.'

'What then? An orphanage?' Harriet asked.

'Perhaps – though it seems to me he needs a good foster home, really – loving people to take the place of his parents. I'll see the almoner, and the Children's Officer from the Council about him, and see what I can do – but there's a shocking shortage of foster homes in this district – '

With an effort, Harriet said, 'A foster home? Does it have to be in this district – I mean, suppose I could find a home for him – would the Children's Officer be willing to consider it?'

'You've done quite enough, Sister – quite enough. No need for you to worry about this. I'll find an answer somehow,' he said.

'But I – I've got rather fond of him,' she said. 'And I feel – responsible.' He mayn't be Gregory's child, she thought bleakly, but he was his wife's child – and Davey has suffered enough. Someone's got to love him.

'No need – ' he began again, but she interrupted him.

'I've got a sister,' she said. 'A vicar's wife. They live in Devonshire, in a huge old house, and they've got three children of their own – as well as foster children – and I think she'd be happy to have him – '

'I must say it sounds eminently suitable – ' he said after a moment. 'Have you already suggested this to her?'

'No, but I could 'phone – and I know Sybil will be glad to have him. She loves children, and she's the sort of girl who wouldn't be able to let him go on unwanted like this – '

'Well – ' He thought for a while, then he said briskly, 'I must say it would solve the problem very nicely. We've got to get him out of here soon. He's physically fit, and we need the bed. Talk to your sister, then, and I'll discuss the matter with the powers-that-be this morning – ' He turned to go, but Harriet put a hand out to stop him.

'Please – Dr Bennett – someone will have to tell him, tell Davey – about his mother. That she's dead. And – ' she drew a shuddering breath, 'I don't think I can do it. I can't – I'm probably the best person to tell him, I know. I've spent more time with him than anyone else, but I can't do it – '

He looked down at her unhappy face, at the pleading eyes, and smiled gently.

'All right Sister. I'll tell him. It might be better, at that. I'm less emotionally involved than you are – '

She watched him as he went down the ward, his tall figure stooping slightly, saw him stop beside Davey, talk to him for a moment, saw Davey look up at him, saw his lips move as he spoke in answer.

Dr Bennett bent, and picked him up, carrying him out to the sunny balcony, empty yet of children, most of whom were still finishing their breakfasts. I hope he manages to help Davey understand, she thought bleakly. But it will be a long time before he really gets over this. Poor Davey. Poor baby.

She reached for the 'phone, and asked the switchboard operator to make a person to person call to Sybil, promising to come down later to sign for the cost of the call, and sat with the 'phone to her ear as she waited for the connection, listening to the clicks and the distant voices of operators as the long miles to Devonshire were covered.

Sybil's voice sounded distant, but warm and friendly as always, and for a moment, Harriet could hardly speak in answer to her 'Hello? Hello?' so suddenly lonely did she feel, so suddenly yearning to be there with her, to see her plump happy face, hug her close.

'Sybil?' she managed at last. 'Sybil darling? It's Harriet – '

'What's the matter?' She could hear the anxiety, the rush of fear that Sybil felt at the sound of her strained voice.

'It's all right – but I need your help. And you said to ask when I needed – ' As quickly as she could, Harriet told her about Davey, told her of his need for a foster home, and finished awkwardly, 'He's – he's more than just a patient to me, Sybil. He – he's connected to someone – someone I know. I can't explain now, but I will.'

'Of course we'll have him, Hattie,' Sybil's voice came quickly. 'Of course we will – as soon as you like. He can share Jeremy's room – Jeremy's the same age, and he loves company. As soon as you like – '

'Bless you, Sybil. I – I'll phone again as soon as I know what the arrangements are – we'll have to get permission from the Children's officer – '

'It'll be all right,' Sybil said reassuringly. 'We've fostered children before, remember – we're registered foster parents. Tell them that – they can check with the Children's Officer at Exeter – it'll be all right – '

After that, things moved quickly. Dr Bennett came back to the office, after settling Davey in bed again, and writing up a mild tranquilliser for him. 'It'll help a little,' he told Harriet as he signed the prescription sheet. 'He took it well – too well. Too quietly. He'll have a storm about it all some time, and this will help him when it happens – '

There was a great deal of telephoning, between the hospital and the Children's officer, the police and the Court official who was responsible for Davey, the Children's Officer in Exeter, and Sybil and Edward in their distant vicarage, but by lunch time, the whole thing was settled. Davey was to go to Devonshire two days later.

Dr Bennett came back to the ward in the early afternoon to see Harriet and tell her what had been finally arranged.

'I've been talking to Matron,' he told her, 'and asked her if she can spare you to take the child to his new home yourself. You're the best person, and the break won't do you any harm. And she's got a Sister to replace you for a few days, so it's settled. And I've told her you've been overworking – ' he silenced Harriet's protest with a raised hand, 'and she's sending the replacement for this afternoon. You take the rest of today off, Sister – I insist.'

Harriet didn't want to go off duty in the least. Without the ward to keep her mind occupied, she would have too much opportunity to think, to remember Gregory's unhappiness, to think about a future without him, for it was obvious that he had meant what he said. That he couldn't marry her, love her though he did. But she was too weary to argue, and she trailed off, leaving a cheerful junior Sister in charge, to make her way heavily across the crowded courtyard, weaving her way past ambulances and hurrying medical students, and out-patients searching for various departments where they had been sent for special tests, towards the Home.

But before she could reach the gate to the garden, hurrying footsteps behind her caught her up, and a hand on her shoulder pulled her back.

'Harriet – what's the matter? Are you ill? You look ghastly – '

She looked up at Paul, at his handsome face, at the eyes full of concern, and shook her head. 'It's nothing – ' she began. 'Nothing – ' and then, to her horror, her eyes brimmed with tears, and her jaw shook so that she couldn't speak, and with a shake of her head, she turned and tried to run away from him.

But he fell into step beside her, followed her through the gate into the garden, and made her stop and sit down on one of the benches under the trees.

He put an arm round her shoulder, and after a moment's resistance, she relaxed, drooped against him, and let the tears run unheeded down her face. He said nothing, just held her, letting the tears fall, mopping gently at her face with a big white handkerchief that smelled faintly of antiseptic and tobacco.

Gradually, she stopped crying, and managed to sit straight again, taking the handkerchief to blow her nose, setting her cap straight on her head.

'What is it, Harriet? What's happened? Tell me, love. This is Paul, remember?'

She looked up at him, at the crinkled eyes looking at her with so much affection, at the broad shoulders, the square jaw, and drew a shuddering breath.

'Yes – ' she said, 'I remember – '

I loved him once, she thought. Not as I love Gregory, but I loved him. He's comfortable, and he's fun, and he loves me.

Her voice came to her as a surprise, as though it were someone else's.

'Paul – do you still – care for me? A little?'

He looked down at her, and his mouth twisted a little wryly.

'I may be pretty volatile, Harriet, but I'm not that volatile. Yes, I love you. Very much indeed. Does it matter?'

She managed a smile then. 'It matters. I – need loving, just now. Need it a great deal – '

'What's happened, Harriet? Has – what has Weston done to you? Is – is it what I thought? Is he married?'

'No,' she shook her head. It's not a lie, she told herself a little defensively. Not a lie. Susan is dead, and he isn't married any more.

'What then?' Paul persisted.

'It – circumstances,' she shrugged a little. 'Things can't always be the way you want them to be. Circumstances – alter things. It – oh, it's such a mess, Paul! Such a mess. And I'm lost – lost and miserable, and I need loving so much – '

His face went blank, and she felt his arm round her shoulder slacken.

'I see,' his voice was flat. 'I see. You still love him, don't you, Harriet? Circumstances haven't changed that, have they? You love Weston?'

She sat very still for a long moment, then she said slowly. 'Yes – I do – I do. It's not like a – a tap. I can't just turn it off because I want to. But I wish I could – my God, I wish I could!' She looked up at him then, tried to smile. 'But it will change, Paul. It must. I – I can't go on like this – '

He rubbed his face, running his fingers through his hair, looking at her with indecision in his eyes.

'You – are you trying to tell me it's finished, Harriet? That you won't be seeing him again?'

Bleakly, she nodded. 'Yes,' she said. 'It's finished. It's got to be – I can't cope any more – '

'Harriet – ' his voice seemed to be pulled from him. 'You asked me if I still cared for you. And I said I did, and I mean it. But – but I can't just pick things up where we left off. I love you – too much for that. Can you understand that, Harriet? I'll always care for you – not always as now, perhaps, not always with a – with a pain. But I always will care. But it's too late, Harriet – '

'Too late?' she stared at him stupidly.

'I wanted to marry you, once, Harriet – wanted it more than anything in the world. But what I want from marriage, what I've got to give – we couldn't have together, not now. Whatever has happened between you and Weston has – spoiled things. I'd never be able to make you happy now, Harriet. And – and you couldn't make me happy. He'd always be there, you see. I – I could never be sure I wasn't second best, never be certain you'd married me because I was me, or whether I was just – just a bolt-hole for you. And I'm not the sort of man to settle for second best. Even with you. Forgive me, Harriet, and try to understand. I do love you – if you can believe that. But it's too late – '

She closed her eyes against the sick pain in her, against the surge of hurt that welled up, and nodded heavily.

'I – forgive me, Paul,' she said 'Forgive me. I – it was an insult. I should have known better. But – you caught me at a bad moment. I hadn't had time to think. Forgive me.'

He put his hand out impulsively, tried to take hers, but she pulled back. 'Oh, God, Harriet – maybe I'm wrong? – I don't know. Maybe it isn't too late? – '

But she stood up, pulling her cape around her.

'No, Paul. You were right the first time. It is too late. Goodbye, Paul – ' she stood for a second looking down at him, at his unhappy face and slumped shoulders, then touched his cheek gently. 'Goodbye, Paul,' she said gently. 'Be happy, my dear.'

And she turned and went, ran across the garden to the Home, leaving him sitting in the bright May sunshine, his hair blowing a little in the morning breeze, sitting still on a bench under a green tree.

14

Sally came to her room at lunchtime, peering anxiously round the door to see her lying on her bed, still in uniform, as she had lain ever since she had left Paul in the garden.

Sally pushed her to one side and sat beside her to look down at the white face on the counterpane with a thin smile.

'Well?' she said.

Harriet looked at her, and managed a smile herself.

'Well,' she repeated.

'So, what's happened? Have you see Gregory about Tod – I mean, Davey?'

Harriet nodded bleakly. 'I've seen him,' she said, and told Sally everything, past thinking about her pride, past anything, except the need to pour out her distress at someone's feet. And she told her why Gregory had asked her to wait, what had happened to his marriage with Davey's mother.

Sally listened in silence, and when Harriet stopped talking, stirred slightly, reaching in her pocket for a packet of cigarettes.

'I think I can understand up to a point,' she said slowly, watching the thin grey smoke curling from the cigarette she lit. 'Once the seven years were up, once he could feel free, he'd have been able to start – fresh – again. But why give up now? I mean, he *is* free – really free. Even after the seven years were up, even if the court had presumed her dead and said he was free to marry again, there would have been a chance she'd turn up again. But this way, it's all right. She's dead.'

'I – think it's because I've found out by myself.' Harriet said painfully. 'I've become involved with Susan, this way. So I'm as much a part of his misery over her, as much a part of his sense of failure with her as – as she was herself. He wants no part of me now because I'm tied up with Susan in his mind, and – and he feels he won't be able to make me happy because he couldn't make her happy.'

'For God's sake, Harriet! What's the matter with the man?' Sally said irritably. 'All right – so his first wife was nearly a nymphomaniac – does that mean every other woman is, that you are?'

'Don't – ' Harriet closed her eyes, tried to close her ears against Sally. 'Don't – '

'Mincing words doesn't help,' Sally said briskly. 'That's what she was, wasn't she? Admit it – and Gregory should admit it too – ' she stopped short, and then said wonderingly. 'There's one odd thing, you know.'

'What?' Harriet muttered, not caring much.

'Well, if she was – like that – why did she live as she did these last years? You say Mrs Ross told you she had no friends – never went anywhere. It doesn't sound very logical, does it? She wasn't the sort of woman to live the life of a celibate – '

'Christ, don't ask me,' Harriet said with sudden violence. 'How can I know? How can anyone know? Perhaps it was because of Davey that she changed, perhaps because this other man – Brooks – left her in the cart. Who knows? She might have loved Brooks – might have changed because he abandoned her. No one will ever know – and I don't want to. I don't want to think about her again.'

There was a long silence, then Sally said, 'What happens now? About Davey?'

'He's going down to Devonshire – Sybil's going to foster him.'

'Good for Sybil. Does she know about the story?'

'Not yet. I'm taking him down there the day after tomorrow. I'll tell her then.'

'And what about Gregory? I mean, is he going to – to take any interest in the child? He must be concerned about him. Why else did he buy those clothes?'

Harriet shrugged. 'I don't know. I didn't even mention the business of the clothes to him when I talked to him last night. There's no – legal reason for him to be concerned. The child isn't his – '

'No – but he is his wife's child.'

'I – I suppose I'll have to ask him. I haven't told them – Dr Bennett, or the Children's Officer – about the relationship between Gregory and Davey's mother, and there's no reason why

I should, or why they'd ever find out. Even though she gave Davey the second name of Weston, it's not too uncommon a name. No reason why anyone should ever connect Gregory with the whole mess at all.'

'But you'll talk to him about it?' Sally persisted.

'I'll – I'll probably write a letter. It'll be easier that way. He – said last night he – wouldn't see me again. I suppose he'll refuse that job here, and go on somewhere else.'

'Always on the run,' Sally said softly, and stood up. 'What about you, now, Harriet? What will you do?'

Harriet sat up, and ran her fingers through her tousled hair. 'I haven't thought about it yet,' she said wearily. 'Stay on here, I suppose. I've got a good job – and friends,' she smiled up tremulously at Sally, 'and I'll settle for that.'

'There's still Paul – ' Sally began, but Harriet shook her head violently. 'No – not any more. I – I'll tell you about that some time – not now. I'm too tired, Sal. But Paul is – finished with me.'

And wisely, Sally said no more.

Harriet slept for most of the remainder of the day, tossing heavily, later to lie awake for the greater part of the night, her thoughts chasing each other through her head with sick monotony. But she was beyond constructive thought, unable to see her way clear, however hard she tried.

'I'll see Davey settled,' she promised herself in the cold light of dawn, when she got up, finally giving up any attempts at more sleep. 'I'll see Davey settled, and then just – see what happens.'

She spent the next day on duty working with automatic precision, going through the motions of showing interest in what she was doing, grateful that Davey slept for most of the day, removed from stress as he was by the tranquillising drugs Dr Bennett had ordered for him. She took no off duty that day, staying in her office to make lists and write down all the information the relief sister would need to run the ward during her absence in Devonshire. She sent most of the nurses off duty early, leaving the ward to the care of herself and one junior as the day came to a weary end at last.

It was half an hour before the night staff were due on duty, when she was sitting beside the bed of one restless child who had had an eye operation that day, that the 'phone rang shrilly in her office. The junior hurried to answer it, and came out to Harriet breathlessly when she had hung up.

'There's a child coming up from Cas, Sister,' she reported importantly. 'Sister there says he's got a – a laryngeal obstruction – and could you get a steam tent ready for him, and Mr Weston'll be up to see him right away – '

As she hurriedly prepared a cubicle for the emergency, sending the junior to get steam kettles, arranging the bed and the tent, checking oxygen cylinders, Harriet found her hands shaking. She had forgotten the possibility that they would meet on duty like this, but she reminded herself that this *was* work, that this child on his way would be the only point of contact between them. There would be no need for any personal talk, she told herself, almost in panic.

The big double doors swung open, and the trolley from Casualty came through it, a porter at the foot, Gregory at the head, holding onto the child on it. Harriet could hear the harsh whooping of the child's breathing, could see the red blankets that covered him heaving as the small body struggled for breath. With the smooth speed of long practice, she helped the porter bring the trolley to the side of the bed in the prepared cubicle, gently helped Gregory lift the child on to the bed, and stood for a moment looking down at the face on the white pillows. His grey eyes were staring, tears running from them, down the grimacing face to the drawn back lips, lips blue with lack of oxygen, and his brown hair was sticking to the sweating forehead in pathetic wisps.

Together, she and Gregory straightened the straining body in the bed, arranged the steam kettles so that the tent of sheets that had been erected over the head of the cot filled with the damp greyness of steam.

But it made no difference. The horrible whooping went on, the harsh sound of air struggling to pass whatever obstruction was nearly closing his air passages filling the small cubicle with sound, so that Harriet felt her own lungs constrict, seemed to feel as though she were herself choking, found herself breathing deeply in an impotent effort to breathe for the ill child in the steam tent.

'It can't be an infective oedema – ' Gregory muttered. 'I haven't been able to look properly – the child's too ill. It must be a foreign body – '

'Tracheostomy?' Harriet asked quickly, and Gregory nodded.

She flew to the sterilising room, to grab the tray that was always ready set up for just such emergencies as these, and hurried back up the ward to the cubicle as though all the hounds of hell were after her.

Gregory was bending over the child, his face white, and for a moment Harriet couldn't think what had happened. Then, she realised. The sound had stopped. The whooping that had filled their ears had gone, and the child was stretched rigid on the bed, his eyes wide, his face an ominous blue.

'It must have moved,' Gregory said desperately. 'The obstruction's complete – I only hope it's above laryngeal level – '

Swiftly, Harriet shoved the sandbag that was part of the tray she was carrying under the thin neck, a neck now rigid with engorged blood vessels, and held onto the child's shoulders as Gregory pulled the cover from the tray, and grabbed the gleaming scalpel that lay nested in a piece of gauze on it.

'Here goes,' he muttered, and with steady fingers, gently set the edge of the knife on the blue skin at the base of the throat. Smoothly, he put pressure on the knife, and the edge split the straining skin so that it parted, probed deeper, opening a channel straight into the child's windpipe.

Blood oozed onto the skin, running in purplish streaks down over Harriet's hands on the small shoulders, and then, as Harriet and Gregory held their own breaths in agonising tension, there was a hissing whistle as the air entered the small incision.

'Thank God,' he said. 'Thank God – it's above laryngeal level – ' and he reached for the narrow silver tube on the tray. Gently he eased the curving section of the tracheostomy tube into the incision, and pushed the inner tube in, making a clear hole through which air could enter. And slowly, the child's face lost its blueness, slowly the narrow chest began to heave as the lungs again filled and emptied with air.

With fingers shaking a little, Harriet threaded tapes through the narrow slits at the edge of the tube, tied them carefully round the thin neck, arranged gauze under the edges so that the delicate skin wouldn't be hurt by the rigid metal, and then straightened her back to look down on the child.

His eyes were closed now, his face smooth again, the look of fear gone as his body greedily took in air, his skin gradually showing a more normal colour.

There was a soft rattle at the door as an anaesthetist came in, pulling his big anaesthetic machine behind him.

'Casualty told me about this kid.' His voice sounded oddly

loud in the small room. 'What gives, Weston?'

'Foreign body,' Gregory said crisply. 'I've done a tracheostomy, 'You're a bit late – '

The anaesthetist grinned cheerfully. 'Wouldn't you know it? Dragged this thing right from the theatres like a carthorse, and now you don't want it – '

'Yes I do,' Gregory said with decision. 'I'm going to find this obstruction right now and get it out before it moves any further. You game?'

'Sure – ' The anaesthetist pulled his machine to the side of the bed, and began to check the cylinders. 'Fire away – '

'Got the gear, Sister?' Gregory didn't look at her, turning instead to the wash-basin in the corner to scrub his hands.

'Yes sir,' Harriet said. 'I'll get it – '

As she rapidly laid a trolley in the sterilising room, putting out the special long forceps that would be needed, the mouthgag and tongue holders, Harriet found her head spinning, a combination of fatigue and tension making her whole body ache. But she pushed the trolley into the cubicle with strong arms, scrubbed her own hands steadily as the anaesthetist carefully connected his anaesthetic tubing to the tracheostomy tube in the child's throat.

'He's ready,' the anaesthetist's voice seemed to Harriet to come from a great distance, as she stood beside the bed, facing Gregory across it.

'Right.' Carefully, Gregory set a mouthgag in position, holding the child's jaws wide, clipped the tongue holders on, jerking his head at Harriet to take the handle from him, to keep the tongue out of the way as he worked.

Then he went behind the bed, to bend forward to peer deep into the child's mouth, gently easing the blade of the big laryngoscope Harriet gave him with her other hand into the small throat. The little bulb on the laryngoscope lit the mouth redly, gleaming on the small milk teeth, and then Gregory grunted in satisfaction.

'I can see it – Forceps, Sister – '

She slapped the long handled forceps into his hand, and moving his fingers with the careful precision of a machine, Gregory probed, tensely clipping the forceps closed on the still invisible object that was blocking the child's larynx.

'Got it!' he said triumphantly, and carefully eased the forceps up and out.

'A marble!' the anaesthetist peered at it, and laughed loudly. 'Little devil – a marble! And a king marble at that!'

The big round marble glinted gaily in the teeth of the forceps, the light swirling prettily on the gaudy red and blue glass, and Harriet laughed shakily too.

'They will do it,' she said, her voice cracking a little. 'They will do it – '

Gregory's voice seemed to come from a great distance as the light in the cubicle began to swirl in front of Harriet's eyes just as the gaily coloured marble had swirled before.

'I'll leave the tracheostomy patient for tonight, Sister – there'll probably be oedema, and we don't want to take any chances. Give him a massive dose of penicillin to avoid any sepsis, and I'll see about closing the incision in the morning. He'll need a special nurse, and frequent suction on the tracheostomy tube – '

'They will do it,' Harriet said again stupidly. 'Tell children not to put things in their mouths, and they will do it – marbles are dangerous – they will do it – '

And then the light swirled more brightly than ever reddening in sickening circles to disappear in a grateful black wave.

15

When she opened her eyes, she was lying on the couch in the dressing cubicle, and she stared round her stupidly, plucking at her collar which was open, aware of the looseness of her belt, which someone had undone.

'The child – ' she said, suddenly remembering. 'The child – ' and she tried to sit up.

'It's all right,' Gregory's voice pulled her eyes round, to where he was standing at the head of the couch. 'The night staff are here, so you're off duty now. He's all right – '

She sat up, her head still spinning a little. 'I'm sorry,' she said. 'I beg your pardon. I – can't think what happened – '

'You fainted.' His voice was strained. 'Have you been eating properly?'

'I – ' she looked up at him, and then dropped her eyes. 'No – I suppose not. Stupid of me.'

'I haven't been eating much either.' He said, and came round the couch to sit beside her. 'Harriet – this was my fault, wasn't it?'

'Yours?' she looked at him, pulled her body away from the nearness of his, suddenly wanting to get away. 'No – not really.'

'I've made you unhappy – more than unhappy. Ill. You look – ghastly.'

She managed a smile at that. 'You're looking pretty grim yourself,' she said huskily. And indeed he did, his face seeming more heavily lined than ever, his eyes grim in shadowed sockets.

'I've been trying to think,' he said heavily. 'Trying to make some sense out of this mess, but it's no use. I can't. You – you're the best thing that ever happened to me, but I'm afraid – afraid to hold onto you. I can't believe that we could ever – ' He stopped, seeming to struggle to find words. 'Already, I've done this to you – made you look ill, made you so miserable you forget to eat, so that you faint – '

'I'll get over it,' she said, pulling the shreds of her pride round her. 'I'll get over it – '

There was a long silence. Then he said heavily. 'I'm right, aren't I? It wouldn't work for us, Harriet. I'm no use to you, any more than to myself. If I thought I had it in me to make you happy, to be the sort of – of husband you deserve, I – I can't tell you what it would mean to me. But I know I couldn't. It's finished, Susan – destroyed me.'

She looked at him, at the face she cared for so much that it hurt, and said gently. 'You're making too much of this, Gregory. Far too much. It would take more than a Susan to destroy you, whatever you think now. She's hurt you – hurt you dreadfully, but you could recover – '

He shook his head, getting up to walk restlessly about the room. 'I can't take the chance. I can't – not when it's you that will suffer. If I married you, and – failed to – '

'God Almighty, Gregory!' Suddenly she was angry, wanted to shake him, locked in a fury that pulled her from the couch to stand swaying a little beside it. 'Is that all you think a marriage is? Just sex? Do you think that that's all I need from marriage? A – a mate, as though I were an animal? If I *were* like that – if I needed sex so desperately, don't you think I'd have found it out about myself before now? I'm twenty five years old, remember? Would I still – still be the virgin I am if I was the same sort of woman Susan was? I know sex matters, but it's not the only thing! Doesn't respect, companionship, simple love, have any place? What do you think I am, for Christ's sake? I'm a woman that loves you – and it's *all* of you I want – not just the – the sexual satisfaction you seem to care about so much!'

He came to stand beside her, to hold her face between cold hands.

'Dear Harriet,' he said softly. 'Dear Harriet. How can you know? How can you? I felt like that once – before Susan. But I know now, as you can't possibly, just how important it is. When you love someone – really love them, sex *does* matter. It mayn't be the only thing – but if that goes wrong, it poisons everything else. Companionship and love and friendship – none of them matter when you can't – express what you feel properly. I saw what the failure of sex did to Susan – and I'm not going to let it happen to you. There'll be someone else for you, Harriet. Someone else will make you happy as I never could. Try to believe me.'

She looked up at him, and her heart seemed to fill with defeat. There was no answer she could make, no argument she could set against the flatness of his eyes, nothing she could do to convince him he was wrong.

And then, almost against her will, thought welled up in her, thoughts that showed her the one argument she could make, the only way she could show him he was wrong.

'All right,' she said, pulling away from him, turning to the glass fronted instrument cupboard to use it as a mirror as she fastened her collar, and straightened her crumpled uniform. 'All right, Gregory. I'll try to believe you,' and her voice sounded cool and composed.

'Thank you, Harriet,' he said. 'That's all I ever seem to say to you, isn't it? But I mean it – '

Without turning she said, 'I'm taking Davey down to Devonshire tomorrow. My sister is going to foster him. I know he's not – not your child, but you are – connected to him. It's only fair that Sybil should know the whole story, don't you think? If she's to help him as he should be helped? Could you – could you come down too, meet her, help me explain to her?'

He stood very still, and then said. 'I see. Tomorrow, you say?'

'Yes.'

'I – I suppose I owe him that at least. Whatever happened, it was none of his doing. I'll – I'll get someone to stand in for me for a couple of days.'

'We're taking the ten o'clock train from Paddington,' she said, and turned to look at him. 'Will you travel with us?'

He nodded. 'Yes,' he said. 'I'll be there,' and he put a hand out towards her, an odd look of appeal on his face, but then dropped it, and turned and went.

Harriet went off duty in a sort of dream, her head filled with only one thought. As she packed a case with the few things she would need in Devonshire, as she bathed and got ready for bed, that thought went round and round.

'If he thinks that sex is all that matters, I'll show him. Prove to him he needn't be afraid. I'll show him – '

But even as she thought, her mind refused to go further. Quite how she would show him, as she put it, she wasn't sure. But she would. Somehow, in the peace of the country, away from London and all the memories of Susan that London held for Gregory, she would show him.

She sat in the window of her bedroom, the room she always had when she stayed with Sybil, staring out at the garden, letting the warm peace that was so much a part of this house wash over her. She could smell the warm drift of flowers from below, see the faint glimmer of white from the big bed of cottage pinks under her window, and she closed her eyes gratefully.

It had been a long day, and she could still feel the sway and rattle of the train journey in her bones, almost smell the oily dusty reek of the long rushing over the miles, still feel the weight of Davey on her lap, as he had sat there all through the long hours, refusing to move from her arms.

Gregory had sat beside her throughout, speaking only of commonplaces, getting food for them from the restaurant car, because Davey seemed to panic at any suggestion that they move from their compartment, helping her feed him, wrapping a rug round him when he fell asleep on her lap afterwards.

Sybil and Edward had met them, Sybil clucking over Davey in a way that seemed to reassure him, so that he had gone to her without demur, allowing her to bath him and put him to bed in Jeremy's room, falling into an exhausted sleep as soon as his head touched the pillow.

And after the children had gone to bed, the four adults sat long over their belated supper, while painfully, Gregory told Sybil and Edward about Davey, leaving out as much as he could about his own relationship with Susan, about the causes of the failure of their marriage.

Edward had said little, only listening, but Harriet felt that he knew somehow, understood what lay behind Gregory's halting words, felt his eyes on her own bent head, aware of the sympathy and affection in them.

And now, the day was over. Sybil and Edward had gone to bed, Sybil hugging Harriet warmly as she went, saying nothing, just holding her close in a sympathetic lovingness that brought tears to Harriet's weary eyes. And Gregory had said goodnight stiffly, and gone up to his own room at the other side of the house, avoiding looking at Harriet, including her in his impersonal politeness.

She opened her eyes and looked round at her room, a room that was home to her. The furniture sat shadowed in the darkness, comfortable and shabby, and the narrow bed with its patched cover looked inviting. For a moment, she wanted just to run to it, to bury her head under the covers, and fall into the oblivion of sleep.

But Gregory was going back to London tomorrow. Tomorrow. If she was to make any effort to hold him, to convince him there was a future for them together, now was the last time she could make that effort. After tonight, it would truly be too late.

She stood up, suddenly cold, pulling her thin nylon nightgown round her, and with a lifted head, moved across the room to pick up her cotton housecoat. As she put it on, she shivered, painfully aware of its flimsiness.

'I can't,' she thought with sudden panic. 'I can't – not me – I'm not like this really. I'm not – I can't – ' But part of her mind said with cold repetition, 'You must. It's the only way. You must – '

The door creaked slightly as she pushed it open, and slipped out into the dimly lit hall, and she stood poised in sick fear, waiting for Sybil and Edward's door to open, desperately trying to think what she would say if they did come out to see why she was prowling about in the silence of the night. But there was no movement, no sound but her own uneven breathing.

Her slippers moved softly over the carpet, as she walked along the wide hallway towards the blank door at the far end, and she tried desperately to control her uneven breathing, tried to stop her legs shaking against the folds of her thin nightdress.

It was as though she were someone else, a tiny Harriet perched high in the corner of the hall, looking down in sick disgust at the figure standing in front of Gregory's silent door.

'What are you?' this small Harriet jeered from her distant place. 'What are you? Are you going to make a fool of yourself – at best, a fool of yourself? Or will you be able to do this? Can you crawl to this man, beg him to make love to you, be the sort of woman who cares so little for her own self respect – can you?'

'I must,' she thought desperately. 'I must. It's the only answer – I must – '

She pushed the door open, stepped inside, and closed it behind her to lean against the panels in numb terror.

The curtains were wide open, moving gently in the breeze from the open window, and the light of a late moon filled the room with a dim radiance. He was lying in bed, his hands clasped behind his head, his eyes staring at the window, and he moved sharply as the door closed behind her.

He reached out, and switched on the small bedside light, so that the moonlight disappeared in a rush of yellow light that made her blink.

'Turn it off,' she said breathlessly. 'God, turn it off – '

After a long moment when he stared at her, he did turn it off, and Harriet breathed deeply in the grateful darkness.

She could hear the soft rustle as he got out of bed, pulled his dressing gown across his shoulders.

Then, with a last burst of resolution, she crossed the room, came to stand beside him, close to him, looking up at his face shadowed in the soft moonlight.

'Gregory – ' she could feel the warmth of his body close to hers, could feel the rise and fall of his chest as he breathed, and she moved closer, putting her cold arms around his neck.

'Gregory, I love you – I love you. I need you, Gregory. Don't send me away – don't – please – '

She couldn't believe this was herself, that this woman straining her body so close to the rigid one she held in her arms was Harriet, that she could possibly be behaving like this.

'Don't send me away,' she whispered again, and put her face up, seeking his mouth with cold lips, pulling his head down into a long kiss.

For a moment he resisted, pulling back from her, rigid with control. Then it was as though a wall had fallen, had burst in her arms, and he was holding her close, kissing her with a violence she couldn't have believed was in him.

'Harriet – Harriet,' he murmured at last, lifting his head to look at her. 'My Harriet – '

And then he was kissing her again, holding her in a grasp that seemed to melt her bones, pulling her against him, so that they fell against the bed, till they were lying locked together in an embrace that seemed to Harriet to last an eternity.

And then she knew, knew she was right. She could feel the passion in him, feel the urgency of his whole body as he held her close, as his hands moved on her cold skin in desperate caresses that made her tremble in answering need, that made her body shiver with sensations she could not have imagined possible.

'Harriet,' he said again and again, the sound of his voice a caress, full of a longing that every fibre of her answered.

And then, suddenly, the curtain at the window moved again, rustling softly against the sill, and it was as though she were pulled out of herself, pulled out of her body to think logically again, to be the person she always was.

She was aware of every detail about her, of her slippers where they had fallen from her feet onto the floor, of the tumbled bedclothes under her, of the way his hair showed tousled against the brightness of the window, of the furniture seeming to stare at her with watchful eyes.

And with every ounce of strength she had, she pulled back from him, away from his arms and urgently caressing hands, to huddle crouched against the door trying to pull her dressing gown around her.

'What am I doing? My God, what am I doing?' she said in a wondering voice. 'What am I doing? – ' and then she was crying, shaking against the door in an agony of shame and fear, her head down so that her hair fell against her cheeks to stick against their wetness in wispy strands.

He was very still, half lying on the bed, staring across the dim room at her huddled figure, his body seeming to shake in answer to her own trembling.

Then he was beside her, picking her up like a child, cradling her in his arms, rocking her gently as he murmured in her ears.

'It's all right, my darling – it's all right – hush, my love, hush – '

Gently he crossed the room, to sit in the deep armchair by the window, holding her on his lap, her head against his chest, soothing her gently.

'I – I wanted – I wanted to show you,' she began at last in a thick whisper as her tears stopped. 'I had to show you you were wrong, but I can't – I can't do it – I love you so, but I can't.'

'It's all right, my darling,' he said again, and there was an exultant lilt in his voice, as he held her close again, rested his cheek against hers. 'It's all right – '

She pulled away from him, to peer into his face in the dimness, and her voice was full of appeal when she spoke.

'I'm not – I'm not really like this, Gregory. Truly I'm not. But I love you, Gregory – I love you. I couldn't bear to lose you, I had to show you – '

'Harriet, my own love,' he said, his voice full of a tenderness she had never heard before. 'I know – I know what you are –

what sort of person you are. I know just how hard it must have been for you to do this – to come to me like this – and oh, Harriet, you can never know how wise you were – '

He put his head down and kissed her, a long gentle kiss that made her shiver and then relax, that filled her with a peace as unlike the passion she had felt before as it could possibly be.

Then he gently pushed her head down onto his shoulder.

'I was so wrong, my love – so wrong. When you came to me, when you held me as you did, you seemed to break down all the misery of years. You've killed all that fear I had, you've made me feel – I can't tell you, my love, I can't tell you. Holding you as I did then, touching you, it was as though – as though we were one person. Not two people battening on each other – one person. You and me, together. We – belonged,' and then he threw his head back and laughed with pure joy. 'It's all right, Harriet darling, it's *all right*! Can you understand? You've made it all right – '

And she breathed deeply, filling her body with the peace she had always looked for with him, feeling the same sense of being one person he had felt, for the first time in her life knowing what love would be, what it could offer her.

They sat together in the darkness, watching the window as the faint light of the moon disappeared as it sank behind the trees, letting the peace and silence of the old house wash over them.

Then, gently, with infinite tenderness, he carried her across the silent hallway, back to her own bed, to lay her softly on the pillow, to kiss her eyes, her mouth, her cold cheeks, wrapping her in love and gentleness.

'Goodnight my darling,' he murmured. 'Goodnight. Soon we won't ever say Goodnight again, my love – we'll never leave each other. Not yet, my love – not yet for either of us. We – aren't the sort of people to spoil things for each other, are we? Not now. But soon – we'll be married, Harriet darling – and then it will be all right – '

And Harriet smiled up at him in the darkness, and with a soft laugh in her throat murmured, 'All come right – just like algebra – ' and she fell asleep as suddenly as a baby.

The Lonely One

1

Bridget sat at the desk at the very end of the back row, staring round the big classroom with miserable eyes. The letter from Matron had told her to arrive at the Preliminary Training School at 2 p.m., and she had decided then that she would try to be the first to arrive. She had a confused notion that the other new girls would arrive accompanied by loving parents, and she wanted to make sure that this time at least she would not have to face the pitying eyes of people who realised she had no parents. All through her schooldays she had shrunk from that all too familiar look on the faces of other girls and their parents, and although she knew quite well that it was no fault in her to be without a mother and father of her own, she felt an obscure sense of shame about it. So she had decided to arrive early, letting later arrivals think her parents had already left.

But, as always seemed to happen to Bridget, her plans had been almost too well laid. She had arrived at just after one, and the little maid who answered the door to her had led her into the classroom and told her to wait there for Sister Tutor.

'You're too early,' the maid had said, somewhat crossly, humping Bridget's big suitcase into the classroom and dropping it with a clatter on to the polished floor. 'Sister's having her lunch, and I better not disturb her – she'll be flaming mad if I do – ' and Bridget, stumbling over her words, had begged the girl to please *not* disturb Sister Tutor, she was fine, really she was, please do not bother about her – And the maid had looked at her with ill-disguised contempt in her eyes, or so Bridget had thought, and gone off with a shrug to finish the illicit cup of tea she had been drinking in the kitchen.

And now Bridget sat and looked about her, frightened as

always by the newness of things, for Bridget was not a girl to find strange surroundings exciting. For her, newness was menacing, something to be faced with screwed-up courage, not pleasure. In one way, the room had a school-like familiarity – the rows of desks, the teachers' dais backed by a blackboard, the smell of chalk and ink, and faint overtones of human bodies that had spent long hours here.

But there were other things in the room that made it utterly strange. The three hospital beds against one wall; the cupboards, glass fronted, white enamelled and chromed, showing rows of instruments, bowls, piles of wound dressings; the charts on the walls depicting very unhuman-looking men and women, with their muscles and organs all too faithfully drawn in ugly blues and reds, and the articulated skeleton that dangled from the little hook in its skull from a big metal stand.

Bridget giggled aloud, a little hysterically, at him, and said softly, 'I wish I were you – ' but the skeleton just hung and grinned mockingly at her.

There was silence, not even a faint clatter of human movement coming from the rest of the building behind the closed door of the classroom. With an effort, Bridget got to her feet, and started to prowl about the room, looking at the strange things, running her fingers over the desks she passed, trying to gain a sense of security from touching these calm inanimate objects.

She stopped in front of one of the glass-fronted cabinets, peering at its contents with a sort of fascinated horror. There were gleaming scalpels, dangling rows of artery forceps, big metal loops that were retractors, though Bridget had not the faintest idea what they were for, let alone what they were called. Tentatively, she put her hand on the fastening of the glass door, and it swung open on well-oiled hinges. With one slightly shaking finger she touched one of the rows of artery forceps that hung from below one of the shelves, and as she did so, the big door of the classroom opened with a sharp click, and someone came in.

Bridget whirled to see who it was, and her convulsive movement made her finger curl and hook into the first forcep in the row. The whole lot slid out of the cupboard to fall clattering to the floor in a cascade of gleaming chrome.

'My good girl, what on earth are you doing?' A tall woman in a dark-blue dress, with a frosting of white at the collar and cuffs, swept forward crossly, and bent to pick up the fallen instruments just as Bridget, with really shaking hands now, bent to do the same. She scrabbled among the forceps, trying to collect as many as she could, and only succeeded in dropping all those she picked up, so that the tall woman, with a cluck of impatience said sharply, 'Do leave them – I'll pick them up,' which she proceeded to do with deft fingers. Then she hung them back in place and turned to Bridget, who was now standing in dejection behind her.

'I'm so sorry,' Bridget muttered. 'So sorry. I was too early – I thought I'd look about – so sorry – I didn't mean to – '

'Well, no harm done,' the tall woman said briskly. 'Just remember in future that these are valuable pieces of equipment and need to be handled with respect. Clumsy nurses are bad nurses – we must teach you to be more careful, mustn't we?'

'Yes,' Bridget said miserably.

'Yes, Sister,' the tall woman said. 'In hospital, we address people with a particular courtesy.'

'Yes, Sister,' Bridget said again, now very near to tears, wishing she could turn and run.

The tall woman seemed to sense her misery, and smiled, a smile that lifted her rather craggy face into softer lines.

'Dear me, but this is an unfortunate beginning for you! But don't worry about it – we all had to start once, and we were all just as nervous as you are!' And Bridget, managing a shaky smile in response, tried to imagine this very masterful woman being as nervous as she was now, and couldn't.

'Well, since you are here early, we'll make the most of the time, and get you sorted out before the others arrive. Come along to my office, now – and you'd better bring your case and leave it in the hall until Margaret shows you your room.'

Bridget picked up the big case and hurried after the tall woman, who was leading the way out across the hall towards a door on the other side of it.

'Have you lunched?'

'Yes, thank you – Sister,' Bridget lied. She hadn't been able to eat for the last two days, so nervous about it all had she been.

'Good – now, leave your luggage there, and come along in.'

Bridget obediently followed her into the office, and sat down in the chair the other woman indicated with a nod of her head, and clasping her hands on her lap, to hide their shaking, waited for what was to come next.

'Now, my dear, let us introduce ourselves to each other. I am Sister Chessman, your Sister Tutor. I will be looking after your tuition here at the Royal for the next three years, and I hope we will be able to be of help to each other. I will do all I can to make a nurse of you, someone of whom the Royal and the profession can be proud, and with interest and intelligent co-operation from you, we should have a very successful and happy three years together.' She leafed through a pile of papers on the desk between them. 'Now, what is your name?'

'Bridget Preston, Sister.'

'Preston – Preston – ah, yes. Here we are.' She pulled one of the sheets of paper out and peered at it. 'I see that you did not come to the Royal for a preliminary interview, because your home is in the North – so we know very little about you. Let me see. You are nineteen?'

Bridget nodded.

'And you have no parents, I see. I'm sorry about that, my dear,' and the all too familiar and hateful look of pity appeared on the craggy face.

'They died when I was a baby,' Bridget began the usual explanation with a spurious ease born of long practice. 'My grandmother brought me up.' She began to stumble a little then. 'She – she died last month – I have a guardian now.'

'I'm sorry,' Sister Chessman said again.

'Well, to tell the truth, she was very old, and I didn't see a lot of her,' Bridget said with a rush of honesty. 'I've been at boarding-school most of my life – I only lived with Grandmother these last two years, and she was pretty much of an invalid – I can't pretend to miss her very much.'

Sister Chessman nodded, looking at the girl in front of her with shrewd but friendly eyes. 'You have had rather a lonely time lately, then?'

Bridget thought of the last two years, the interminable hours in the dingy, big house in the depths of Yorkshire, the hours spent doing such small household tasks as her grandmother's dour housekeeper had allowed her to do, the hours of reading through the ancient collection of dreary books, of solitary walks across the bleak moors, the emptiness that had been her life. But she made no attempt to explain all this. She just nodded.

'Why did you decide to be a nurse, Miss Preston? What attracted you to the profession?'

Bridget bit her lip momentarily. How could she explain that to this severe, self-assured woman? Explain the look of rather impatient benevolence on the face of Mr Lessiter, the solicitor her grandmother had appointed as her guardian, when he had come to collect her from her grandmother's house the day after the funeral?

'Well, Bridget, my dear,' he had said briskly, as they sat in the train that carried them both towards the Lessiter home in Edinburgh. 'And what are you going to do now? I'm afraid you'll have to take some sort of job, you know. Your grandmother's income died with her – it was an annuity – and the sale of the house will just about cover the expenses of her illness and funeral and the legacy she left to her housekeeper. Much as Mrs Lessiter and I would like to support you, we aren't in any position to do so unless you make some contribution yourself – '

Bridget had understood the situation at the Lessiter's very quickly, almost before she had been in the house an hour. Mr Lessiter was a busy man, much too occupied with his work to care to have a girl like Bridget cluttering up his life, and Mrs Lessiter, childless as the couple were, had filled her life with her job as an advertising executive, and had no more relish for her unwanted task as joint guardian to Bridget than had her husband.

It had been Bridget herself who had solved the problem. She had remembered the rather nice girl who had come to the house to nurse her grandmother during the last week of her life, the little she had heard from her about being a nurse, and had decided, on the basis of this flimsy knowledge that she, too, would be a nurse.

She had said to the Lessiters, with some diffidence, that she would like to work in a hospital, and the patent relief on their faces, the warm pleasure with which they had greeted this suggestion, had made it clear to her that she had been right.

'An excellent plan,' Mr Lessiter had said, almost with gaiety. 'Excellent; you'll be far more comfortable living in a Nurses' Home with a lot of girls your own age than with a pair of old fogies like us, eh Elizabeth?' and his wife had smiled back at him and agreed heartily.

Now, Bridget tried to answer Sister Chessman's question with some honesty.

'I – it seemed the best thing to do,' was all she managed.

'Do you know anything about nursing?'

'Well – no, not very much. But I liked science at school – I got quite good O levels in it – though I got A levels in English – '

'Your educational qualifications are quite satisfactory – we have a record of all that here on your application form. No, I want to know *why* you chose nursing. Do you like people? Want to help them?'

'I – I think so, Sister.' Bridget tried again. 'I – I haven't seen much of people, really, not since I left school, and even then, it was a very small school – I didn't get about much. I just worked.'

Somehow, at school, she had never been very good at making friends. The other girls had been so full of their home doings, chatter about their parents, their brothers and sisters, their friends with whom they spent their holidays, that Bridget, lacking these subjects of conversation, had retreated into a quiet, bookish world of her own, a safe world, free from any emotional tangles of the sort other girls seemed to get into. No boy-friends, no violent crushes on other girls at school had ever disturbed the even tenor of her life.

Mercifully, Sister Chessman seemed to understand some of her difficulty in explaining, and said no more about the matter. She busied herself with asking rather more practical questions, about her health, explaining that she would be having a general physical examination by one of the hospital physicians, to make sure she was physically fit for the arduous job of nursing, telling her that she would spend the next three months in the Preliminary Training School, visiting the hospital's wards one day a week, and that if she studied hard, and passed the examination that would be set at the end of that three months, she would be admitted to the Royal as a full student nurse.

'And looking at your scholastic record, I would say you should have little difficulty in coping with your studies, as long as you work hard and don't slack the weeks away. Now, I rather think I hear some of the other girls arriving. If you go to the hall, Margaret, the maid, will show you to your room, and you can unpack. You will have to share a room with other girls while you are here in the Preliminary Training School, I'm afraid – we are very short of single rooms in this building, but later, when you move to the Nurses' Home proper, you will, of course, have a room to yourself. Off you go now, and ask Margaret to send the next arrival in five minutes – I must sort these papers out first.'

Obediently, Bridget turned to go, and was called back just as she reached the door.

'I hope you will be happy with us, Nurse Preston. It will all seem very strange at first, I know, and probably frightening. But we at the Royal understand that, and we want to help. Don't be afraid to come to me if you have any problems. I don't bite – and I do care a great deal about the happiness of every girl in the training school. An unhappy girl makes a bad nurse, and we want you to be a good nurse, as well as a happy person. Remember that, won't you?' She smiled her transforming smile again. 'Welcome to the Royal, Nurse Preston. We are happy to have you with us.'

And with a sudden uprush of emotion Bridget could only smile shakily and nod, before escaping to the hall outside.

There were about half a dozen girls in the hall, none of them with parents accompanying them, yet Bridget felt her heart fail her for a moment. She was so bad at making friends, so unable to chatter easily to strangers, as these girls clearly could. They were talking together as though they had known each other all their lives, heads together, leaning against the radiators in the hall in relaxed attitudes that Bridget envied heartily.

The maid came across the hall as Bridget closed the office door behind her.

'Please, Margaret,' she said. 'Sister Chessman said would you send the next one in to her in five minutes?'

The maid nodded, and one of the girls leaning against the radiator detached herself from the group and came over to Bridget, who was standing a little helplessly next to her suitcase.

'What's she like?' the girl asked.

Bridget looked up at her, a girl taller than herself by a couple of inches, with thick fair hair that curled becomingly into a springing bob round a pointed face, large blue eyes, well made up to show the thick brown lashes to advantage. She had a smooth skin, clear of any blemish, and a neat figure that was perhaps a little too well displayed in a tightly fitting jersey suit. Her legs were long and beautiful, and she wore high-heeled, very fashionable shoes that made Bridget painfully aware of her own sensible Yorkshire brogues.

'I – I beg your pardon?' she said awkwardly.

'What's she like?' the girl said again. 'The old she-dragon in there? Is she a real old battle-axe, or one of those nice motherly types you can push around?'

'She's very – nice, I think,' Bridget said. 'I mean, I hardly know – I've only been with her a little while – She's a bit – a bit scary, really, I suppose.'

The girl nodded, resignedly. 'I get you. Battle-axe.' She turned to the others.

'We're out of luck,' she announced to them. 'She seems to have scared the pants off this one, anyway.' She turned back to Bridget. 'Who're you? I'm Roberta Aston – Bobby to my friends. And this is Judith Mayer – that tall one with the red hair over there, and this dolly face with all the black hair is Liz Cooper, and that's Dorothy – Jackson, isn't it?' – a quiet-looking girl in a blue coat nodded shortly – 'and this is Mary Byrne, and this is Jean McDonald. I gather from the maid there're four more to come yet. Not exactly a big class, is it? Who're you?'

'Bridget Preston – er, how do you do?'

'And how do *you* do?' Bobby said gaily. 'Look, Margaret says we can share out the rooms how we like – there's one four-bedder, and Liz and Judith and me have already opted to share – and you can join us if you like. You look nice and quiet – do you snore?'

'I don't think so.' Bridget stared fascinatedly at this elegant and loquacious girl, who already seemed to have the whole place organised. 'Have you been here before?' she asked tentatively. The dark girl called Liz moved lazily away from the radiator towards them and laughed huskily.

'Not a bit of it, Bridget,' she said, with an amused note in her voice. 'I've met this type before. Give her five minutes in a place, and she knows it all – who to get things out of, who to avoid, the back way out, and the secret ways in, all the useful things like that.'

Bobby grinned complacently. 'Got it in one, ducky,' she said. 'If you don't look after yourself in this wicked world, no one's going to look after you – take it from one who knows and 'as suffered sumfin' crool,' and she struck a mock heroic pose that made them all, including Bridget, laugh.

There was a faint sound from beyond the closed door of Sister Chessman's office, and the maid nodded at the quiet girl called Dorothy, and opened the door for her to go in.

'I'll show you others your rooms, then,' she said. 'And mind you don't make too much noise, or Sister Chessman'll be after you. Come on – '

As Bridget followed the maid and the other girls up the wide, polished, wooden stairs to the bedrooms above, she felt a little better. This gay girl, this Bobby who seemed so self-assured, who had all the qualities that Bridget herself lacked but longed to have, she seemed to like Bridget already, certainly enough to let her share a room with her and the other two girls she had chosen to be her friends. Perhaps life at the Royal wouldn't be too bad, after all. Above all, she reminded herself, as she dropped her suitcase on to one of the beds in the big room Margaret showed them into, above all, it was safe. There was nowhere else to go. The Lessiters didn't really have room for her in their lives, and there was no one else to help her, she told herself practically, but without self-pity. The Royal, or a hospital just like it, was the only answer. It might as well be the Royal as anywhere else.

So, lifting her chin with an effort, she turned to look at the other three girls and the room she was to share with them for the next three months.

2

Bridget spent the next weeks in a state of startled happiness that left her almost physically breathless when she thought about it. Everything about her new life was so enjoyable – the lectures were interesting, and with the habit of study and reading she had developed during her schooldays, presented little difficulty. In a way, the ease with which she coped with her work enhanced the greatest pleasure of all – her friendship with the other three girls with whom she shared a room. In the area of study and work, she was superior to them, and in only this. They were gay – particularly Bobby – they had a brand of high spirits that spilled over into their everyday speech and seemed to the hitherto lonely Bridget to be sparkling wit, and they were so pretty.

It was wonderful, Bridget thought, to be like that, admiring these qualities in them without envy. But despite her whole-hearted pleasure in their company, her genuine lack of envy, it was equally wonderful to be able to answer any question that Sister Chessman threw at the class, wonderful to sail through a test paper and sit back with the feeling of having produced well-written answers while the others breathed heavily over their pens, and muttered at each other about the hellishness of study.

Liz and Judith, and particularly Bobby, rapidly discovered that Bridget found the work easy, and seized on this ability in her to make their own lives easier. Bobby told Bridget gaily that it was uneconomic, to say the least, for all of them to wear their delicate brains out with work, when she could do it for them. And Bridget, delightedly, agreed. At first, she took her careful lecture notes, made her clear diagrams, and handed over her notebooks after lectures so that the others could copy them at their leisure, while they sat in class and passed silly notes to each other, giggling softly, and looking at Sister Chessman with limpid innocence in their eyes when she caught sight of them in the back row obviously not working at all. By the end of the second week they found an even easier way of keeping their notes up to date. They just handed their books over to the willing Bridget who would copy her own notes into them. Bridget didn't mind in the least, for not only was she helping her friends – she found it helped her to learn her work very quickly. By the time she had written out the notes four times, made four sets of diagrams, she knew the material backwards.

There was only one aspect of their life in the Preliminary Training Scool that worried her, only one in which the other three were better than she was. This showed on the day each week when the eleven students, awkward in the white coats that the PTS students wore, were shepherded over to the hospital to spend time in the wards.

On the first of these days, Bridget, together with Bobby and Liz, was sent to the male surgical ward. She stood at the door of the big ward, her heart beating thickly, her face white under its dusting of freckles, feeling her knees shake. How could she face a ward full of men, ill men? She knew there were thirty of them, that the long ward held fifteen beds on each side, and she dreaded the thought of having to walk down that ward, with thirty pairs of eyes fixed on her. But Bobby and Liz had no such fears.

'Cor!' Bobby said in her mock cockney accent. 'Cor – Thirty lovely men – just think of it!' And she tightened her white belt around her slender waist, shook her fair hair into an even more becoming casualness, and walked into the ward, with Liz beside her, her slender hips waggling in very conscious provocation, the frightened Bridget scuttling shyly in their shadow.

Sister was at the far end of the ward, standing beside a bed, as the three students walked towards her, and her round young face creased into a faint frown as she heard the decided wolf whistle one of the patients produced at the sight of the beautiful Bobby, walking down the ward with her fair hair swinging, her big eyes fixed on Sister's face with apparent unawareness of the stir she was creating among the patients.

But Sister was young enough, and had a sufficiently satisfying private life of her own, to lack the vindictive jealousy of a young pretty student some of the other Sisters at the Royal occasionally displayed, and contented herself with a wry comment on the length of Bobby's hair, advising her that she would have to have it cut or wear it up before she came to this ward again. And Bobby demurely agreed, knowing full well that she looked as good with her hair piled on her head as with it swinging loose round her ears.

Bobby and Bridget were sent to give drinks of hot milk and cocoa to the men, while Liz, much to her digust, was taken by Sister on a tedious tour of the ward cupboards. Her only comfort was that Bobby and Bridget would have to do this on the next visit, while she would be able to talk to the patients.

By the time the two girls had loaded the trolley with cups and saucers and the jugs of drinks, Bridget felt a little better. She had something to do, and perhaps the business of pouring the drinks would make it possible to avoid the men's eyes as they went round.

'You pour, I'll dish 'em out,' Bobby said quickly, as they rattled their way out of the kitchen into the big ward. And Bridget was only too glad to agree. Industriously she filled the cups with steaming milk, while Bobby happily tripped from trolley to bed and back again, giggling at the men, joining in with their chatter, and generally enjoying herself while producing a very enjoyable performance for the delighted patients. Sister was out of earshot with Liz, the staff nurse was occupied in a corner with a tricky dressing, and the other nurses who belonged to the ward had gone off to drink their own morning coffee. Bobby had the field to herself, and made the most of it.

But just before they had finished the round, when Bobby was standing by the trolley, holding her hand out to Bridget for the next cup Sister appeared at the ward door with Liz in tow. And at this same moment, one of the up-patients passed by the trolley, a young man with a plaster cast on one arm, and he pinched Bobby's bottom as he shuffled by. Bobby yelped with a mixture of surprise and pleasure, throwing out one arm. Bridget, nervous and startled, lurched backwards, and a jug of hot milk went splashing messily all over the polished floor, sent there by her flying hand.

'Oh, for heaven's sake, you stupid girl!' Sister bore down on Bridget with rage all over her face. 'This floor was polished this morning, and now look at it! How clumsy can you get! Go and get a mop from the kitchen at once and clean it up, go along now! And you – ' she turned to Bobby. 'Even if you were splashed with hot milk, there was no need to make a noise like that! Are you scalded?'

And Bobby, with a sharp glance at the flaming-faced and miserable Bridget said, 'Er – no, Sister, thank you – I'll help Nurse Preston, shall I?'

'You'll do nothing of the sort. She was stupid enough to make the mess, she can clear it up. You come with me, and Nurse Preston – hurry up with clearing that mess you've made!' And she sailed off down the ward, with Liz and Bobby behind her. Bobby cast an apologetic look over her shoulder at Bridget, standing mortified with shame and a sort of helpless rage, in a pool of slimy hot milk, and shrugged slightly.

Bridget spent a dreadful half-hour on her knees, mopping up milk and re-applying the polish the spill had removed. The obvious sympathy of the men made her feel worse. Even when the boy who had started it all by pinching Bobby's bottom came over to tell her how sorry he was, that it hadn't been her fault, she kept her head down, refusing to look up or answer him, so that he shrugged and went away, leaving her to her shame and misery.

Later that day, when the four girls reassembled in their bedroom, Bobby had the grace to apologise to Bridget.

'I am sorry, Bridie, love, truly I am – ' she said winningly. 'But I couldn't tell that Sister it was me that spilt the milk, could I? If I had, I'd have had to tell her that boy started it by getting fresh, and then she'd have given the boy hell, and we're supposed to look after the patients, aren't we? It wouldn't be good nursing to shop a patient, now would it?' And Bridget, though she was still smarting a little from the episode, found herself laughing, completely disarmed, as usual, by Bobby's undoubted charm. They spent the evening in a visit to a local cinema, and Bridget tried to forget the whole business, only grateful it would be another six days before she would have to face a ward again.

Unfortunately for Bridget, however, the episode had been reported to Sister Chessman, not because the Ward Sister was still particularly annoyed about it – her temper, while hot, cooled rapidly – but because it was usual practice to report fully on each student that came to the wards from the PTS. And Sister Chessman made a mental note that this girl Preston would bear watching. As she told Matron, on her weekly visit to the lady's office to report on the progress of the school, 'I'm a little doubtful about Nurse Preston. Her background isn't all it might be – these quiet girls of strict upbringing tend to run wild when they get to hospital, in my experience. And she spends her time with three very giddy people.'

'Are you worried about the other three, too, then?' Matron asked.

And Sister Chessman, frowning a little, said slowly, 'I'm not sure. They have very high spirits, but they are the sort that can be guided. I think. I much prefer high spirits to this quietness – you just don't know where you are with Nurse Preston. She doesn't talk to me very much, though the others chatter away freely enough. I could be being unfair – maybe she was just clumsy from nervousness, though Sister on the ward thought she was making a scene for attention's sake.' Altogether, it was unfortunate for Bridget that the Ward Sister was as young as she was. An older, more experienced, woman would have recognised that Bridget was nervous, not an attention seeker.

As the weeks wore on, Bridget got to know a little more about her new friends. They showed little interest in her background, though Liz once or twice asked her about the sort of life she had led before coming to the Royal. But Bridget had shrugged her questions away, and Liz didn't persist. But they talked about themselves a good deal, and Bridget listened fascinatedly, particularly to Bobby.

She was the only daughter of fairly rich parents, and as far as Bridget could tell, had never had to ask more than once for anything she wanted. Bridget got the impression that her parents had little time for their only child, regarding her with a sort of impatient affection, discharging all their parental duties by spending money. There had been nannies, expensive boarding-schools – several, for Bobby admitted unashamedly to being expelled from one after the other – foreign holidays, gay Mediterranean cruises. And Bobby liked her life as it was very much. She had come to the Royal because she wanted to live in London on her own, and somewhat to her surprise and chagrin, her father had balked at her demand for an allowance to run a flat of her own. He had told her that she either had to live at home in Surrey, or get a job living-in where she would be supervised. And as Bobby said with a grimace, 'That meant nursing. So here I am.'

Judith, the one of the three Bridget found least approachable, for all her surface gaiety, was the daughter, surprisingly, of a parson in a market town in the Midlands. She too, Bridget discovered, wanted to get to London, and the only way she could do it was by nursing – and as she said smoothly. 'The parents think it's a "Good" thing to do – service to others and all that guff. My God, but it's good to get away from that bloody vicarage – ' and Bridget had felt chilled at the coldness, the calculation of her.

Liz, too, seemed to find Judith's attitude to her parents rather distasteful. Her own parents were apparently happy, friendly people with a shop in a country town in Devonshire, and they had been delighted when their daughter had decided to become a nurse.

'They're not too well off,' she explained, almost apologetically. 'This way, I earn my own living, and get a career as well – they think it's a great idea. And with two sisters younger than me, they've got a lot of expenses – ' and Bridget had smiled at her across the room, and poured out another cup of coffee for her, feeling a warmth for this pretty, friendly girl, who seemed so normal, somehow, the one of the three somehow most like Bridget herself.

It was about half-way through the three months in the PTS that Bobby at last made the contact with the medical staff she wanted. As she had said firmly one evening, when the four girls were sitting in their room over cups of coffee made on the gas-ring each room was provided with, 'Life in this hospital will be pretty drear if we don't get to know some of the men around the place.'

'The patients?' Bridget asked, remembering the boy who had pinched Bobby's round bottom.

'Not on your life, my pretty,' Bobby had said, stretching catlike on her bed, and grinning across at Bridget. 'I mean *real* men. I mean, what are we here for?'

Judith chuckled fatly from her own heap of pillows. 'I know what I'm here for,' she said, peering into the mirror she was holding as she combed her thick red hair into a sleek style. 'I want to get married as fast as ever I can. And not just to anyone. I want a man who can keep me in the style to which I have every intention of becoming accustomed as fast as ever I can.'

And Liz, from across the room agreed. 'A nice handsome doctor with prospects and a private income if it's at all possible,' she said dreamily. 'Someone who will think I'm God's gift to doctorkind, who'll devote all the time when he isn't saving lives to my special welfare. There ought to be a few of 'em around a hospital this size to choose from.'

'Oh,' said Bridget, startled. 'I – I hadn't thought of that.'

Bobby sat up and stared at her. 'Come off it, little one! I mean, I know you *look* like a schoolgirl, and behave a bit like one sometimes, but surely you aren't really as green as that! Don't you want a man of your own, or are you odd or something?'

'I – I'm not odd, of course I'm not,' Bridget said hastily. 'I – well, I just hadn't thought about it, I suppose.'

'Well, it's time you did, sweetie,' Judith said. 'Why on earth come to work in a hospital, for God's sake, if not for the – social opportunities? Don't tell me you're like that dreary Dorothy Jackson, all religion and a burning vocation to help suffering mankind, and all that rubbish.'

'Of course I'm not!' Bridget said indignantly. She, too, found Dorothy Jackson, with her sanctimonious voice, her tendency to smarm round Sister Chessman, and her self-righteous and very obvious departure for Church each Sunday, unpleasant. 'It's just that I hadn't thought – I hadn't thought about – getting married,' and her voice faltered on the words. Indeed, she never had thought about marriage. She hadn't even thought about having boy-friends. She had never had the opportunity to meet any boys of her own age, and so found men rather frightening people. The thought of having boy-friends of her own, of ever getting close enough to a man to even think of marriage made her boggle.

Bobby laughed softly. 'We'll have to take you in hand, Bridie, my pretty, 'deed and 'deed we will! You're not bad looking, and with the right clothes and a bit of know-how you'll go a long way.'

'I haven't got much in the way of clothes.' Bridget found the thought of being dressed in the sort of clothes the others wore decidedly attractive suddenly, despite her fear of men, her diffidence towards the idea of marriage.

'All for one and one for all!' Liz said gaily. 'You do our notes for us, and the least we can do is show you how to dress and lend you some gear – ' and Bridget smiled gratefully at her. Of all the three, Liz was certainly the most appreciative of Bridget's help with their work, and had an easy generosity of nature that was extremely appealing.

So, when a few weeks after this conversation, Bobby came bursting into the PTS sitting-room with triumph all over her face, Bridget knew what was coming.

'I've done it, I've done it, I've done it!' she cried.

'Don't tell me, let me guess!' Liz looked up from the pair of stockings she was darning. 'The most famous surgeon in the place has just fallen on his knees at the sight of your gorgeous orbs, and begged you to take him and his little all for ever and a day!'

Dorothy Jackson, sitting in lonely state at the other side of the room, with text-books spread ostentatiously all round her, sighed loudly, and collecting her equipment, left the room to the four friends, disapproval written all over her straight back as she went. Bobby stuck her tongue out at the slam of the door behind her, and then jumped gaily on to an armchair. 'Listen, you lucky, lucky people. Your Auntie Bobby, who has the welfare of each and every one of you dear creatures firmly ensconced in her kind heart has made a social arrangement for you. Say thank you nicely.'

'Thank you nicely,' said Judith promptly. 'What is it?'

'*Well*,' said Bobby, with theatrical emphasis. 'I was just walking quietly across the hospital courtyard on the way back from that nice little errand Sister Chessman sent me on, and what should come across the said yard but the most *beautiful* piece of man I have ever clapped these young eyes of mine upon. To put it in a nutshell, and without any vulgarity, he was gorgeous!'

'So?' Liz was getting impatient.

'So,' Bobby said. 'I, without a moment's hesitation, and knowing full well that you three dear souls were sitting here positively languishing for the company of a few males, did my famous imitation of a lady tripping over a stone. And the gorgeous object caught me! Never even noticed there wasn't a stone there! Cor, but I'm a talented creature – admit it!'

'We admit it.' Liz was nearly bouncing with impatience. 'So what happened?'

'So we're all invited to a hospital party tonight as ever is! Doctors' common-room, nine o'clock sharp, in your best bibs and tuckers! How's that then!'

'All of us!' Judith said. 'All four of us?'

'Sure!' Bobby said. 'He wanted to go and buy me some coffee in the canteen, to get me over the shock of my fall, you see – ' She smirked wickedly. 'And I told him I had to get back to the kind care of Sister Chessman, or I would have loved to drink coffee with him – you know, a delicate mixture of interest and maidenly modesty. It always gets 'em. Anyway, he said in that case, come and have something a bit stronger by way of restorative tonight, so *I* said – more maidenly modesty, and general nice mindedness – that I had three very nice friends over here in the schoolroom without whom I couldn't *possibly* go anywhere, so he said, with charming promptness, Bring 'em along!' She giggled, her eyes sparkling very attractively. 'He said if they were half as nice as me, they'd be very ornamental about the old common-room, so I assured him you were all much *much* nicer! Cor, was I modest today! The strain is killing me!'

'But so late!' Bridget felt fear rising in her as she thought of herself going to a party. 'We can't possibly go – we have to be in here at ten o'clock – you know they lock up then!'

'Bridie, Bridie, dear!' Bobby cooed across at her. 'Be your age, my little one. A couple of bob in Margaret's outstretched palm, and the back door will be ever so conveniently forgotten tonight – and even if it isn't, I'm a dead ringer at climbing into first-floor windows up fire escapes. Let's live dangerously, girl! Fear you not, we'll get in again! It's the least of our problems.'

Amid the general hilarity of the other three, Bridget was silenced. She was definitely afraid, mostly of the thought of going to a party where there would be lots of people she didn't know, partly because of the fear of being caught out of the building after the curfew set by Sister Chessman. But she said no more about her feelings, for she knew that Bobby's high good humour could rapidly deteriorate into irritation, and she had no intention of upsetting Bobby. Bobby happy was a wonderful and exciting person to be with, and could make them all feel marvellous. But Bobby in a bad mood could plunge them all into gloom and despondency, so strong was her effect on them.

So, at eight o'clock that night, she let the other three lend her clothes, let them show her how to put on some make-up, let the clever Liz comb her hair into a very becoming new shape, and said not a word about her nervousness. When they had finished with her, she stared in the mirror at the new Bridget, and at what she saw there found a sort of excited pleasure battling with her apprehension.

Her thick dark-brown hair was swept on each side of her face into gleaming wings, the ends turning up slightly so that the light caught the tips with a gleam of gold. The big, grey eyes under fine-winged eyebrows looked deeper and somehow larger, thanks to the smudge of eye-shadow Liz had expertly applied to the lids and the touch of mascara on the lashes. Even her freckles, something she had always disliked on herself, looked different, attractive somehow, dusting her nose and cheeks above the soft, rose-coloured lipstick Liz had found for her. She was wearing one of Judith's dresses, a deep green one that fitted her well, showing her long waist and pretty tilted bust to perfection.

'Oh,' she breathed softly, as she stared at herself, and impulsively, Liz hugged her. 'I look quite – nice,' Bridget said wonderingly.

'Of course you do, mouse!' Liz said affectionately. 'You've got lots of potential. You've just got to learn how to develop it, that's all! You're as nice to look at as the next person – and don't you forget it! If you feel pretty, then you'll *look* pretty – it never fails. You'll have lots of fun tonight – come on.'

And with pleasurable anticipation at last overcoming her nervousness, Bridget 'came on', and followed her three friends as they slipped silently down the wide staircase towards the back door. Bridget was going to her first party, with her first real friends, and Bridget was a very happy girl indeed.

3

Bridget had never seen so many people crushed into one room before. It was not a big room, either, as far as she could see through the crowd and the dim light and the thick drift of tobacco smoke that clung to the ceiling and sent tendrils down among the close-packed bodies beneath. She was still feeling bewildered. When they had walked into the doctors' common-room, Bridget hiding behind Judith, they had been greeted with a boisterous shout from a tall man who had been busily working with bottles and glasses in one corner.

'Hallo! – Then you managed to escape from your wardress? Well done! Clive, David, Ken – meet some of the new lambs!' and he had taken Bobby's hand, thrown one arm across Liz's shoulders, and with Judith and Bridget following, led the four girls towards a group of men who had been leaning against the makeshift bar. There had been introductions, to which the other three girls had made gay response, only Bridget seeming in the least bit shy of these strangers, not that anyone seemed to notice her shyness. Someone had thrust a glass into her hand – the contents of which she had not attempted to taste – and in seconds, Bobby and Judith were dancing, while Liz was chattering to one of the men as though she had known him all her life.

The room filled with people very quickly, one or two of the girls in uniform, some of the men in white coats, and the noise increased in proportion. A record-player ground out raucous music that made Bridget's head swim a little, and people chattered at the tops of their voices in an attempt to make themselves heard above it. But despite the noise, and the smell of smoke, Bridget was enjoying herself.

She sat perched on the arm of a chair, against the wall, and watched the dancers and the chatterers with wide eyes. She was quite happy to be by herself in the middle of it all – indeed, her pleasure would have been diminished if she had not been able to sit quietly and watch, turning her still untasted drink in her hands.

Bobby, twisting merrily in the middle of the room, her fair hair swinging round her flushed cheeks, was a joy to watch, and when one of the other men, with a neat movement, ousted the tall man with whom she had been dancing, taking his place with a mock bow, Bridget chuckled. The tall man, without any apparent annoyance, made his way through the crowded scrap of dance floor towards Bridget's corner, and flopped into the chair whose arm she was occupying.

'Between ourselves, sweetheart,' he said, grinning up at her, 'I'd had about enough of that. Me, I wasn't made for these energetic type of dances. Give me a nice smoochy blues any day. What say you?'

'I – er – I don't really know,' Bridget said awkwardly. 'I've never done much dancing – '

'No? We'll have to remedy that!' He leaned forwards, and pulled her round to look at him. 'Now, which one are you? You *are* one of the new lambs, aren't you? Didn't you come in with Bobby and the others?'

'Yes – ' Bridget looked at him properly for the first time. He had a square face, with deep clefts in each cheek, clefts that had obviously started out as dimples when he had been a child, a wide, friendly mouth with very even white teeth, brown eyes that were crinkled with laughter-lines under slightly untidy eyebrows, and crisp dark-brown hair that was cut close to a well-shaped head.

'I seem to have missed out on the introductions,' he said, his smile deepening as he noticed the ready colour climb into her cheeks. 'I'm Josh Simpson. My misguided parents named me after a rather dull Biblical type, but try not to hold it against me. Anyway, Joshua will be an excellent name for me when I get my knighthood, don't you think? Sir Joshua Simpson, don't you know – surgeon extraordinary to the Queen – very extraordinary!' And he struck a heroic pose that made Bridget gurgle with laughter.

'I'm Bridget Preston,' she said, in response to his questioning face. 'And I did come with Bobby and the others. It – it was very nice of you to ask us.'

He stood up, and smiled down at her. 'But I *am* nice – very nice. Nicest man in this here mess of men, believe me. Come on – let's find a nice smoochy blues record, and try you out on that – ' and he pulled her to her feet, took her glass from her hand to put it down on the cluttered bar, and dragged her behind him to the record-player in the corner.

'Here you are,' he said, rapidly scrabbling through the untidy pile of records. 'Here's a gorgeous one – ' and he put it on the turn-table, and led her to the middle of the room.

As the other couples, some with loud shouts of disagreement at Josh's choice of music, moved towards each other to dance, and others, only interested in the fast, twisting records, made their way towards the drinks, Josh put his arms round Bridget, and started to dance. She had only ever danced with girls at school before, but she had a natural sense of rhythm, and despite her nervousness, the music soon relaxed her, and she found herself moving smoothly, matching her steps to his.

'That's better.' His voice came very close to her ear. 'Relax and enjoy it! Come on, now – ' and his arms tightened round her, and she felt his cheek against her hair, could feel his breath warm on her skin. For a moment she resisted the closeness, but then as the music swelled, and slid into a more definite beat, she did indeed relax, and danced as she had never danced before.

It was odd, the way she was able to anticipate each move he made, the way her feet seemed automatically to go the right way, the comfort she found in his firm clasp. She danced on, eyes half closed, the soft wail of the trumpet in the music sending a delicious sleepiness through her, a sleepiness that in no way altered her pleasure in the dance. When the music stopped, she stood surprised for a moment, still held closely by Josh's strong arms, before suddenly feeling all her shyness come surging back, so that she pulled herself awkwardly from his arms, and stood blinking at him.

'Th – thank you – that was fun – ' she managed, and he laughed at her obvious confusion.

'Bless the child, but she's a shrinking-type violet! Are you really as shy as you seem to be?'

She bit her lip. 'I'm sorry,' she said. 'I – I've never – well, I'm not really used to parties. I am sorry.'

'Don't apologise, my pretty!' He touched her face then, gently running his finger down the curve of her cheek. 'Believe me, sweetheart, you make a more than refreshing change. I'd forgotten there were girls in the world like you. I only ever meet the other kind. Come on – let's have a drink, and find a nice cosy corner, and you can tell me the story of your life – '

As he pulled her towards the bar again, she caught a glimpse of Bobby and Liz and Judith across the room. Almost to her horror, she saw that Judith was sitting perched on one man's lap, while Bobby was busily parrying the attentions of a man who, even to Bridget's inexperienced eyes, seemed to be rather full of drink.

'You see what I mean?' Josh's voice came from above her, and she turned startled eyes on to his face. 'Shy girls are at a premium these days – ' and he, too, looked across at the others, but without any of the shocked surprise on his face that Bridget had felt. 'Not that those friends of yours aren't crackers – gorgeous types, hmm? Can't say I blame David.'

'David?' Bridget asked, as they arrived at the bar, and Josh began to mix drinks for them both, more to say something than because she really wanted to know which one David was.

'David is the one who's working so hard with your Bobby,' Josh said over his shoulder. 'Tell me, how far will he get with her, do you suppose?'

Bridget, for all her inexperience, was not completely ignorant, and as she saw David make an even more determined lunge at Bobby, this time succeeding in kissing her very thoroughly, a success that she could see Bobby did not object to with any real strength, she blushed scarlet.

'I – I really don't know,' she said stiffly, and Josh, the drinks now ready, turned and looked across the room too.

'Whoops! My money's on David, lucky dog!' he said, laughing. 'That's some girl.'

'She's very nice!' Bridget was suddenly angry with this handsome, tall man beside her. 'She can't help it if – some drunken – drunken ass makes a nuisance of himself!'

He looked at her, and his face softened. 'I'm sorry, Bridget. I didn't mean to be rude about your friend. I'm sure she's a very nice girl – '

'Oh, course she is!' Bridget said hotly. 'She can't help it if she's so pretty people make a fuss of her, can she?'

'I suppose not – ' Then he laughed again. 'Come on – let's find a corner somewhere and wrap ourselves round these highly restorative-type medicines, and you can prove to me just how shy you really are – '

And obediently, Bridget followed, still smarting slightly about his implied criticism of Bobby, but attracted to him far too much to willingly abandon his company.

They settled themselves on a corner of a couch, and Josh put a glass in her hand, and looking at her over the top of his, said softly, 'Skol!' and Bridget, unable to refuse the drink, smiled stiffly back and said, 'Skol!' too, swallowing a mouthful of the cold, sweetish mixture he had given her.

'Come on, now,' he said, his face serious for the first time. 'I truly would like to know about you. Are you as shy as you seem? Or is it a pretty pose? My instincts tell me it's the real Macoy. Let me guess, hmm? Straight from school, and loving parents, and never been out on your own before.'

Bridget, suddenly not caring about the possibility of pity said, 'I left school a couple of years ago – I'm nineteen, you know – '

'Honestly?' He looked genuinely surprised. 'I'd not have given you a minute over seventeen – though that's silly, isn't it? I mean, you have to be eighteen even to start nursing here, don't you?'

Bridget nodded. 'Mmm. And I have no parents. Died when I was a child. I lived with my grandmother till *she* died a couple of months ago.'

There was none of the pity she hated on his face, and for this alone she warmed to him. 'Sounds a dullish sort of life. Was it?'

She took another sip of her drink, and felt the warmth of the gin in it slide into her veins. 'Pretty dull. It's – it's marvellous to be here – to – well, to be on my own. Not that I'm lonely, of course. I've got my friends,' and she said it with a sort of pride that made Josh suddenly feel the pity that she had thought she had managed to avoid – not that Bridget noticed it. She was looking dreamily across the room at the others. 'They are such fun,' she said with a sudden rush of confidence. 'They do all the things I'd like to do – they're marvellous – '

'Don't let them change you too much will you?' Josh, too, looked across at the other girls with their three escorts. 'You're fine as you are, Tiddler.'

She flushed, and with a courage born of the drink she was now steadily swallowing said, 'Why not? You said yourself I was dull.'

'Nothing of the sort!' he said indignantly. 'I just said you'd had a dull life – but *you* aren't dull – not a bit of it! You're sweet – '

And she blushed hotly again at the warmth in his brown eyes, and dropped her own gaze to her glass.

Bobby's voice above them pulled her back from her confusion. 'Help!' she said gaily, flopping into the couch beside them. 'That David's quite a character, Josh! Shouldn't he have a keeper or something? A girl isn't safe with someone like that!'

Josh laughed, and leaning back, threw a negligent arm across Bobby's shoulders. 'He's all right – just gets all excited when he meets gorgeous girls. Can't blame him for that, can you?' And with a return to his mock heroics, he pulled her to him, and held her close.

'What a woman!' he proclaimed, winking at Bridget over Bobby's smooth head. 'Is this the face that launched a thousand ships, the face that set the hearts of every medico for miles around beating with unrequited passion? Woe is us! You'll have us all leaping into sterilisers or something to drown ourselves and our sorrows, you and your luverly big blue eyes!'

Bobby gurgled with pleasure, and said with a pretended severity that convinced no one, 'And don't you start, Buster! Just you be a good doctor and go and get me a drink. I need one.'

He got to his feet with a deep sigh. 'You see?' he said to Bridget. 'One word from this luscious creature and we all run. I go, Madam, I go forthwith,' and with another deep bow, he turned and shoved his way through the mob towards the bar.

'He's nice, isn't he?' Bobby's voice sounded slightly sharp to Bridget, and she turned and looked at her in some surprise.

'Josh? Mmm. Very nice.'

'Well, listen, Bridie, my love. I saw him first, hmm? You know what I mean?'

Bridget stared at Bobby, at the faint line on the smooth brow, and said awkwardly, 'Saw him first? What do you mean, Bobby?'

'Just this, my lovey.' Bobby leaned forward. 'I know you haven't been around much, so you can't be expected to know the rights and wrongs of – shall we say, social behaviour? I saw Josh first, just that. I met him in the courtyard, and if I hadn't, we wouldn't be here tonight. And I like Josh – he's my type. So just hands off, hmm? I'd hate us to spoil a beautiful friendship just because you don't know enough to leave another girl's friends alone – and Josh is *my* friend first. OK?'

Bridget stared at her, her mind whirling with gin and surprise. 'I'm sorry, Bobby – please, don't be cross! I wasn't – wasn't trying to – I mean, I'm not like that, really I'm not!'

Bobby smiled cheerfully then, the faint displeasure on her face that had so chilled Bridget disappeared. 'That's all right then, lovey!' She hugged her briefly. 'I should have known better, shouldn't I? You're a *real* friend – not the sort to pinch another girl's men – sorry I mentioned it – '

'Here you are, beautiful!' Josh reappeared with a glass in his hand. 'Long and cold and full of gin, just like the Chief of Staff's wife! Drink up!' and Bobby took the glass from him, and drank up, smiling brilliantly at Josh over the rim.

When she had finished it, she put the glass on the floor beside her, and stood up, holding her hands out to Josh.

'Can you Madison, Josh?' she asked gaily. 'I've just learnt how, and I'm longing to show off – come and help me – ' and Josh, apparently nothing loth, followed her on to the dancing area to join her in the steps of the Madison, leaving Bridget with a warm smile over his shoulder.

With a smooth ease that Bridget found herself admiring, Bobby collected Liz and Judith and the other three men at the end of the dance, and brought them back to Bridget's corner, managing to arrange them all so that Bridget found herself sitting next to the now rather morose David. But as the evening wore on, he seemed to accept the fact that Bobby was not very interested in him, and turned his attentions to Bridget, who found herself dancing with him several times. She was a bit frightened of him at first, but he made no attempt to treat her as he had treated Bobby earlier in the evening, only holding her close while they danced. Bridget was grateful to him for seeming to realise that she didn't really like being held too close, relaxing his grip on her as soon as she pulled back slightly from him.

Liz and Judith both seemed very happy with their two partners. Liz with the one called Ken, a man as fair as she was dark, seeming particularly happy.

It was past twelve before Bobby made any move to go, when she said with a regretful move in Josh's direction. 'We'd better be moving, Josh. We'll have to climb into the PTS as it is – '

With much hilarity, the four men escorted them across the courtyard towards the PTS building, and with many giggling shushes from Bobby, helped them creep up to the back door, and kept watch for them as they slipped into the dark and silent house. Liz and Bobby were the last two to come in, and Bridget couldn't help noticing the look of smooth pleasure on Bobby's face as she brushed her hand across her smudged lipstick.

Why should I care? she asked herself reasonably, as the four of them silently undressed in their dark bedroom, and slid into their beds. If he wanted to kiss her goodnight, that's their business – and Bobby saw him first –

But she couldn't help caring a little. Josh had seemed to her to be so very nice, so much nicer than David with whom Bridget had spent the end of the evening. But there it was. If he was meant to be Bobby's friend, he was, and that was all there was to it. Bridget fell asleep at last, her mind a confused mêlée of thoughts about Bobby, about her friendship and how much it meant to Bridget, and thoughts about Josh, and how nice it could have been if it had been Bridget who 'had seen him first'.

4

The final exams of the PTS came on them suddenly, and for a week, Bobby and Liz and Judith spent every spare moment poring over books, feverishly repeating facts to themselves and groaning because they hadn't worked harder from the beginning. With infinite patience, Bridget helped them, listening to their halting recitals of the various facts they should know – and didn't know – correcting written answers for them, and generally nursing them through the actual week of examinations.

To her own delight and embarrassment, Bridget was second in class when the results came out; only the sanctimonious Dorothy had beaten her to first place. Mary Byrne, a quiet and hard working Irish girl came closely after Bridget in third place, and the rest of the class marks strung out reasonably until the list showed Bobby's, Liz's, and Judith's marks. They had scraped through by the skin of their teeth; indeed, had Judith had one mark less, she would have failed, and that would have been that. Sister Chessman made it quite clear that the Royal had no room for people who couldn't pass their examinations.

But the three of them escaped with nothing worse than a severe reprimand from Sister Chessman, and a strong recommendation to work harder in the future.

Bobby said shrewdly, after they had been released from Sister Chessman's office, 'Not to worry, my beauties. That there old basket is the sort that likes gay people like us. She might tell us off for laziness because it's the right thing to do, but inside, she likes us. I know that.'

Bridget heard this, and felt her heart sink. She too, had realised that Sister Chessman, while scrupulously avoiding any hint of favouritism, preferred the gaiety and charm of her three friends to Bridget's own quietness. She had noticed Sister Chessman looking at her with a sort of baffled irritation on her face when she sat with the class conducting free discussion sessions, sessions during which Bridget had never been able to say a word. Bridget felt, not without just cause, it cannot be denied, that she would have to watch her step where Sister Chessman was concerned.

The very first morning they spent as real students at the Royal came at last, and Bridget sat with the rest of the class at the big round table behind the dining-room door – the one specially reserved for each new intake, and consequently called the Lambing Pen by the rest of the nurses – and shook inside. It had been so strange to wake that morning in a small room of her own, not to see Bobby's crumpled bed across the room, not to hear Judith and Liz muttering as they crawled crossly out of their beds. And then, getting into uniform – that had been odd too. Instead of the white coat she had worn for the past three months, there was a striped dress, with complicated fastenings at the front, an apron that rustled with starch, a cap so stiff that it would hardly stay on her smooth hair, a collar so crisp that already it was reddening the soft skin of her neck. But she had managed to dress at last, and now there she sat in the dining-room, at her first breakfast, watching the big room fill, too nervous to touch the scrambled eggs and toast that were offered, settling for a cup of tea.

It was like an aviary full of blue and white birds, she thought, watching wide-eyed. Some hundred nurses came fluttering into the dining-room, white aprons flapping as they moved, white caps bobbing like crests on black, brown, and red heads, slender, black-stockinged legs twinkling as they carried their breakfasts from the hot plate to the tables. There were some lordly staff nurses with black belts gleaming with silver buckles, caps embellished with lacy bows and strings, who sat in casual elegance while a maid brought their breakfasts to them, the only nurses in the room accorded this privilege.

And the noise – the rattling of dishes, the high, chattering voices, the hiss of steam from the big boiler that provided hot water for the big teapots, the noise battered against her ears. Somehow, despite her nervousness, her fears about where she would be working, her shrinking dread of the day on the wards ahead of her, Bridget felt suddenly safe, and warm, a sense of belonging in this aviary, for after all, wasn't she as bird-like as the rest of them? And she smoothed her shaking hands across the smooth starch of her apron, under the table, and tried to relax.

Liz grinned at her across the table, seeming to read her thoughts.

'It's a giggle, eh, Bridget?' she said softly. 'I mean, get us! All dolled up like nurses – anyone who didn't know any better'd think we *were* nurses, just to look at us. And if anyone were to faint in front of me, or be sick, or anything, so help me I'd do exactly the same. Are you going to eat that egg? Because if you aren't, hand it over – I'm building up my strength against the horrors that lie ahead,' and she leaned over and scooped Bridget's uneaten meal on to her own plate.

The dining-room slid into silence suddenly, as a blue figure came bustling in and made her way towards a little dais at the end of the room.

'Night Sister,' breathed Bobby softly. 'Come to call the roll and tell us where we're to work.' Night Sister looked sharply across at the junior table and said dryly, 'We do not talk once I arrive to call the roll, Nurses. Remember that, please.' And of course it was Bridget who blushed scarlet as Sister's eye fell on her, while Bobby merely sat and looked the picture of innocence.

The recital of names was quick, each nurse replying with a mumbled, 'Yes, Sister,' and at the end of it, Night Sister read out where various people were to work. To her horror, Bridget found herself allocated to Men's Surgical – which caused the others to make envious faces in her direction – while Bobby was sent to Casualty – she brightened visibly at this – and the other two to women's wards.

In strict order of seniority, the nurses began to leave the dining-room, the lordly staff nurses first, the new class straight from PTS last of all. And Bridget scuttled unhappily in the lee of her classmates, and found all her old misery coming back. How could she face that ward full of men? All her other trips to the hospital from PTS had been to women's wards, and children's wards, apart from that one disastrous afternoon on the male surgical ward, and she wished with all her heart that she could change places with Liz or Judith, both of whom would willingly have changed places with her. But it couldn't be helped, and she arrived at the door of her new ward just behind the last of the senior nurses, and stood in the lobby for a moment, clutching her cape in cold hands, looking around for someone to tell her what to do.

A thin-faced girl in a rather grubby uniform came towards her at last, and said. 'Preston? I'm Barnett – next after you, I was junior pro till this morning, but now you're down among the dregs – and you can have it. Come on – I'm to show you around, and there's one hell of a lot to do before Sister gets here to take the report from the night staff. Come on – shove your cape in the linen cupboard – '

And Bridget followed her into the ward at a trot, her head down. The ward looked different this morning – not so tidy for one thing. Two of the night nurses were feverishly making beds, one eye on the clock, while the senior night nurse sat at the desk, her cap sideways on her untidy head, scribbling away in the report book for all she was worth. There were men lounging about, some of them very unshaven, others looking fresh and clean as they emerged from the bathroom at the end of the ward. A lackadaisical maid was collecting dirty breakfast dishes from the bed-tables, and a couple of the day nurses were rushing around with screens and trolleys, getting patients ready for the first operation list of the day.

'Come on,' Barnett said fretfully. 'Ten beds to make, and the ward to get cleaned in the next half-hour – come *on*.'

Bridget had no more time to think of how she felt, for she was rushed into a whirlwind of activity by the morose Barnett. They galloped from bed to bed, pulling on blankets, beating pillows into submission, while patients either mumbled or grumbled or tried to flirt with them, depending on their age, their illness, and the moods they were in.

Bridget was a little puzzled at first at the difference between the technique of bed-making she had learned in the PTS and the rapid sketchiness of the bed-making Barnett seemed to expect of her, but she soon realised that there wasn't any time for the leisurely perfectionism of the classroom, and she followed Barnett's quick movements with gradually increasing speed of her own.

And then, there were lockers to polish, bed-tables to wash, empty water-jugs to be collected, washed, and refilled, and Bridget scuttled after Barnett through these jobs like a giddy little squirrel. It seemed impossible to Bridget that the untidiness and general bustle would ever settle before Sister arrived on the ward at eight o'clock, half an hour after the rest of the staff, but somehow, every job seemed to get done at once. When Sister arrived, cool and crisp in her blue uniform, the patients were all in bed, the maid was busily pushing each bed back against the wall, having finished her sweeping, a senior nurse was checking the injections to be given to the patients waiting, red-blanketed, white-capped, and meek, on their trolleys to go to theatre for their operations, and Barnett and Bridget were bringing the last of the flowers in from the kitchen, where the staff nurse had been rearranging them.

The other day nurses finished tidying the beds, made sure the last locker was in position, and all of them, day and night nurses, came to cluster round Sister at her desk to hear the day's duties, and an account of the previous night's activities. As she stood in line with the others, at the very end as behoved her lowly position as junior pro, Bridget carefully put her hands behind her, as the others had, painfully aware of the smudge of dirt on her apron, put there by a dirty ashtray she had removed all too hastily from a particularly cluttered locker, and feeling her cap wobbling insecurely on her head.

Sister let her eye run along the line of nurses, stopping at Barnett and Bridget.

'I realise that as juniors, you two have rather dirty jobs to do – but that doesn't mean you can go about my ward looking like ragamuffins,' she said severely. 'If you can't keep cleaner than that, you'd better wear plastic aprons when you do your cleaning. How do you suppose patients feel having to look at people as messy as you two?' She looked at Bridget then. 'Now – you're fresh from PTS, so we mustn't be too hard on you, must we? But remember, this is a clean ward, and my nurses must be clean – ' She peered closer at Bridget then. 'Heaven help us, aren't you the clumsy one who used hot milk to wash the floor when you came here?'

Bridget blushed scarlet, and mumbled, 'Yes, Sister. Sorry, Sister.' And Sister threw her eyes up in mock horror and said to the other nurses, 'Keep an eye on this one, Nurses – she'll need training not to break and spill everything in sight.' Which was hardly fair, Bridget thought miserably. Anyone can have one accident, for heaven's sake –

The other nurses giggled obediently, clearly seeing that Sister expected them to, and one of the senior nurses winked companionably at Bridget, which made her feel better, while the morose Barnett sniffed at her side.

Sister then plunged into her reading of the night report, and Bridget listened carefully, trying to make some sense out of what she heard. The man in bed one was well, he'd slept well, and his colostomy had worked well – what was a colostomy? wondered Bridget – and pushed the word to the back of her mind as Sister went on inexorably. Bed two, Herniorrhaphy for today's list, slept well last night, ready prepped this morning. Bed three second on the list for a lumbar sympathectomy, needed sedatives in the night, very nervous man – and so it went on, till Bridget's head reeled with patients' names, with unfamiliar diseases, odd abbreviations – what was Mag. Tri. Co., for pity's sake? – feeling hopelessly that she would never in a million years learn enough to understand what it was all about. The things she had learned in PTS – about the structure and function of the heart, for example, and about the workings of a sewage farm – had no apparent relevance to any of the things she had heard this morning.

But before she could think about this further, Sister was reading out the day's off-duty rota. 'Let me know what days off you want by tomorrow at the latest, please, Nurses, and I'll do my best to oblige – ' She smiled up at Bridget then, her really rather pretty face smooth and young in the morning sunshine. 'You'll find me very good about off-duty, Nurse Preston – ' The others nodded in eager agreement. 'If you want any particular off-duty for a special date, or a party or whatever, let me know, and I'll do my best to help – but I expect you to be willing and cheerful about changes if I have to make them in an emergency. Fair enough?' And Bridget, confused and blushing again, nodded speechlessly.

'For the rest,' Sister went on, 'all I ask of you on my ward is willingness to learn, *constant* thoughtfulness for the patients, and a modicum of commonsense. If there's something you don't understand, come and ask me – for God's sake don't take chances on doing things if you are in any doubt. Nurse Barnett there, now. Last week she gave a man a drink of water ten minutes before he was due in theatre – the whole list had to be rearranged. So remember, if you're in any doubt, *ask*. And don't mind even if I'm angry at the time. I may bark, but I've never been known to bite, right, Nurses?'

'Right,' the others chorused, even the sulky Barnett, and then scattered about the morning's work, some to be off duty till lunch-time, others to finish getting the ward ready for the morning's operation lists, and consultants' and registrars' rounds. Bridget was sent to tidy herself, change her apron, and drink her morning coffee, and to come back immediately after that. Her off-duty time was to be that afternoon.

When she came back to the ward, half an hour later, it was quiet, the men reading papers or dozing in their white-counterpaned beds, the long, polished floor gleaming in patches as sunshine poured in through the tall windows and lit the long room to a bright butter-yellow. She stood for a moment, looking down the ward, and suddenly she liked what she saw, forgetting her nervousness. It was quiet, a nurse moving softly along the beds, distributing morning medicines, another at the far end taking 10 a.m. temperatures, while a clatter of dishes came from the kitchen where Kitty the wardmaid was washing up. It all looked and sounded so peaceful, so safe, like an ovesized nursery full of oversized babies.

And then sister came up behind her – Nanny? thought Bridget wryly, still with her nursery simile – then banished the thought as sister said crisply, 'Now, Nurse Preston, I'm going to start the morning's dressing round, and you are going to come with me. I will do the dressings, and you will help me, and *learn*. Listen to what I say, store the things I will tell you in a tidy corner of your mind, and you will be glad of it when your final exams come round. We'll set the trolleys now, and then start.'

Together, Sister and Bridget put masks over their mouths and noses – Sister lecturing Bridget severely on the technique of using masks meanwhile – and Bridget stood in awe and admiration as Sister deftly removed steaming bowls and instruments from the huge steriliser in the sterilising room at the end of the ward, using long forceps, moving the things about on the trolleys with the ease of long practice.

And then they began. From bed to bed, removing stitches, shortening drainage tubes, cleaning infected incisions–the tasks were many, often extremely unpleasant, sometimes decidedly smelly. Bridget was sent scuttling from bedside to sterilising room, clearing used trolleys, emptying receivers of their dirty dressings with averted eyes–they really were so very unpleasant, some of them, particularly the colostomy one. Bridget told herself with heartfelt certainty that she would never again have to ask what a colostomy was. And then Sister would arrive like a young tornado behind her chivvying her to hurry, sending clouds of steam bellying through the room as she laid her next trolley, shooing the now almost exhausted Bridget in front of her.

The dressings began to get nastier and dirtier. As Sister explained, surgically clean dressings were done first – others, the kind that showed infection quickly, like prostatectomy incisions, were done later. As she stood beside the beds, Bridget began to feel decidedly queasy. Some of the wounds they were dressing really did look very nasty, some of the smells – of the lotions on the trolleys as much as those of the dressings – so unfamiliar and pungent that her head swam and she wished with all her being that she had been able to eat something at breakfast that morning. Somehow, she told herself hazily, it would have been better if I didn't feel so horribly empty.

It was while they were doing a complicated dressing that involved Bridget having to hold a pair of forceps to keep part of the original dressing out of the way while Sister clipped stitches and shortened the red rubber drainage tube in the wound, that the screen behind Bridget parted. She could not look round, even had she wanted to. It was taking all her will power to keep her swimming head up, to keep her shaking hands holding the forceps, to just keep on her feet, so wobbly and sick was she feeling now.

'Morning, Sister! How's my favourite Sister this morning?' said a cheerful voice. 'As beautiful as ever?'

Sister bridled and her eyes crinkled above her mask as she smiled, and the patient grinned too, relieved at the interruption. He wasn't really enjoying her ministrations very much.

'Good morning, Mr Simpson,' he said, equally cheerfully, as Josh came round from behind Bridget, still bending over her forceps. He peered interestedly at her, above her mask, for Josh was a man who looked at every girl he ever came across as a matter of course, and the clefts in his cheeks deepened suddenly as he grinned at her.

'Well, blow me, if it isn't the Tiddler!' he said. 'First day in the slaughterhouse, is it?' and he winked at the patient, who winked back, and laughed hoarsely. This was his fifth operation in two years, and he had been in and out of this ward so often that he felt a proprietary interest in the lives of all the people who worked in it.

'Ain't she a quiet little mouse, Mr Simpson?' the patient said, grinning at Bridget. 'Never said a word yet, she 'asn't.'

Bridget felt rather than saw Sister's displeasure, and the faint frown that appeared between her smooth eyebrows. But Bridget was feeling much too ill to care now, her head whirling as the people and things around her seemed to swirl and dip in sickening waves.

And then, another nurse put her head round the screens, and said urgently to Sister, 'Matron's on the 'phone, Sister – wants to speak to you at once – '

And Sister, muttering slightly at the interruption, said, 'I'll have to go – Nurse Preston, just hold those forceps like that, and I'll be right back – sorry, Mr Simpson – and you, Mr Jeffcoate, mind you keep your inquisitive fingers away from that dressing while I'm gone – ' and she slid away between the screen to go purposefully up the ward to the telephone. Josh perched himself on the side of the bed, and with a wink at Mr Jeffcoate, said to Bridget, 'Well, Tiddler? How goes it? Do you think you'll last the next three years?'

But his voice came to Bridget from miles away, seeming to echo in her ears, as waves of blackness and speckles seemed to wash over her. She just heard Mr Jeffcoate say indignantly, ' 'ere, watch out will yer – ' before she passed clean out.

She came round almost immediately, to find Josh holding on to her, gently pulling her away from the bedside, while the indignant Mr Jeffcoate held protective hands across his abdomen. He had only just prevented Bridget from falling heavily on to it, and was still shaking with reaction from the fright she had given him.

'Silly Tiddler – why didn't you say you'd come over all queer like? It happens to all of us some time or another – didn't eat any breakfast this morning, I'll bet you.'

Bridget leaned against him gratefully, feeling his broad shoulders behind her, his hands on her arms, holding her firm, and managed a watery smile. 'No – ' she murmured. 'I didn't, I am afraid – and then all the dressings – '

He nodded sympathetically, but she could feel the laughter bubbling in him. 'I do wish you could have seen Mr Jeffcoate's face,' he said, still holding her firm. 'Thought you were going to squash him flat, he did, didn't you, Mr J?' and the patient, now reassured he was safe from any such accident, grinned back.

At this point, Sister reappeared behind the screens, to look at the little scene that met her eyes with a very definite frown on her face.

'What's going on here?' she asked icily. 'Nurse Preston, I told you to keep that dressing out of the way, and now look what's happened.'

'Not to worry, Sister,' Josh said soothingly. 'No harm done – and the poor little scrap couldn't help it – fainted she did! No breakfast, and then a lot of dressings – too much for a novice, especially one as tender as this.'

At the implied rebuke, Sister coloured up hotly under her mask. 'They have to learn, Mr Simpson, and the sooner the better. We can't cater to adolescent squeamishness, you know. I'm running a ward, not a girls' boarding-school, and these nurses must be trained and the patients looked after – '

'Of course, of course,' Josh said, soothingly again. 'And this girl is a silly little goose – still, I'm sure you'll make a nurse of her in time, Sister – look, I'll take her to the office, and get someone to give her a cup of hot milk and a biscuit or something, and then I'll do the round with you – all right?' and before she could answer, he pushed Bridget ahead of him and led her shaky steps down the ward towards the office and a chair.

As Kitty went scurrying off at his command to get Bridget something to eat, he plonked her down in a chair and stood looking down on her bent head.

'Poor old thing,' he said softly. 'You've had a horrible morning, haven't you?'

She nodded wordlessly, and then he squatted on his haunches in front of her and took her chin in his square, warm hand, and Bridget was aware of the faint scent of antiseptic and tobacco on it.

'Tell you what, Tiddler – I'll buy you a slap-up supper tonight to make sure you're well stoked up against tomorrow's horrors – pick you up at the home at nine – you'll be off at half past eight – and don't bother to dress up. I can only afford the local fish restaurant, anyway. OK? Take care of yourself till then – '

And with a last, friendly grin, he disappeared back into the ward, leaving Bridget mortified with shame, delighted and excited because he had asked her out, dreading facing Sister again, and wondering what on earth to do about Josh. After all, Bobby had said she'd 'seen him first' and so she had. What on earth was she to do?

5

She got through the rest of the day somehow, dreadfully aware of Sister's displeasure, more and more aware of the fact that her feet ached with a steady, nagging insistence, worried yet happy when she remembered Josh's invitation to supper. Had she heard Sister discussing her in the Sister's dining-room that lunch-time, she would have been even more unhappy.

'I've been landed with a right little monkey,' Sister Youngs confided to the Theatre Sister, with whom she shared a table. 'One of those quiet, demure ones who looks as though butter wouldn't melt in her mouth. And do you know what she did? I turn my back for one moment, and she promptly faints in Josh Simpson's arms!'

'She shows good taste, then,' Theatre Sister drawled. 'He's one of the best-looking men we've had here for years.'

Sister Youngs sniffed. 'Precisely! If she'd fainted while I'd been there, I'd not have given it another thought – I mean, first day on the wards is a bit of a so-and-so – I know that – but the neat way she waited for someone interesting to faint on! Too smooth by half.'

Theatre Sister laughed. 'I'm damned grateful I don't get 'em fresh from PTS like you ward wallahs do. At least, by the time they're sent to theatre, the worst of the corners are rubbed off.'

'I'll rub a few corners off this one, that I will,' Sister Youngs said grimly, and put a third lump of sugar in her coffee. Sister Youngs was beginning to get decidedly fat, Theatre Sister thought smugly, and passed her a jug of cream, just to help her along. Even at Sister level there were rivalries at the Royal, and Theatre Sister and Sister Youngs had had their respective eyes on the same consultant for the past year now, and it was Sister

Youngs who was making most progress with him. Hence the cream.

Bridget almost fell off duty that night. Even the three hours afternoon off-duty that she had spent in the sitting-room with her shoes off and her feet propped high on a stool, had not relieved her fatigue. Now, at half past eight, she was exhausted.

The four girls had adjacent rooms in the main Nurses' Home, and when Bridget toiled her weary way to hers, she found the others were already there, Liz and Judith sprawled on her bed, Bobby sitting at her dressing-table peering at her face in the little mirror.

'I think I am going to die, right here and now,' Judith said dramatically, lying with arms outstretched.

'Well, have the decency to do it on your own bed,' Liz said, pushing her away irritably. 'Why do you have to lie around on Bridget's bed?'

'Same reason you do,' Judith said. 'My room looks like Paddy's market – I haven't even made my bed yet.'

'You'll have Home Sister on to you like a ton of bricks, if she spots that,' Bobby said from the mirror. 'My God, just *look* at my hands! They'll be like a washerwoman's after another day like today. I've done nothing but scrub and clean and mop floors and generally act like a char – ' Then she grinned reminiscently. 'Not that Casualty doesn't have its compensations. There're some very nice men about – '

Bridget, sitting on the only remaining chair in her room, easing her shoes off, took a deep breath at this.

'Josh Simpson turned up on my ward this morning,' she said, her head down, apparently absorbed in undoing her shoes. 'Asked me out for supper tonight – coming here at nine, he said.'

There was a brief silence, then Liz said, 'Well, get our mouse! First day on the wards and she gets herself a date! I must study your technique, sweetie!'

Bridget looked up miserably at Bobby. She didn't know whether to apologise, or say she wouldn't meet Josh – though she felt that would be discourteous in the extreme, apart from her own inclinations – and was relieved and rather surprised to see that Bobby was smiling with a cat-like satisfaction.

'Well, now, there's a coincidence!' she drawled. 'David – you remember David, Bridget? – he asked *me* out to supper. Picking me up here at nine o'clock as ever is. We'll have to make up a foursome, eh, Bridie, my love?'

And Bridget smiled in relief. She had been so afraid that Bobby would be cross, would withdraw the warmth and friendship that Bridget treasured so much, also afraid she would not be able to see Josh, which she wanted to do very much indeed. And now Bobby wasn't a bit cross, and she could still see Josh. Even her feet seemed to ache less, suddenly, so happy was she.

Judith grinned across at them, and said admiringly, 'I don't know how you do it, so help me I don't. I could no more keep a date tonight than fly to the moon. Me for a hot, hot bath and blissful bed – '

'Me, too,' said Liz, and slipped off the bed to stretch and yawn hugely before padding away to her own room. 'Anyway, I've got a date with Ken for the day after tomorrow – he asked me this afternoon when I met him in the corridor on the way to dispensary – there's a lot to be said for errand running – at least you meet people and get away from those God-awful women in the ward – 'night, you lot. See you at breakfast,' and she went, followed by Judith yawning even more widely than Liz, if that were possible.

'I'll change fast,' Bobby said cheerfully, grinning at Bridget. 'Put a move on, Bridie, my love, and we'll go down together to meet the men – '

Bridget felt suddenly very shy indeed as the two of them came down the stairs twenty minutes later to see Josh and the tall, lean David leaning against the radiator waiting for them. It was Bobby, looking particularly feminine, as only she could, in tight black ski pants and a heavy red-and-yellow sweater, who ran gaily down the stairs towards them, smiling and sparkling in a way that made Bridget almost ache with envy. If only she had Bobby's gay insouciance, and her social ability, she told herself miserably, following her. Even her choice of clothes was so good, Bridget thought, painfully aware of her own sedate green skirt and matching twin set. But Josh grinned at her and said, 'You two look charming – much nicer than you do in uniform, and that's saying a lot, because you both look *very* nice in all that starch and those sexy black stockings.' And Bridget felt better, grateful to him for the ready understanding in him that was only slightly masked by his easy charm.

Almost without discussion, they went out of the building together, taking it for granted they would be a foursome. It was unfortunate for Bridget that Sister Youngs met them on the steps outside, as she came late off duty, and noticed with her sharp eye for such things that it was Josh who appeared to be squiring Bridget. The meeting only confirmed her belief that Bridget was a sly-boots who knew just how to set about getting what she wanted.

They spent an hilarious evening. Bobby and Josh were both in fine form, capping each other's jokes and sallies with ever more outrageous comments, sparkling at each other in a way that made Bridget giggle helplessly, even made the silent David smile. Bridget soon realised that David was not a man to talk much – his moroseness at the party had not been entirely due to the fact that he was drunk. He was just a man who talked little, who sat in smooth silence, observing, missing little of what went on about him. As the evening progressed, and they ate fish and chips and huge pickled onions – which Bobby and Josh both seemed to adore, even spending a noisy five minutes trying to see which of them could get the most of one particularly large onion, stuck up on a fork between them – David and Bridget became more and more like an audience, rather than participants in the evening's entertainment.

Bridget didn't mind this a bit. She was more than happy to sit in a bemused and fatigued silence, picking at her meal, watching the others – particularly Josh. She watched the way his eyes crinkled when he laughed – which was often – the way the light reflected off the fine hair on the back of his hands, the shape of the square, well-kept nails, the way his cheeks deepened into clefts when he smiled or spoke. And almost without realising it, she began to feel that this attractive man was the sort of man she liked more than any other sort. She stole a glance at the silent David, at his deep-set eyes, his narrow mouth, unsmiling and shut as tight as a trap, at the faint blue shadows under his eyes and on his temples, and thought confusedly. 'How can two men be so unlike? I wish I could be like Bobby, and talk and giggle with Josh like she does – ' But she was content just to sit and watch.

When it was time to get back to the hospital – and it was more than the curfew that decided this, for even Bobby was beginning to wilt at the end of her very long, hard day – they all walked back together. But it was Bobby who put her hand companionably into the crook of Josh's arm, and Bridget who found herself walking beside David.

And when they stood on the steps of the Home, there was a silent, slightly embarrassed moment, until Bobby, moving very imperceptibly nearer to Josh, put her face up towards his and said softly, 'I must *reek* of pickled onions. Is it very bad – or can't you tell, because you're in the same state yourself?' And Josh, finding this very pretty face so conveniently near to his, and being a man of very friendly tendencies, accepted the clearly implied invitation, and kissed Bobby very thoroughly. And Bridget, seeing Bobby's arms go up round his neck, seeing the dark head she had come to like so much so near to Bobby's fair one, felt a stab of almost physical pain and unhappiness.

But she had no time to think about it, for to her complete surprise, David, beside her, suddenly whirled her round, held her very close, and kissed her extremely thoroughly, in a way that bruised her mouth, and made her want to pull away from him. But she couldn't move, so firm was David's grip.

When he released her at last, she pulled back, her hand against her sore mouth, and looked at him over it, her eyes shadowed in the dimness.

'Thank you for supper – er – both of you – ' She stopped, unable to look at Josh and Bobby, aware that Bobby still had her arms twined about Josh's neck, that she was holding on to him as if she had no intention of ever letting go.

'Goodnight, David,' she said again, just as David seemed about to make another lunge at her, and turned and almost ran through the door into the Home.

Josh, looking over Bobby's shoulder at the flick of green skirt disappearing, felt a sudden twinge of something rare for him – embarrassment. He had always taken his pleasures easily and gaily, not being in the least perturbed if another couple were about when he kissed a girl goodnight. After all, why should he? None of the girls he ever met had mattered to him very much, except as delightful creatures who were fun. Why care? But this quiet, shy child, as he thought of her, somehow embarrassed him, making him see himself, for a fleeting moment, through someone else's eyes.

But then Bobby put up her inviting lips again, and David muttered a glum 'Goodnight' before making his way across the garden towards the courtyard and the doctor's commonroom, and Josh, left with a very pretty and willing girl, forgot his moment's embarrassment and enthusiastically co-operated with Bobby.

It was twenty minutes later when Bobby came upstairs, by which time Bridget was already in bed, lying in the darkness and staring at the dim shape of the window, trying to sort out her confused thoughts, still feeling David's experienced and alarming kiss on her mouth.

Bobby put the light on, and sat down beside Bridget, smiling at her in a warm friendliness that brought all Bridget's need for her friendship and approbation bubbling up inside her.

'Hello, love,' Bobby said softly. 'Are you at all annoyed with me?'

'Why – why should I be?' Bridget said lamely.

'Well, it was *you* that Josh asked out – and we did change partners, didn't we?'

'He – he only asked me out of pity – because I fainted,' Bridget said honestly. 'I mean – I'm not his type, am I? He – he needs someone like you, who can talk like he does – '

Bobby, with a sort of rueful smile on her face, said, 'Well, I think you could be right, lovey – '

'And you did see him first, anyway – ' Bridget was trying not to remember the sharp pain she had felt when she saw Bobby kissing Josh, trying to forget the way Josh had looked in the restaurant, the way his eyes looked when he smiled, the warm notes of his voice, the way his hands had felt on her shoulders that morning, when he had caught her and stopped her from fainting all over Mr Jeffcoate.

'Oh, please – ' Bobby seemed suddenly embarrassed. 'I know I said that at the party, but I'd had a drink or two, you know, and – well – I mean, if I thought Josh liked you best, I wouldn't *dream* of trying anything with him. I mean, a girl's got her pride, hasn't she? But it just seems to me that really David likes you better than he likes me – he *did* kiss you goodnight.'

'That was just because I was there,' Bridget said, with a surprising shrewdness. 'I think he's the sort who doesn't really notice people – I mean, a girl is a girl – not a *person*.'

'Nonsense!' Bobby scoffed. 'Of course he likes you best – and I rather think that Josh likes *me* – which is tidy and convenient, to say the least!' She smiled with sudden reminiscence. 'He certainly *behaved* as if he liked me, downstairs just now – ' and Bridget dropped her gaze, feeling the sharp pain of acute – what? She didn't know, but she certainly felt it. Maybe it was shame, she thought miserably, because it *is* shaming when a man asks you out from pity, and then prefers someone else's company. 'I'm so tired I could sleep for a week – I'm for bed, sweetie. And Josh says there'll be another party in the mess next week, and of course we're all invited – Liz'll be tickled to death. She's mad about that Ken of hers – 'Night, Bridget. See you at breakfast.'

' 'Night,' Bridget echoed, and then lay in the dark for a long time, staring at the window, trying to sleep, but too mixed up and almost too tired to.

She woke next morning feeling heavy-headed and leaden-limbed, dragging herself on duty to face another day of hard work, of Barnett's nagging, who as next in seniority was Bridget's guide about the ward, to face Sister's now definite dislike of her, to the sounds and sights and smells of the ward that seemed so dreadful to her.

But she survived the day, the long hours of running about the ward, the bed-pan and bottle rounds, the sluice scrubbing, the fetching and carrying, the bed-making and locker polishing, the serving and collection of meals, the washing of patients – everything. And she survived the next day and the next, till suddenly she realised that it wasn't quite as hard work as it had been, that the patients were no longer an amorphous crowd of frightening people, but individuals, some nice, some unpleasant, some cheerful, some perpetually moaning.

She began to like the work she did, to take a real pleasure in the muttered 'Thank you' from a man whose bed she had made more comfortable, to enjoy the appreciation with which a very ill patient sipped the orange juice she had prepared for him, to appreciate the way a man would be grateful for a friendly word from her while she cleaned his locker. Even the really difficult jobs, like helping a grown man with a bedpan, a man so miserably embarrassed by her ministrations that he almost wept with it, became worth doing. She learned, gradually, how to help the men lose their shame, learned how to be relaxed and make *them* relaxed.

She became quicker in her work about the ward, more deft, and managed to avoid the clumsiness that so enraged Sister Youngs, so that that lady began to develop a grudging respect for Bridget, began to wonder if she had misjudged her.

'Certainly,' she told Sister Chessman, at the end of Bridget's first month on the ward. 'She learns fast. And she seems to care about the patients as people, which is important. I know they like her, which is a good sign. I mean, if she was just putting on a show for me, when I was around, the men'd soon see through it, and let me know they didn't like her – Apart, as I say, from a possible tendency to be a bit of an exhibitionist when it suits her, I think she'll make a fairly good nurse – ' And Sister Chessman marked Bridget's file with a query, and sighed, wondering whether she too, had been misjudging Bridget. This was, after all, a good ward report, compared with some she had received on others in the new class.

Rather to Bridget's relief, the projected party in the mess had to be cancelled, because of a sudden epidemic of flu among the medical staff – so many men were off sick there was no time for a party, even if any of them had wanted to have one without their missing colleagues. For the same reason Bridget saw little of a very busy Josh, only sometimes scuttling past him on ward rounds, while she ran one of the lowly errands that were her lot, blushing when he managed a friendly wink in her direction.

And then, one morning in early May, when there was at last a real hint of summer in the air, Bridget was in the little cupboard that ran off the lobby of the ward – the cupboard used for testing urine specimens – scrubbing the shelves and relabelling the bottles. She was singing under her breath, quite enjoying the job, taking an almost housewifely pleasure in the tidy shelves, the freshly scrubbed wooden working surface, the gleam of the chrome taps over the tiny sink.

Josh put his head round the door and grinned at the flushed face that met his eyes, the roughened hands that were busily rubbing at a recalcitrant spot on the wooden shelf above her.

'Hello, Tiddler. Thought I heard your mellifluous tones as I hurried by on my errands of mercy – going to give the push to at least three of your patients this morning, I am – how's things in your little world?'

She felt her heart lurch sickeningly inside her at the nearness of him, the smile in his eyes so close to hers, and swallowed.

'Er – er, hello,' she said awkwardly, avoiding his eyes, and scrubbing busily at the now vanished spot. 'Fine, thanks. How are you?'

'Worked to death as usual,' he said, leaning against the door, and smiling down at her obvious confusion. 'Honestly, Tiddler, you are sweet. I've never met anyone as shy as you are – really I haven't.'

She didn't answer, wishing desperately that she could, but

completely unable to think of the sort of flippant, gay thing Bobby would have said in the same situation.

'You know, Tiddler.' He was almost serious suddenly. 'I never did apologise for what happened that night we all went out to supper.'

'Apologise? What for?' Bridget was genuinely surprised. It had never occurred to her that Josh had anything to apologise for. Admittedly, he had taken her out, and should, in all courtesy, have spent the evening concentrating on her, but if she herself was too dull to interest him it was hardly any fault of Josh's – or so she argued within herself.

'Well, never mind,' he said, a little shy himself for once, and then smiled again. 'Listen, let me make it up to you – what say we go out for a drive somewhere tomorrow? Hmm? Spring is really and truly here at last, and we could get out to the country in no time in my old jalopy – poor but hard working, like me, that car. What do you say?'

She looked at him then, part of her aching to say, 'Yes – oh, yes please!' and his eyes looked down at her in a way that made her head swim suddenly, delightfully. But almost without thinking about it, she heard Bobby's voice in her mind's ear, 'I mean, a girl's got her pride, hasn't she? – if I thought Josh liked you best, I wouldn't dream of trying anything with him – he certainly behaved as if he liked me – '

And even though I'm dull, Bridget thought desperately, looking up at the face above hers, a face she was coming to care a great deal for, even if I am dull and a bit stupid about men, I've got my pride too. He only asked me out of pity the first time – and now he's asking me out of pity again, because he really likes Bobby better than me, and thinks I might be hurt –

'No – no thank you,' she said baldly, and dropped her gaze before the look of surprise on his face, dropped her eyes too soon to see that he was hurt as well as surprised.

'Phew – !' he said after a moment, his voice a little strained. 'Well, that's me told off! I didn't mean to make you as mad as that, you know. No need to bite my head off – '

She could have wept at that. If he'd only understand how hard she found it to talk to men, how little experience she had of saying 'no' gracefully –

'I didn't mean to be rude – ' she managed. 'It's just that – well, I'm rather busy just now – '

'Oh, well, not to worry!' he said, with an apparent return of his usual cheerfulness. 'Sorry I bothered you – see you!' and he was gone, on into the ward to drink coffee with a friendly Sister Youngs, and go through the notes of the patients to be discharged. And Bridget was left in her little cupboard, still scrubbing shelves, but with every scrap of sunshine gone out of her day. But a girl's got her pride, she told herself stubbornly. And I can't bear to be pitied. So that's that.

6

Spring made its reluctant change to summer, and suddenly, their first three months as full students at the Royal were past, and Bridget and her class found themselves in the heady position of having a class junior to them in the hospital. They moved from the Lambing Pen, in the dining-room, behind the door, to the next table up, where they ate their meals in gay and relaxed postures, so that the new juniors at the table behind the door could steal admiring and awed glances at them, just as they had themselves in the days when they had been fresh out of PTS.

The new class meant, too, that a reshuffle of staff was necessary, and Bridget found herself assigned to the Casualty department. Bobby was sent to the Male Surgical ward, a move which delighted her, Judith to the Out-patient department, and Liz to one of the Children's wards, which pleased her rather – she had a genuine liking for children, and found that most of them liked her, which was half the battle in any form of child care.

In one way, Bridget was relieved to be away from Male Surgical. It meant she would see less of Josh, who, as senior surgical registrar, inevitably spent a lot of time there. Ever since that day when Bridget had so baldly refused to go out with him, he had seemed to Bridget to change somehow. He was still friendly, still gay, and amusing when he met her, but in an oddly distant way. He didn't call her Tiddler, for example, a nickname she had liked to hear on his lips, made no further attempt to talk to her on her own. And this helped a bit – but not much. For Bridget couldn't deny to herself that Josh had become a very important person in her life, yet she knew she had no right to regard him as anything other than an acquaintance. Every time she saw him, she felt her knees shake, something deep inside her taking a sickening lurch, felt her face flame with a hot blush. But even as she felt so, she reminded herself sternly that he was Bobby's friend, not hers. It was Bobby he took out, Bobby he kissed 'Goodnight' on the Home door-step, Bobby who always sat next to him when they went out in a crowd, as they often did.

This was the hardest part of it all, she would tell herself bleakly. They often went out in a noisy group of eight, the four girls, with Josh escorting Bobby, Ken escorting Liz, and a fresh-faced young anaesthetist called Clive Damant escorting Judith, and the silent David always with Bridget. It was odd, really, she would tell herself, undressing wearily after these evenings out. David has never once asked me out in so many words – he's hardly said more than a few words to me, anyway. Yet we seem to be stuck with each other.

And indeed, so it was. Bobby, still the prime mover in the tight little group, would come bouncing into her room, to tell her cheerfully that they were all going out to a cinema, or on a country pub crawl, or to eat hot-dogs and hamburgers at the fun-fair in Battersea, or whatever she and Josh had planned between them. Neither Liz nor Judith had the least objection to having plans like this made for them, as long as they were assured that Clive and Ken would be there, and when Bridget once said to Bobby that she didn't want to go, Bobby had flown into a furious temper.

'But I just don't want to go out tonight – I'm tired – we've been terribly busy on Cas, and I want to go to bed early – ' Bridget said pleadingly.

But Bobby wouldn't hear of it. They were all friends weren't they? she asked in a voice that made the tired Bridget shiver suddenly.

'And if we are, it means we do things in a crowd – we like to be together. If you want to turn into a drear like that Jackson, or a swot or something, just say the word, and we'll keep out of your way. If you don't want us, we don't want you – '

And inevitably, Bridget went out with the crowd, to sit again with David, to listen to the others chatter, to try not to watch the way Bobby snuggled close to Josh at every possible opportunity, to try not to see the way he would drop casual kisses on her upturned face, or would sit with an arm round her waist.

Even the way David took it for granted that she, too, wanted to neck, like the others, was something she learned to tolerate. She couldn't pretend, even to herself, that she really liked his kisses, or even accorded him more than the casual regard she had for any of the others – except Josh of course. But she couldn't bear the thought of being shut out of the company of her three friends. Even though she had been at the Royal for more than six months now, she had made no other friends. The four of them were so self-contained, there had been no real opportunity for her to make friends among any of the other nurses. They had formed their own groups and cliques and there was no room for Bridget in any of them. If she had not had Bobby and Liz and Judith, she would have been quite without friends, and the thought of returning to the loneliness of her previous existence made her shudder.

But in spite of the ever-present ache about Josh, in spite of the depressing tedium of having David kiss and fondle her, she was happy. Casualty was an exciting and interesting place in which to work, and as she became more senior, she was taught to do ever more complicated work in the department. She learned to apply dressings, to bandage wounds and help put plaster casts on broken limbs, to give injections, to assist in the minor operating room attached to the department, and she gloried in her new skills, and took a real pride and interest in her work. Casualty Sister seemed to like her, which was refreshing to say the least, after the sort of armed truce her relationship with Sister Youngs in Male Surgical had been.

She found time, too, to study, to keep up with the lectures that they attended during the week, to plan her work for the next study block the class would go to, just before their Preliminary State Examinations. She would spend hours of her daytime off-duty in the classroom, reading and studying for the sheer pleasure of it, enjoying tracking down information about a patient she may have seen in the course of her work in Casualty; but she never told the others about the time she spent thus, knowing quite well that they would laugh at her, sneer almost, for all three of the others had short patience for the people they scornfully labelled as swots.

And then, late one evening, just before she was due off duty, she was in the department rolling bandages ready for the next morning's dressing clinic, alone with one of the very few juniors from the class after hers, while Sister was off duty for the evening, and the staff nurse in charge had slipped off to have a quiet natter with a friend on one of the wards. The department was completely empty of patients, and the staff nurse, a rather giddy girl with a decidedly underdeveloped sense of responsibility, told Bridget that if anything came in, she was to cope if she could, and if she couldn't, to send the junior to find her.

Bridget was enjoying herself. The department was so clean and quiet, the junior singing unmelodiously in the sluice as she washed that day's dirty bandages, and Bridget was at peace. The late sunshine of a summer evening slanted across the tiled floor, lighting the flowered cubicle curtains to an incongruous gaiety, glancing off the chrome and enamel of the instrument cupboards, while the sterilisers hissed contentedly in the corner, and the distant sounds of people in the courtyard outside came through the big double doors. Bridget was to have a day off next day, and as none of the others had days off to coincide, she had planned to spend it all alone, sight-seeing around London, for as a Northerner there was still a delight for her in behaving like a tourist in London.

She had just tucked the last bandage into its box, and was stretching in luxurious relaxation, when the rough, urgent peal of an ambulance bell cut across the peace of the big department. Bridget felt her heart fall with a sickening thump; an emergency – and Staff Nurse wasn't here and would be furious if Bridget sent for her before finding out just what the case was. Perhaps it's for the Maternity department, she told herself with hope, even as she hurried across the big floor to open the curtains of one of the cubicles, to get it ready for a possible case. Her hope was short-lived, for the big double doors swished open and two ambulance men almost tumbled through, pushing a trolley as fast as they could.

'Bleeding – ' one of them muttered, as he manoeuvred the trolley towards the opened cubicle. 'And he's damn' near 'ad it, I reckon – where do you want 'im, Nurse? – '

Bridget stared down at the patient on the trolley, almost paralysed with fear, all her new-found skills and knowledge seeming to melt away. 'What do I do now?' she asked herself in desperation. 'What do I do now – '

There was a youth on the trolley, a fair boy, with straight hair flopping into half closed eyes, with faint rims of blue showing under the lax eyelids. He was waxen white, his skin showing the faint blue-green tinge of extreme blood loss. One arm was clumsily wrapped in a big bath-towel, and the gaudy reds and blues of the pattern on the towel seemed smudged with the much brighter red that was spreading over it with ominous rapidity.

'Put him on the couch,' Bridget managed. 'I'll help you – '

Behind her, she heard the double doors swish open again, and she looked up, praying it was Staff Nurse come back, but it was a woman, a woman with the same sort of fair hair as the boy on the trolley, a face twisted with fear, and streaked with tears, yet obviously enough like that of the patient to make it clear she was a relative.

'If you'll just wait in the waiting-room,' Bridget said, with the automatic brightness she had learned to use when dealing with anxious relatives, 'I'll call the doctor, and he'll see you as soon as he's examined the patient – '

'Hurry 'im, then – please, get the doctor quick – he's a bleeder, see, he's a bleeder – it won't stop, no matter what, it won't stop – told 'im I did, been telling 'im all 'is life – you're a bleeder, I told him, don't go playing with things what might start you off, but' e won't listen, you know what boys is, and 'e wouldn't listen – make the doctor 'urry, Nurse, get 'im quick – e's a bleeder, see, like my dad – a bleeder – '

Bridget stared at her in bewilderment while the ambulance men fussed over the boy on the trolley, lifting him on to the couch.

'A bleeder?' she said stupidly. 'A bleeder – like your dad?'

'That's right – ' The woman came close, and putting her hands on Bridget's arms, shook her in urgency. ' 'e's a *bleeder* – 'e needs some of that snake stuff – do 'urry – for Christ's sake, *'urry.*'

And then, something she had read in one of her long mornings in the classroom came back into her head, and almost without thinking Bridget called quickly to the nervous junior who was standing hovering on the outskirts of the little group.

'Get the surgeon on duty, Nurse Stead – and then call Staff Nurse – as fast as you can – ' and as the junior scuttled for the phone, Bridget ran across the big room towards the tall medicine cupboard on the far side.

'Please God, let there be some. Please God, let there be some,' she prayed urgently under her breath, as she scrabbled through shelves, not completely sure what she was looking for, but hoping she would know it when she saw it. She could feel the stillness behind her, the urgency in the ambulance men and the fair woman, all standing helplessly watching her, and she let her eyes run across the shelves, looking desperately for something she prayed she would recognise when she saw it.

And then, tucked at the back of a shelf, she did see it. A small box with a dimly written label. 'Russell's Viper Venom. Packed in Fibrin gauze. Sterile.'

With hands shaking with a mixture of fear and relief, she grabbed the box, and almost slid across the floor in her hurry. The ambulance men without a word stepped back, one of them leading the frightened woman away towards the waiting-room while the other stationed himself behind the couch, ready to help Bridget.

With infinitely careful fingers, her heart seeming to be in her mouth, she began to unwrap the now completely bloodsodden towel. As the last fold came away from the arm, she could see the really comparatively small cut that was causing the trouble, a mere inch long, but from which blood was pouring, an ominous bright-red, completely unclotted, liquid. The towel that had been wrapped round it showed no sign of a clot anywhere, unlike most blood-soaked things Bridget had seen before.

With her lower lip clenched between her teeth, she mopped at the cut with a big swab from the little table ready set up beside the couch, as in all the cubicles, and with a sign to the ambulance man, let him hold the swab firmly over the cut while she opened the precious box she had found in the cupboard. The pads of sponge-like yellow fibrin gauze tumbled out into the dressing-bowl on the trolley, and with a pair of forceps, she picked up one piece after another – there were three – and pressed them on to the wound, dropping the already-soaked swab on to the trolley beside her. Then, she piled thick pads of cotton wool on top, and strapped them down with sticky tape the sensible ambulance man had cut ready for her as she worked. And then they both stood there, staring down at the dressing, not much whiter than the skin of the arm against which it lay.

Bridget stood, absurdly aware of the sounds from the courtyard outside, the clatter of wheels and drums as the sterilising porter went by with his load of drums to be baked in the big autoclaves of the main operating theatres, the high voices of children passing by in the street outside, on the other side of the department. As she stared at the makeshift dressing she had put on, her eyes never shifting from it.

A patch of blood appeared in the centre, spread slowly. She found herself praying, confusedly – 'Please let it work – please let Staff Nurse come back soon – please let it work – '

Then, after a long pause, she let out the breath she had been unconsciously holding.

'What do you think?' she asked the ambulance man, still standing silently beside the couch. 'What do you think?'

'I think you done it, Nurse – that patch hasn't changed last minute or so, has it?'

'I thought it hadn't – ' she murmured, and stood staring still. But the patch didn't grow any bigger, just remaining in the middle of the snowy cotton-wool dressing as an uneven splodge of vivid red. Maybe she *had* done it – ?

The doors swished, and footsteps clattered purposefully across the terrazzo tiles, and the cubicle curtains billowed as Josh appeared at the side of the couch.

'What gives?' he asked gaily. 'Some hysterical child on the phone rang the common-room with some garbled tale about a blood-bath down here – I'm not on Casualty call, but I thought I'd better come – oh, hello, there!' and he grinned in a friendly way as he recognised Bridget standing still, leaning over the silent pale boy on the couch.

'Bleeder, sir,' said the ambulance man with cheerful officiousness. 'Got a call from the other side of the railway station there – found this feller goin' like a stuck pig – 'is mum said 'c'd been muckin' around with a hammer and chisel – anyway, he was damn near right out then, and by the time we got 'im 'ere, 'e was right out – and bleeding! – cor, never saw so much blood in all my natural, and I've seen a bit in my time, I can tell yer!' He grinned with a sort of horrible relish – 'Bleeding like a stuck pig, 'e was – you should just see our ambulance – '

'Mmm – ' Josh pushed him to one side with an inoffensive gesture, and the ambulance man gave way, leaving Josh to bend over the boy, one hand on his pulse, the other lifting one eyelid with a practised gesture.

'My God, but he's exanguinated – ' he muttered.

Bridget lifted her eyes for the first time from her dressing, in which the tell-tale splodge of blood had made no change, smiled shakily at Josh, and said, 'He must be – that towel was wrapped round him – ' and she indicated the sopping-wet towel on the floor at the foot of the couch.

Josh looked at it, and nodded crisply. 'What did you do?' he asked, as he touched her dressing on the lax arm with delicate fingers.

'I – I hope it was right,' she said, suddenly remembering just how junior she was, frightened in case she had done the wrong thing. 'His mother said her father was the same, and I thought – I read it somewhere – I put Russell's Viper Venom on it – '

'You were absolutely right – ' He smiled at her warmly. 'I've seen this boy before – he's a haemophiliac all right. If you hadn't put the venom on he'd have been dead by now – as it is, he's in a pretty bad state – well done, Tiddler – '

And then, Staff Nurse came clacking across the department, summoned from her cosy chat on the ward by the frightened junior, her face a picture of guilt.

'Sorry, Mr Simpson,' she said, lying bravely. 'I had to go away for a moment – '

'Not to worry, Staff,' Josh said, grinning at her obvious confusion. 'Your deputy here did nobly and well. A proper little life-saver, eh?' and Bridget felt the all too ready blush climb into her cheeks.

'Better get this boy to a ward,' Josh said. 'And we'll need some blood for him – chase up his notes, Staff, will you? There's a record in them about his blood group, and I'll take some from that sopping towel for a cross match – jump about now!'

And in record time, the boy was whisked away to a medical ward, while a medical registrar came and relieved Josh of his cross-matching job. By the time the night staff arrived, and Bridget was free to go shakily off duty, feeling desperately tired as a sort of reaction to the fright of the past half-hour, Josh too was free to go.

He hurried across the courtyard after her, and caught her up at the gate to the Nurses' garden.

'You did very well, Tiddler,' he said, his voice warm. 'You showed a presence of mind not many as young and inexperienced as you could have managed. Well done.'

'Thank you,' she murmured, agonisingly aware of his warm hand on her arm. 'I – I'm glad I remembered – '

'He'll be glad too, I imagine,' he said dryly. Then, with a pressure of his hand, he held her back, as she started to try to go on through the gate. 'Listen, Tiddler – isn't it time you and I got to know each other a little better? When we're with the crowd, I never get the chance to talk to you – '

She bit her lip. 'I – I'm sorry – ' she said awkwardly.

He smiled then. 'You're always apologising,' he said, and his voice was teasing. 'Nothing to apologise for. What say you and I take an evening out on our own, hmm?'

She looked up at him miserably, at the handsome square face, the friendly eyes looking at her so warmly, and let her own gaze slide away.

'I can't,' she said. 'There's Bobby – and David.' Why she said David's name she wasn't quite sure. Somehow, she felt obscurely ashamed. Josh knew, knew perfectly well, that she and David had spent time necking, that he had kissed her and fondled her, just as Josh himself had behaved the same way with Bobby, and she wanted to explain how little she cared for David, feeling that quite apart from Bobby's claim on Josh, she could not possibly go out with Josh if he thought she cared for David at all. But he misunderstood – and why shouldn't he? she thought miserably – I'm so bad at explaining.

Misunderstand he certainly did, for his hand dropped from her arm and his face closed suddenly.

'Yes – yes, of course – ' he said. 'Sorry to be so silly – I'll see you around, then,' and he turned and went, striding across the now dusky courtyard back towards the lights of the main hospital. And Bridget stood at the gate on the edge of tears, feeling a mixture of reaction to the episode in Casualty, kicking herself mentally because of the way she always said the wrong thing to this man, a man she cared far too much about for her own peace of mind.

7

The last brown leaves from the trees carpeted the courtyard with dangerous wet drifts, and the November wind sent them swirling messily in all directions, as the four girls hurried across on their way to the main hospital. Bridget felt her knees shake as she thought of the interview to come, though the other three chattered cheerfully enough. She could not tell them how scared she was or even why, since they seemed so unconcerned. And why should I be scared? she asked herself with an attempted reasonableness. Everyone has to see Matron to get their second-year belts – but it made no difference. She was scared.

The four weeks of the Preliminary State Block were behind them, the examinations had been written, the vivas struggled through, and now the results were out. Bridget hadn't found the exams too difficult, the long hours of study she had spent standing her in good stead. And the other three, needing constant help as usual, had badgered her to hear their learning, to check their notes for them, and this had helped Bridget's own studies, too. It was odd, somehow, how quickly the past year had gone, yet how slowly too. It seemed to her she had spent her whole life at the Royal, that she had known no other existence. It had been a happy year, most of it, except for the ever constant ache about Josh. For the status quo was maintained. The four girls and their regular escorts still went about together, their relationships with the men seeming to change little, though it was obvious that Liz and Ken were very deeply in love with each other – certainly more genuinely attached than any of the others were.

Bobby still went about with Josh most of the time, though Bridget knew she also went out with other men on the staff, and, while on holiday, with men from her home town in Surrey.

Bobby was rarely in her room during her free time – always out with someone, and in a way Bridget was glad she had so many boy-friends. It made her dates with Josh less hurtful somehow. Maybe one day Bobby will tire of Josh? she would think sometimes, and then push the thought away. Even if she did, it would make no difference. Since that evening in Casualty he had never again made any attempt to ask Bridget out on her own, made no sign that he regarded her as any more than just one of the crowd.

David was a problem, though. Still morose, still not particularly communicative about himself, still he seemed perfectly happy to escort Bridget on all the group outings, still took it for granted that they would make casual love at the end of the evening. She had come to loathe those silent hours spent in the front of his car, or in the Nurses' garden, sitting on a bench under a tree. She often tried to tell him she didn't really like necking with him, didn't want to go out with him. But she could never find words, and anyway, he would take no notice, stopping her from speaking by seizing her and kissing her. There had been a couple of occasions when he had tried extremely hard to go a great deal farther than just kissing, moving his hands over her body in a way that made her go rigid with fear, once even made her pull roughly away from him and run stumbling across the garden to the safety of the Nurses' Home.

She had hoped, after that evening, that he would at last realise how she felt, and make no further attempts, but he behaved as though it had never happened. And when Bridget tried to tell Bobby that she didn't really like David, that she didn't want to go out with him any more, even if it meant not going out with the group at all – which would have been the best solution for Bridget, meaning she would not need to see Josh with Bobby – Bobby had become very angry. It was odd, she thought sometimes. I need Bobby and Liz and Judith, and I know I need them. Life without them would be dreadful. But why does Bobby need me? She must, or she wouldn't get so angry when I try to opt out of going out. I suppose she *must* need me and the others, though I can't think why. She could make friends with anyone, she's so gay, and so much fun –

No doubt about it, the happiness of the past year had nothing to do with Bridget's private life. It was in the time she spent working that she found pleasure, a deep, very real pleasure that almost surprised her. She found a sort of love, compounded of pity and, of practical sympathy welling up in her when she was with patients, an enormous satisfaction in being able to make ill people comfortable, do something real and constructive towards making them healthy again. And when someone who had been very ill walked out of the ward, on their way back home, she would feel that everything she had done for them, be it only emptying bed-pans, making beds, or dusting lockers, had been infinitely worth while.

As the months went on, she learned more skills, was given more complex jobs to do, and gloried in these new abilities, gloried in the increasing responsibilities that they brought with them. Her only regret was that so few of the senior staff seemed to like her. When she was assigned to a new ward, she found the Sister there often cool, on one or two occasions actively hostile, and she could never understand this, for though she made no conscious efforts to please them, she knew her work to be well done. They *should* have liked her.

She would have been less surprised had she been able to listen to some of the gossipy conversations the Sisters indulged in in their sitting-room at nights. They talked about the nurses endlessly, and as a group, tended to form opinions based on others' experience and stick to them. And Sister Youngs, on Bridget's first ward, had disliked Bridget, said so loudly, and convinced all the others that the reserved, quiet girl wasn't just shy – which was the truth – but that her silence hid slyness, and that her watchful look was not born of interest in her work and concentration on it, but was rooted in a nasty sort of selfishness.

It was perhaps because of her awareness of the dislike she had engendered among the Sisters that she was so nervous now as she followed her friends along the corridor to Matron's Office. In a hospital the size of the Royal, the nurses saw Matron rarely – she had too little time to have close contact with her junior nurses she would have liked to have had. She depended heavily on the judgement of her Sisters, and Bridget knew this.

One by one, the nurses who were due to receive the striped belt that would proclaim the fact that they were now second-year nurses and had passed their preliminary exams, went into the office, and came out self-consciously smoothing the stiff, new belts round their middles. Liz and Judith and Bobby went in before Bridget, and while one other girl took her turn before

Bridget herself, they stopped to whisper to her as she stood nervously waiting.

'She's a right old tartar,' Bobby giggled. 'Told me I'd scraped through by the merest fluke, and I'd have to wake my ideas up a bit before finals – but I don't much care. If you pass by a fluke or with flying colours, what's the odds? As long as you *get* through.'

'She doesn't miss much,' Liz said, blushing a little. 'Asked me if I was planning to get engaged or anything before finals – '

Judith grinned. 'She didn't ask me – how do you suppose she knows? I mean, that you and Ken are such love-birds, and that Bobby and me are playing the field?' For Judith, too, had boyfriends apart from Clive. 'Maybe she'll ask you if you're marrying David?' she said to Bridget, and grinned wickedly at Bridget's hot blush. 'I bet you do, for all you say you don't really like him. And he's not a bad catch, you know. Clive says he's got a private income and that's quite a thing – '

To Bridget's intense relief she didn't have to answer, for the other girl came out of the office and stood back to let Bridget take her place. And with her heart in her mouth, she walked in, crossed the wide expanse of carpet to the desk, and stood meekly in front of the woman sitting there with head bent over a folder of notes.

There was a short silence, in which Bridget found herself intensely aware of the distant sound of traffic from the main road far below, found herself stupidly counting the loud ticking that came from the clock on the mantelpiece.

'Sit down, Nurse Preston,' Matron said at length, and as Bridget obediently subsided into the hard chair at the front of the desk, looked at the apparently composed young face with a faint line between her brows.

'Are you happy here, Nurse?' she asked abruptly. 'Do you enjoy your work?'

'Yes, thank you, Matron,' Bridget said. Enjoy it? I wish I could explain how much, her thoughts murmured, but she said no more than that meek 'yes', which sounded unconvincing even in her own ears.

Matron leaned back, and looked across at her thoughtfully. 'You puzzle me, you know, Nurse Preston. Your examination results are uniformly excellent, your actual work on the wards appears to be satisfactory, yet somehow, the Sisters with whom you work find you – difficult, shall we say?'

'Difficult?' Bridget repeated, letting her eyes slide away from Matron's face, too shy, too nervous to look directly at her. Which was unfortunate, because it made Matron herself wonder if Bridget was sly, unable to meet her gaze because of a lack of honesty in her.

'A nurse needs sincerity, you know, Nurse Preston.' Matron's voice sharpened. 'Her first thoughts should be for her patients' welfare, not her own concerns. Some of the Sisters seem to feel that you are too wrapped up in yourself – that your good work is due not to a concern for patients' welfare but to a concern for your own needs. Is that true, would you say?'

No, no, her mind clamoured. It isn't. I'm just bad at talking to people, I can't make the Sisters understand that – I can talk to patients, but not to the Sisters – but all she said aloud was 'I don't know, Matron.'

'For Heaven's sake, girl – you ought to know! Do you think of your patients as you should, or don't you?'

'I – I try to, Matron,' Bridget said miserably. 'I try to. I – I like looking after them, truly I do – '

'Hmm.' Matron looked at her sharply. 'I realise that I have no right to interfere with your private life except inasmuch as it affects your work. But I gather you lead a – a fairly gay life, shall we say? I have often seen you and your friends at hospital parties and dances. I hope – I hope you are – sensible about your private relationships.'

Bridget felt her face go hot, and in an attempt to freeze her shaking lips into stillness set her face into a mould that looked to Matron to be decidedly mulish. Poor Bridget, with her positive gift for giving people the wrong impression. She wanted to please this woman very much indeed, respected her as a person and as the individual who was ultimately responsible for her work and welfare, and would have given anything to be able to talk to her freely, to relax and tell her really how she felt. For a mad moment, she wondered if she could blurt out to Matron about her private difficulties, ask her how to tell David she didn't like him, how to tell Josh that she did, very much indeed, like him. But even as she thought it, she knew she couldn't and said only, 'I try to be sensible, Matron.'

The older woman sighed sharply, and leaned across her desk to pick up the striped belt that was ready for Bridget.

'Well, Nurse Preston, here is your belt. I must remind you that you have an even greater responsibility now that you have it, that patients will depend on you to a greater and greater extent, and that it is up to you to make yourself worthy of their dependence. Try to be – warmer, more thoughtful, and see if you can get better reports from the Sisters with whom you work from now on. Good afternoon, Nurse Preston.'

And Bridget almost stumbled from the room, clutching her belt in a cold hand.

She was glad the others had not waited for her, and went back across the courtyard to her room with her head whirling. It's not fair, she thought desperately, not fair. Why can't they understand, why can't any of them understand? I'm just not a person who can explain to people how I feel, I'm not made that way –

She locked herself in her room when she got there, to lie on her bed in the dusk of the early winter evening, to think and, to soothe her smarting feelings in privacy. Liz came and battered at her door and tried to open it, but she lay still, ignoring her. She heard Liz calling to the others that Bridget wasn't there, that she must have gone out somewhere, and Bobby's reply that she was going out with one of the new registrars, so she'd see Bridget in the morning, and Liz's footsteps clattered away down the corridor. Still Bridget lay on her bed, heard the other three chatter and giggle as they scampered in and out of each other's rooms to get ready to go out, heard the silence wash back into the building as they at last clattered away down the stairs towards their evenings out.

And as she lay there, long into the evening, her hands behind her head, staring at the dim square that was her window, she began to think about herself, about her relations with the three girls who were her friends, about David and Josh, about her work. Part of her knew perfectly well that in a way Liz and Judith and Bobby were bad for her. She had warmed to them first because they seemed to have all the qualities she herself lacked, and had wanted to be with them so that she could learn to be like them, warm and gay and friendly. Yet all that had happened was that she became, if anything, quieter, shyer, less capable of coping on her own, clinging to them as lifelines rather than because she really enjoyed their company – and then she pushed all her thoughts firmly to the back of her mind. It was no good thinking about it. I am as I am, she told herself and there it is.

They were put on night duty the next night, and for Bridget, this was an intense relief. Although Night Sister had a reputation of being a very stern woman, on night duty, one saw little of her – far less than one saw of a Sister on day duty.

She enjoyed night duty, the greater freedom to be with patients, the way she found herself doing complicated procedures that on day duty were done by third-year nurses, enjoyed being in charge of a ward at night, with a third-year nurse on call from a neighbouring ward for emergencies, and just a junior with her to cope with everything. She enjoyed the last round of the night, tucking patients down, turning off lights until only the shaded light over the desk in the centre was left to illuminate the big ward, enjoyed moving silently from bed to bed as the night wore on, checking that all the men in the ward were sleeping, giving warm drinks to the wakeful ones, even enjoyed the hectic rush of dressings, treatments, breakfasts, and bed-making that the morning brought. It was a male medical ward to which she had been assigned, and the work was heavy, many of the patients being old, needing a great deal of bedside nursing.

Everything seemed to be going very well, until she had been on the ward for about a month. She came on duty, a few days before Christmas, to find the Day Sister and nurses scurrying about busily. The Christmas decorations were already up, tinsel and paper chains swinging lazily from the light fittings, the huge Christmas tree sparkling with lights and coloured baubles, sprigs of holly and laurel drooping from the chart-racks above each bed. Some of the men, well enough to be up, were clustered round the big radiator, drinking some beer that Day Sister – a kindly woman – had allowed them 'because it was nearly Christmas.' But at the bed at the far end of the ward, there was a scurrying of nurses, screens pulled round to hide the patient from prying eyes, and a faint hiss of oxygen could be heard above the soft, murmuring voices of the other patients.

Bridget hurried down the ward to see what was going on while the junior set about the first jobs of the night, and slid round the screens to where Day Sister was leaning over the bed.

An oxygen tent was set up, translucent folds of polythene masking the occupant of the bed, the huge cylinder of oxygen beside him gleaming dully in the light.

Sister straightened, and nodded at Bridget. 'Evening, Nurse Preston. Hope you slept well,' her usual greeting, given with a sort of absence that made it clear that she was not really very interested.

'This man was picked up by the police down by the railways this afternoon. He's a tramp – very ill indeed. Clearly hasn't had much to eat for days, and Dr Winkworth thinks he's a meths drinker into the bargain.' She wrinkled her nose with distaste. 'He certainly smelled pretty ghastly when they brought him in. Anyway, he has lobar pneumonia – very nasty – both bases are completely full, by the sound of him, and his breathing is very poor indeed. Keep this oxygen going – there's plenty of ice in the cooling system, and see to it that you watch it carefully – it'll probably need renewing about midnight. He's on four-hourly tetracycline and you can give it straight into the drip.'

She indicated the tall stand beside the bed, where a bottle of glucose saline hung, red tubing running from it to the invisible arm inside the oxygen tent.

'Keep the glucose saline going, and watch him – I doubt he'll last the night, but he just might. There's a full cylinder of oxygen in the ante-room, though this'll last well into the small hours. All right?'

Bridget nodded, and watched Day Sister make the last check on the patient before following her out of the screens down to the desk to take the rest of the report.

'Half-hourly pulse on that man – don't know his name, by the way – no one's identified him yet, and I doubt very much if the police'll find anything about him – and keep an hourly blood-pressure chart, too. And an intake and output record. Right?'

She rattled through the rest of the report – and to Bridget's relief there was no other very ill patient in the ward, which meant she could concentrate on the pathetic wreck in bed seventeen – and pulled on her cuffs at last.

'I must go,' Sister said. 'There's a dress rehearsal for the Christmas show tonight, and I'm in it, God help me. Hope all goes well, Nurse – watch that man – and of course, you know about the general precautions? I've warned the men they mustn't smoke of course – see to it they don't. Don't want that tent going up in an explosion, do we? Though between ourselves, poor devil in it would hardly know if it did. He's right out. Anyway, I'm off. Goodnight,' and she bustled away, the last of the day nurses following her wearily.

Bridget hurried through the routine, settling the men, warning them again of the danger of smoking when there was highly inflammable oxygen in the ward, and when they were all settled, sent the junior to the kitchen to prepare the breakfast trolleys while she went up the ward to bed seventeen.

For the first time, she could see the patient inside the tent.

He was very old, his face deeply lined, the grooves in his sallow cheeks still showing dirt deeply ground in. Obviously, it would take a great deal of washing to get that out, she thought. And he was in no condition for such niceties. He was unshaven, the narrow cheeks covered with rough grey stubble, and his scrawny neck stuck out pathetically from the neck of the hospital's pyjama jacket. He lay with his head on one side, propped high on pillows, inside the tiny world of the oxygen tent, his lax lips crusted, his chest hardly moving as he breathed.

She slipped her hands carefully through the sleeves at the side of the tent, making sure that no oxygen escaped as she did so, and checked his pulse, made sure he had a clear airway, and with a sudden access of pity, stroked the grimy old face with a gentle finger.

Odd, she thought feeling something perilously close to tears in her throat. He was a baby once – it doesn't seem possible – such a wreck. I wonder what he was like when he was younger, why he's like this, who he belongs to, or who belongs to him –

But the old man just lay mutely, his closed eyes deep in his dirty thin face, the hollowing of the temples that indicated the severity of his condition making his head look skull-like.

And then, sighing sharply, she sealed the tent again, checked the cylinder and the ice, and began to enter the readings of his blood pressure and pulse on to his chart.

As she finished, and hung the chart back at the foot of the bed, she raised her head sharply, and sniffed. There was no mistake about it – she could smell cigarette smoke, somewhere near.

Moving with all the speed she had, she came out of the screens, and peered round the ward. The men were all lying humped in their beds, apparently snoring, and she could see no tell-tale glow – and then, a tall figure appeared at the end of the ward, sihouetted against the light. As it came towards her, she, too, hurried towards it, for she could see the bright glow of a cigarette held in its hand. I must put a notice at the door for the doctors, she thought anxiously, and then, she was face to face with the man who was smoking.

'Hello,' he said, his voice thick and blurred. ' 'S'me – David. How're you, sweetheart?'

She peered up at him in the darkness, and whispered sharply, 'David – I've got an oxygen tent going – put that cigarette out – ' and she reached for it.

He laughed, loudly, so that one or two of the men stirred in their sleep, and teasingly held the cigarette high out of her reach. 'Whatsamatter, lovey? Want to smoke?'

'Give me that, you idiot,' she said, louder now, her voice thin with her fear for the oxygen she could hear still hissing behind her. 'I've got a tent up, don't you understand?'

'Aha!' And he laughed again. 'Florence Nightingale on the war-path – scared there'll be an accident?'

'Of course I am!' She was nearly crying now. 'Are you too drunk to care, you lunatic?' for he was obviously very drunk indeed.

'Got it in one, sweetheart. Been a nice big party in the mess, and I'm as sloshed as a newt – ' and he raised his other hand high, and she could see the light glint on a half full glass in it.

Almost sick with terror now, she did the only thing she could do. She turned him by sheer force, propelled him as fast as she could down the ward towards the doors at the end, while he slithered on the polished floor in front of her. They reached the door, and there he set himself against the jamb, and managed to stop her headlong rush.

'Now go easy, sweetheart,' he said, his voice ugly suddenly. 'I only came to say hello to you, give you a nice Christmas kiss – '

He lurched towards her suddenly, just as she managed at last to wrench the cigarette from his hand, and as he lurched the glass in his hand fell tinkling to the floor, to splash her apron as it went. She smelled the thick reek of whisky, as she ground the cigarette out. And then, off her guard, his arms were round her, and he was pushing her head back in a violent kiss that hurt her mouth, that made her head swim with the fumes of the whisky he had been drinking. He pulled at her uniform, so that her collar burst open under his onslaught, and the bib of her apron tore from the pins that held it to her dress, and her cap fell to the floor as he tried to run one hand through her hair.

'Stop it, you idiot – stop it – ' She managed to get her hand away from his, tried desperately to pull right away from him.

And then, suddenly, he pulled away from her himself, and stood awkwardly straightening his tie as he stared over her shoulder.

She turned herself, fumbling with her collar, agonisingly aware of the torn apron she was wearing, the stain of whisky on her skirt, her cap lying at her feet, to see Night Sister staring at her with a face rigid with shock, blue eyes icy with rage.

8

David seemed to have been shocked into sobriety by Night Sister's sudden appearance.

'Evening, Sister,' he said, and his voice sounded almost normal, though there was still a faint blur about the sibilants. 'Just going – ' and he made a move towards the main outer doors of the ward, while Bridget stood in dumb misery, trying to do up her collar, fumbling with the pins on her torn apron.

'I'd like to speak to you, if you don't mind, Dr Nestor,' Sister said, not taking her eyes from Bridget. 'You will wait for me, please – outside the ward,' and meekly, David nodded, and with a quick glance at Bridget, slid out of the little group and went to the door. As it swished shut behind him, Night Sister said to Bridget, 'Where is your Junior?'

'In – in the kitchen, Sister – laying the trolleys for – '

Night Sister pushed the kitchen door open, and called the junior out. 'Go into the ward, Nurse,' she said curtly, 'and stay there until I tell you what to do,' and with a startled look at the dishevelled Bridget, the junior scuttled into the dimness of the big ward.

'Now, Nurse, come in here. Tidy yourself up at once.'

Under Night Sister's icy-blue gaze, Bridget started to tidy her uniform, to set her crumpled cap back on her head, and when she had managed to make some semblance of order, stood still to wait for the onslaught of Night Sister's tongue.

There was a long pause, and then Night Sister said, her voice thin with controlled anger, 'Now, perhaps, you can offer some explanation of that disgraceful scene?'

Bridget took a deep breath, and swallowed hard. She was shaking with reaction, with tears very near the surface, and for one ghastly moment, as she opened and closed her mouth, she thought she wouldn't be able to speak at all.

'He – he was smoking,' she managed at last. 'Smoking. And there's a tent up. I was frightened. And he wouldn't – he wouldn't put it out. I *had* to make him put it out – there was oxygen – '

'Well? That still doesn't explain what I saw, does it?'

'He wouldn't put it out,' Bridget said desperately. 'He just wouldn't. And – and when I took it away from him, he – he – ' but she couldn't go on.

'Is Dr Nestor a friend of yours?' There was a world of scorn in the way Night Sister said the word 'friend', a scorn that made Bridget squirm sickly. A friend of hers? How could she possibly explain the relationship that existed between her and David, the unwillingness she felt towards that relationship, the reasons for its continued existence? She couldn't. All she could say was, 'A – sort of friend, I suppose – a sort of friend.'

'I can imagine what sort,' and now Sister was really sneering. 'I can well imagine. However, that is no concern of mine. You can explain the rest to Matron in the morning. In the meantime, since you are clearly not to be trusted in charge of a ward, you had better spend the rest of the night in Casualty where Staff Nurse can keep an eye on you, and I will send someone else here. And you will go to Matron as soon as you are off duty in the morning, do you understand? Go to Casualty now, and ask Staff Nurse to send Nurse Jessolo here to take over from you. And keep out of my sight for the rest of the night. I don't want to see you – you make me *sick*!' and she held the kitchen door open for Bridget to pass her.

Outside the ward, David was leaning against the wall, obediently waiting for Night Sister, and as Bridget went past him, he put a hand out to stop her. But she looked at him with such anger, such loathing in her face, that even he, unperceptive as he was, dropped his hand in confusion, and let her go.

The rest of the night dragged for Bridget. A curious Night Staff Nurse, down in Casualty, tried to get her to explain why she had been banished from her ward. But Bridget only shook her head, and refused to talk, which annoyed the Staff Nurse enough to make her send Bridget to the sluice to spend the long, dark hours cleaning equipment and making dressings ready to be packed in the big drums for the morning.

There were not even any accidents during the night to break

the monotony, to keep the department and Bridget busy, so she had nothing to keep her thoughts from their sick repetition of anger, of fear and a sort of shame. She knew perfectly well that it had been David's fault that the whole thing had happened. He had been drunk, and behaved outrageously. But part of her mind kept reminding her that he would never have behaved so if it had not been for the relationship between them, the memory of the hours she had spent necking with him. He had every right to expect her to behave as badly as he had himself, she told herself miserably. Every right.

The long night came to an end at last, and Bridget dragged her aching and miserable body to Night Nurses' supper at nine in the morning, to sit next to the other three, trying to eat the cold meat pie and boiled potatoes and cabbage the hospital provided for this dull meal. Already, she discovered, everyone on night duty knew what had happened. The junior on the male medical ward had overheard Night Sister talking to David, after Bridget's departure for Casualty, and had lost no time in recounting – not without embellishment – the details of the whole sordid business as she knew it.

Bobby was highly amused by it all, though Liz was sympathetic. Judith, as usual, simply followed Bobby's lead, and laughed at Bridget's misery with her.

'Oh, come off it, Bridie!' Bobby said at length, staring at Bridget over the rim of her coffee cup as they finished their meal. 'Why all the glummery? So you got copped having a quiet snog – you aren't the first, and you won't be the last. Matron'll give you a bit of a nagging, and that'll be that! No need to behave as though the world had come to an end! Cheer up, love!'

'Oh, leave her alone, Bobby,' Liz said, uncomfortably, looking at Bridget as she sat slumped dumbly in her chair, her untouched food in front of her. 'I'd be scared too. You know what a tongue Matron's got – and I bet it wasn't Bridget's fault, anyway – was it, Bridie?'

Bridget looked up at her and said quietly, 'No it wasn't – ' and she warmed to Liz, managing a smile at the friendly face across the table.

And then, it was time to go to Matron's Office. She stood outside the door, hearing the faint sound of Night Sister's voice inside as she gave the night report, seeing the morning bustle about her with unseeing eyes, but aware of the incongruity of the

Christmas decorations that bedecked the long corridor, of the chilliness of the wintry morning.

Night Sister came out of the office, and stood back, grimfaced and tight-lipped, to let Bridget go in, and summoning all the strength she had, Bridget walked across the carpeted floor to stand in front of the big desk at the far end of the room.

Matron looked up at her, and at the sight of the pinched, white face, the misery in the big, grey eyes, much of the anger that Night Sister's account of the night's happenings had roused in her dissipated. She had expected to meet – dumb insolence perhaps, a perky insouciance, regret at having been caught rather than regret that the episode had happened at all. But this girl was clearly deeply unhappy, terrified, and Matron, instead of showing the anger with which she had intended to speak, smiled at Bridget, and said gently, 'Sit down, Nurse Preston.'

Her gentleness was too much for Bridget. She stared at the older woman, and then, the tears that had been so near the surface all night at last broke bounds, and came tumbling down her face, filling her throat and nose with tight misery, so that all she could do was collapse into the proffered chair, and bury her head in shaking hands.

Matron said nothing, letting the storm subside, and gradually Bridget brought herself under control again, and wiping her eyes to a puffy redness, at last sat silent, head bowed in front of the big desk.

'Now, Nurse Preston. Tell me what happened last night. And why it happened. Because that is what really matters.'

Bridget took a deep and shuddering breath. 'Dr – Dr Nestor came to the ward last night,' she began. 'And he was smoking. I could smell it. And – there was an oxygen tent up, and I was frightened.' She looked at the older woman who just nodded encouragingly. 'I told Dr Nestor – about the tent – but – but' – she wanted to say, 'he was too drunk to care – too drunk' but this was impossible. For all her anger towards David, she knew that to say he was drunk and came to a ward would get him into very severe trouble indeed, and a streak of loyalty in her made it impossible to pile any more on to David than she had to. So she said, 'I – I don't think he understood – not properly. Anyway, I took it away from him, and put it out. And then – then – '

Just as when she had tried to explain to Night Sister, she balked at this point, but Matron just raised her eyebrows at her, and sat silently, clearly waiting for her to go on. So she tried again.

'He – it was Christmas, he said.' Perhaps the fact that it was Christmas would constitute some sort of excuse. 'And – and he – well, he grabbed me, and – and he' – she closed her eyes and swallowed. 'I tried to stop him, really I did. But – he's very strong.' As she said it, she could feel the almost brute strength of his arms round her. 'And when I tried to stop him – my apron got torn, and – everything. And then Night Sister came,' her voice trailed away into silence.

Matron stirred. 'That is what happened,' she said at last. 'But not *why*. When I talked to you a few weeks ago, when you got your second-year belt, I asked you then if you were – sensible about your private life. This episode – this shows that perhaps you are not as sensible as you might be.'

Bridget said nothing, just sitting staring at her hands clasped on her lap.

'Look, Nurse Preston. I know perfectly well that young women like you need boy-friends. I know how much it matters to you to have a boy-friend. But let me assure you that there is no need for any girl to – put up with the attentions of a man she does not really care for just for the sake of having such a boy-friend. Do you understand what I mean?'

Bridget raised her head and looked at her. 'I – it isn't that I specially want to – to – '

'There are plenty of other people around from whom you can choose friends, you know. If you don't really care for this man, and he does not really care for you – and I can't think that he really does, for if he did, he would never have allowed last night's scene to happen – '

But Bridget, to her own amazement, interrupted. 'How do you know I don't really – like him?' she asked wonderingly.

Matron laughed at this. 'My dear child, I am not nearly as stupid as some of you girls think I am. I am not a Matron of a hospital like this one as – as a freak of nature, you know. I *do* know something about people, about their needs, and behaviours, and listening to you explain what happened last night makes it clear – to me at any rate – that this Dr Nestor is not someone for whom you care very deeply. I suspect that – that your friendship is something that happened to you, and that it is not one you sought for yourself.'

Bridget nodded miserably, 'Yes – ' she murmured. 'Yes.'

'I am beginning to realise that you are a person to whom things happen, Nurse Preston. You are not – not fully in control of your life, shall we say?'

Bridget nodded again, and at the warmth in the face across the desk said breathlessly. 'That's exactly it, Matron, really it is. I'm – I'm not very used to people – ' She stopped, and then said with a sort of ruefulness, 'I never really had the chance to learn how – '

Matron nodded. 'And you let other people push you about – even get the wrong impression of you, and you do nothing about it – the Sisters think you are silent because of insolence. That you are self-absorbed. Are you?'

'Oh, no, Matron, really I'm not,' Bridget said eagerly. 'I – I'm just not good at – well, explaining to people. So I don't try. And then – then – '

'Then they don't try to understand *you*,' Matron finished. 'Now listen to me, Nurse Preston. You are not a child. You are a grown woman, nearly. And you must learn how to control your own life. You must not let events and people take hold of you. Do you understand that? If a particular friend seems, after you have known him for a while, to be the wrong friend for you, then do something about the situation. Don't just drift. This time, it is all right. I can see that what happened was not entirely your fault – except inasmuch as you *should* have been in better control of matters than you were – so we will say no more about it. But I shall be more than disappointed in you if you allow such an episode to happen again. Do you understand? I am not going to tell you to break off a friendship if you do not want to – I have no right to do so. But if I hear that you are still drifting, as you clearly have been, I will suspect that you are not fit to continue to train at the Royal. A girl who cannot control her own life will never make a nurse. Now go to bed, and come on duty tonight ready to make a new start. I will explain matters satisfactorily to Night Sister – but it is up to you to convince her that you are to be trusted in future.'

Bridget got to her feet, smoothing her apron in front of her. 'Thank you, Matron,' she said. 'Thank you – ' For a moment, she wanted to explain to Matron that it wasn't because she just wanted to have a boy-friend that she put up with David. That it was because she needed other friends – and that without a willingness to be David's friend, she feared that the other three would shut her out – and that it was that that mattered to her. But already Matron was reaching for the pile of paper work on her desk, and Bridget allowed her inherent diffidence to override her need to explain.

Outside the ofice door, she leaned against the wall for a moment, trying to collect her thoughts. The darkness behind her closed eyes swirled momentarily, and she took a deep breath before opening them.

And as she opened them, and stood straight, she saw Josh standing in front of her, his friendly face smiling a little, his head on one side as he looked at her.

'Hello, Tiddler,' he said gently. 'On the carpet?'

At the sight of him, her still very shaky control slipped again, and to her horror, she found tears welling up into her eyes again. Josh's own face altered at the sight of her distress, and with a quick movement, he took her arm, and hurried her away down the corridor.

'Come on, Tiddler. Can't have you weeping all over the place –come and tell your Uncle Josh all about it – ' and he led her towards the hospital coffee shop, while she tried desperately to push her tears back down inside her again.

He chattered cheerfully as he settled her at the table in the corner, giving her time to regain control, and she was grateful to him for his quick understanding. Then, when they were settled with steaming cups in front of them, he leaned forwards and smiled at her.

'Was it that business last night the old girl was wigging you about Tiddler?'

She looked at him quickly, and then dropped her eyes to her cup.

'Yes – ' she said in a low voice. 'And she was right, really.'

'David should have been shot, the idiot. He was drunk as a lord, and he shouldn't have come anywhere near the wards in that state.'

'I know,' Bridget said wearily. 'But he did.'

'Did – did you tell the old girl he was drunk?'

She shook her head. 'I thought there'd be a row for him if I did.'

'You're damn' right there – he'd have had the book thrown at him.' Josh looked at her sharply. 'You're a good lass, Tiddler. Old David doesn't know how lucky he is, I reckon. There aren't many who'd carry the can back like you've done.'

She shrugged. 'It doesn't matter,' she said, and suddenly felt desperately weary. 'It doesn't matter.'

'But he is lucky,' Josh said softly, and put a hand out towards her. 'Any man with a girl like you to care for him is lucky, you know that?'

She looked up at him, at the face that was so achingly familiar, and all the feeling she had for him suddenly bubbled up inside her so that her mouth trembled, and her eyes brimmed with tears again. She put her hands in her lap, to avoid his touch, feeling that the warmth of his hand on hers would be more than she could cope with.

'I – I don't care for him,' she said baldly. 'I – don't. I – hate him.'

He looked at her uncertainly for a moment. 'Hate him? I thought – you said once that – I don't understand. You've been going about with him for a long time, Tiddler. Or is it just that now you're angry with him? You've every right to be.'

'I – it was – ' She took a deep breath. 'It just happened. I never did specially care for him. Not really. He was – just one of the crowd.'

'Oh, for God's sake, Bridget!' He sounded angry suddenly. 'Don't tell me you just went around with a man out of habit – I don't believe it. Some girls would – but you?'

'Well, it's true.' She hated herself then, hated her own weakness. 'The others – they got mad if I said I didn't want to go out with David – so I did. That's all there ever was to it. I never want to see him again – and I don't care what the others say. I just don't care – '

'Did it matter so much to you?' he asked curiously. 'What the other girls said?'

'I never – I never had friends before them,' Bridget said softly, 'and they were such fun, and so gay – I – I wanted to be like them. But – well, I was wrong. I'm just not like them, and I never will be. I – I guess they'll have to take me as I am. If they don't like me that way, that's all there is to it.'

He sat in silence for a moment. Then he said gently, 'Tiddler – tell me something. If you don't care for David Nestor, is there anyone else you care about? Anyone at all?'

She looked up at him, at his warm smile, at the deep clefts in his cheeks, and every fibre of her ached to say 'Yes – yes. I care for you – for you.' The words trembled on her lips for a brief second and then, across the crowded coffee shop, she saw Bobby appear at the door, her fair hair swinging over the thick sweater and tight trousers she had changed into.

The words died unspoken, and she sat in silence as Bobby saw them, and came swinging over towards them.

'Hello, Bridie, my love. Hello, Josh, my angel,' and she dropped a casual kiss on to Josh's head as she slid into the vacant chair beside them. 'So what happened, Bridie? Did the old girl have your guts for garters? Old David had a hell of a pasting from Night Sister. She threatened to tell the Chief of Staff all about his wicked ways, but he persuaded her to show a little of the milk of human kindness – poor old David – he's feeling awful about it all this morning.' She laughed then. 'He's got the father and mother of a hangover, and he's been looking everywhere for you to apologise, and he couldn't find you. He's on his way to a clinic now, so he'll have to wait to make his peace with you till later. I just met him in the courtyard.'

'I don't – I don't want to see him, not now or later,' Bridget said, her voice low, but firm. 'I just don't want to see him.'

Bobby hitched her chair closer to Josh, and linked an arm through his, and winked at him. But he was looking at Bridget and made no response.

'Don't be nasty to him, Bridget!' Bobby said. 'He didn't mean to get you into hot water – put it down to your lovely eyes. He just wanted his Bridget, I suppose.'

'Stop it, Bobby!' Bridget said violently. 'I tell you I never want to talk to him again. I've had enough, do you understand? Enough.'

Bobby frowned sharply. 'Oh, come off it, Bridget. No need for all the dramatics. So you got caught necking! So what? The old girl hasn't fired you, has she?'

'No – but that's got nothing to do with it. Nothing at all. I'm – I'm finished, that's all. Finished,' and she felt a wave of relief wash over her as she said it.

'Give the poor old devil a chance, Bridget!' Bobby said. 'Look, he just wants to apologise, that's all. It's not fair not to let him, is it? Listen, Bridie' – she leaned over the table – 'we've all got nights off next weekend – and Ken and Clive and Josh are off too – I've already arranged it, haven't I Josh? We're going down to my people's place for the weekend – a real breath of clean air and peace, down in the country. And I just asked David, and he says he'll come, as long as you do. Now, please, Bridie – don't spoil things for everyone – it's all fixed, eh, Josh? We'll have a ball, and a real rest, and it'll be fun. Now don't be difficult Bridie – nothing to get difficult about. Come down with us, and give old David another chance.'

Bridget looked up at her, at her wheedling face, and then at Josh, still sitting silently across the table, and felt all her newfound resolve crumbling in her, as it always did when she was faced with Bobby's charm.

'I don't want to, Bobby,' she said with a sort of desperation – and knew as she said it that it was no use. 'I'd rather not, truly.'

And then Josh leaned forwards, and smiled at her. 'Listen, Tiddler, Bobby has got a point, you know. Even if you really are going to give David the push, you ought to tell him so. You can't just – disappear. Not in a place like this. If you're going to do it, do it clean. Come down for the weekend with us. And then start from scratch.'

Bridget looked from face to face, and then closed her eyes in sudden weariness. 'All right. I'll come. But that's it. Never again after that. I've had enough.'

'Good girl,' Josh said softly, and then with a quick glance at Bobby closed his mouth firmly. And Bobby grinned triumphantly and said cheerfully, 'You'll change your mind, love. You see if you don't. David's a nice old thing, really – just gets a bit wild sometimes. You'll change your mind.'

And Bridget took herself off to bed, leaving Josh and Bobby in the coffee shop, her last sight of them sitting close together making her grateful Bobby had come in time to prevent her making a complete fool of herself. For she was sure, seeing them together, that they were meant to be together, that her own feeling for Josh must never be allowed to show itself. Josh and Bobby belonged together, and there was nothing Bridget could do about it.

9

She managed to avoid seeing David at all for the rest of that week. He had more sense than to come to her ward at night, keeping well out of Night Sister's way, and Bridget made sure she avoided all the places where he might be during the day, refusing to join the others for morning coffee in the coffee shop, going straight to her room and bed as soon as she came off duty. Bobby and Liz and Judith, with a rare tact, said nothing to her about what had happened, only chattering of their plans for the Christmas weekend they were to spend at Bobby's home.

There was one bad moment for Bridget, at supper one morning when, listening to the others, she discovered that the weekend was not to be spent, as she assumed, in the company of Bobby's parents. They were away on a winter cruise, and when Bridget heard this, she said baldly that she wasn't going.

But Bobby was angered by her demurs. 'For Christ's sake, Bridget, what's the matter with you? You aren't going on a dirty weekend or anything! There's to be eight of us – eight of us! No one's asking you to do anything you shouldn't! We've a big place – and everyone's got a room of his and her own! I'm not running a – a bawdy house, you know!' and she looked so indignant at the implied insult Bridget had offered her that Bridget perforce gave in.

'Anyway, it's the last time,' she told herself firmly, as she packed a case for the weekend. 'If Bobby and Liz and Judith decide to do without me, that's too bad. After this weekend, I'm on my own. I'll do what I want to do when I want to do it, and that's that. I *will* control my own life – after this weekend.'

It was a lovely house. Bridget had always known that Bobby's parents were rich, but she had not expected anything quite as beautiful as the country house in front of which the two cars drew up after the two-hour drive from London. It had been a silent journey for Bridget, in David's company for the first time since the episode in the ward. She and Bobby and David had travelled down in Josh's car, while the others came in Ken's, and she had sat in stony silence next to David all the way. He, after one look at her face, had made no attempt to speak to her or touch her, and she was grateful for this, at least.

The house was an old one, with rambling corridors, unexpected steps up and down in odd corners, and big, comfortably furnished rooms. As Bobby had promised, each of them had a room of their own, Bridget being allotted Bobby's old nursery, while the men were accommodated in the four maids' bedrooms at the top of the house.

'The folks only have a housekeeper these days,' Bobby said gaily, as she showed them all round. 'And a couple of dailies from the town. But they're all on holiday too, so we'll have to fend for ourselves. More fun, anyway. Can you cook, Josh?'

'Like an angel,' he assured her, cheerfully. 'I'm a dab hand with a boiled egg, I promise you!'

'Some Christmas dinner that'll be!' Bobby jeered. 'I've ordered a flipping great turkey from the farm – so someone'll have to cook it – '

'I can cook,' Ken said unexpectedly, 'and with Liz to peel the vegetables, you'll get a meal fit for a king,' and he kissed Liz resoundingly. 'She'll have to learn sooner or later – if she's going to marry me, what say you, Liz?' and Liz laughed and blushed a little and looked up at him adoringly.

And even now that they were all at the house, Bridget managed to keep out of David's way. They unpacked their clothes, and all went down to the local pub for a drink, filling the small country bar with noise and laughter, so that the regulars looked across at them with indulgent grins, and joined in the teasing of Liz and Ken, neither of whom minded the laughter a bit. Only Bridget, sitting as far away from David as she could, and David himself, were quiet. But Bridget could not help noticing that David was, as usual, drinking a great deal more than was good for him, while she sat with the same untouched drink for the whole evening.

When the pub closed, the eight of them went singing back through the dark wintry lanes, and Bridget, the only one not merry from the effects of the drinks they had had, listened to them and watched them with a sort of cool surprise.

'I can't think what it was I saw in them all,' she told herself wonderingly. 'Ken and Liz – they're nice. I could have been Liz's friend anyway, and she wouldn't have demanded so much from me. But Bobby and Judith – they – I don't even *like* them – '

She looked across at Bobby as they arrived at the house, dropping coats and gloves in a disorderly pile in the big hall, collapsing laughing and shouting in the big armchairs in the drawing room. Bobby, her fair face flushed with excitement and drink, sprawled across a somehow quiet Josh, a Josh who seemed to Bridget to have only a surface gaiety tonight, lacking the sparkle and warmth that he usually had, seeming to force his jokes and laughter. She looked at Bobby, and wondered at herself.

The fascination that had held Bridget so firmly for this past year seemed to disappear suddenly, to melt like snow in a morning's bright sunshine. She was noisy, she was gay – but she was shallow, Bridget told herself. She gives nothing but a spurious friendship, but she takes everything everyone has to offer. And with a flash of insight, Bridget realised suddenly that Bobby was essentially a very lonely person, even lonelier than Bridget herself. For Bridget at least realised that she was lonely, that she needed friendship. Bobby doesn't know, Bridget told herself. She doesn't know a thing about herself.

With a sigh, Bridget left the others to wander off in search of the kitchen. She needed coffee, and so did the others, even if they didn't realise it. She found the kitchen at the back of the house, and rooted in cupboards and drawers for the equipment to make black coffee for them all. She took her time, in no hurry to return to the others, and when the kettle boiled, poured the steaming water over the coffee grounds, and filled cups on a tray.

It wasn't until she had made her careful way, with her loaded tray, back to the drawing-room, that she realised that silence had descended on the big house. She put the tray down on a low table near the door and straightened up to peer into the dimly lit room.

Only one light was burning, a small table-lamp, and the only other source of light was from the logs burning with uneasily flickering flames in the wide, brick fireplace. For a moment, she thought the room was empty, and told herself ruefully, 'I've made all that coffee for nothing,' not stopping to wonder why the others had gone. And, then as she turned to pick up her own cup, a movement in the shadows brought her whirling round.

David was sitting sprawled in an armchair by the fire, his head slumped deep into his shoulders, his brooding eyes staring out at her from his silent face. She looked at him for a moment, and then turned away, meaning to go to bed.

But he stood up, and came round in front of her, barring her way to the door.

'I want to talk to you,' he said, and his voice was thick.

'I'm afraid I don't want to talk to you, David,' Bridget's own calmness almost surprised her. 'There's nothing to say.'

'Oh, yes, there is,' he said, and came closer, so that she could smell the whisky on his breath. Uncertainly, she stepped back, and said again, with rather less conviction, 'I don't want to talk to you, David. Not now, or ever.'

'What'sa matter with you, for Christ's sake? What you coming the prude for all of a sudden?' He sounded angry, his voice thick and blurred. 'A year you've been going around with me – a year! And now all of a sudden, you don't want to know! So there was a row at the hospital – !' His voice changed suddenly, became placatory. 'Look, I'm sorry about that, I was drunk, and I don't deny it, and I got you into a row, and you covered up for me, and I'm damned grateful. I'm ready to apologise – really I am – no need to get all chilly and nasty, is there?' and he put his hands out to grasp her arms.

She shrank back from him, now frankly loathing the thought of his touch, no longer able to merely tolerate him.

'Keep away from me! I tell you I don't want to talk to you. The only reason I agreed to come here this weekend was so that I could finish all this. I don't want to talk to you now or ever. You've apologised. All right. I accept your apology, and all I want from now is to be left alone – just to be left alone – '

'What's the matter with you?' he said, angry again. 'Why the prudery all of a sudden? You came down here for the same reason the rest of us did – and don't go getting girlish and pretending otherwise – I don't fall for that sort of guff, do you hear? All right. I behaved badly, and I said I was sorry, and I am, if it got you into trouble, so let's forget it now, and have some fun – come on – ' and he lurched towards her, so that she had to back away from him if she was to avoid him.

He was really furious now, his eyes blazing in his white face, and as he forced her back into the hall beyond the big drawing-room doors, she felt real fear bubbling up inside her.

'Keep away from me – keep away from me!' she said, her voice cracking a little, her eyes wide with terror. 'Don't touch me – don't – '

But he was too quick for her, and his arms, the arms whose strength she had fought in the past, were round her, and his whisky-reeking breath hot on her face. She squirmed, twisting her head away from his face, but he put a steely hand under her chin and forced her head back, his own face coming closer. She did the only thing she could do – turned her head sharply and bit his hand hard, so that he yelped with the pain, and in a sudden rage, pulled his arm back and hit her, so that her face stung, and her head whipped back on her neck with a sharp crack that made her whole body hurt.

'You little bitch!' he said, and his voice was now without the blur of drink. 'You bitch! Stringing me along like some – if you think you're getting away with that, you're mistaken – ' and once again he made a grab for her, this time pulling at her thin dress so that it ripped right away from her shoulder.

She struggled, heard her own voice shouting, heard herself almost screaming with fear, and then, suddenly, there was a clatter of feet on the stairs, a rush of light as someone put on a switch upstairs, and she felt, rather than saw, someone pull David away from her.

'What in God's name are you doing, you lunatic!' It was Josh. Josh, in a dressing-gown pulled untidily round him, his usually neat hear ruffled above his wide face. He was holding on to David from behind, both arms held tightly, while David tried to pull away from him.

'You keep out of this, Simpson!' David shouted, managing to get out of Josh's firm grip, to turn and glare at him. 'This is none of your bloody business!'

'What's going on down there?' Bobby's voice came coolly from the head of the stairs, and Bridget looked up to see her standing there, a thin dressing-gown pulled negligently round her, her bare legs under its shortness making it obvious she was wearing nothing else.

David looked up at her, and laughed loudly, without humour. 'What's going on? What's going on? Your *friend* here has decided she doesn't like the idea of this weekend after all –

changed her mind. She knows bloody well why we're here, and now she doesn't want to play. And your boy-friend has decided to muscle in on what doesn't concern him — that's what's happening — '

'It does concern me,' Josh said, his voice very even. 'A private argument becomes public property when you can hear it for miles around — and if — if Bridget didn't need help, she wouldn't have screamed like that.'

Bridget was leaning against the staircase now, clutching at her torn dress, still shaking with fright as she stared at the two angry men, and as the other four, hearing the row, appeared at the top of the stairs, she shrank even closer to the stairs. Bad enough Josh had to hear what David was saying, without everyone else being an audience. But David had no such qualms. He was shouting again.

'Don't be so bloody sanctimonious, Simpson! You've got what you want, haven't you? You came down here for the same reason I did — you've got a willing girl, so never mind anyone else, is that it? It's all right for you to have a toss, but hard luck on anyone else with a girl that isn't quite so accommodating! After the last year, believe me, I've got every right to get mad — she's no more than a — '

'Watch it, Nestor — ' Josh cut in sharply before David could finish his sentence. 'You're drunk, and you don't know what you're saying — '

'I know what I'm saying all right, believe me I do. She's been playing me for a complete idiot, and she isn't going to get away with it!'

'Listen, you damned idiot!' Josh shouted at him. 'Drunk you may be, but it doesn't mean *you* can get away with anything you want to! Be your age, man!'

'Oh, Josh, for Heaven's sake!' Bobby came down the stairs, her face creased with irritation. 'Leave them alone. What's it got to do with us, for God's sake? Bridget's a big girl — she can look after herself. Come back upstairs, and leave them to sort out their own arguments.'

'Yes, why don't you?' David said, sneering. 'Your girl's all ready and waiting for you. Why not leave me to sort out mine?'

And now Bridget managed to move. 'There's nothing to sort out,' she said dully. 'I'm sorry, Bobby. Sorry for the noise. I'll leave now. I'm going back to London,' and she moved towards the stairs, grateful for the way Josh moved forwards to cover her from David as she did so.

But David made no move to touch her, this time. 'You go,' he said shortly. 'You go. I wouldn't want you if you were the last female going, believe me. You go running back to London and find another mug to play your pretty games with,' and he pushed past Josh and went back to the drawing-room to pour himself another drink at the bar in the corner.

Bridget dragged herself up the stairs, past Liz and Judith, both standing with Clive and Ken, staring at her. Bobby stood back as she passed her, and said shortly, 'Well, I hope you're satisfied. You've ruined everyone's weekend, you with all your fuss.'

And now Bridget, almost for the first time in her life, lost her temper.

'I didn't want to come – you know I didn't!' she said, blazing at Bobby. 'When I heard your parents were not going to be here, I said I didn't want to come, and you said it was all right! All right! You – you're as bad as he is, do you know that? You've got the morals of – of a tom-cat, and I was a fool not to see it sooner! You sleep around if you want to – that's your business! But don't try to make me do the same! I'm going back to London, and I never want to speak to you again – ' and she pulled away, and ran up the stairs towards her room.

Liz followed her, and stood hesitantly at the door as Bridget, moving as fast as she could, changed her dress, and threw her things into her suitcase.

'I'm sorry about this, Bridget,' she said, her voice ashamed. 'I – I thought you knew, really – I didn't know you truly didn't like David – '

'Whether I like him or not hasn't anything to do with it. I'd need to feel rather more than that to – to spend this sort of weekend with him – ' Bridget said roughly.

Liz winced at that, and went a hot red. 'It's different for me and Ken,' she said, her voice almost apologetic. 'I mean, I'm not like Bobby and Judith. They're fun to be with, so I – well, I strung along. But Ken and I are going to be married soon and – and well, we don't get a chance to – to be together much really. So we came. But we aren't like them – '

'It doesn't matter,' Bridget said, closing her case, and shrugging her coat on. 'It doesn't matter. I was a damned fool not to see what the set-up was long ago. Well, now I know. Leave it at that,' and she pushed past Liz, and went purposefully down the stairs.

The drawing-room door was shut and she breathed a sigh of relief at that. She wouldn't have to see David again, at least. Josh was sitting on the bottom step, and she went past him without a word.

'I persuaded you to come,' he said in a low voice. 'I should have known better. I'm sorry.'

She stopped by the front door, and said without turning, 'There's no need for you to apologise. I should have known myself. And thank you for – for your help.'

He came and stood beside her, putting a hand on her arm.

'Please, Bridget. Can I tell you something? Why I wanted you to come here this weekend?'

'I've told you it doesn't matter,' she said dully.

'It matters to me,' he said. 'Listen. I – I've always liked you, you know. I said you were different, and so you are. You're sweet, and innocent – '

'Innocent!' She laughed shortly at that. 'Innocent! Ignorant and stupid, and pushed any way anyone wants to push me – '

'No,' he said softly. 'Innocent. That's why this happened, really. And I respect that in you. Very much. I'd hoped that this weekend – well, that I'd be able to find out for certain whether you cared for David – whether it was anger that made you say you hated him, or whether you meant it. It – it mattered to me to find out. Do you understand what I'm saying?'

She turned and looked at him then, and her grey eyes were level in their gaze.

'I thought you had come for the same reason everyone else seems to have come here. For – for cheap sex, for "fun", for a "giggle" – ' she said evenly.

He reddened. 'I deserve that, I suppose.'

'Don't you? Are you trying to say that you came here for any other reason. As David said – Bobby is ready and willing. Why don't you go and find her? She'll – she'll be getting angry, no doubt.' And she was amazed at the cold anger in her own voice.

'Listen to me,' he said, his voice hard and even. 'I can't deny that I've been having – "fun" as you put it, with Bobby. For God's sake, Bridget, what do you think I'm made of? If a girl is – like Bobby, and seems to – want a man's company, then only a very odd man would refuse what she puts on a plate for him! And

I'm – a very normal sort of man. I take my pleasures where I can. But pleasure is one thing – and – and feeling is another. That's what I'm trying to tell you. I've – oh, for Christ's sake girl, I'm beginning to feel a great deal for you, and it's that that matters to me! I wanted you here this weekend to – to see if there could be a chance to talk to you properly. Whenever I've tried to get anywhere near you at the hospital, you've sheered away, slipped out of my fingers! Here, being down here for three days, I thought I'd stand a better chance of – of getting to know you. So now you know. And I'm damned if I'll apologise because I've been sleeping with Bobby – and I don't deny I have. She's – '

'I don't want to know – I don't want to know,' she cried, and then pulling blindly at the door, she ran out into the cold of the December night, running as fast as she could. Anywhere – she didn't care where to. Just to get away from the sound of his voice, the implications of what he had been saying.

10

It was odd, somehow, the way everything about the Royal seemed to change, now that Bridget was no longer one of the four. It was the same hospital, the work was the same, the same people worked in it, but now, everything was different. She would come off duty alone, go to her room alone, spend her free time alone. The other nurses in her year all had their own friends, had had for a year or more, had made lives for themselves that included their friends, and there just wasn't any room for Bridget.

The strangest thing was the way Bobby and Judith would pass her in the corridors, or in the dining-room, without a word, not appearing even to see her. It wasn't that they set out consciously to 'send her to Coventry'. It was simply that they had no further use for her, and as such, she just didn't exist. Liz would speak to her, however, when they did happen to meet, though even she seemed unwilling to do more than exchange casual greetings. Bridget knew that this was partly because of Bobby and Judith. She accepted that Liz felt a loyalty towards them, even while she did not really share their view of the world. And it was partly because of her ever-growing preoccupation with Ken. They were to be married as soon as Liz finished her training, and this was general knowledge among the nurses.

Bridget didn't mind her solitariness nearly as much as she had feared she would. Many times she would marvel at the old Bridget she had been, so frightened of loneliness, and would smile in her new-found maturity when she remembered how she had been at first. For Bridget had undoubtedly changed a good deal. The affair at Bobby's home at Christmas, as well as the episode on the ward with David before that, had pulled her up sharp, as it were, made her aware of herself and her responsibilities as she had never been before. The Sisters with whom she worked now told each other that that Nurse Preston was a different girl – that training had decidedly knocked the corners off, that the silent, still face of the old days had given way to a warmth, a friendliness. She was still reserved, but much of the diffidence of the old days, a diffidence that had looked like dumb insolence, had gone, as she developed both as a nurse and as a person. For she loved her work more and more, taking intense pleasure in every aspect of it. To her own surprise, she had a very real vocation for it – which, as she told herself wryly, was fortunate, seeing I took up nursing for any reason but that!

She saw little of the men, either. David, much to her relief, left the Royal shortly after Christmas, as his appointment was over and he was not offered a new one. Bridget wondered vaguely if the fact that he had come drunk to a ward had actually reached the ears of the senior medical staff, and whether this had anything to do with his not being reappointed, but dismissed the thought. She just wasn't interested, and that was that. David Nestor was a thing of the past, to be as forgotten as thoroughly as nursery school experiences.

Sometimes, she would see Josh crossing the courtyard, meet him in a corridor, or see him in the coffee shop, but she would merely nod, and hurry on when this happened. Once or twice he tried to stop her, to speak to her, but she would pull away, say she was in a hurry, and couldn't stop. She didn't know whether he was still going about with Bobby – and as the only gossip she ever heard was the general gossip that occupied the nurses in the dining-room or in the sitting-room at night, she had no way of finding out. She certainly didn't intend to ask.

She pushed the memory of what he had said that night at the house in Surrey firmly to the back of her mind. He had said enough to make her realise that he did, in fact, care a little for her, that it hadn't been the pity she abhorred that had prompted his kindness to her back in her early days at the Royal. And though she knew that she loved Josh Simpson very much indeed, that part of her always would, she had decided to cut her losses. It was impossible to follow up what he had said that night, impossible to allow her feelings for him to sway her. What was past was past. She had only one idea now; to finish her training, and then to leave the Royal for ever, and start a whole new life for herself somewhere abroad.

And then, half-way through her second year, she was sent to work in the operating theatres. She was alarmed at first, memories of her trips to that august department as a ward nurse stirring in her, but then she told herself sensibly that everyone who went there was new; they all had to learn, and she would learn too. And learn she did. Her days were a rush of sterilising, of running about as 'dirty nurse' for small cases, then larger and more complex cases, and the interminable cleaning that was so much a part of the work. And then, after her second month in the department, Theatre Sister sent for her.

'Now, Nurse Preston,' she said briskly. 'You've been on this department for eight weeks, hmm?'

'Yes, Sister.' Bridget felt a momentary sinking as she wondered whether she had done something wrong. It was not often Theatre Sister found time to call individual nurses to her office like this.

But Theatre Sister went on cheerfully, 'You seem to have an aptitude for this work — I've been watching you, and you're quick and deft — which a theatre nurse needs to be. Now, Nurse Jessolo is off sick — which means that the second theatre needs a new senior. Do you feel capable of coping with such work?'

Bridget gulped. The second theatre was the one which handled the smaller lists, the straightforward work like appendicectomies, herniorrhaphies, varicose vein ties, and the senior nurse there was the one who 'took table', who scrubbed up with the surgeons, handed instruments, and generally acted as the boss of the small theatre, under Sister's supervision.

'I — I think so, Sister,' she said. 'I'd certainly like to try.'

'Good,' Sister said briskly. 'Now, this is a good time for you to start — we're not too busy at present, and I've time to really teach you — the first list today is a small one — an appendix, excision of lipoma, and a hernia. You will scrub for it and I will act as your dirty nurse — so I'll be there to help if you get stuck. Come along now, and we'll get your instruments out, and check the layout.'

Bridget enjoyed that morning thoroughly. It felt odd at first to scrub up, to put on the sterile gown, to stand still while Sister tied the tapes, to put on the smooth, brown rubber gloves, but after the first few moments of strangeness, she forgot herself, and became absorbed in the operation. She found she knew more than she had realised that she knew. Almost without being told, she handed the surgeon — one of the younger consultants — the sponge forceps for the preliminary swabbing of the skin, spread the sterile towels over the area, clipped them into place, and swung smoothly into the routine of the operation.

When the last stitch was tied, and she took off the towels to fasten the dressing in position, the surgeon grinned at her cheerfully above his mask.

'First case, Nurse?' he said, as he stripped off his gloves and dropped them into the bowl of saline beside him.

'Yes, sir,' Bridget said, looking at him sideways for signs of annoyance.

But he grinned even more, his eyes crinkling above the white line of his mask. 'Well done, then. To the manner born, eh, Sister?' And Sister, busily changing trolleys round, ready for the next case smiled too, and nodded. 'A credit to me, sir!' she said, they both smiled at Bridget in a way that made her glow with pride.

Within a week, Bridget was in full control of her new job. She found the work difficult enough to extend her fully, which was enjoyable, but not so difficult that she could not cope with any aspect of it. Sister, realising this, put more and more complicated operations on to the second theatre's lists, and by the end of a month Bridget felt herself to be the complete theatre nurse.

One of the best things about working in the second theatre was that Bridget hardly ever saw Josh at all. In the first eight weeks on the department, when she had been 'dirty nurse' in the main theatre, she had seen him almost every day, for he worked there constantly. But although there had been no occasion for them to talk to each other, except on purely professional matters, his presence had been distressing to her. Every time she had caught sight of his square shoulders, the muscles moving sleekly under the white gown as he worked, she felt her heart lurch, the painfully familiar sense of sheer physical excitement that he could arouse in her.

Sometimes she had caught his eyes as she moved about the theatre, when he looked up momentarily from his work to ask for something, once or twice he had turned his head towards her so that she could mop his forehead, as he sweated slightly under the hot, shadowless light, and these moments had been electric for her. It would take a long time for her to get over the way she felt about this man, she knew that, and seeing him so closely and so often only exacerbated her feelings. So it was an intense relief that she no longer had to see him, tucked away as she was in her own little second theatre.

And then, late one evening, just as she was going off duty, Theatre Sister called her from her office.

'Look, Preston, can you help me out tonight? There's a bit of a panic on in the private wing theatres – Sister there has flu, and her staff nurse has a septic finger, blast her, and can't scrub. So I've got to cover for them tonight. And Night Sister is off duty, and her deputy can't take any theatre cases if any emergencies come in, because she just isn't a theatre nurse. So that means I've got to put a middle-year nurse on call here tonight – what with Staff Nurse Casey being on holiday this week. Do you think you can manage that? The chances are nothing'll come in, of course – but it could happen, and if it does, someone from the department will have to be on call. Do you feel able?'

'I think so, Sister,' Bridget said slowly. 'I've scrubbed for most of the sorts of emergencies we get, haven't I? And if I get really stuck with something, I could get the junior to phone you in the wing to give advice?'

'Of course you could – and I'll probably be there all night God help me. They've got five labouring women in Private Maternity, and Sister there has warned me it's odds on two of them will need Caesars – *two* of them! Honestly, it never rains but it pours – '

'I hope I don't get a Caesar over here.' Bridget was alarmed. 'That's one thing I've never taken – '

'No, you should be all right there. General Maternity is full, and any new cases will have to go somewhere else on the Emergency Bed Service, and none of their people are likely to come here for anything. I've checked – the most they anticipate are a couple of high forceps, and they cope with those themselves – look, I'll have to go. They've still got a list going over in Private Theatre and none of their people have had any off duty today, they're so short-staffed – I'll tell Night Sister you're on call – and here's hoping nothing comes in for you – 'Night, Preston. All the best!'

Bridget checked that all was clear in the theatres before taking herself off duty, also praying that nothing would come in. She was tired already – it had been a long day, and much as she enjoyed her work, she did not relish the idea of being dragged from a warm bed in the middle of the night to take another case.

She checked the list of surgeons on call before leaving the hospital for the Nurses' Home, and at what she saw there, prayed even harder that nothing would come in for theatre, for Josh was on call for main theatres that night, too.

But at the back of her mind, she knew something would come in. It was almost inevitable – her first time on call, and Josh on call too. And she was right.

At half past two, the night staff nurse came and shook her briskly, pulling her out of a confused dream about taking a Caesar all on her own, to tell her of a case that needed urgent surgery.

'I'm not sure what it's all about, Preston,' the night staff nurse said. 'It's all a bit hush-hush. All I know is it's a member of the staff, and whoever she is, she needs a laparotomy. I can't imagine *why* there's such a fuss, but there it is. They want the theatre ready for a laparotomy in half an hour, anyway. And Mr Simpson said to be ready for a pretty major job. He told me to tell whoever was on call to put out practically everything she could think of. I've put the sterilisers on for you – so jump about a bit!'

Bridget dressed with chilled fingers, her heart trembling within her. Of all things that could have come in, a laparotomy was the most terrifying. The patient needed an exploratory operation – and once the incision was made, and the condition explored, almost any operation might be needed. There was just no way of knowing what. She would indeed have to put out practically every instrument there was.

By the time she had arrived at the theatres, the junior on night duty had laid up almost completely, which was one comfort. Bridget had merely to select her instruments, get them boiling, and lay her trolley. She checked the theatre carefully for details before scrubbing up herself, and as a precaution, told the junior to prepare a small trolley for an intravenous infusion.

'This could be anything,' she told the scurrying junior, over her shoulder, as she scrubbed her hands and arms at the big white sink. 'And it's odds on the patient'll need some sort of IV – saline and glucose almost certainly, possibly blood. When you've done the trolley, ring the lab and see if any blood has been cross-matched for her, whoever she is.'

'Will they know, if I can't give them a name?' the junior asked, busily slapping bowls and instruments on to a small trolley.

'Probably,' Bridget said. 'They'll know who the emergency is, anyway. Unless there's another case for the Private Theatre – anyway, ask them.'

'Someone told me it's one of the nurses,' the junior said chattily. 'But I can't find out who – Night Sister was flying around like a flea in a fit, and no one dared ask her – you know what she's like when she's in a flap.'

Bridget laughed, and began to dry her hands on the sterile towel that lay ready for her. 'I do! But there usually is a fuss when it's staff that gets sick, you know that. We'll know who it is soon enough. Probably turn out to be an appendix, anyway – ' and under her breath, she muttered, 'I hope – '

She shrugged into her gown, and said without turning, 'Do up my tapes, Nurse, will you, before you make that phone call?'

But as she spoke, the big door of the sterilising room shushed open, and footsteps came purposefully across the floor.

Josh's voice made Bridget stiffen. 'I'll do it, Nurse. You go and make your phone call, whatever it is – '

Bridget felt his hands behind her as he took the tapes of her gown and began to tie them.

'I didn't know you were on call,' he said, and his voice was so low she could barely hear it above the hiss of the sterilisers.

'There was a shortage of staff over in the Private Theatres,' Bridget said evenly. 'So I had to cover here while Sister covers them. I can cope.'

'I'm sure you can.' He stood still watching her while she pulled on her gloves, and when she had finished, and turned to go into the theatre to arrange her instruments on the trolley, he said in a strained voice, 'Wait a minute. I – I want to talk to you about this case.'

Obediently she stopped, and picked up a sterile towel to wrap her gloved hands in, to keep them sterile while she waited for him to speak.

He stood undecided, his mask dangling below his chin, a white cap covering all but a rim of hair above his creased brow.

'Do you know who this patient is?' he asked abruptly, after a pause.

'No – only that it's a member of the staff. What's all the fuss about? I gather there *is* a bit of fuss going on.'

He nodded, then dropped his eyes. 'It's Bobby,' he said flatly.

Bridget felt sick for a moment. Not just because the patient they were preparing for was Bobby, but because of his obvious distress. Even though she knew that she had no hope – or even intention – of ever becoming any sort of friend, or more, of this man's, it hurt to discover that he still seemed to care something for Bobby, despite what he had said about his feelings for her that night last Christmas.

'I see,' she said, after a moment. 'What's the matter? Is – is she very ill?'

'Very ill indeed,' he said, and then looked up at her, his eyes shadowed so that she couldn't see the expression in them. 'And you might as well know now as later. She – she's been very stupid – ' He swallowed. 'She was pregnant. And – and she's procured an abortion. I don't know the details, but I suppose she went to some botcher in a back street somewhere. Anyway, she's in a pretty bad state. God knows what we'll find when we open her up – '

Bridget stared at him, her thoughts swirling. Bobby, pregnant? An abortion?

He turned away, and with a vicious gesture, pulled his mask over his face and started to scrub his own hands.

'I know what you're thinking,' he said above the swish of the water. 'But – '

The big doors moved, and the junior came scurrying across the terrazzo floor.

'I say, Nurse Preston,' she gasped, heavy with her important news. 'I say, there *is* some blood cross-matched, and do you know who the patient is? It's Nurse Aston, and – '

'I know,' Bridget said heavily. 'I know. Get my instruments out of the steriliser, please, Nurse. We're in a hurry.'

As she sorted out haemostats and clamps, sponge forceps and needleholders, laying them in neat rows on the trolley, as she broke tubes of cat-gut, and laid the hanks of smooth, brown ties ready on a swab, she felt strangely numb. Part of her was distressed to think of Bobby being so ill – angry and hurt though she was whenever she thought of Bobby, badly as she felt Bobby had treated her, still, they had been friends, of a sort. And to think of the gay, noisy Bobby as anything but bubbling with good health was sad.

But what hurt most was the way Josh had behaved when he told her the news. It seemed obvious to Bridget that the pregnancy Bobby had tried so disastrously to terminate was due to Josh. Why else should Josh seem so upset? But was he distressed because of the pregnancy, or because he had known – had allowed – Bobby to procure that abortion?

She remembered his voice as he said, ' – I don't know the details, but I suppose she went to some botcher in a back street somewhere – ' Was he telling the truth? Did he really not know? Or had he himself sent her to that botcher?

She tried not to think about it. One of the things about Josh that she had admired most was his approach to his work. He was gay, he joked with patients, he led a noisy and hectic life on as well as off duty – but somehow she had always been aware of his deep care for his work, his feelings about its importance. Had his relationship with Bobby so poisoned his attitudes that he had lost all ethical ideas? It was more than she could bear to think about.

And then, the big doors of the theatre swung open, and the trolley with its white-sheeted form trundled in, the porter at the foot, a weary anaesthetist guiding the head, while the junior pushed the big anaesthetic machine alongside. As the trolley came up to the table under the big, shadowless light, Josh came through from the sterilising room, and stood back to let the porter and junior nurse lift Bobby on to the table.

Bridget looked down at her, at the white face, crumpled and half hidden under the dark-green rubber of the anaesthetic mask, at the fair hair escaping from the white cap that was supposed to be covering it, at the rim of white showing under the half closed eyelids, and felt a wave of pity wash over her. To see the pretty, gay Bobby like this, helpless under her anaesthetic, her skin blotched red by the pressure of the anaesthetic mask, the half dried tears on the white skin of her cheeks, the tears that often accompanied unconsciousness, was agonising in its pathos.

'She's bloody low,' the anaesthetist grunted, lifting one eyelid with a practised finger to peer into the blank, blue eye beneath. 'She's in a high fever – and that doesn't help. I've given her a massive dose of penicillin, as an umbrella, but it's my guess you'll find a mass of infection there – she's been sitting on this for a week or more.'

'You managed to get some details?' Josh asked sharply, as he took the sponge forceps from Bridget, and began to swab the wide swathe of skin over the exposed abdomen with red mercurochrome.

'Yup.' The anaesthetist, a dour Scot, gave a quick snort of humourless laughter. 'I cheated. Gave her some of her pentothal, and then asked her a few questions before I put her right out. Christ, man, we had to find out *something*. She wouldn't tell us when she was first brought in, so what would you have me do? Maybe it's unethical, but she's too ill for me to give a good goddam about ethics.'

'So?' With a sign to Bridget, Josh began to spread the big

towels in place, clipping them to expose just the square of the operation area.

'She was three months pregnant – her parents were away – on a tour or some such, and she was on holiday at home. So, she tried everything from quinine to gin to hot baths with no effect, and then went to some dirty old woman she heard of – God knows where from, but they always do hear somehow. She had a sort of operation eight days ago – and I gather she had no anaesthetic, poor little devil – and started to feel ill a day or so later. Seems a daily help her family employs came to the house to get it ready for her parents' return, and found her collapsed in the bathroom – and had the sense to get in touch with a doctor. Who sent her back here. And that's about it – '

Josh stood very still for a moment, and then said, 'Well, at least we know. I couldn't find out anything. She wouldn't talk to me. All I could get out of her was that she – she had been pregnant and now she wasn't.' He took a deep breath, and then thrust a hand at Bridget. 'Can we start, McPherson?'

'She's as fit as she'll ever be,' the anaesthetist said. 'And the quicker you start the sooner you'll finish – so get on with it, man.'

With cold fingers, Bridget put a gleaming scalpel into Josh's hand, and watched, her face rigid under her mask as he made the first sweeping incision, from umbilicus to pubis. As the orange-painted skin parted, and the first small blood vessels spurted vividly, she found her head swimming. She had seen this many times before, but this was Bobby, Bobby – and then, as though from a distance she heard Josh snap, 'Spencer Wells – Nurse, Spencers – ' and she pulled herself together, and slapped a pair of forceps into his hand, so that he could clip the vessels.

Soon, the wound sprouted a twinkling fringe of forceps, and with deft fingers Josh tied each bleeding point and discarded the used forceps for the junior to collect and reboil for later use. Bridget, her hands moving automatically, helped, swabbing, handing instruments and ties, acting as assistant surgeon, because there was no other doctor available at this hour to assist in her stead.

She felt like an actor in a weird film, one of a group of white-gowned, head-bent people, encapsulated in the glare of the big light, while a soft-footed nurse padded busily about in the shadows beyond the focus of the table, helping the anaesthetist set up a blood transfusion. Her hands and Josh's, so similar in characterless brownness, moved easily and smoothly about their work.

Then, Josh straightened, and grunted softly, angrily:

'The uterus is perforated – and she's full of pus. You were right about that, McPherson. I – I don't think I can suture it – it's a huge tear – and both tubes are heavily infected – '

There was an agonising silence. 'Well, man, you've got a consent form signed, haven't you? The girl's over twenty-one – just. She was fit to sign it – so you'd better do what you've got to do,' McPherson said heavily.

'Twenty-one – ' Josh said. 'Christ, I can't – '

The anaesthetist leaned forwards and said grimly, 'I know how you'll be feeling, but use your head, man, not your sentiments. Even if you do suture her, what'll happen? At best, you'll get a uterus so scarred she'll have no hope in hell of ever conceiving again – and with both tubes as far gone as those are, even if her uterus *is* salvaged, will she ever manage another baby? I doubt it. And at worst, suture it, close her up, and with all the antibiotics in the world, it's likely the thing'll break down, and she'll have to come to theatre again to have a hysterectomy then – use your head, man – '

Josh raised his head and looked miserably at the anaesthetist. The theatre was absolutely silent except for the faint hiss of gas from the anaesthetic machine. Slowly, Josh turned his head and looked at Bridget, and she felt her throat constrict at the agony in his eyes.

Then he said thickly, 'You're right – but it's a hell of a thing to have to do – '

'Ay, it is,' the anaesthetist said briskly. 'One hell of a thing. But she'll hardly survive at all if you don't, and you know it – '

Josh nodded, and with a glance at Bridget, said grimly, 'Right. Hysterectomy it is. Uterus and tubes – though I think it'll be safe to leave the ovaries – they seem healthy enough, thank God – Nurse – '

And Bridget handed him a big retractor, and watched him make the first steps towards ensuring that never again would Bobby have a pregnancy, wanted or unwanted. And she felt tears slide down her face as the operation went on, to sting her cheeks with pain for Bobby.

11

The hospital seethed with gossip, knots of nurses standing chattering in corners in the courtyard, scattering guiltily when Sisters went by, only to reassemble like flocks of starlings when they had gone. Despite the attempts of the administrative staff to keep the facts quiet, everyone knew that Bobby Aston had nearly died, and exactly why, and they all knew, too, that she had had a hysterectomy, and it was this that made them talk in frightened awe, yet with the sort of relish that such gossip always engenders.

Matron, deeply distressed, not only because of what had happened but because she felt she had had so little insight that she had been unable to see that Bobby was a girl to whom such a thing *could* happen, managed to derive some small comfort from this.

'Perhaps it's as well they do know,' she told Sister Chessman as they sat one morning over coffee, discussing the whole business. 'I'd have preferred to have kept it quiet, if only for Nurse Aston's sake – but perhaps it'll have a deterrent effect, I mean, the fact that the poor child had a hysterectomy. I don't believe in trying to keep young girls on the straight and narrow by using fear, by warning them of the "horrid consequences" when they do go wrong, but there's no doubt this has stopped a few of them in their tracks.'

Sister Chessman nodded. 'Mmm. I've been listening to them chatter – and there's not one that doesn't see what an awful thing it is to lose all hope of having children of your own when you're only twenty-one. What's happening to Aston?'

Matron sighed, and lit a cigarette. 'I've seen the parents – and a right pair they are! You can see why Aston's the sort of person she is. No regret about it – not a bit. No feeling on their part that they let her down, that they just didn't take enough interest in her – just annoyed it's happened – it gets in the way of their private plans, I gather. They'll have to take her off to convalescence somewhere now – and it was much simpler to have her safely tucked up here – so they thought. My God, some of these parents!'

'Any idea who – who the father was?' Sister Chessman asked curiously.

'I haven't asked her,' Matron said. 'It's happened, and if she doesn't want to tell me off her own bat, I can't pry.'

'I'm wondering if it's Mr Simpson, frankly.'

'Who can say? I know they did go about together a good deal – but according to the ward Sisters, they haven't been seeing as much of each other as they once did.'

Sister Chessman laughed shortly. 'They should know. Honestly, the gossip that goes on in the Sisters' sitting-room – '

Matron smiled grimly. 'I know, I know. And perhaps I shouldn't listen to as much as gets to me – but if I didn't I'd know all too little about what goes on – and I feel I should – '

Bridget, intensely unhappy, moved through the days, working automatically, sick with reaction whenever she thought of Josh and Bobby. She assumed, reasonably enough, that the relationship had gone on as before, that Josh and Bobby were still enjoying their full-blown affair, and that inevitably, Josh had been the father of the child Bobby didn't want – so desperately didn't want.

She managed to understand, much as it hurt her to think of it, why the affair existed. Bobby was 'available' and as Josh had said to her that night, it would be an odd man who did not take advantage of the fact. She found it impossible to realise, however, that such an affair could exist in the absence of love on Josh's part. Bridget, still very inexperienced in the ways of men, took it for granted that a man functioned as she did – that he could only sleep with a girl he loved – for she was an intensely feminine person, and knew instinctively that for her, at any rate, such love-making and real love were indivisible. One could not exist without the other.

So she went about her work in a state of numb misery. However much she told herself that there was no possible chance of her ever being able to think of Josh and herself as a unit, which in her heart of hearts she knew she wanted more than anything else in the world, she still could not help feeling bereft when she thought of his love for Bobby – which she was convinced he felt.

And yet, she would tell herself, sick at heart, and yet, he let her do this dreadful thing to herself, despite the fact he was a doctor, despite the fact that he loved her. How could he? How could he? she would ask herself with dreary insistence. How could he?

So, when Josh came to the second theatre late one evening, to talk to her, she made every effort she could not to respond to him.

He came and stood at the door, barring her from leaving and she stood rigid on the far side of the narrow operating table and looked at him, at the unwontedly unsmiling expression on his face, and said desperately, 'Please, go away. I don't want to talk to you – I just don't want to talk to you.'

He shook his head at that. 'But you're going to – *you are going to*. There – there are things I've got to tell you, and I must tell you. For God's sake, Bridget, be fair. I care about you – do you understand? I've *got* to talk to you – '

But she blazed at him, her cheeks showing high spots of colour, her eyes sparkling with anger, an anger that was the only thing that prevented her from crying out, from throwing herself into his arms, from telling him that she loved him, and didn't care about anything else – she loved him –

But she used her anger to push her feelings down, and said between clenched teeth. 'I *won't* talk to you – I won't – after what has happened – after Bobby – No!' and she crossed the theatre, to push him forcibly away, so that he had been unable to keep her there.

She wondered for a while whether the best thing for her to do would be to leave the Royal altogether. Somehow, it was all such a mess. She would sit in her room, alone, staring out of the window into the garden, thinking till her head swam.

Liz came to her there, one afternoon, while she was sitting with a textbook in front of her, making a poor pretence at studying, and stood diffidently at the door, hovering anxiously as she looked at Bridget sitting still by her window.

'Can – can I come and talk to you?' she said, her face a little flushed. 'I – I've got a message for you.'

Bridget stood up awkwardly. It had been so long since there had been any real contact between Liz and herself that she felt almost as awkward and strange as she had on that very first morning in the Preliminary Training School, so long ago now.

'Of course – of course,' she said. 'Er – shall I make a cup of tea? I wasn't going to go to tea in the dining-room – and I'm due back on duty at five – ' She was talking just to make conversation now, as she looked covertly at Liz'z strained face.

'Er – er – no thanks. I'm not really thirsty – ' Liz came across the room to perch uncomfortably on the edge of the bed, and began to twist her fingers in her lap.

'Look, Bridget – ' she began. Then stopped.

'Well?'

Liz took a deep breath. 'I've got a message for you – from Bobby.'

Bridget stiffened. 'Oh?' she said politely, her face smooth, not wanting to let Liz see how she felt about Bobby.

Liz leaned forward impulsively. 'Oh, Bridget, please – don't be angry. She knows she treated you badly – but she's truly sorry – I think – and she wants to talk to you. She – she needs a friend, you know. Very much.'

Bridget raised her eyebrows at that. 'Oh, come off it, Liz. She doesn't need *me*. What about you – and Judith?'

'Judith!' Liz put a world of scorn into the name. 'Judith makes me *sick*. She won't go near Bobby. Scared Matron'll think she's the same sort of person Bobby is, and terrified the old girl'll tell her parents – and you know what her father's like. Not that that's any excuse. Because Judith *is* like Bobby. I mean, Judith – well, she's been behaving just as Bobby did. The only difference is, she's been lucky, and got away with it. It's Bobby who – got caught.'

'Hasn't she even been to see Bobby in the sick bay?'

'Not her! I tell you, Judith has dropped Bobby as though she never even met her! She's going around the place as though butter wouldn't melt in her mouth, too bloody good to be true. And you can bet your bottom dollar she'll go on that way. No, Bobby's got no friend in Judith.'

'What about you, then?' Bridget said evenly. 'Or are you scared to admit that you're a friend of Bobby's, too?'

Liz flushed. 'No! It's not like that at all! I – I haven't been as close to the others as I was before – before last Christmas, I mean. Ken – well, he and me – we were both so sick about what happened – I mean, we had no idea that you didn't care for David Nestor. We thought you did – and that – oh, I don't know. It's funny, really. When – when you're really in love with someone, you think every other couple is the same as you are. Ken and me, we both thought that you and David, and Bobby and Josh, and Judith and Clive were like us. In love, you see, and – and only wanting to be – together *because* you were in love. And when we realised that you – that Bobby had sort of engineered you into coming down that weekend, that you didn't even know what she was up to, we felt sick. And since then, I just haven't been so friendly. I mean – I didn't *drop* them or anything – I'm not like that. I just haven't been so friendly.'

'And now, you don't want to see Bobby at all,' Bridget said flatly.

'Oh, let me finish, Bridie, please!' Liz said urgently. 'It's not that at all. Look, Ken has a new job – he goes to Scotland next month to a junior consultancy – it's marvellous, really. I mean, we'll be able to get married almost right away. And I've asked Matron to arrange for me to finish my training at the same hospital where Ken will be. They don't mind married students there, Matron says, and she'll – give me a good reference. So I won't be here, you see. So, like I said, Bobby – needs a friend.'

Bridget stood up, and began to prowl restlessly about the room. 'Look, Liz. I know you mean well – but how can I just – just go and see Bobby as though nothing ever happened? I – I thought you three were such wonderful people – especially Bobby. You were everything I ever wanted to be – gay and relaxed and happy – you know? And I needed you all as friends so much. That was – why it all happened, really. I was so scared you'd not want me if I didn't go along with you – with Bobby, really, though I thought you were all the same, I suppose. And then – then you – she let me down. It hurt. A lot. I've – got used to being on my own again, like I always was. It doesn't matter so much any more. I don't think I could bear to start again. Not after what's happened.' She stopped by Liz, then, and said earnestly, 'Please, don't think – that it's a *moral* thing. That I – don't approve of what Bobby did. I mean, I *don't* – I think it's – awful. Sickening. But I'm not the sort to turn my back on someone just because I think they've been stupid, and behaved badly. It's just that I don't think I *could* be a friend of hers again.'

'Poor Bridget,' Liz said softly. 'I just didn't know. That you were so – lonely. I thought you were reserved because you *liked* to be that way. You were – sweet and quiet, and I left it at that. I never thought very much about what went on behind people's faces – not till I met Ken and – fell in love with him. I've grown up a bit since then. I'm sorry about it all, really I am, Bridie. If – if I'd *known* what Bobby was like, what she would do to you, I'd never have just sat by. But I didn't know, truly I didn't.'

'I believe you,' Bridget said.

Liz smiled crookedly at that. 'Well, that's something. But about Bobby, Bridget. I see what you mean – but couldn't you at least go and see her? She wants you to – and the least you could do is to tell her yourself how you feel.'

There was a long pause, then Bridget said unwillingly, 'All right. I'll go and see her. But only to make it clear that I can't just pick up again where I left off.' Impulsively, she leaned over, and hugged Liz warmly.

'And I'm awfully pleased about you and Ken, Liz, truly I am. I hope you'll both be very happy, and – and have a marvellous life together up in your Scottish hospital.'

Liz lit up at the thought of her bright future.

'Isn't it marvellous? I'm so lucky, Bridget, and I know it. Ken's a wonderful person – '

She glowed as she thought of her Ken, then looked shrewdly at Bridget. 'What about you, Bridie? I know now that you never cared for David, but isn't there anyone else on the horizon for you? It's so lovely to be in love – I sort of want to see everyone else as happy as I am.'

'Me?' Bridget managed a smile. 'Oh, don't think about me! I'm not the marrying sort, I suppose. I mean, when you all used to talk about meeting doctors here, and marrying one, I never really saw it as you all did – '

Liz made a face. 'Don't remind me about the way we used to talk. I – don't think I meant it, really. I used to talk like the others did because it seemed the – smart thing to do. I didn't set out to – to catch Ken, honestly I didn't. It just happened.'

Bridget laughed then. 'I believe you,' she said again, and Liz, too, laughed, and relaxed a little.

They talked of casual things then, and when it was time for them both to go back on duty, they walked across the courtyard in companionable silence. At the door to the main block, where they parted, Bridget to return to Theatre, Liz to go back to the Gynae ward she was now working on, Liz said impulsively, 'I'm sorry I'm going away, in one way. I mean, you and I could be real friends I think. Will you write to me?'

'I will,' Bridget promised, and smiled. 'And knit things for your babies too.'

Liz laughed. 'Plenty of time for that,' she said. 'But I hope I have dozens some day.' She sobered then. 'Poor Bobby – '

'Yes – ' Bridget said. 'I suppose so. Poor Bobby – '

There were no cases that evening on Theatre, only a mass of clearing up from the day's lists, and Bridget settled to the long tedious chores with a sigh. She had promised Liz she would go and see Bobby, and she would keep her promise. But she didn't relish the idea of facing her one bit.

'I'll go tonight, after I get off duty,' she told herself, as she industriously scrubbed instruments, and laid them in neat rows in the gleaming cupboards. 'Better get it over with – '

When she went up to supper, an hour before she was due off duty, she stopped at the porter's lodge in the main hall to see if there were any letters. The only letters she ever got were the monthly, short, typewritten notes from Mr Lessiter, who wrote out of a sense of duty about his guardianship, notes which Bridget as dutifully answered. One of these letters was due, so Bridget thought she might as well go and see if it had arrived.

It had, and she took it from the porter with a brief thanks, and turned to go, tucking it into her apron bib.

But he called her back. 'Nurse Preston! There's something else for you – ' He leered at her. 'By hand, this one – ' and he gave her a thick white envelope, with her name written across it in a firm hand.

She stared at the envelope, and said wonderingly. 'For me?'

'You're the only Preston we've got, ducks!' the porter said. 'It's for you, all right – '

She tucked it into her apron with the other letter, and went on to supper with a faint frown on her face. Though she had no idea who the letter was from, not recognising the handwriting, she felt obscurely that this was something to be read in privacy, that it was somehow too important to read in public. So she hurried through her meal, and went back to the peace of the quiet theatres to perch on a tall stool in the sluice, out of Sister's way, to slit the envelope in peace.

'My dear Bridget,' she read. 'Since you flatly refuse to talk to me, this is about the only way I can communicate with you. For God's sake, Tiddler, *read* this. Don't just screw it up. That would be childish, wouldn't it? And I don't think you are as petty as that, even if you do refuse to talk to me.

'In a way, it's easier to write all this than to say it. When you stand and stare at me with those big, grey eyes of yours, all icy, I find myself almost at a loss for words – which is an extraordinary way for *me* to be. But that is the effect you have on me – if you didn't, believe me, you wouldn't be able to get away from me as you always do.

'Tiddler, dear Tiddler. I've been trying to tell you for a long time that I care a great deal for you – I've watched you this past year or more, watched you with David, and since, on your own, and I have ached to know you better. There is something about you that makes me – I don't know. I've certainly never felt about any other girl as I do about you. And that brings me to what I must say to you.

'From the beginning, I've spent a lot of time with Bobby. I don't for a moment intend to pretend otherwise. But I want you to know that she meant no more to me than any other girl has ever meant – someone who was – fun, if you like. You must try to understand, Tiddler. Ever since I was little more than a kid, I've liked girls. And they've liked me. Does that sound big-headed? I suppose it does. But there it is. I've slept around – my God, but that looks revolting in cold print! But it's true. If a girl was willing, then I was too. But if you can understand this, it never meant anything to me more than a passing affair. Fun. Immoral, I suppose – but I've no great claims to being a great moralist. I've seen sex as – as an appetite like any other, one to be satisfied where and when I could.

'But now, I feel very different. I don't want any more of these grubby affairs. For the first time in my life, I'm in love. And now I've said it. I'm in love, with you, my own Tiddler, and somehow, I've got to make you see that, got to make you see me, if you possibly can, with new eyes. Try to forget that I was the man you knew, who carried on an affair with a friend of yours. Can you forgive that? Can you try to see me as a man who loves you very much indeed, and wants nothing more than to spend the rest of his life with you?

'And to make sure the slate is clean, to help me more than you really, there's something else I want you to know. This grim business about Bobby. I had no part in it – to put it bluntly, her pregnancy was not due to me. I *know* that. That night at Bobby's place last Christmas finished things as far as I was concerned. I can still see your face that night, and I feel sick with anger whenever I remember it. You must believe this, Tiddler, you must.

'Please, my own love, please, think about this. And talk to me about it. I love you. And even if you feel now that you can't forgive me, please give me a chance. *Talk* to me. Let's spend some time together. Give yourself a chance to get to know me. Then, if you can't love me, I'll try to accept the fact with the best grace I can muster. But somehow, I'm going to *make* you care for me as I care for you. I *must*. You're the most wonderful thing that has ever happened to me. Josh.'

She sat for a long time, after she had folded the letter and put it back into her apron bib. A long time, not thinking, just sitting staring at the tiled wall of the sluice.

Then, she took a deep, shuddering breath, and dropping her head into her hands, wept bitterly. It was almost more than she could bear. That Josh should write as he had, that he loved her – nothing else mattered. The past, his and Bobby's, was dead, and a bright, a glittering future stretched ahead of her. And she wept as though her heart would break, her mind whirling with the pain and the joy of it all.

12

She went off duty at half past eight, leaving the theatres clean and quiet behind her, smiling so brilliantly in response to Theatre Sister's 'Goodnight' that the lady told herself in surprise that young Preston looked positively beautiful tonight. And then sighed sharply as she remembered the days when she, too, had been able to look like that.

Bridget stood undecided outside the big double doors for a moment. What she wanted to do was to go over to her room to re-read Josh's letter, now sitting warmly inside her apron, feeling as heavy as if it were written on a clay tablet. But she had promised to go and see Bobby. And somehow she felt obscurely that until she had seen Bobby, made the break with the past complete, as it were, she could not really think properly about what Josh had written.

So she straightened herself, took a deep breath, and walked purposefully along the corridor towards the doors that led to the little complex of private rooms that was the staff sick bay.

There was a staff nurse on duty there, sitting writing a report in her little office, and she nodded in response to Bridget's request to visit Nurse Aston.

'All right. She's much better – probably going convalescent in a week or so, and Matron said she could have visitors. Nip along – she's in the end room on the right.'

At the door, Bridget stood for a long moment, then took another deep breath, and tapped on the panels.

'Come in,' Bobby's voice came muffled from the other side, and Bridget opened the door and went in, to close it behind her so that she could lean against it.

Bobby was sitting up in bed, the only light in the room coming from the bulb above her head, a light that cocooned her in brightness, lighting her fair hair to a gleaming sheet of blondeness.

When Bobby raised her head, Bridget gasped a little with shock. The beautiful round face, the sleek health that had always invested that face with a peach-like bloom, had gone. Her cheeks were thinner, her eyes so deeply shadowed in their sockets that they seemed to be violet in colour. Her temples were translucent, giving her face a mask-like look that aged her immeasurably.

There was a long silence, while the two girls stared at each other. Then Bobby said huskily, 'Hello, Bridget.'

'Hello, Bobby.' Bridget managed a narrow-lipped smile. 'How are you?'

Bobby stretched her arms above her head, letting the diaphanous sleeves of her blue nightdress fall back, so that Bridget could see that even her arms had become stick-like in their thinness. 'As well as can be expected. Isn't that what they always say?' Bobby said, and dropped her hands on to the covers again. 'It – it's nice of you to come, Bridie, love.'

Somehow, the familiar expression made Bridget want to cry. This girl was such a wreck of the old Bobby, so different, that to hear familiar words on her lips was eerie, somehow.

'Liz – said you wanted to see me,' she said baldly, sounding curt in her effort to control the rush of feeling Bobby's greeting had roused in her.

'Come and sit down, Bridie,' Bobby said. 'There's a chair over there.'

Obediently, Bridget brought the chair, and came and sat beside the bed, folding her apron neatly on her lap for something to do – anything to avoid looking at Bobby.

'Bridie – I – I owe you an apology. I've owed it to you for a very long time. And I – wanted to tell you so.'

'Please – ' Bridget began. 'Please, Bobby, don't – '

'But I must,' Bobby said, almost fretfully. 'I must. I treated you badly, Bridie, and I know it. I shouldn't have – I shouldn't have let you think that weekend was going to be anything other than what it was – '

Bridget bit her lip. 'Well, I suppose I should have realised,' she said slowly. 'I – was a bit naïve, to put it mildly.'

'Honestly, Bridie – I didn't know. I truly thought you *liked* David – I had no idea he'd turn so – nasty. If I had known – '

'Oh, Bobby, for God's sake!' Bridget was angry suddenly.

'Don't try and tell me that. I mean, if you really *were* surprised, as you suggest, when he – he got so nasty – you wouldn't have told Josh to – leave us alone. And you did. That's what hurt me most I think. I mean, David – David tried to – to – '

'To force you to sleep with him,' Bobby said, watching Bridget as she said it.

'Yes. And when Josh interfered, you told him to leave us alone – to let us sort it out for ourselves. And that – wasn't kind, to put it at it's mildest.'

'I know – I know.' Bobby began to pleat the sheet between her fingers. 'I – I didn't think.'

'And you told me I'd ruined the weekend, remember? Ruined the weekend! You didn't seem to care – care about what might have happened to me – '

'Please, Bridie, don't,' Bobby said. 'I'm truly sorry, really I am. Can't you forgive me? Can't we be friends again?'

Bridget looked at her, at the appealing expression in her shadowed eyes, and said abruptly, 'Tell me something, Bobby. Why did you ever want me to be one of – of your set? I mean, I wasn't a bit like you. I needed *you* all right – I know that. I was lonely, and awkward, and shy, and you three – specially you – you sort of dazzled me. But why did you want to include *me* in your life? I don't understand it. I was – dull. Naïve. Always trying to back out of things. Yet you kept on at me – got mad when I tried to – to tell you I didn't like David, made me go on with him, because if I hadn't you'd have dropped me. That mattered to me – a lot. But why should it have mattered to you? I don't understand.'

Bobby shrugged slightly. 'I don't really know. I – just liked you, I suppose.'

With a sudden shrewdness, Bridget said, 'Was it because I helped you all with your work? Did your notes and all that?'

Bobby had the grace to blush slightly. 'A – little, perhaps. But it was more than that. I *did* like you – I still do – you were calm, and quiet, and I suppose I needed that.'

Bridget laughed shortly. 'You needed me for that? Not really. Bobby. Not really.'

Bobby looked at her sideways, through lowered lids, then with an apparent effort said. 'All right. I'll tell you. And you won't like it.'

'I'd like to know, all the same.'

Bobby let her head droop, so that her hair swung forwards and hid her face, while she watched her fingers at their incessant pleating of the sheet.

'It was Josh,' she said in a low voice. 'Josh.'

Bridget felt herself go cold suddenly.

'I knew – he liked you,' Bobby said. 'At that party – do you remember that first party in the mess? He – he looked at you. And I knew he liked you. And – I liked him. Very much. I – wanted him. And I knew enough to see that the only way I could make sure he'd – go on seeing me for any length of time was if you were included in the things we did. If you were around. So – so I planned it so that you always were.'

Bridget stared at her, her heart sick. 'And you pushed me at David – '

'I pushed you at David so that Josh could see he was wasting his time yearning after you. It was easy then – he was attracted to you, I knew that, but not so much that he'd march off or anything if he saw you with someone else. I thought if he saw you with David, he'd give up, and settle for me.' She raised her head then, and looked at Bridget, her eyes glinting with something of the old Bobby. 'And he did, didn't he?'

'Yes,' Bridget said in a low voice. 'He did.'

'I suppose I've mucked it all up for you, Bridie, and I'm sorry.' Bobby's voice was smooth. 'If I hadn't been around, you and Josh – maybe you would have got somewhere with him. But I *was* – '

Bridget closed her eyes. To look at this girl, to hear her admitting that she had set out to take away from her the only man she had ever really cared about was dreadful. But the voice went on, inexorably.

'It's too late for you now, Bridie. Josh is mine now.'

Bridget opened her eyes then, and looked at her with a startled expression.

'Yours?'

'Of course.' Bobby smiled, sleekly. 'He's – an honourable type, old Josh. He – won't leave me in the cart now. Not after – what's happened to me.'

'What – what do you mean?' Bridget's own voice sounded cracked. 'What do you mean?'

Bobby opened her eyes widely at her, and smiled. 'Well, it's obvious, isn't it? I know I'm not having the baby – won't ever have a baby' – and at the sight of the sudden pain that crossed

Bridget's face, she laughed aloud – 'no need to look like that – I'm not cut out for motherhood – it doesn't matter to me that I'll never be saddled with brats – but even though I'm not having his baby, Josh isn't the type to leave me to dree my own weird, as they say – '

'His baby?' Bridget whispered. 'His?'

'Who else's?' Bobby put a pained expression on her face. 'My dear Bridie, who else's?'

'He – does he know?' Bridget said.

'Of course he does! Poor old Josh – he was sick when he realised I'd gone to that ghastly woman, and saw what she'd done to me, but he knows I did it for him. He doesn't want kids any more than I do – '

Somehow, Bridget got to her feet, somehow, managed to walk to the door.

'Don't go, Bridie – ' Bobby sat in her pool of light and looked across the room to where Bridget stood shaking and almost in tears.

'Can't we let bygones be bygones?' Bobby said sweetly. 'Can't we?'

Bridget shook her head. 'No – Bobby. No,' she said, almost in a whisper. 'Not now. Goodbye, Bobby,' and she pulled the door open, to almost fall out into the corridor.

And behind her, in the quiet room, Bobby snuggled deep into her pillows, her arms behind her head, and smiled up at the ceiling.

Bridget reached her room, the haven of her room, almost without knowing how she got there. And then sat in her chair by the window, staring out at the winking lights of the hospital, away over the garden, feeling as though she were so much dead flesh, not a person at all. He had lied to her. Lied to her. The words thumped and twisted in her head until she wanted to scream. He had lied to her. The happiness that had so short a time ago seemed so close within her grasp had gone, gone for always. There was nothing left.

She slept fitfully, tossing on her bed, sinking into vague and terrifying dreams that brought her sitting bolt upright, shaking, her eyes wet with tears. And so odd was the night, so confused her feelings, that when the night staff nurse suddenly appeared at her door, to switch the light on and fill the room with dazzle, she wasn't even surprised.

'Sorry to get you out, Preston,' Staff Nurse said. 'But there's an emergency call.'

Bridget blinked at her stupidly from her pillows. 'An emergency?'

'There's been a multiple smash-up on the motorway – four lorries and a motorbike and a couple of cars – a right holocaust. The police want an emergency medical team, and the ambulance depot can't help because their team is out on another call at a factory some place. Night Sister says they need two good surgical nurses – and the Casualty Department is full, so we can't send any of our people. And the theatres are working tonight on top of it. There's only you and Jessolo available, so you'll have to get up – Come on, girl – it's an emergency!'

Almost in a dream, she dressed, climbing into slacks and a sweater rather than uniform, for the staff nurse told her that this was the best clothing for what she would have to do, and followed the impatient older girl across the dark courtyard to the hospital.

There was a hospital ambulance waiting there, its engine ticking over, and as Bridget arrived, Nurse Jessolo appeared behind her, her eyes still thick with sleep, also in slacks and a sweater.

The ambulance driver leaned over, and hauled the two girls in beside him.

'Come on you two – the doctors are in the back – we'd better get moving – ' and as they huddled themselves into the small space beside him, the engine roared, and with a wide sweep of its headlights that threw the walls of the courtyard into glittering brilliance, the ambulance shot out of the hospital gates and on its way.

They sped through the silent streets, past shops with windows blank behind their blinds, along the shining tarmac, wet from the thick mist that lay close to the ground. As the ambulance reached the flyover that led on to the motorway, the fog seemed to thicken, to swirl in patches that made Bridget's eyes smart, and set Jessolo coughing.

They came on the scene of the smash-up almost with shock. One minute there was nothing but the patches of fog, the brilliance of the headlights on it, then there was noise, and light, and people.

One lorry lay on its side, two more piled drunkenly alongside it. Police, with huge emergency spotlights, and firemen, their black coats seeming to gleam yellowly in the light, were clambering over the wreckage, while alongside, on the grey-looking grass of the verge, three bodies lay under police greatcoats, ominously still.

The ambulance drew up alongside the lorries, its wheels screaming in protest at the sharp braking, and the girls tumbled out, Bridget bewildered and frightened at the noise, the suddenness of it all. At the back of the ambulance, the driver fumbled with the doors, and three men jumped out, to stand blinking in the light for a moment. Two of them, grabbing the bags of equipment the driver tossed out, made a beeline for the people lying on the verge and one, as he passed Bridget and Nurse Jessolo called out, 'Hey – you two – '

It was the senior RSO, and still in her dream-like state, Bridget, with Jessolo close behind, followed him and the other man towards the side of the road.

A policeman seemed to materialise from out of the fog and stopped them.

'Hospital? Thank God you got here – listen – two of them are dead, far as we can tell. T'other's pretty rocky – out cold, and breathing bad. Chest stoved in, seemingly – '

The RSO nodded. 'Right – Prater' – he nodded at the other doctor with him – 'take one of the nurses and have a look – '

'And there's a car under the other side of that lorry,' the policeman went on. 'And there's someone in there moaning – woman – can't get much out of her but moans – and the other car's over there – and the motor-cyclist – got a kid under it. They're trying to get him and the driver out now – '

'Right – ' the RSO said crisply. 'I'll take that car. Simpson – you take the other nurse, and see about the woman – get on – ' and he ran across the road to disappear into the yellow mud of the fog.

For a moment, Bridget stood rigid, for the first time realising that the last of the three men who had been in the back of the ambulance was Josh. Then, as Dr Prater ran towards the men at the side of the road, with Nurse Jessolo loping awkwardly behind him, she felt his hand on her arm.

'Come on,' he said briefly. 'Work to be done – ' and she let him pull her along with him, to the far side of the crumpled lorries, her feet icy with cold, her body shaking with fear, in anticipation of what she might see.

The car was a little red mini, looking like a toy as it lay crushed under one huge wheel of the articulated lorry almost on top of it. The side nearest the driver was miraculously free, and Josh dropped to one knee beside the fireman who was beside it, working to free the jammed door with an acetylene blow-torch.

'Nearly got it,' the man grunted, his face lit to a ghastly blueness in the light of his torch. 'Nearly got it – '

She could hear the unearthly moaning that was coming from the car, above the noise of the torch, above the sounds of shouting voices and engines that filled the night with hideous sound. A rhythmic even moaning that filled her with sick terror.

'Got it,' the fireman said, and the door swung back on its ruined hinges, to lean drunkenly against the bonnet.

Josh, his back straining, moved swiftly. Bridget could see his arms flex, the muscles strain hard, as he backed away from the car, a woman held awkwardly in his arms, her head thrown back against his arm, her mouth wide and red as she moaned and moaned interminably.

'Easy does it, girl, easy does it,' Josh was murmuring. 'We've got you, lovey, we've got you – easy does it now – ' He straightened, and moving with cat-like smoothness, carried her to the side of the road, to lay her down on the big tarpaulin a policeman had laid ready.

Bridget, following, dropped to her knees beside the tarpaulin, and as Josh felt for her pulse, and then started to straighten the bent legs, she leaned over the moaning woman, and murmured, gently, as though to a crying baby, 'It's all right, my dear, it's all right – we've got you – there's a doctor here, and we've got you – don't cry, we've got you – '

The woman opened terrified brown eyes, the whites showing all round the edge of the iris, and her moaning changed, became gasping.

'Baby – baby – baby,' she said, her voice rising to a scream at the end of it. Then she arched her neck, and opened her mouth wide to scream in agony once more.

Bridget looked up, to where Josh was kneeling beside her, pulling the woman's coat from her sides, and as she did so, his face whitened in the fitful light.

'Oh, my God, she's pregnant – ' He put a hand on the distended abdomen, and leaned towards the woman's face.

'Listen, my love – listen – don't scream, try not to scream – tell me – how far on are you?'

She opened her eyes again, to stare at him in terror, and her lips pulled back over her teeth in a feline grimace.

'Eight – eight months – baby – eight months – ' she said, and again, arched her neck, and screamed.

Bridget, clutching at the woman's icy hands, held on to her like grim death, feeling utterly helpless, only able to offer her own physical presence as a help in the woman's agony.

Josh's voice came crisply, 'That's a contraction – and a strong one – she's gone into labour – how long was she under that lorry?' and the policeman's voice above them said gruffly, 'Close on half an hour since it happened, sir.'

'Rig me some sort of screen, will you?' Josh was pulling the woman's clothes back out of the way. 'Get a set of emergency gear from the ambulance – she's going to deliver – we'll never get her to the hospital before she does – Nurse – here – '

He indicated to Bridget, with a curt gesture of his head, to come to the other side of him.

'Hold that leg – hold her, do you hear? Bend the knee – that's it – here, you – ' The young policeman who had been standing on the other side dropped to his knees on the other side of the woman, who was moaning again, her neck once more extended in a long arc. 'Hold that leg – like Nurse is – bend the knee –that's it – now hold her – other hand on her pelvis – at the side – hold her firm – got her?'

The policeman who had gone for the emergency case reappeared out of the fog, and with quick fingers, Josh undid the covers, and with careful movements, opened the packets inside.

'Bloody sterile this'll be,' he muttered. Then, as the woman once more stiffened and let her moans rise to a scream, said loudly, 'Easy does it, lovey, easy does it – we've got you – '

He fumbled in his pocket for his stethoscope, and with a swift movement, pushed the woman's torn clothes away, and set the bell on to the high dome of the abdomen.

'Foetal heart's all right – thank God for that – and here's another contraction – '

Bridget watched him, her heart pounding in her chest, as he pulled a pair of gloves from the emergency pack on to his wide hands, and heard him tell the woman, 'Now, listen, lovey, take it easy. I'm going to examine you – see how near this babe of yours is – easy now – ' and his hands moved gently but firmly, as he felt for the baby's head, while Bridget held on to one leg, and the young policeman, head averted, hung on grimly on the other side.

'Ye gods, she's crowning – ' Josh said loudly. 'Here we go – ' and under Bridget's terrified stare, the crumpled scalp, with black hair lying on it in even waves, like those left in beach sand when the tide goes out, appeared. The woman stretched herself again, pushed her legs hard against Bridget and the policeman, and the rest of the head appeared, the face looking furiously angry in its crumpled dusky redness.

There was an apparently interminable pause, and then, as the woman gave a deep grunt of intense effort, the rest of the baby's body appeared, the cord attached to its abdomen thick and gleaming in the glare of the spotlight. Josh held it high, both feet firm in a brown-gloved hand, and the baby squirmed, opened its wide, red mouth, and squalled lustily, its head held back in a sort of imitation of its mother's position just before it was born.

'It's a boy – a right lusty little so-and-so, too,' Josh said exultantly, grinning from ear to ear in relief that the child was all right. 'Hear that, mother, lovey? It's a fine boy! Prem, but a good six-pounder, I'll bet – here, Bridget – give me a towel from the pack.'

And Bridget did, and held it carefully as Josh laid the still-squalling baby into it, to wrap him carefully, and hold him still, while Josh clipped and cut the cord.

'Give him to his mother,' he said. 'And tell her to hang on. We'd better deliver the placenta before we move her, if we can – '

And gently, Bridget knelt on the muddy grass of the verge, the fog moving sluggishly round her, to lay the baby beside his mother, who was now lying, her head at rest at last, with closed eyes in her white face.

'There he is, my dear,' Bridget whispered, and the woman opened her eyes, and looked at her, and then at the baby, wonderingly.

'All – all right?' she whispered, and as the baby opened his mouth to shout his rage at his unceremonious arrival, Bridget smiled and said, 'Listen to him – '

The woman's face lit into sudden brilliance, and she fumbled for the child, to peer eagerly into his creased face, to touch the streaked cheeks with a gentle finger.

'Here's the placenta – ' Josh said at length, as the woman gave one more effortful grunt, and then he worked in silence for a while, eventually to stand up and sign to the ambulance man on the other side of the hastily rigged tarpaulin screen.

'Get her back to the hospital fast, will you?' he said. 'Got an ambulance to spare?'

The man nodded. 'Three more just got here. This is the last case, anyway – we've got all the others away. You comin' back with us?'

'If there's nothing else to do here – have the rest gone back?'

'Gone with their patients – and the dead ones – shocking business – shocking.'

Josh nodded. 'But at least we've got one extra – very much alive – listen to the little devil,' and the baby squalled louder.

Together, Bridget and Josh rode back to the hospital, sitting beside the sleeping and exhausted mother, while Bridget cradled the baby warmly in her arms. And when Josh caught her eye, and smiled at her, his face warm, and with a question on it, she dropped her eyes, to look at the baby's crumpled little face. She could not look at Josh for the life of her.

13

When they got back to the hospital, Casualty was seething with activity. Every cubicle was full, every one of the staff, including a few extra nurses collected from less busy parts of the hospital, running about as though all the hounds of hell were after them. In the waiting-room, two trolleys with grimly covered shapes on them, waited for porters to take them to the mortuary, and a theatre trolley arrived to take the most severely injured straight to Theatre, just as Bridget and Josh and their two patients arrived to swell the throng.

The RSO, his hair ruffled and his face creased with fatigue, took one look at the small bundle Bridget was carrying, and his face dropped.

'Christ, not a *baby* as well. Was it injured?'

Josh grinned. 'Looks fine to me. Born on the edge of the road – '

'That's all that I was short of,' the RSO said wearily. 'How's the mum?'

'Pretty exhausted – but as far as I could tell, no other injuries. Bloody miracle – '

'Mmm. Look, don't bring 'em in here. Get her straight to Maternity – tell them to put her in a single room and barrier nurse until they're sure she hasn't picked up an infection – '

'I should think she must have done. I mean, delivery in the gutter isn't exactly an aseptic technique,' Josh said.

'Yup – tell the Maternity people to put her on penicillin. I'll send a radiographer up to take some films – better make sure she's got no bones broken – and I'll come and see her as soon as I can. Oh, and the baby'd better be in isolation, too.'

'It's prem – about thirty-two weeks maturity, to look at it.'

'Well, the midwives'll know whether it needs an incubator. Get them off, will you, Josh? I'm a bit pushed here – ' and he disappeared back into a cubicle, to deal with the motor-cyclist, who was now regaining consciousness, and making a great deal of noise about it.

Josh turned to where Bridget was standing, still clutching the baby, and said crisply, 'Right. You go on ahead, will you? I'll follow with Mum – '

The midwife on night duty looked startled, to say the least, when a trousered and dirty-faced Bridget arrived with a baby wrapped in a now oil-stained towel. Until she saw the look on the midwife's face, Bridget had no idea how very odd she looked, but she caught a reflection of herself in the glass front of a cupboard, and despite her fatigue, grinned slightly as she handed the baby over to the midwife.

'Mother's on the way – ' she began, and then the trolley with Josh at the head came rattling along the corridor from the lift. Succinctly, he gave his instructions to the midwife, who with a nod, swept into efficient action. Just as the trolley was being wheeled into one of the single wards at the side of the corridor, the mother turned her head, and putting her hand out, touched Bridget.

'Nurse?' she whispered hoarsely. 'Are you a nurse? The one who was with me?'

Bridget smiled, and held the hand warmly. 'Yes – and the doctor's here, too.'

The woman turned to look at Josh, and murmured, 'Thank you – thank you. Is – he all right?'

'I think he is, lovey,' Josh said, smiling down at her. 'He looked fine to me. They'll have a good look at him here, and tell you all about him properly – but I don't think you need worry – '

She bit her lip, to stop herself from crying tears of weakness and sheer happiness. 'What's your name, Doctor?'

He grinned widely. 'Joshua, I'm afraid.

'And yours, Nurse?'

'Bridget Preston.'

And the woman nodded. 'That's what I'll call him then. Joshua Preston Burke. Nice name. Thank you both so much – '

And the midwife pushed her away to her warm bed and to the rest she so sorely needed.

There was a long pause, then Josh said softly, 'There. A baby named after us. Isn't that nice? An – omen, perhaps?'

But Bridget turned away, and began to walk towards the lift. He fell into step beside her, and said softly, 'Bridget? Tiddler?' She shook her head wordlessly. All that had happened the night before, so very long ago now, it seemed, his letter and the way it had made her feel, the conversation with Bobby, came back to her, and misery washed over like a palpable thing.

But before she could open the lift gates, he took her arms, and pulled her away, leading her into the small linen room that was alongside.

He stood with his back to the door, and said firmly, 'Now, listen. I know it's the middle of the night – damn' near morning – and we're both dead on our feet' – his voice softened – 'you look exhausted, my love – ' and she turned away, and shook her head again.

' – but I *must* talk to you. I must. You – got my note?'

She swallowed, and then said huskily, 'Yes, I got it.'

'Well?' and his voice was urgent. 'Well?'

'Please, let me go. I – I'm tired,' she said.

'So am I,' he said grimly. 'And another few minutes won't make much odds. Please, Tiddler, what have you to say about that note?'

And his voice, the nearness of him, was too much for her exhausted body to cope with any more. She felt huge tearing sobs start deep in her throat, felt her shoulders shake, and leaning against the little table covered with sheets and towels in the middle of the room, wept as though her tears would tear her apart.

His arms were round her then, holding her close, holding her against the roughness of his tweed jacket, holding her shoulders so that their shaking was stilled, so that she felt warm and safe again.

Slowly, the tears subsided, and she managed to pull away from him, to stand pressed against the wall as far away from him as she could get.

'You lied to me. You lied to me,' she said flatly, and her eyes were huge in her pinched face.

'I lied to you?' He looked genuinely puzzled. 'Lied? My love, what about? I told you all I could tell you in that letter – that was why I wrote it – to – clear the slate – to start new – '

But she shook her head stubbornly. 'You lied,' she said again, feeling the dreary persistence in her voice. 'I know now.'

'Know what?'

And at the continued puzzlement in his voice she became angry, and clenched her fists and almost shook them at him.

'I saw her last night – Bobby – and she *told* me – '

His own eyes glittered at that. 'Bobby? She told you something last night?'

'Yes!' she blazed. 'So you can keep your lies for *her* in future. I want no part of it – '

His hand shot out, and gripped her wrist in a grasp so strong it hurt her, and he bent his head close to hers, and looked directly into her eyes, eyes full of pain, and anger.

'I don't know what she told you – that girl is a pathological liar – but whatever it is, *I* told you the truth in my letter. You *must* believe that – '

She closed her eyes wearily. 'Oh, God, I don't know what to believe – I just don't know – '

He dropped her hand, and stood back, then after a moment said shortly, 'We're both tired out. And the only way I'll ever convince you is to get this business about Bobby sorted out properly once and for all. Tomorrow – today – we'll go and see her – '

'No – no, I couldn't – not again – '

'Yes!' He almost shouted it at her. 'Yes! Together, we'll go and see her. And then you'll find out for certain. Now, go to bed. And at two o'clock this afternoon, I'm coming to the Home to collect you and we'll go over to Sick Bay and see that – girl. And if you aren't waiting for me, so help me God, I'll come and drag you out of your room – and don't think I don't mean it.'

And he turned on his heel and left her, listening to the lift clatter away to the third floor and the doctors' quarters.

It was half past one in the afternoon when she woke from a thick and troubled sleep to find one of the Home maids standing grinning down at her.

' 'Allo, Nurse – 'ow are yer, love? Better for a good kip, I'll be bound – ' she plonked a tray of tea and toast down on the bedside-table and crossed the room to open the curtains. As the afternoon sun came streaming in, Bridget blinked, and rubbed her face, aware of the stiffness of fatigue that was still in her.

'Cor, but you're a right one, you and your pal, aren't yer? Evenin' papers is full of it – two plucky little nurses from the

Royal, that's what it says, two plucky little nurses, and three doctors all out in the fog in the middle of the night, savin' lives – an' that baby – ain't that a thing though? Was 'e a nice baby?'

'Very nice,' Bridget said absently. 'The papers?'

The maid grinned, basking in the reflected glory of it all.

'Not 'arf! All over the front pages it is – not much other news about, see? Makes quite a story. They had men 'ere today – wanting pictures of you and Nurse Jessolo, but Matron wasn't havin' any. "They're sleepin'," she told 'em, "and they're not to be disturbed," that's what she said. And 'ome Sister says to tell yer you're off duty rest of today, and not to go back till termorrer mornin'. So you just drink your tea and have a bite o' that there toast, and rest up. Lovely day, too – bit of an airin'd do you all the good in the world,' and she bustled away to tell the other maids about the way poor little Nurse Preston looked when she woke for her tea and toast.

Bridget swallowed her tea and toast with a relish that almost surprised her, and then took a hot bath that brought some of the exhaustion out with the steam. She dressed slowly, and was still combing her hair when the maid reappeared, grinning even more widely, if that were possible.

'There's someone waitin' downstairs for you. An' 'e says to tell yer if yer don't come down right now, 'e'll be up 'ere to get you. 'E's standin' on the bottom step, and 'e looks as if 'e means it – ain't 'e a looker, though? Smashin' feller – you'd better 'urry, Nurse. If 'e comes up 'ere 'ome Sister'll 'ave you on toast – '

And under the grinning maid's eye, Bridget couldn't help herself.

She walked down the stairs with all the dignity she could muster, all too aware of the maid watching her from the landing at the top.

He was standing as the maid had said, staring up at her as she came, his hair neat, his face fresh-shaven, looking as rested as though he had spent the past twenty-four hours in bed, rather than a bare five or six.

'Hello,' he said softly. 'How are you?'

'Very well, thank you,' she said stiffly.

He took her arm, and then walked out of the Home into the garden, and by one of the benches, he stopped and pulled her down to sit beside him.

'Will you come to see Bobby, Tiddler?'

She looked up at him, startled.

'You're – asking me? I thought – '

'I'm not going to force you to do anything against your will,' he said soberly. 'Last night – this morning – I was tired, and – upset – you seemed so – so bitter about me. But now – well, if you don't want to come, I won't force you. But I do ask this. I've told you one thing. Clearly, Bobby's told you another. And though it hurts to have to admit it, there's no reason why you should believe me rather than her. I've not exactly shown myself to be – a suitor *sans reproche*. On past showing, you're entitled to believe me a liar as well as – a tom-cat – '

She winced at that. 'Don't – '

He laughed a bitter little laugh. 'Well, wasn't I? It was your own term – you used it to Bobby, and my God, you were right to – no, I shouldn't say that. Whatever else Bobby may be, I've no right to call her names. I – was as much a party to her behaviour as she was herself, I suppose – '

He looked at her, and smiled crookedly. 'I don't like myself too well, at present, Tiddler. It never mattered before, you see. But now, I feel – ' and he moved his shoulders in a gesture of distaste.

She sat in silence, looking with unseeing eyes at the wide lawn, the early flowers nodding in their beds, at the thin spring sunshine glancing off the white-painted walls of the garden. Then she said, with sudden resolve, 'You're quite right. Of course you are. The only thing to do is go and see Bobby – and – ' She stopped, and looked at him, smiling a little. 'I – want to know. It's – important to me. I'm feeling less emotional this morning – afternoon, I mean – than I was. Last night I hated you – '

'And now?' He put his hand out, and held her chin between strong warm fingers. 'And now?'

She bit her lip, not meeting his gaze. 'Now, I – I want to know.'

'Come on, then. We'll get it over – '

They walked in silence across the courtyard, managing to avoid the few nurses and doctors who seemed to want to stop and talk to them about the night's exploits, and still in silence, walked along the corridor that led to the sick bay.

Bridget felt herself go cold again, a familiar sick feeling, as she thought of having to see Bobby again. And Josh would be with Bobby again, just as he used to be. She stole a look at him, at the rigid face, as he walked head high, beside her, and told herself – no. He'll be there, but not as it used to be.

Sister on sick bay looked at them curiously when they arrived and asked to see Nurse Aston. But she gave her permission, and watched them covertly as they went down the little corridor to the room at the end. She would have given a great deal to have been able to hear what was going on there – and wished, not for the first time, that the sick bay was an ordinary ward, instead of single rooms. It would have given her a better opportunity to 'keep an eye on things' as she told herself mendaciously.

It was Josh who knocked at the door, who opened it in response to the high 'Come in!' in Bobby's unmistakable voice. And it was Josh who walked in first, while Bridget, her nervousness rising in a huge wave, lingered behind for a second.

She heard the warmth, the almost caressing note in Bobby's voice as she said in surprised delight, 'Josh!' and wanted to turn and run.

But Josh stood aside, and put a strong hand out, and led her in so that she was standing beside him in the doorway, looking across at Bobby in her nest of pillows.

She was looking better than she had – or perhaps that was because Bridget had already seen the change in her, and could no longer be shocked by it. Her hair was tied back with a wide, blue ribbon, which gave her an appealing little-girl look, and the matching bed jacket showed off her fair skin to advantage.

But when she saw Bridget, her face altered, the warm welcoming smile that had wreathed her lips giving way to a sort of petulant surprise.

'Bridget?' she said uncertainly. 'You here again – '

Josh closed the door firmly, and said evenly, 'Yes, Bobby. Again. And I want you to repeat to her again whatever it was you told her last night. Now. While I'm here to listen.'

Bobby stared at him, and frowned sharply. 'For heaven's sake, Josh, what is all this? If I say anything to Bridget, it's my affair – I don't see that it's anything to do with you – '

'I rather think it is,' he said, and stood still, his hands in his white-coat pockets, his head bent in a watchful way. 'I rather think it is. Will you repeat whatever it was?'

She slid down in her bed a little, and made a *moué*. 'Why should I? Anyway, it was true – ' but she sounded unconvinced.

He looked at her with distaste, his mouth turned down. Then without turning his gaze away from Bobby, he said softly, 'Bridget, will *you* tell me now what Bobby told you last night?'

She gasped a little, looked at him appealingly, and for a fleeting moment, he looked at her, his eyes stern.

There was a long silence, then, almost against her will, Bridget heard her own voice.

'Bobby says the – the baby she got rid of was yours. That you knew. That you knew she was going to get rid of it, and that she did it for your sake.'

The silence this time was electric, and Bridget felt, rather than saw, the muscles of Josh's face go hard as he clenched his teeth. Then, in a voice thin with the control he was putting into it, he said slowly, 'That baby could not have been mine. On your own admission, Bobby, you were three months pregnant. The – the last time I – could have been responsible was well before three months ago. According to your history, and the information you eventually gave the Gynae registrar, that child was conceived at about Christmas-time.'

Bobby said nothing, lying quite still, staring at him with her shadowed eyes, her mouth a thin line.

'And you know as well as I do what happened at Christmas. When Bridget left the house that night, I went shortly afterwards – and very angry indeed you were about it. What happened that night, Bobby? Because it was then, wasn't it?'

Still she said nothing, only lying still and staring at him unwinkingly.

'I know what happened that night, Bobby. You don't need to tell me. Because you forget that David Nestor was not a man to care what he told to who. You know that, don't you? One of the boasters, David?'

Bobby closed her eyes at that, 'No – '

'Yes – yes, Bobby, he told me. With a great deal of relish. As he put it, I'd – "spoiled his weekend" ' – his voice grated in anger – 'so he sorted out things for himself. Didn't he – ? And until you were brought in that night last week and I was sent to see you, I had not the least idea of what had happened – not that you were pregnant, or what you had done about it – '

Bobby pulled herself up then, to lean forwards, her face twisted with rage.

'All right – all right – ' she screamed. 'So what? So bloody what? You walked out and left me high and dry, to run after your sweet little – bitch' – she almost spat the word – 'so what would you expect? And who cares, anyway? What's it to do with you?

Don't tell me I was the first – or that I'm the last either – ' and she looked at Bridget with such loathing and such spite in her eyes, that Bridget shrank back in sick fear.

Josh was breathing hard now, and put a hand out to hold on to Bridget, filling her with strength as he touched her.

'I'm sorry, Bobby,' he said. 'Very sorry. Not just because – of what's happened to you, but because of the sort of person you are. You'll never be happy, will you? Not unless the world always goes your way. And I doubt if it will. It hasn't this time – I had an affair with you, and it ended – a long time ago. And it's no good trying to pick up the pieces, because there aren't any left. I – ' He looked down at Bridget. 'We both wish you well, Bobby, believe it or not. Don't we?' and he looked at Bridget again. But she couldn't move or speak, just standing still and silent beside him.

'I'm sorry,' he said again. 'Sorry to have made you – admit all this to both of us. But I had to. Goodbye, Bobby – ' and with a gentle pressure on Bridget's arm, he opened the door, and led her out, closing it behind him with a sharp click.

Bridget stood in silence beside him for a long moment, ignoring the curious stare of the nurse who rustled past on her way to the sluice at the end. Then she looked up at Josh and said miserably, 'That – that was horrible.'

'We can't talk here,' he said, and moving purposefully led the way back down the corridor towards the main courtyard and the Home garden.

Neither of them said a word as they walked, and the silence persisted even after they were back on the little wooden bench under the tree, back among the spring flowers and the sound of birds twittering desultorily above the distant roar of traffic from the main road far beyond them.

Then Bridget said again, as though there had been no gap at all, 'Horrible – '

'I suppose you're thinking I'm a – pretty dreadful person. To have made Bobby tell you that way?' he said, his voice expressionless.

She remembered the look of anger on Bobby's face, the shrill sound of her voice, and said heavily, 'She's – had enough to cope with. No matter what else she may have done, she's had a lot to cope with. And now – it was like – oh, I don't know. Like standing by and jeering while somebody was whipped – '

'I know, I know,' he said roughly. 'But it was the only way.

She's a devious person, Bridget. Bobby can't tell the truth, even if she tries. She tailors what she says to each occasion and the person she is talking to. And the only way to convince you of what happened was to put her in a situation where she couldn't lie. Which was why I did it.'

Bridget moved fretfully.

'I don't understand – I don't understand,' she said. 'The night she had her operation – you were so – miserable – so distressed. I thought – I thought it was because you loved her. That you – cared. And now this – '

'Of course I was distressed – of course I cared. Damn it, I'm a doctor! Do you think I *liked* what I saw when I examined her that night? Liked to do a hysterectomy on a girl of her age? I'd have to be – a completely callous person not to have cared – and though I may sound a bit callous about her now, I still care about what's happened to her,' he said savagely.

She closed her eyes against the brightness of the sunshine, and said miserably, 'What *will* happen to Bobby, Josh? What will happen to her now?'

'Oh, God, I don't know!' He sounded irritable suddenly. 'Who can say? She's – promiscuous, immoral – who can say what will happen to her?'

'And you don't care.' It wasn't a question. Just a statement.

'I – can't pretend I do, not now, apart from – the medical aspect,' he said with painful honesty. 'For me, as a person, rather than as a doctor, she was – an episode. Just an episode. I'm sorry for her, in a remote sort of way – but that's all.'

She leaned back on the hardness of the wooden bench, and looked down at her hands twisted on her lap.

'And what will I be? Another – episode?'

He twisted in his seat then, to sit close beside her, to hold her chin in his hand again, forcing her to look at him.

'No, my love. You – you're special. Even if you decide right now not to have any more to do with me, if you get up and walk away from me at this moment, you'll always be special to me. Do you believe that? Can you believe that?'

She sat very still, feeling the warmth and strength of his fingers on her face, seeing the truth of what he said in his eyes, in the set of his wide mouth, tracing every line of his face with her own eyes. Then she said tremulously, 'I've got to believe you – I've got to – '

'Got to?' and his voice was infinitely gentle.

'I love you, Josh,' she said simply, and looked at him with a clear look that made him drop his own eyes, made him sit back on the wooden bench almost trembling, his hands lax on his white coated knees.

'Thank you – thank you,' he said at length, and then looked at her, his mouth twisted into a rueful half smile.

'That's a feeble thing to say – ' and he moved closer to her, to put his arm round her, so that they sat side by side in dumb happiness, the soft breeze moving her hair across his face, just sitting in a sort of exhausted peace.

He stirred at length, taking a deep breath.

'It's going to be wonderful, Tiddler. Wonderful,' and his voice had an exultant lilt in it. 'We'll be married – soon – we'll be married – '

'I – give me time, Josh – time – ' She felt a sudden wave of anxiety then. Married? It was what she wanted more than anything in the world, but somehow, it couldn't be thought of. Not yet. Not too soon.

'I know,' he said softly. 'I know. You need time – to be sure – isn't that it?'

She nodded dumbly.

'Sure that I love you?' He sounded oddly mischievous, almost little-boy, and she laughed shakily in spite of herself.

'I think that *is* what I mean – ' She turned and looked up at him. 'I – I think I've loved you for a long time. A very long time – but – '

He smiled at her, all his love in his eyes, spilling over her in a wave of feeling that was almost a concrete thing. 'And I have loved you for a long time. And there's plenty more time. You'll see, my love, Bridget my love. You'll see – ' and at the confidence in his voice, she relaxed, to sit still in the circle of his arm, confident too, knowing that the future was opening before her, wide and full of the promise of all she had ever wanted.

And beyond the quiet garden, the hospital went on its own organised, impersonal way, offering life and death, beginnings and endings, to the people who came to it, the people who worked in it trying in the only way they knew how to comfort the sick, to give the peace and freedom from pain the sick demanded of them.

'Comfort,' Bridget said suddenly. 'I came here looking for comfort – I didn't know, but that was what I wanted – '

'You brought it with you,' he said softly. 'It's a two-way thing. You brought it with you – for me, for the people you looked after, for the people you worked with – '

'I shall go on nursing,' she said, with a sort of discovering in her voice. 'I want to go on – I will, won't I?'

'For a while,' he said. 'For a while. And then – ' He took a deep contented breath. 'No matter. There's all the time in the world to talk about it. All the time in the world – '

The Private Wing

1

The man in bed four rolled over again, and, finding sleep no nearer on his left side than it had been on his right, gave up trying to sink back into the blissful slumber that had been so unpleasantly shattered by the snores coming from the bed opposite. Wadding his pillow beneath his head, he lay staring at the dim ward across the humped shape of his own feet under the red hospital blanket, and wondered. Sneak out of bed quietly for a crafty smoke in the john? Call plaintively to the junior nurse next time she came padding past his bed in the hope she'd take pity on his insomnia and slip him an early cuppa? Or just lie here watching the senior girl write her report?

Certainly she was worth watching, the man in bed four thought approvingly. Sitting cocooned in the light thrown by the discreetly shaded lamp over her desk, she looked good enough to eat. Not a small girl, by any means. Bed Four began to catalogue her interesting points. Must be a good five foot seven, and there's plenty of her to go with it. Long legs, a neat waist, but a most agreeably rounded pair of hips – he remembered how delightful it was to watch those hips swing past his bed when she made her round just after coming on duty – and a definite bust. No, no disappointing twigginess about the senior night nurse. She'd be worth getting hold of, she would, a real armful, Bed Four told himself lasciviously. And nice hair, too. He liked the way it curled round the edge of her cap and on the nape of her long neck, and he'd always had a taste for hair that colour. A brown so deep it looked black except when light hit it, like now. Now it showed definite dark reddish bits – very nice. Funny, thought Bed Four, I've never noticed the colour of her eyes. Really funny, that. Been here a week, and watched her every night, and never noticed.

Almost as though she heard his thoughts, the senior night

nurse looked up from her report writing to sweep a watchful glance along the rows of beds, and Bed Four grinned in the dimness. Of course! How could he think he hadn't noticed? Marmalade eyes, that's what she had. A sort of brownish yellow with specks in. Very tasty altogether.

He slid the pillow more comfortably under his head, and a little drowsily began to construct a conversation in his head. As long as he could get at her without one of the other girls around, it shouldn't be too difficult. When's your day off coming? he'd ask her, and she'd tell him, and then he'd say Well, that's a coincidence, me too, and how about a nice day out – say the races, eh, and a bit of dinner afterwards – and what his wife didn't know wouldn't hurt her and no one'd blame a man fancying so splendid a –

At the desk, Tricia suddenly yawned hugely, and then rubbed her nose hard, to help keep the sleepiness away. Worst time of the night, this was. Half past four, and the sky still black in the tall windows that looked out over the main courtyard, the air chill as it crept in through the open fanlights above them. Another hour, and she'd be busy enough, heaven knew. Seven for the top theatre list to be prepped, a drug list as long as your arm, and a dressing round to get through before breakfasts and blanket bathing and bedmaking. Three hours of hard slog lay ahead, but right now, just dimness, and the breathing of the men lying asleep around her and a subdued rattle of dishes from the ward kitchen where the junior was cutting bread and butter and laying trays for breakfast.

She yawned again, and stood up, and tucking her chilled hands into the bib of her apron began one of her regular prowls from bed to bed. Mr Southcott sleeping well. Good – she'd thought he'd be wakeful, with a major operation to look forward to in the morning. Mr Baskomb and young Jeff, both involved in the same road accident, but both getting on nicely and sleeping rather noisily but deeply. The man in the next bed woke with a start as she passed him, and said in a thick drowsy whisper, 'Hallo, beautiful! Come and talk to me, won't you? Can't sleep a wink, I can't . . . '

'Move over and I'll show you how,' Tricia whispered back tartly, and moved on to the next bed. Unpleasant man, that. He'd been making passes at every nurse in the ward ever since he'd come round from his anaesthetic and they'd all be glad to be rid of him. These gay Lothario types, making such bores of themselves; there was always one in any wardful. That at least would be something she wouldn't miss, if she got theatres.

She checked the rate of the drip on the blood transfusion running into the ankle of the man in bed seven, and then relaxed the clip very slightly; the third pint should be started before 8 a.m. Sister had said, and this one was still barely a third through; and thought again about theatres as she checked the blood pressure and pulse rate.

Theatres. She'd be hard put to it to say why she wanted so much to finish her three years at the Royal as a student nurse working in the operating theatres. It would be hard slog – theatre staff always seemed to work harder than anyone else – and trying to study for Finals in the middle of it all would be no picnic. But she wanted theatres all the same. It wasn't that she didn't like ward nursing. This night duty had been marvellous, for instance. To be senior night nurse on the busiest men's surgical ward in the hospital was great. Lots to do, masses of responsibility (Night Sister was so busy she was only too happy to leave a capable person to get on with the job) and some interesting patients. But there was so much more that was interesting in theatres. Ward nurses – especially on day duty – had to spend too much time on dingy jobs like bedmaking and getting people in and out of bed. But theatre nurses, even when they were only scrubbing instruments after a case, were always doing something really important.

Day duty. It would be funny to get back to sleeping during the night and working during the day, after three months of the other way about. She checked the third drip at bed nineteen, found it running smoothly, and padded past the last eleven patients and back to the desk. All were sleeping well; even poor old Mr Suckling, who was dying and was a great deal too wise a man not to know it, was sleeping shallowly instead of lying staring into the dimness as he usually was at this hour of the morning.

'Thinking of the infinite, I am,' he had told Tricia one morning at this time when she'd murmured a mechanical 'Penny for 'em!' as she'd flipped his pillows to a more comfortable position. That had made her shiver slightly. She never had been and she never would be able to come to terms with death, no matter how often she saw it. That would be something else to be glad of, if she got theatres.

She made a few more notes in the report, and then sat with her elbows on the desk, resting her face against her fists so her cheeks crumpled up like a chipmunk's, and thought more. Day duty. That would mean being able to see a lot more of David. Lovely, said a corner of her mind, obediently. Is it? retorted a more rebellious corner. What's so lovely about being nagged more than ever? But look what he's nagging you *for*! said the obedient corner, rather primly. To marry him! Like, can that be bad? He's gorgeous, you know that. He loves you, the dear Lord only knows why, and as Ngaire keeps pointing out, he's very well off. I mean, who are you to complain at being nagged to marry a man with as much money as he's got? Oh, I don't know, said the rebellious corner. And of course I care for him. I mean, I'm not the sort to marry someone just because of their money. No, no, soothed the obedient bit of her mind, of course not. It's just one of the attractions I was pointing out, that's all, and there's another thing –

'Pss't!'

Tricia jumped, and stared round, peering into the darker corners of the ward, and the surge of fear the sound had raised in her settled into a sharp annoyance as she saw the faint glimmer of a white apron in the doorway of the sluice at the far end of the ward, and she marched swiftly towards it.

'Honestly, Ngaire! Are you out of your tiny excuse for a mind? You'll get shot if Dracula's daughter catches you doing this again. You know what she said last time – '

Ngaire perched herself awkwardly on the edge of the washbasin, and digging into her dress pocket brought out half of a chocolate bar wrapped in crumpled paper.

'Have a bit – ' she said invitingly, and produced one of her wide disarming smiles that crinkled her face so that all her freckles seemed to run together. 'I know – I'm awful, aren't I? But it's so easy, having the fire escape to nip up when I want to see you – I'm sorry, this is a bit soggy, isn't it?'

Tricia wiped her fingers on a paper towel, and said crossly, 'Well, what do you expect? If you keep chocolate in your pocket of course it melts – '

'I used to stick it up my knicker leg when I was at school. It got a lot soggier there,' Ngaire said cheerfully. 'Hey, listen, what do you you think of my hair? We're ever so quiet on women's med, so I nipped into the linen cupboard and had a go with a razor. Good, eh?'

She pulled off her cap, and turned her head to and fro, to show the jagged edges of her black hair. On anyone else it would have looked disastrous, but on her neat round head the hair sat like a sleekly uneven helmet framing a ridiculously pretty face, dark blue eyes, freckles, and the incredibly white teeth that showed when she smiled — which was practically all the time.

'Not bad,' Tricia said judiciously, and then turned to peer round the door into the ward. But the men were all still sleeping, and she came back to Ngaire who was busily licking the last of the chocolate from the silver paper wrappings.

'But couldn't you have waited till breakfast to show me? I mean, it isn't going to grow that much in the next couple of hours.'

'Well, no. I mean, that isn't the only reason I nipped up — '

'I had a feeling it mightn't be.'

'Well, look, you didn't think I'd let it go just like that, did you? He's a lovely guy, and I had to let him know my next off duty, didn't I?'

'Oh, come on, Ngaire — you've done this so often! You see a patient in the ward, you fall hook line and sinker, and then when you go out with 'em after they're discharged, you fall out again as fast as you fell in. Do me a favour — don't make me go through it all again!'

'Oh, I know — it's funny, isn't it?' Ngaire said happily. 'Like I told one of 'em — that Canadian boy you remember? — they look so different with their clothes on — but Jeff's different. I mean, he's a real beaut — Don't you think so?'

'I hadn't specially noticed,' Tricia said tartly. 'I've only nursed him for two of the weeks he's been on the ward, after all. How could I do as well in that time as you did in a mere three nights of relieving me?'

'It's experience that counts,' Ngaire said, quite unabashed. 'So, look, give him this note for me, hey? He wanted to know what my name means, so I've signed it Daughter of the Morning. To tell you the truth I made that up, because I don't know what it means — I never did get all those Maori names sorted out, but it sounds good, doesn't it? And tell him if he dares spell it N-Y-R-E-E when he writes back, I'll never speak to him again. I want it spelled the right New Zealand way. All right?'

'Oh, all *right*! You and your affairs — you fall in and out of love like a yo-yo. It's getting awfully boring. And for God's sake get going. If the old bag comes round and finds your ward with only a junior on it she'll have your guts for garters – and serve you right, too.'

'Right. I'm going.' Ngaire slid to the ground and smoothed her crumpled apron, before heading for the fire escape door.

'By the way, have you got any news on the Change list?'

'How could I have? We won't be told till breakfast,' Tricia said. 'But I'm keeping my fingers crossed like mad.'

'I tried to get a peep when I went to the office to pick up my D.D.A. key, but the old bat came in before I could get the desk drawer open,' Ngaire said cheerfully. 'Told me I'd know soon enough, and to get on with tonight's work, and never mind tomorrow's. I told her I'd cut my throat if I was down to go somewhere like Emergency Services or Theatres, and all she did was say "Wait and See." Like doom. I bet she makes sure I do go somewhere like that, just so as to make me cut my throat. Tell you what – if I do, I'll cut it in front of her, and she'll get smothered in my berlood, and I'll die with a horrible gurgle, right at her feet.' Ngaire crossed her eyes sickeningly, and let her tongue loll out of her mouth, while her head drooped to one side. 'Then she'll be sorry – '

'Oh, go back to your ward, you – you antipodean nut!' Tricia said, and laughed, and Ngaire winked at her, and slid out of the door to rattle her way cheerfully down to the floor below.

And for Tricia, the next three hours or so passed with incredible speed, activity building to a crescendo of rush to have the ward ready for the day staff at eight-thirty. With her junior nurse and the second year girl who shared her time between Ngaire's ward and Tricia's, she dressed the previous day's operation wounds, organised the operation preparations for the seven men to have surgery that day, dished out medicines, gave injections, served breakfasts, her sleek black legs almost twinkling under the blue and white of her uniform, as she bustled from bed to bed, kitchen to sterilising room, sluice to ward office.

And all the while, as she exchanged the usual badinage with the livelier of the patients, and sent her junior scurrying about her jobs, she found herself thinking, 'Last time – my last night duty as a student nurse. With a bit of luck, maybe my last time as a student ward nurse – if I get theatres. Maybe I'll stay on theatres as a staff nurse, too, after Finals. That'd be great. Maybe even manage Theatre Sister before too long – '

But that thought she pushed away, almost as briskly as she snapped her wrist as she shook down thermometers before tucking them under the tongues of the patients who sat like obedient baby birds, mouths open, waiting for them. Because that was really the whole problem, as far as David was concerned. And that had to be faced pretty soon. She couldn't keep him quiet much longer.

And when she went off duty, her junior trotting behind her, to say a polite Good-bye to Night Sister (an absurd tradition for people going off night duty, since everyone saw night sister every day anyway at breakfast time, but one that was jealously upheld) she had the rare pleasure of being told, 'I'll miss you, Nurse Oxford. You have proved an extremely efficient and capable person to be in charge of a ward at night. A great improvement on the way you were during your first night duty!'

Remembering one or two of the things that had happened then, Tricia blushed.

'Yes, indeed, you've coped well. I hope you do as well in your next assignment, whatever that is.'

'Which only goes to show what a hypocritical old Dracula's Daughter she is,' Tricia said to Ngaire as they followed each other in the queue that shuffled along the servery counter in the dining room, loading plates with scrambled eggs and toast. 'Seeing she knows perfectly well where we're all going. I wish the Royal'd come up to date and post Change lists in advance the way they do in some of the other hospitals.'

'That'll be the day, me old mate, I tell you. This place is as about as up to date as gaslighting when it comes to things like that. I mean, great on the old medical and surgical sides, but when it comes to really modern ideas like good staff relationships and that – ' Ngaire sounded very disgruntled.

'Well, you asked for it,' Barbara Lloyd said from her place in front of Ngaire. 'Honestly, Trish, would you believe it? This screwy friend of yours only took herself up to the medical staff quarters on her way up to breakfast, and when the old bat saw her and did her nut, Madam Ngaire's only answer was to open her eyes wide and say "she only wanted to see a friend of hers". I ask you!'

'Ngaire, you didn't!'

'Well, look, why not? I wanted to tell Skip Peters I was coming off nights, and he could reach me at the Nurses' Home if he wanted to, and – '

Tricia, following Ngaire to the table under the window in the corner, said in an exasperated voice, 'But my dear girl, what about young what's-his-name – Jeff? That boy on Men's Surg. Three. I thought you were going great guns with him?'

'Well, so I am, but what's that got to do with anything? I mean, Skip's a real dishy guy, you know? And he drives a great car, one of those things that goes vroom-vroom all over the place, and so I just thought – '

'She just thought she'd pop up and see him,' finished Barbara. 'How you ever managed to get as far as the end of your third year without someone getting desperate enough to dig a hole deep enough to drop you back home again, I'll never know. Trish, you remember that time she climbed in one of the Private Wing windows? and nearly under Matron's nose?'

'Well, for God's sake!' Ngaire protested, her mouth full. 'I had to, didn't I? I mean, how else was I to get to know him? All that week he'd been making signals at me across the courtyard – it wasn't my fault I was on Radiotherapy and the kitchen window looked straight across at his – '

'I'm not so sure,' Jennifer Cooper leaned across from the other side of the table. 'I was on Radiotherapy with you, remember? And no gorgeous private patients never made any signals at *me* through the kitchen window.'

'They feed 'em something special in New Zealand,' someone said from the end of the table. 'Brings 'em on faster than your common or garden English rose – '

'Seeing you're Irish, Mary Margaret, how do you know?' Ngaire said equably. 'Anyway, you're right of course. They do feed us better at home. Tamarillos and feijoas and – '

'And passion fruit,' said Tricia succinctly, and they all laughed with the somewhat exaggerated hilarity that goes with fatigue while Ngaire, unperturbed, buttered her fourth slice of toast, and smiled happily at them all.

'Just jealous, that's what you lot are,' she said, her mouth full. 'Me, I'm happy as a box of birds. All I ask is that they've put me somewhere nice to work this next three months. Not much to want, is it?'

'Nice meaning not too much work, or nice meaning lots of interesting men for you to add to your collection?' Barbara Lloyd asked.

'Why, both of course!' Ngaire said, opening her eyes very wide.

And then the big dining room stilled as Night Sister came in, clutching a clipboard, and the ninety night nurses put down their cups and rose to their feet with a crisp flutter of starched aprons.

'Good morning, Nurses,' she said, her voice sounding almost as starched as the aprons.

And 'Good morning' they chorused back 'for all the world like great babies in Sunday School' whispered Ngaire in Tricia's ear, and turned a limpid gaze on Night Sister's frown in her direction.

'Change list, Nurses.' Night Sister said. 'Ten senior night nurses, ten intermediate, ten juniors are to change to day duty as from 4.30 p.m. this afternoon. Listen carefully, as I do not intend to read any name more than once.'

The ritual began. Tricia found herself sitting with her fingers crossed under the table, and then, annoyed with herself, consciously relaxed. It was ridiculous to care so much about where she was to be posted. Damn it, it was all part of the job, wasn't it? Wherever they sent her, she'd still be nursing at the Royal, wouldn't she? But how much better it would be to be working somewhere she really wanted to be. It did matter, like mad, and she couldn't deny it. And not least because it would be much – well, not easier, but say less difficult – to stick to her guns as far as David was concerned if she was posted somewhere she knew she'd enjoy, where she'd be able to do a really good job.

'Nurse Lloyd, Children's Medical,' Night Sister intoned. Across the table, Barbara grinned hugely, and joined her fists in a successful boxer's salute; she loved children's nursing so much that she intended to go on to get her paediatric certificate as soon as she had finished her general training, and clearly Matron had remembered this and allocated her accordingly. Tricia smiled back at Barbara in congratulation. Maybe this augured well for herself, she thought hopefully.

'Nurse Mullins, Out-Patient Department, Nurse Nanson, Gynaecology One, Nurse Noone, Fracture Clinic, Nurse Oxford, Private Patients' Wing, Third Floor, Nurse Rawlings, Male Surgical Three, Nurse Taylor, General Theatres, Nurse Throgmorton, Emergency Services – '

And as the list droned to its end, and Night Sister left her staff to finish their breakfasts in a clatter of cups and a roar of chatter, Tricia and Ngaire sat and stared at each other miserably.

2

'But my God! Theatres! Me!' Ngaire wailed. 'They must be clean round the twist! I mean, can't you just see it? I'll fall over everything, I'll drop all the instruments, I'll give the surgeons the screaming abdabs, and – '

'Oh, give it a rest, Ngaire!' Mary-Margaret Noone said from the deep armchair near the fireplace where a cheerful early morning blaze crackled and spat, for it was still cold enough for fires even at the end of April. 'You've been grizzling ever since breakfast. And what have you got to moan about anyway? Theatres are fun! Not like rotten old Fracture Clinic where they've stuck me. I'll spend the next three months up to my behind in plaster of paris, and I'll develop muscles like a boxer and hands like – like old kippers!'

'It's all *wrong*!' Tricia said furiously, and got out of her chair to begin to prowl about the sitting room, from bookcase to fireplace and back again. 'I mean, for God's sake, why can't we have some sort of say in where we work? We're senior students, aren't we? Here's Ngaire terrified out of her socks because she's got to go to Theatres, and me, I'd give my eye teeth for it. Why can't we just change places? Ngaire'd adore being on the Private Wing, but me – it makes me sick to just think about it! Damn it all, I didn't go into nursing to act like a glorified chambermaid or a nanny or something to a bunch of spoiled stupid idiots with more money than sense who aren't proper patients at all, but just fancy a week off in bed in a fancy expensive private hotel – '

'They aren't all like that,' Mary-Margaret said mildly. 'I did Private Wing last year, and some of them were – '

'Oh, I know, they get the occasional patient that really is ill, I suppose, but most of them – you've only got to look at them strolling around the corridors in their mink and maribou negligees to know that they're – '

'Mink and maribou? Oooh gorgeous,' Ngaire said. 'And just think about the fabulous men you'd meet! I mean, I can just see it – there's this smashing disc jockey, flat on his back, in agony and helpless – '

'Sounds like a classic case of slipped disc to me,' Barbara Lloyd murmured sleepily from the other side of the fireplace.

'Yeah – why not?' Ngaire said agreeably. 'Anyway there he lies, a complete pushover for a girl with reasonable legs in sheer black stockings – '

'With or without runs and holes?' Barbara asked sweetly, staring pointedly at Ngaire's legs, but Ngaire was too well established on her daydream to hear her.

'He'd lie there, and he'd have all these fabulous visitors, and I'd nip in and out with champagne glasses and flowers, and – ooh, it'd be *gorgeous*! Why can't we change, Trish? I mean, no one would notice, would they, as long as someone turned up in each department? We could pretend we made a mistake, and by the time they found out, hell, it'd be too late to change things again, so we'd all be happy – '

'Oh grow up, Ngaire,' Molly Throgmorton said crushingly. 'Even you can't be so daft as to think you'd get away with that!'

'No – I suppose not,' Ngaire said. 'But it's a great idea, all the same, isn't it? Never mind, Trish. You can have the Wing. Only do me a favour. Remember your old friend. I mean, I'll bet those private patients are all so stinking rich they give their nurses fabulous presents when they leave after a week of brow-soothing, and although I wouldn't say I was exactly mercenary, I have to tell the truth and say I'm usually pretty broke, which reminds me – can anyone stake me to – '

'No!' Several people said very firmly and at the same time.

'And if you think I'm going to let any of those rotten lazy stupid idiots hand out their condescending tips to *me*, as though I really were a chambermaid, you've got another think coming!' Tricia said furiously.

'Not that it's likely to be offered if you go on like that, Trish,' Mary-Margaret said. 'I mean, why get so mad about it? It won't be that bad, surely? I know it's not like Theatres one bit, and that you'd enjoy that more, but it'll still be interesting and anyway, nursing means a bit of everything doesn't it? Including private patients.'

'I know what's the matter, Trish,' Ngaire said shrewdly.

'You'll be the lowest of the low up there, won't you? A bit of a comedown after being in charge of Men's Surg. Three for your last night duty. All those staff nurses on the Wing – why, it'll be like being a junior pro all over again – bedpans and all – '

Tricia scowled, and opened her mouth to argue, and then closed it again and stood up, shrugging her cape around her shoulders. 'Oh, the hell with it. I'm going to bed. Anyone coming?'

One or two people yawned, and then one by one, they stood up. Collecting their capes and night bags they straggled out of the big sitting room where the night staff always congregated for an hour or so after breakfast, and followed Tricia up the stairs to their respective bedrooms.

And as she bathed, and cleaned her teeth, and prepared a fresh uniform for the afternoon, and for a while after she climbed into bed, Tricia went on turning her disappointment and anger around in her head. Private Wing! It's downright degrading, she told herself. That was why she was so upset. It wasn't – was it? – that she would again be a junior instead of enjoying the responsibility and status of the senior student. But really, she was too honest to be able to keep up that pretence for long. Of course Ngaire had been very perceptive (and she often was a good deal more aware of realities than her flibberty exterior manner suggested) in pinpointing the real cause of Tricia's irritation. It would indeed be miserable to be back where she had been almost three years before, at the start of her training.

Inevitably, she slept badly, waking at every sound; a thoughtless junior clattering up the stairs at lunchtime on her way off duty, the buzz of vacuum cleaners as the domestic staff made their desultory way around the big building that was the Nurse's Home, the distant shrill insistence of the telephone. At four o'clock as she dressed and pinned on her cap, and filled her pockets with scissors and pens and notebook, not even the bright afternoon sunshine pouring into her room cheered her. She ate very little at teatime, settling for a cup of tea and one of the rare cigarettes she allowed herself, and listening glumly to the chatter of the others around her. And seeing Ngaire in the short white socks, white plimsolls and close fitting white cap that marked out the theatre staff didn't help at all.

By the time she walked across the courtyard to the red brick building that carried over the main door a plaque that read 'St

Cuthbert's Wing for Private Patients Endowed by Sir Samuel Costerd 1931' (and irreverently labelled 'St Custard's' by most of the medical students), she was in a thoroughly unpleasant mood. Her eyes felt sandy and hot – legacy of inadequate sleep after a hard night's work – and the irritation in her was barely contained.

So it wasn't much help to be stopped at the lift gates in the flower-bedecked entrance hall by the bustling and officious hall porter who sat in his small cubbyhole of a lodge in the corner.

"Ere, nurse – where you goin'?'

'Up to the third floor,' Tricia snapped irritably. 'Why? What does it matter to you?'

'A lot, *Nurse* whateveryournameis. On account of I'm the 'all porter 'ere, and it's my instructions to stop the lift being used by the nursing staff and the junior medical staff, on account of the fact that this lift is used for patients and their visitors all the time, and staff – except for the senior medical – 'as to use the stairs. Matron said, so there it is. I've got to report anyone as doesn't do as I say about that there lift – '

'Oh, go to hell – ' Tricia muttered under her breath, and leaving him still talking ran up the stairs. And as she passed the first and second floors, her nose wrinkled in disgust at the composite smell of expensive perfume and cigar smoke and flowers mixed up with the more familir hospital odours of antiseptics and soap, floor polish and food. She'd complained sometimes about the smelliness of Men's Surg. Three, especially after one of the patients had smoked a home-made cigarette or one of those bubbly old pipes so beloved by elderly men, but this was worse somehow – it reeked of money, and Tricia was in no mood to find that in the least tolerable.

The third floor was quiet when she arrived and stopped just inside the double doors, leaving them swinging behind her. On each side stretched the long polish-gleaming corridor, lined with heavy wooden doors each embellished with a glassed central square, and with vases of elegantly arranged flowers set in the occasional niches between them.

Outside one of the doors a red light glowed, while a white one winked steadily outside another. She could her the muffled sound of a radio coming from somewhere, and then a telephone began to ring in the office which faced the main entrance to the floor, and she started forwards and then hesitated. Should she answer it? Not much point, really, seeing she knew nothing about the work of the floor as yet, and had no idea where she'd find someone who did. The phone rang on insistently, and again she stepped forward and again hesitated.

Then, sharply, the door outside which the red light was burning opened, and a tall woman in Sister's uniform swept out and hurried along the corridor towards the office. She threw a sharp glance at Tricia as she went past, and said irritably, 'Nurse Oxford, I suppose? And how long must a telephone ring before you decide to do something about it?' and not waiting for an answer swept into the office and picked up the phone.

Tricia, furious, set her jaws. Stupid old bag, she thought angrily. You'd think her own commonsense'd tell her why I didn't answer it – I'll soon tell her –

With a clatter the phone was recradled, and then Sister came out of the office and stopped in front of her.

'Well, Nurse Oxford? I am Sister Cleland to whom you should have reported on duty – ' she looked at her watch 'five minutes ago.'

'I was here five minutes ago, but I didn't know where anyone was to report *to*!' Tricia said sulkily. 'And about that phone – '

'No excuses, Nurse! I have no time to waste on them. Just remember, on this floor we believe the old proverb – "qui s'excuse, s'accuse". Now, put your cloak in the nurses' changing room, down there, put a pleasanter expression on your face, and then come back to me here and I will deal with your duties for the rest of the day. Hurry along now!' and she turned and went swiftly back to the room with the red light, leaving Tricia fuming.

This was really going to be choice! Bad enough to be lumbered with the Private Wing without having to put up with such an old battleaxe of a floor sister into the bargain. As she put her cape on a hook in the changing room, and tweaked her cap straight, Tricia was very close indeed to tears.

And the next half hour was a pretty miserable one, too. In her office Sister Cleland briskly reeled out a mass of information that Tricia could only just listen to, let alone absorb; patients' names and diagnoses; the location of such important places as the sluice, the linen cupboard, the sterilising room, the drug cupboard; times of patients' meals, visiting arrangements, rules about flowers, about talking to visitors, about reporting on and off duty. And at the very end:

'There is one other very important rule on this floor, Nurse, that I want you to understand clearly. On occasion some patients take it into their heads to give the nurses gifts – and while I cannot really object to the occasional chocolate, I object very strenuously to anything more. Any nurse that accepts a gift in money or kind on this floor will – '

'I wouldn't dream of doing such a thing!' Tricia interrupted, outraged. 'It's bad enough being stuck with private patients without being accused of – '

'Oh?' Sister Cleland raised her elegant black eyebrows at that. 'So nursing private patients is not to your taste, is it? How unfortunate! And you are too lofty a personality altogether to consider accepting gifts? How remarkable! Well, let us see just how both these statements stand up to the test of the next three months. I have no further time to waste on you now, so go along to the linen cupboard and help sort out the fresh linen delivery. Hurry along now! I have some important *nursing* work to do, whatever you may think goes on in a private patient's wing!' And she swept Tricia to one side and went swiftly along the corridor to disappear into the room outside which a white light blinked.

Seething with temper, Tricia marched along the corridor to the linen cupboard, which was actually big enough to have been dignified with the label of room. Certainly it held not only shelves full of linen, when Tricia pushed the door open, but three other nurses besides, and crowded though it was there was still room for Tricia to join them. And she, a third year student, sent to sort linen like any junior pro, she thought angrily. It was outrageous.

'Hullo! You our new student nurse? I only hope you're a bit quicker off the mark than the one who's just gone!'

Tricia looked with distaste at the very pretty plump little blonde who was perched on one of the shelves, her legs swinging, and her cap on her lap as she teased and tweaked her hair to a more becoming arrangement.

'I'm not anybody's property, as far as I know. I'm a Royal student nurse, but that doesn't mean I belong to you or anyone else on this floor. And as for the student nurse who was here before me – if you've any complaints go and make them to madam Cleland. I've no doubt she'll be only too happy to listen to you – '

A small girl, in an all white uniform, busily folding sheets on the far shelf, laughed softly. 'Oh, boy! Has she started on you already? Poor old you! She always has to have someone to have a go at. Never mind, me love. It's not as bad here as you'll be thinking it is. Take no notice of old Jensen there. She's as much sense as a fly, the silly ijjut – but what can you expect from one that trained in the wilds of – where was it, Jensen? Birmingham, did you say? Or some such place – '

'Better than being chucked up out of a bog in the much wilder wilds of Connemara or wherever it is you slept your training years away,' Jensen said without rancour, and pinned on her cap, peering into the tiny mirror that hung crookedly on the back of the door. 'Anyway, Miss Royal Student, don't get so uppity. We're all in the same boat, really – stuck with a stinker like Cleland, is it any wonder we have to insult each other to get rid of our spleen? Listen, Gallon, it's as near five thirty as makes no matter, and I for one am not about to hang around this haven of hygiene one minute longer than I have to. Not unless they dish out some overtime pay, and since they won't do that, I'm off. Coming?'

The other nurse, a rather sleepy looking redhead, moved forwards from the narrow wall against which she had been leaning at the far end.

'Are you kidding? If I don't get to bed soon, I'll die. It was a hell of a night last night, and no way to prepare for a day with Cleland. Aren't you coming, Bridie?'

'There's the linen to finish yet – '

'Ah, let little thingy here do it. You're supposed to be off at five thirty, too.'

'Well, I'll hang around a bit. Just to show her the ropes. What's your name, me love?'

'Oxford,' Tricia said sulkily.

'Well, Nurse Oxford, I'm Cavanaugh. Now let's see how fast we can get through this little lot – you go on, you two. I'll see you in the changing room, maybe – '

The other two went, leaving the door swinging wide behind them.

'Are all the staff here like that?' Tricia asked, as the other girl handed her the ends of a sheet.

'Like what?' Together they expertly flipped the sheet into a neat parcel, and started on the next.

'Well – I don't know – clock-watchers. So – so – *offhand*. I suppose I was a bit snappy to that one – who is it – Jensen – when

I came in, but damn it, that Sister Cleland is enough to make anyone ratty. But apart from that, she doesn't seem at all like the people I'm used to working with. I mean, going off and leaving something unfinished just because the time says off duty – that's – '

Cavanaugh laughed, and began to separate pillow slips and dressing towels into neat heaps. 'Ah, listen to the starry eyed little darlin'! Look, we're all like that when we're students. And that's as it should be. All eager and interested – but not everyone stays that way, d'you see. Ingrid Jensen, now – she's a midwife, you know? That's her thing, and I've no doubt when she gets back to her mums and babes she'll be as eager as the next one. But right now – well, she's after earning some cash, you see. On account of she's away to the States as soon as she's raised enough money. She's an agency nurse – she and Prue Gallon too.'

'Agency nurse?'

'Ah, it's a whole new thing that's crept in in the past few years. There are these agencies, d'you see, who find staff for hospitals that can't get 'em. And they pay a girl a deal more than she'll get in a staff job – so, the hospitals have to pay the agency to get the staff, and the girls can work as much – or as little – as they please. Take Gallon, now. She's getting married in a few months, and her man's away in Germany – Army, he is – so she's working her fool head off to raise money for their weddin'. That's why she's so tired all the time.'

They finished the pillow slips and dressing towels and started on the operation gowns and pyjamas.

'How do you mean? She didn't seem to me to be exactly working her fool head off just now,' Tricia said waspishly.

Cavanaugh smiled. 'Maybe she did not – but she's doing nights with a dotty old lady over in Knightsbridge somewhere – and don't you be tellin' anyone that, or there'll be all hell let loose.'

Tricia stared. 'Do you mean she's doing days *and* nights?' she almost squeaked it. 'She can't be!'

'Indeed she is – here, sort out these theatre socks, will you? – and making a small bomb out of it. Well, I don't blame her. 'Tisn't every day a girl has a weddin' to save for – '

'Well, if that doesn't prove it!' Tricia exploded. 'I knew that was how it would be – just chambermaids, that's all – '

Cavanaugh looked up from the laundry list she was checking 'What are you talking about? Proves what? Who's a chambermaid?'

'Well, for God's sake – just what *is* private nursing? Nothing, that's what! If someone can do day *and* night duty she can't be doing any real nursing, can she? I've just finished nights on a male surgical ward, and take it from me no one could work there *and* do a day job. Those were *real* patients. People worth looking after! Not like these so-called patients over here, just sitting around feeling sorry for themselves and not a blasted thing wrong with 'em! It may suit people like Jensen and Gallon to run after such spoiled stupid objects but it doesn't suit *me* – '

'Well, thank you, me old darlin',' Cavanaugh said softly. 'Seeing' as I'm working here too, I take it I'm cut out of the same piece of cloth?'

'Oh – hell, I'm sorry. I mean, I didn't mean to be rude to *you*. I suppose you've your reasons for being here, just as they have – but it's the *patients* I'm objecting to – or non-patients'd be better. Damn it all, I'm in training! I'm supposed to be learning and a damned lot of learning I'm likely to do on this excuse for a – '

'Well, well, well! What a knowledgeable young lady, to be sure,' Tricia jumped and whirled and her face flooded a deep crimson as she met the steady gaze of the man leaning against the open door of the linen cupboard. About as tall as Tricia herself, but stocky and square so that he looked rather shorter, and with sleek fair hair, marked with lighter streaks, combed back from his forehead to finish fairly long on the back of his neck; heavy dark rimmed glasses behind which startlingly deep brown eyes gleamed, his hands thrust into the pockets of a crisp white coat.

'Very knowledgeable indeed,' he said, and his voice had a cold mocking note that made Tricia's face go redder still, if that were possible. 'Do tell me what else you know about our patients. I have not the least doubt that it would be of inestimable value to me.'

'Ah, don't be like that, Dr Kidd,' Cavanaugh said cheerfully. 'The girl didn't mean any harm – '

'I'm sure she didn't!' Dr Kidd said. 'I could tell how sincere she was in her opinions from half way down the corridor. It's my guess everyone within shouting distance did. I'm not complaining about her comments. Far from it! I'm just interested to know on what observations she bases her judgement of the private patients you and I and a few other people here spend – I'm so sorry – waste our time with. Do tell me!'

'I – er – I – ' Tricia muttered, and then stopped, looking

appealingly at Cavanaugh, who was clipping the completed laundry list to a board hanging from the far shelf.

'She's hardly had time to find out yet, and that's the truth,' Cavanaugh said. 'Poor girl's just come off nights, d'you see, and – '

'Ah! I thought I hadn't seen her around before,' Dr Kidd said smoothly. 'Clearly, a remarkably percipient nurse, eh, Cavanaugh? To have so much knowledge so soon?'

'Oh hello, Adam! – er Dr Kidd!'

Behind him, Sister Cleland had appeared. 'Were you looking for me? Sorry. I was with Mrs Kester. I'm a bit concerned about her drip – '

'Good afternoon, Sister,' Dr Kid turned. 'I'll have a look at her, then. I was about to do the round – but I'll tell you what. I won't bother you. I'll take this young lady – Nurse – er – ' He turned back to Tricia, his eyebrows raised enquiringly.

'Oxford,' Tricia muttered.

'Nurse Oxford. Yes.' He smiled at Sister Cleland. 'I have a feeling she could do with a little more information about the patients we have in at present. And I'm always delighted to take my share of *teaching* – ' he threw a swift glance at Tricia again, ' – since it is so important a part of what I'm here for.'

Sister Cleland looked sharply from Tricia's intensely embarrassed face to Dr Kidd, and her mouth thinned.

'Well, of course, that is up to you, Dr Kidd – if you want to. Although if you don't mind I'd like to give you some report results first. They're in the office.' She turned sharply and walked away down the corridor, and Dr Kidd moved after her.

'Don't go away, Nurse Oxford. I'll be ready to start my round very soon,' he said crisply, and went, leaving the two nurses standing silently in the linen cupboard.

'Oh, boy, young Oxford, now you've been and gone and done it!' Cavanaugh said softly. 'You young ijjut! Now you'll really have her gunning for you! She's got more than a passing fancy for him, d'you know that? She'll be fit to be tied! The only time I've ever seen her look half human is when she's got her precious Adam to talk to!'

'I couldn't help it!' Tricia whispered back. 'How was I to know there was anyone listening to me? And anyway, I'm entitled to an opinion, aren't I? We're taught to use our own ideas at the Royal.'

'Oh, sure, me love! But you weren't usin' ideas, were you? You were just soundin' off a lot of nonsense. And now you've copped it. Ah, well, she can't eat you!' Cavanaugh grinned, and then patted Tricia's shoulder. 'At least, not all at once! I'll be away to my off duty. This'll be no place to be the next few hours. All the best! Let me know in the morning how things went.'

And she went away leaving Tricia feeling a good deal more apprehensive than she would have thought possible. And when Dr Kidd came back, pushing a small trolley on which case notes were piled, and said curtly, 'Well, come along, Nurse Oxford! Let's go and look at these non-patients,' she followed him along the corridor towards the far end with her knees shaking with nervousness. And catching sight of Sister Cleland's malevolent gaze as she passed her office didn't help her to feel any better.

3

'Oh, Ngaire, it was *hell*!' Tricia said piteously. 'I never want to face another day like it. What am I going to do?'

Ngaire sat curled up in the armchair by the window, her hands wrapped round a steaming mug of coffee, and she looked sympathetically across at Tricia, sitting woebegone and half dressed on her bed, and said as cheerfully as she could. 'Finish getting changed, for a start. David'll be down in Reception waiting for you in a bare ten minutes. And first things first – '

Obediently, Tricia finished smoothing her knee high white socks over her calves, and began to climb into her yellow trouser suit.

' – and then dig out your sense of humour, Trish! So you put both your feet right in it! I've done that a million times, at least, but it's always come out right in the end. Mind you, I'm expected to behave like a nut, so no one's ever surprised. But you – hell, you're the one who always gets *me* out of trouble! When my Ma writes from home she always asks after "that nice sensible friend of yours". And now I'm the one who's supposed to give you advice – it's funny, hmm?'

She drank some coffee and then said reflectively, 'Anyway, what's the flap? You've had trouble with Sisters before. Who hasn't? Remember old Screwball on Children's Med? Now, there was a miserable place to be! She ran you ragged – you and everyone else. And from all accounts, Cleland's another of the type. You just sit it out – she'll come round. Even Screwball did by the time you left her – '

Tricia, brushing her hair at her dressing table, dropped the brush and swung round to sit with her elbows on her knees. 'Oh,

I know! It's not her so much – it's this foul man Kidd. If you'd heard him! As snide and as sarcastic and – and – *beastly* as he could be. He made me feel three inches high and covered in something nasty, honestly he did. And he's there most of the time, as far as I can tell. He's the Registrar to the Wing and – '

'So, that's why I've never come across him before!' Ngaire said, 'And here's me, supposed to know every interesting and eligible man in the place. But if he never comes over to the General side, I suppose – '

'Interesting! My God, Ny, not even *you* could see anything to fancy in that one. He's the most disagreeable, ugly, nasty, foul piece of – '

Ngaire raised her eyebrows. 'Hey, easy does it! The lady doth protest too much and all that. If it weren't that you were supposed to be engaged to David, I'd say you found the Kidd more than a little fanciable yourself – '

'Me? I'd have to be pretty desperate to fancy anything as hateful as he is! There's more to a man than – than just being a man, as I've told you more often than I can count.' Tricia returned to the mirror and began to brush savagely at her hair again. 'And what do you mean – *supposed* to be engaged to David? I am! Well, almost. It's just a matter of settling – things.'

She stopped brushing for a moment and frowned at her reflection in the mirror. 'Anyway, that's neither here nor there. What I want to know is whether I can persuade Matron to shift me somewhere else. But what's the use? If I go complaining to the old girl, she'll want to know the whys and wherefores, and if it comes out I behaved so – well I can't deny it, I was damned stupid – not that I was all that wrong, mind you.'

Again she turned and looked at Ngaire. 'Honestly, Ny, they *are* a pretty dismal bunch of patients, really they are. I was a bit over the top, I admit. There's a Mrs Kester with secondary growths of her spine who's as pitiful a woman as you'll ever see. And only forty or so. Poor creature – she had a lump in her breast, apparently, and was too scared to see a doctor about it. Till it was too late. And a couple of appendix people, and a boy with asthma who seemed pretty ill – but some of them!'

She warmed to her theme. 'There's a ghastly great fat man, something in the fashion business I gather, who's sitting there being dieted. I ask you! All that's wrong with him is sheer greed, and he has to come into a private room and be supervised like a baby to try to get some of the blubber off him – '

'Oh, I don't know,' Ngaire murmured. 'Obesity's a pretty dangerous disease, you know that, and maybe he's got a psychological problem or something – '

'Ah, not this one,' Tricia snorted with disgust. 'He's just a self indulgent slob! I had to take him his supper, after the round was finished, and he made me sick! Tried to make a pass at me for a start, and then tried to persuade me to "slip him some toast or something". Just a slob, that's him. And then there's a girl who's so sorry for herself she never stops ringing her bell and moaning – and do you know why she's there? She had her nose altered! Her nose altered! These plastic surgery patients – do you expect me to take *them* seriously? And debby girls in for abortion – we've got one of those. There's another right cracker – a woman who had her varicose veins stripped, and she should have gone home a week ago. And do you know why she's still sitting there, all wrapped up in fancy bedjackets, and her room so full of flowers it looks like Kew Gardens? Because her housekeeper's on holiday and she can't possibly, my dear, go home with no one to look after her, and she doesn't really want a private nurse she doesn't know, because there's nothing like staff that really knows one, is there, and anyway she has to wear pressure bandages for a long time, and my dear, they're *so* hideous, she'd rather stay safely tucked up here where no one can see her than venture out – yuk! You should have heard her!'

'Ooh, slow down! You'll explode in a minute!' Ngaire said mildly. 'What's to get so agitated about? I daresay there's more to it than you think, with these people. Come on, Trish, don't be so po-faced! You get people like that on the general wards, too! they can't all be at death's door. I'm glad of it, myself. It's pretty depressing when you get a wardful of really desperately ill types – the occasional nothing-much one makes a great change. I'd rather be where you are, whatever the patients are like, than where I am. I spent the afternoon sluicing swabs and scrubbing instruments. Honestly, I've worn out at least three layers of epidermis – ' she held out her hands pathetically '– and according to the other people there, that's about all I *will* be doing for a month. You know Baumfield? That second year girl with the big feet? She's been on Theatres two months now, and if you'd heard the relish with which she told me that seniority on the theatres goes by how long people have been working there, and not how senior they are in training! So while I'm scrubbing she's bustling about, all hoity-toity, running for the second theatre on an emergency ectopic. Believe me, Trish you'd have hated it – '

'No, I wouldn't. Nothing could be worse than – come in!'

The face that appeared round the door belonged to a junior who looked as shy and tentative as her knock on the door had sounded.

'Please, Nurse Oxford, there's a man asking for you, down in Reception – he says please to tell you he's double-parked and can you hurry up – '

'Oh, lawks!' Ngaire scrambled to her feet. 'Is there another chap down there – long hair, tall – looking fed up?'

The little junior giggled and said breathlessly, 'Ooh, Nurse Taylor, there's ever such a funny looking boy – he's got hair right down to his shoulders, and he's wearing a sort of nightgown thing with every colour you can think of painted all over it, and his trousers are sort of leathery and only reach to his knees but with fringes right down to his feet, and he's got no shoes on and his feet are ever so dirty, and he's fast asleep and Home Sister says if no one's claimed him and he isn't gone out of there in fifteen minutes, she'd better call the police to get rid of him. She's seen some funny specimens in her time she says but this one takes the biscuit – '

'I didn't think he'd look quite as way out as that,' Ngaire said dubiously. 'I knew he was an art student, when I said I'd go out with him, but he had ordinary enough pyjamas on – I suppose it's my date?'

'He's hardly anyone else's,' Tricia said, smiling for the first time since she'd gone on duty that afternoon. 'Look, I'll tell him you're coming and soothe Home Sister – and I'll see you at breakfast.'

David was leaning against the Reception desk and staring with a look of profound distaste at the sprawling sleeper in the best armchair. She stood at the top of the stairs for a moment, looking at him. Really, he is so incredibly *right*, she thought. His hair, not straight, but not too curly, a discreet and agreeable brown, neither so short as to look dreary nor so long as to seem way out –rather like horrible Kidd's, came the inconsequential thought, which she pushed firmly away – a comfortable six feet, slim but not scrawny, well dressed but not too slick. Altogether, the sort of man any girl ought to be thrilled to bits to have. And I am. Of course I am.

He looked up then and saw her, and a slow smile spread over his face, and he lifted his chin towards the sleeper and raised his eyebrows, asking her to join in his scorn of so absurd a character. And she smiled back, but went over to the armchair and gently shook the young man's shoulder.

'Chuck? Hello. Ngaire asked me to tell you she'll be right down. And – er – look, I'd suggest you wait out in the garden there. Home Sister – she's a bit of a nagger, you know?'

The young man shook his head in a dazed way, and then woke up properly and grinned at her. 'Hello there yourself. You must be Trish – Ny told me about you. Said you were a real dolly – and she's right, from where I'm sitting. Outside, you say? Oh well, I'm getting used to it. She doesn't like my gear, this Home Sister of yours? Boy, oh boy, these old birds – they do jump around their conclusions, don't they? I'm so square it isn't true – working like a lunatic and all that, but I like to dress gear. Still, I'll get out of the way.' He stood up and stretched. 'Come with? We're going to a great gig – and there's plenty of room for one swinging dolly more – '

'Hello, darling.' David's hand was firm on her arm. 'Ready? I'm double-parked – '

'Hello, David. This is Chuck – a friend of Ngaire's. Chuck, this is David Talbot – '

'Hi. Great to be you – your's must be the E-type I saw – the yellow one? And a real dolly to go with it. Great,' Chuck said, and David nodded back rather icily and said, 'Er – yes – Nice to meet you. Ready darling?' and firmly manoeuvred Tricia away and out of the door. She looked back apologetically at Chuck who waved a hand, and then spread both wide in a gesture of amused and understanding defeat.

'You didn't have to be quite so snappy with him,' she said, as they went towards the courtyard and the main gates. 'I suppose he did look a bit scruffy, but so many people do now, and anyway – '

'Not my sort of people,' David said firmly, and then gave her arm an affectionate squeeze. 'How are you, darling? You look a shade peaky – too much night duty, that's what it is – '

'Well, thank you very much, Mr Talbot,' Tricia said frostily. 'There's nothing makes a girl feel better than being told she looks a mess.'

'I didn't say that.' He held the passenger door opon invitingly and helped her in before going round and climbing into the driver's seat. 'I was simply trying to express a legitimate concern with the way you look. Beautiful. Infinitely desirable. But tired.' He crinkled his eyes at her, and then leaned over and tipping her chin with one finger kissed her gently, then more firmly. But when he raised his head, there was a faint line between his eyebrows. 'Yes. Very tired. Come on. You need some food and peace and quiet.'

He drove through the thick evening traffic with the expert care she had learned to expect of him; making the most of his opportunities to get through quickly, but never breaking even the most minor of the rules of the road. And as the car climbed the hill towards Hampstead Heath and the small very intimate and far too expensive (in Tricia's estimation) restaurant they usually went to, she let her mind go back to the afternoon. To Dr Kidd's oh-so-polite words yet oh-so-insulting manner, to Sister Cleland's icy ill temper, and the thought of three months to be spent in so unpleasant a way.

She wondered for a moment if it would be worth discussing the whole thing with David, but then told herself drearily that there would be little point. To pour out her woes wouldn't make her feel any better, and it would give David the chance to start again on his nagging technique, and she was in no mood to face that. And somewhere deep within her she also knew that now, while she was at a pretty low ebb, he might well persuade her to see things his way; and what a waste of all these past months and years of effort and swotting and hard work that would be –

Smoothly, David manoeuvred the car into the last parking space on The Mount, and turned to look at her in the dimness, for it was now nine o'clock and the last of the April evening light had given way to a deep blue dusk through which the elegant old lamps in front of the pretty well-kept houses glowed softly.

'Bit better?' he said softly.

'Better than what?'

'Not so annoyed with me? I'm sorry, sweetheart – but some of these hippy types – they do get on my nerves. But I shouldn't have been so rude to him. Any friend of a friend of yours and all that. Forgive me?'

'Oh, David, of course,' she said and was swept with remorse. 'I'm sorry to have been so snappy, too. I suppose I am a bit tired, really. I didn't sleep much today, and I was on duty from half past four – '

'And you look beautiful on it.' He kissed her again, and this time she softened and let her mouth relax, and then his arms were round her, harshly urgent, and she emerged breathless from as passionate a kiss as she could ever remember from him.

'Hey!' she said, her voice a little uneven. 'Give me warning next time you feel quite so – so – '

'In love,' he said, a little huskily. 'As if you didn't know.'

He took a deep breath, and then said in a firmer voice, 'And you need some dinner. Come on, sweetheart. Your table awaits you.'

They walked down to the restaurant hand in hand, his grasp firm on her chilly fingers, and were welcomed to the restaurant like old friends by the eager Cypriot waiter who, chattering incomprehensibly (and they exchanged amused glances; they'd never been able to understand his rather twisted English) led them to a candlelit table in the corner, screened from the rest of the small restaurant by a trough of exuberantly growing plants.

'David, my dear man! This all looks very elegant!' Tricia said, looking at the avocado pears filled with succulent pink prawns, that stood ready at each place, and then at the dented but gleaming ice bucket that stood beside David's chair, a gold-topped bottle nestled in a white cloth lying invitingly in it. 'What are we celebrating? The end of my night duty?'

The waiter deftly thumbed the cork from the bottle and filled their glasses with the faintly bubbling pale amber liquid and nodding and bobbing cheerfully went away, and David picked up his glass and looked at her over the top of it.

'You've forgotten,' he said softly.

'Forgotten? David! What!' she said, suddenly worried. 'My God, it isn't your birthday? No. No, of course not. That's not till July – I don't – forgive me if it's a special day. Night duty makes anyone's memory haywire – '

'Two years ago tonight, sweetheart, I allowed myself to be dragged along to a medical student's party at the Royal. I'd had a hectic day in the surgery, and a bigger one booked for the next day. But I went because young Harry was so keen I should. And I stood there in all that awful din and guffawing great rugger-playing beer-swilling medical types, and wondered how soon I could get away. And then I saw a girl on the other side of the room. Tall – leggy – a little bewildered in the middle of it all. But then, she was just a young first year student, after all. And I stayed at that party till everyone else had gone, and took the leggy student nurse back to the Home – '

She smiled then, and relaxed. 'Is it really two years? I suppose it must be. I'll be old soon, at this rate – '

He refilled both their glasses and she watched the bubbles rise and thought confusedly, 'Two years. And most of the time we've been engaged in an unofficial sort of way – it's ridiculous.'

Almost as though he'd read her mind, he said, 'It's absurd, isn't it? Darling, eat your pear. There's a duck with orange waiting after this.'

'All my favourites,' she thought, as obediently she sank her spoon into the delicate pale green of the pear. 'Oh dear. Please don't David, not tonight. I'm so tired. Not tonight – '

He didn't say any more about the anniversary as they ate the duck and crisp salad, and finally the delectable cream-filled chocolate profiteroles, and finished the bubbling wine, only talking of amusing general things, about an absurd patient he had had that day, and what she had said when he told her she really would have to lose her teeth; about the incredibly silly relief dental nurse the agency had sent him, and the way he had worded an advertisement designed to get a really good one; about the new equipment he and his partner in their thriving West End dental practice had ordered. And Tricia listened, and laughed and listened again, and relaxed.

'Too many calories altogether, David!' she protested when he tried to persuade her to take another helping of the profiteroles. 'I'll get enormous!'

'Never too enormous for me. And anyway, I'll tell you as soon as I think you're in need of taking care,' he said, and looked down at his coffee, busily stirring it, and went on in a studiedly offhand way. 'Some girls have a problem when they start a family, of course. I remember how my sister suddenly plumped up after young Jeremy was born – but she's dieted it away very well now – '

Abruptly, all the relaxation the food and wine had given her vanished, and she felt herself tense up. And he looked up and saw her face, and said with sudden irritation, 'Ye Gods, Trish! What do you want of me? I asked you to marry me a bare two months after I met you. And you agreed, and I thought – well damn it, *do* you love me? I love you more each month that goes by. Is it asking too much of you to set a date? To let me give you a ring, announce the engagement, start planning? In another three months you'll have finished your training – and though I never did see any point in it, and still don't, I agreed you'd finish it before we got married. And yet – *do* you love me?'

She looked at him, at the square handsome face creased now with anxiety, and affection for him welled up and spilled over and she put her hands out and took one of his between them. 'Oh, David, don't – don't look like that. I don't mean to be selfish, really I don't. But – oh, I suppose I'm stubborn. I set out to train as a nurse, and once I'd started – it's like reading a book, in a way. I mean, once I start one, I have to finish it even if I hate it – '

He looked at her sharply. 'Do you hate it? Nursing. I mean?'

'No – darling, no, of course not.' She struggled with her conscience for a moment. 'Not everything I do is as much fun as it might be, I can't deny. They've put me on the Private Wing, and I can't pretend I like it much. But I have to finish what I start. It's the way I'm made.'

He smiled a little lopsidedly. 'I should be grateful for that, I suppose. At least I've the reassurance you'll marry me eventually. But when is eventually? We agreed you'd finish training – '

'I've told you since, though, that I'd feel sort of – well, incomplete if I never used it. My training, that is. I'd like to do something – '

'Darling, I've told you, once we're married, you won't need to work! It's not as though I *have* to send my wife out to work to make ends meet. Damn it all, dentistry is – '

'I know. It's a pretty affluent sort of career. You've told me before.'

'And you aren't one of these militant feminist types, are you? These women overflowing with ambition – they don't know what they're missing – '

'I'm not militant, of course not,' Tricia said and stopped and thought for a moment. 'I want to marry, and have children just like anyone else, I suppose, but I've plenty of time, haven't I? I'm only just twenty-two, after all, and I'd like to – well, be a Sister for a while before I take to the kitchen sink.'

'Darling, being a mother is worth being ninety-nine Sisters. And being my wife won't mean tying yourself to the kitchen sink. I've been looking at houses, and – '

'You've been *what?*'

His jaw hardened. 'Looking at houses. The lease of the flat is up in a couple of months anyway. And the houses I've seen are all biggish – with room for resident domestic help. I know such people are expensive, but I think you're worth it. You're worth everything, anything you want – ' He leaned forwards and cupped her face between his hands. 'Don't you understand? I love you. And that means I *need* you. Every time I see you it gets worse. I'm a one woman man, and you're my woman. And for a year now you've been so – so wrapped up in your blasted nursing you've no energy or time for me, it seems. What am I supposed to do? Live like a monk for ever? I have – for two years now. Because I *love* you. I could do what some other people do, I suppose. Find some easy-going girl to keep me – company – until you're ready to settle down, but that's not my way. Doesn't that mean anything to you?'

'A great deal.' Gently she took his hands away from her face, and held them warmly. '*You* mean a great deal to me. You're so marvellous to me, you make me feel like a complete bitch. But – '

He leaned back, and his face hardened, and he pulled his hands away from hers, and thrust them into his pockets.

'But what you start you finish. And you haven't finished with your bloody career yet. So hard luck, Talbot. Is that it?'

'Well, what's wrong with having a career?' she flashed into anger suddenly. 'I'm not the only one who's stubborn, damn it all. I've told you, over and over, that if you'll agree to let me go on with nursing for a couple of years, we could get married as soon as the Final results are out. But – '

'I've told you. No wife of mine is going to work.'

'Just how antiquated a set of ideas can a man carry, for God's sake? It's not that I'm not interested in domesticity and motherhood and the rest of it. I am – but not to the exclusion of everything else. All I want is a chance to be *me*. Me, Tricia Oxford, SRN, not just Mrs David Talbot, LDS. Is that so much to ask?'

'If you really loved me you'd have no need to want to be – '

'Love has nothing to do with it. I do love you, as far as I can tell. But I want more from life than just love. Would you give up dentistry just to marry me?'

He frowned sharply. 'What do you mean, "as far as you can tell"? Either you love me or you don't.'

She closed her eyes wearily. 'I mean I've never felt about anyone else the way I feel about you. I like being with you. I like being kissed by you, I feel comfortable, and safe, and at peace with you. Except when you nag me like this – '

She opened her eyes and looked at him then, and suddenly, it was all too much to cope with; her fatigue, the way the elation the wine had created had ebbed, leaving a flat weariness behind, the expression on his face. And her eyes filled with tears, and she swallowed hard and took a deep tremulous breath.

'Oh, darling, I'm sorry!' He was all contrition. 'I'm a louse to go on at you about this tonight. You're dead on your feet – you must be. No wonder you're being so – look, let me take you back. It's gone eleven, and you need your sleep. And phone me tomorrow, yes? And we'll go out and talk properly another time. When you aren't so tired, and I'm not so – well, never mind. I'll tell you next time we meet. All right darling?'

She nodded, and sniffed noisily, and then laughed shakily as he gave her his handkerchief. 'I'm sorry – that did sound horrible, didn't it? I must be more sleepy than I thought. Yes please, David. Take me back. And I'll phone you tomorrow to let you know my off duty, I promise. Tomorrow.'

4

It helped a little to come on duty next morning and find that Sister Cleland was away at a ward sisters' Study Day. Tricia took a deep breath of relief when she saw Bridie Cavanaugh sitting at the office desk, the report book in front of her, ready to give the day's instructions to the staff. She would be much nicer to work with than unpleasant Sister Cleland.

Tricia was feeling a good deal less weary than she had the previous day, for she had slept heavily and dreamlessly, but she was still depressed, not least because of the episode with David. He had been so tender, so solicitous as he drove her back to the hospital, had kissed her goodnight so gently, and now she was filled with remorse as she remembered how she had treated him.

He had gone to all that trouble to arrange their dinner date, had tried so hard to celebrate what should have been as important an anniversary to her as it was to him, and she had thrown it all back at him. How could she be so unkind to someone who so patently loved her so well?

And as she looked along the line of nurses waiting for Cavanaugh to start the giving of the report, she couldn't help feeling that perhaps David was right after all in his dismissal of her career ambitions. One of the joys of the nursing life had always been, as far as Tricia was concerned, the camaraderie of being one of a group of people with shared aims and interests. The feeling of belonging, of being a 'Royal Nurse' wasn't one she had ever thought about much, but now she realised just how much it mattered to her. For the first time in all her almost three years of training, she was with a group of nurses who were not tied by such bonds, who were simply doing a particular job because it suited them.

She looked at Ingrid Jensen's withdrawn expression, at Prue

Gallon's weary one, at the other so far unknown nurses and wondered if this was all she was working towards; a rather dull job with spoiled uninteresting patients. If it were, David's offer of a comfortable, easy marriage, a life filled with peace and pleasure rather than effort, had a greater attractiveness than it had ever before exerted on her.

'Now, me dears,' Cavanaugh said briskly. 'To the day's news. Mrs Kester in room 301 had a poor night – drugs as usual, and dressings prn. She'd best be specialed today, I'm thinkin', Jensen, so I'll ask you take her and only two others. Mr Scott-Lanyard for one – he had his last bladder washout at six a.m. – '

Swiftly, she went through the list of patients, and Tricia realised as she listened that the system the Floor used was to allot to each nurse her own complement of patients for whom she was fully responsible. She perked up a little at that. At least she wouldn't be just a little junior runabout, as she'd feared she would be as the only student among a staff made up entirely of qualified girls. But her hopes were dashed as Cavanaugh came to the end of the report and looked up at Tricia with a slightly lopsided smile.

'As for you, young Oxford – I'm afraid you're goin' to be havin' a rather dull time of it. I've firm instructions here from Sister that you are not to have your own case load, in the usual fashion, but to assist generally as and where you're wanted.' She looked down at the slip of paper pinned to the cover of the report book. ' "Until I can be sure she is capable of being trusted fully" she's written here. You daft ijjut, Oxford, to go and upset her like that, your first afternoon on the Floor! Ah, well, can't be helped. We'll do our best for you, will we not, me dears?' She looked up at the others. 'As long as you don't go doin' anything too silly, we'll make a point of telling Sister what a grand nurse you are, yes?'

'As long as she is,' Jensen said sourly. 'We all know you, Bridie. Softer and sweeter than a doughnut. Well, I for one am not about to go upsetting the Cleland by pleading the cause of anyone other than myself. Call me a selfish old bag if you like, but I've learned to keep out of her way. Anyway, I'll make first claim on your services, Oxford. Mrs Keston is by no means a light patient to nurse, and she's in a good deal of pain, so I need a strong pair of arms to help turn her and make her bed. And you look tough enough.'

'Ah, take no notice of old Ingrid,' Cavanaugh said easily. 'She's just snapping because she missed her breakfast. Look, when Mrs Kester is finished, I'll want you to help with my two up-patients, Oxford. There's young Sandra in 309 and Miss Galt in 317. If I'm not about, just go on in and make their beds, will you? And check that Sandra used the bidet this morning, and if not see to it that she does, will you?' She saw Tricia's puzzled look, and said, 'She's the T.P., remember?'

'I'm sorry,' Tricia said stiffly, hating to have to admit ignorance. 'I don't know what the letters stand for,' and couldn't help adding, 'We're not allowed to use abbreviations on the general side, not in the report, anyway.'

'Ah, the perfection of the student!' Pru Gallon murmured. 'Are we going to have to spend the next three months listening to the "right way to do things, according to the laws of the Medes and the Persians and the Royal"?'

'She's quite right, of course,' Cavanaugh said equably. 'But we've a good reason for it here, Oxford. We can't always be in the office, where the notes and the report book are, and any visitor might take it into their head to go pryin'. So now and again, we use a code, for the patients' own good, d'you see. T.P. –termination of pregnancny.'

'Oh. An abortion. I see,' Tricia said.

'And do please spare us your comments on the rights and wrongs of *that*, if you don't mind, young Oxford.' Jensen said irritably. 'I'm in no mood for it. As far as I'm concerned, the reasons a consultant has for terminating a pregnancy are between himself, his conscience and the patient – and the law. Now, can we please go and start Mrs Kester? If you don't mind!'

Furiously, Tricia opened her mouth to retort, but Jensen swept out of the office, and sulkily, Tricia followed, to collect fresh linen from the cupboard as Jensen told her to over her shoulder, before going into room 301. It was shaded against the bright morning sunshine, and Tricia had to stop momentarily to adjust her eyes to the dimness when she went in. Jenson was there ahead of her and just about to give an injection to the frail woman in the bed.

Almost against her will, Tricia warmed to the little blonde nurse as they worked together, gently washing Mrs Kester, and making her bed while moving her pain-racked body as little as they possibly could, Jensen moved so easily and deftly, with no apparent sign of the skill that went into the way she handled the sick woman with the thin face and the deeply set violet-shadowed eyes. And when an unguarded movement on Tricia's part made her accidentally kick the leg of the bed, and Mrs Kester winced and closed her eyes in agony, Jensen said softly, 'I'm sorry, Mrs Kester. That was my fault. I guess I didn't have enough sleep last night hmm? I had a date – ' and went on to chatter cheerfully about her evening's entertainment until the sick woman smiled and seemed, for a while at any rate, to be able to step outside her own illness and remember the reality of the living busy world outside her hospital room.

When they finished, and had left the room tidy, with the flowers that had been out in the corridor overnight put back in their places, Tricia said awkwardly, 'I'm sorry I was so clumsy, Nurse Jensen. It – er – it was nice of you to take the blame for me.'

'I wasn't taking the blame for *you*, Oxford, and don't you think it. But I know Mrs Kester, and she's very easily irritated – is it any wonder – and she can take a mistake from me and forgive it because she knows me, but a bit of clumsiness from a strange nurse would be something she'd brood over for hours. And she needs all the help she can to be cheerful this morning, because her son comes to see her at lunchtime today – they bring him from his boarding school twice a week – and she needs to put on a good show for him. He's only twelve, and she wants him to remember her as reasonably like her old self as she can make herself seem.'

'Is that why you told her all about your date last night?'

'What date?' Jensen said. 'That was a pure invention, all of it. But it helps her, so I make it up as I go along. Now, you'd better go and see to Sandra for Bridie. If Mrs Kester's bell goes – watch for the red lights to see which room is ringing – find me to go to her. I'll be in 303, or 304. And put this linen in the sluice as you go past, please – ' and she whisked away, leaving Tricia surprised and not a little ashamed of herself.

To know one was dying, and yet to be concerned to put on a 'good show' for other people; that was something remarkable, she thought sombrely as she collected yet another load of fresh linen and went towards room 309. And suddenly remembered Mr Suckling on Men's Surg. Three. How was he? And was he still thinking of the infinite, she wondered?

In 309, she found a small girl with a great deal of untidy fair hair trailing over her face and shoulders sitting hunched on the window sill with her arms hugging her knees and her chin resting on their boniness. The window was open, and the girl was staring out at the busy street below, for this side of the Wing faced out to the traffic-heavy main road, over the Casualty entrance.

'I've come to make your bed,' Tricia said to the girl's unresponsive back, but the girl took no notice, so, still thinking about Mr Suckling and Mrs Kester, Tricia set to work, stripping off the bed sheets, and shaking up mattress and pillows before putting on the fresh linen.

'Those sheets were clean yesterday.'

Tricia almost jumped at the sound of the husky little voice, so sunk had she been in her own thoughts.

'What did you say?'

'I said those sheets were clean yesterday. So why are you changing them? I haven't had to have clean sheets every day so far.' The girl had not changed her curled up position, only turning her head to stare at Tricia from behind the tangled fringe that almost hid her blue eyes.

Tricia had assumed that all the patients had daily clean linen, and made a mental note to check with Nurse Cavanaugh. But now, her mind still on Mr Suckling, she just shrugged and said abstactly, 'Well, no harm. You can't be too clean – ' and then, as she tucked in the last corner of the counterpane added, 'By the way – have you used the bidet this morning?'

'What's that to do with you?' the girl said challengingly.

'I beg your pardon?' Tricia said, a little startled at the hostility in the young voice.

'I know what you're thinking!' The girl moved swiftly, then, and turned so that she was sitting tensely on the edge of the windowseat, her knuckles white as her hands held on to the edge. 'You're standing there thinking I'm a filthy rotten thing, aren't you? That's why you had to change all my sheets again, isn't it? That's why you're like all the rest, always going on at me about using that stinking bidet and washing, washing, washing all the time – I know!' Her voice rose shrilly. 'I knew that was how it would be! I told them it would be like that when they made me come here! You can't just get rid of things just like that, can you? I kept telling them, but it made no difference! Well, if that's what you all think, that's that, isn't it? I'm bad and filthy and nothing you do is ever going to make any difference, is it? Well, don't you waste any more of your time on me, you clean scrubbed bitch! If

I'm that dirty, I'll make myself even dirtier, that's what I'll do — I'll give you something really horrible to clean up — you'll see — '

And to Tricia's horror she turned abruptly, and scrambling awkwardly because of the long dressing gown that wrapped itself around her ankles, thrust her head, and then her body out through the window, swung her legs over till she was sitting precariously on the outer sill, staring malevolently back over her shoulder at Tricia, who was standing frozen with disbelief beside the smooth, freshly made bed.

'For God's sake — come in — what do you think you're doing?' she cried after an agonised moment in which it seemed her voice was as frozen as the rest of her. 'You'll fall — ' she added stupidly. 'Come in, you idiot — what's your name — Sandra, come in at once — '

'I'll give you something really horrible to clean up,' the girl said again, and her voice rose even more shrilly. 'I'll splatter myself to — to a jelly down there — ' she turned her head and looked downwards, and for one sick moment swayed slightly forwards, and that galvanised Tricia into a jerky movement that brought her to the foot of the bed.

The girl looked back at her over her shoulder and cried, 'No! you keep still — you stand there or I'll jump now — right this minute, you hear me? I'll be as horrible and dirty as you think I am anyway — '

'But I don't think you're dirty!' Tricia said helplessly, standing obediently still, terrified to move a muscles. 'I hardly know you, for God's sake! This is my first morning here, how can I think anything about you?'

'You were here yesterday, with the doctor. I saw you. Looked at me like — as though I were too revolting even to look at, I saw you — '

'But that was nothing to do with you!' Tricia tried to keep her voice calm and level, tried to remember everything she'd ever been taught in her psychology lectures in her second year block. 'Truly, I know nothing about you! But last night — well, I'd just come on duty, and that doctor — he — I did something that annoyed him and he made me go round with him and it was awful. And if I looked a bit miserable or sulky, that was why — '

Keep talking, a little voice whispered inside her. Anything, say anything, but keep talking, so that I keep her busy and she doesn't jump, and someone must come soon, mustn't they, soon

– 'I mean, what do you do for a job? Hasn't it ever happened to you that someone in charge takes a dislike to you and has a go at you all the time? Well, that was what happened to me, as soon as I came on duty it started, you see – '

It seemed to go on for hours, the two of them alone in the world, as she stood at the foot of the bed, chattering on and on, and the little girl in the bundled dressing gown sitting poised so precariously on the edge and listening and sometimes speaking herself.

'I'm still at school,' she said abruptly at one point. 'I'm fifteen, I'll be sixteen soon, and then I'm leaving. I'll show them.'

'Show who?' Tricia said, and tried a relaxed smile, and very tentatively bent her knees until she was perched on the edge of the bed, and prayed she looked more at ease than she felt. Reassure her, whispered the little voice. Let her think you aren't going to move. Someone must see, soon, from down there, mustn't they? Send a mesesage up here? Someone must come in soon, surely? And please let them come in quietly so that she isn't startled and falls. Please, please, please –

'Everybody – ' the girl seemed to brood for a moment, and then looked forwards and downwards again, and from the foot of the bed, Tricia stiffened, feeling her eyes widen with fear as the girl again swayed sickeningly. But then she looked back over her shoulder and Tricia hooded her eyes as she looked away from the girl's face, and went on with her ceaseless silent internal praying. Wouldn't someone come, soon?

'The staff. My father. And him. Him especially.'

'Tell me about him. Why are you so – why do you want to show him?'

'Because of what he did.' She moved then, awkwardly, and again a great wash of fear came up in Tricia. 'This window sill is bloody hard,' the girl said petulantly.

'Then why not come in? It'd be easier to talk in here anyway.' Do I sound as relaxed as I'm trying to? the little voice inside Tricia whispered. 'And anyway, I can't hear you properly with all that noise from the street. It would be much quieter with the window closed.'

Behind her, she caught a faint sound, and stiffened. Someone was very gently opening the door, and she took a deep breath and went on talking, rather more loudly. 'Mind, if you don't want to you don't have to. But can I come a bit closer so that I can hear you properly? Standing here, it's a bit of an effort to catch everything you say – '

'No you don't!' the girl cried out. 'You come a step nearer, and I will, I – tell you – I will – '

'Good morning, Sandra!' The voice from behind her made Tricia stiffen and then relax so much that she felt her legs shake, and she knew that if she hadn't already been half sitting she would have fallen as her knees gave way. 'How are you this morning? You're looking pretty fit.'

Adam Kidd walked past Tricia as though she wasn't there, his head bent as he ostensibly looked at the open case notes in his hands. Sandra turned her head further to stare at him, and Tricia watched, cold with fear, as he walked calmly to the window and put his hand firmly on Sandra's elbow.

'Come over to the bed, will you, Sandra, please? I want to check your blood pressure and your chest. That was a nasty cough you had after your anaesthetic, and I want to be sure you're quite clear of it before I'll let you go to your convalescence. Come along, now – '

And obediently, Sandra swung her legs back over the window sill and let Adam Kidd lead her towards the bed, as docile as a baby being led towards her dinner.

'Close that window, will you, Nurse Oxford? Bit cold in here. And then fetch me a sphygmo – and ask Nurse Cavanaugh to come and help me with Sandra's examination.'

He looked up at her across Sandra's back as he helped her out of her dressing gown, revealing the pitiful thinness of her bony shoulders poking out the thin fabric of her nightdress. 'Hurry along, now! Sandra's car will be here shortly, and we've a lot to do before she can go – '

Almost mesmerised by his direct gaze, Tricia moved, and shakily went to the door, and managed to open it and get through without showing how she felt. And outside she closed the door behind her and leaned against it, breathing deeply, and shaking in every muscle.

'Ye Gods, what happened in there?' Tricia opened her eyes and stared round her, at the several nurses clustered by the door, at Cavanaugh's anxious face very near her own.

'He wants you and a sphygmo,' Tricia said faintly. 'Quickly, he said. Oh, my God – I'm going to be sick – '

And she pushed past Cavanaugh to run down the corridor

towards the sluice, to hang weakly over the basin being as sick as any patient she had ever cared for.

It seemed to go on for a long time, the nausea and the waves of faintness, and then she was standing leaning against the tiled wall, wet with a cold sweat and feeling weak but in some control of herself.

Nurse Jensen was standing there, and reached up to wipe Tricia's damp face with a wadded paper towel.

'Now that's over, you'd better come and sit down in the office,' she said calmly. 'Come on. And for Gawd's sake don't go flaking out on me half way up the corridor because plump as I am, you'd flatten me, you're that much taller – '

Tricia managed a grateful smile, and nodded and let the other girl grasp her elbow competently and lead her along the corridor to the office. And almost fell into the small armchair in the corner.

One of the other nurses came in with a cup of tea, then, and Tricia took it and drank it thirstily, as the other two watched her.

'Well, what *happened*?' Jensen demanded. 'First thing we knew, one of the Casualty people phoned up here to say there was one of our patients sitting outside on a window sill, and half North London down there staring up at her, and what was going on? And Dr Kidd was here, and swore like a trooper when we realised who it was from the description of the patient Casualty gave us, and told us to keep out of the way while he went in. And then you come out looking as green as pea soup, and bring up your heart in the sluice – what *happened* in there?'

'I don't know,' Tricia said, and put the cup and saucer down, and wiped her lips shakily. 'I was making her bed, and she said something about having clean sheets, and then I said about the bidet – and the next thing I knew, there she was, on the window sill, and it was wide open, and – oh my God!' Her eyes widened. 'He told me to shut it – Dr Kidd, I mean – and I didn't. It was all I could do to get to the door. Oh, no! I forgot – or I was just too – '

'All right, nurses. The panic's over, and there are bells ringing all over the floor.' Dr Kidd's voice cut across, and he came in followed by Nurse Cavanaugh, and immediately the other two went out.

He came and sat at the desk, and reached for the phone, and Tricia stood up to go out, too, but without looking at her he said brusquely, 'Stay where you are, Nurse. You're clearly in no state to do anything useful anywhere at the moment, and anyway I want to talk to you. Bridie, get that child's gear packed, will you, while she's out of the room with Nurse Gallon. By the time she's back from X-ray the car should be here – '

He dialled quickly, and Bridie Cavanaugh leaned over and patted Tricia's shoulder kindly, and then bustled out. And Tricia leaned back and stared at Dr Kidd's broad shoulders as he talked.

'X-ray? Kidd. Listen, I've sent you a child for a straight chest X-ray. Just go through the motions, will you? She doesn't need a film, but she's a psychiatric patient and I want to keep her occupied while we sort out arrangements for her urgent transfer – thanks a lot. Yes. Yes – that's it.'

He clicked the receiver rest, then dialled again, and Tricia listened, almost dreamlike, as he talked on.

' – yes, Sandra Ryman. Age fifteen. I'm afraid I've had to mislead her, but I thought it justified in this case. She's a good deal more agitated than we had realised – tried to do a jump from her window this morning – precisely. A very big gesture indeed. I've told her you're a convalescent unit – well, I know. But I can't keep her here, we've no facilities for adequate supervision. She's in a private room – I know, I know, but the father was adamant. He's one of those types that thinks it's enough to spend money. Mmm. I couldn't agree more. Anyway, you'll contact him? Fine. You've got his office phone number, haven't you? Good – good. I'm sending notes with her, of course, and I'd like to know how she gets on. She's a very pathetic little creature – yes. Oh, yes, absolutely. Fine. Goodbye, then –'

He cradled the phone with a clatter, and then turned in the swivel chair towards Tricia, to sit with his hands thrust deep into the pockets of his white coat, his eyes sombre and his gaze very direct.

'Well, Nurse Oxford! And what have you to say about this morning's little episode?'

'I don't know what happened, or why,' Tricia said wearily. 'I realise I upset the patient in some way, and I – I'm sorrier about it than I can say, but – '

'I don't want lots of self explanations and apologies. There's no need for that. What I want to know is what happened. What she said, how she looked, what happened *exactly*. In detail. From the beginning. It's the patient I'm interested in, not you – except inasmuch as you had an effect on her. Now, from the very beginning.'

Nettled, Tricia sat up a little straighter. 'I went in to make her bed, and she said – '

'No, no, that won't do. In detail, I said. How did you look when she saw you?'

'How did I look? I don't know! I didn't stare in a mirror!'

'Your expression, Nurse, the expression on your face! Friendly, or as dour as you've looked ever since you reported to this floor? Approachable or sulky? How?'

'I have not been dour, as you put it!' Tricia said furiously. 'It's not my fault – well, not entirely – that everything has gone so wrong since I started here! I don't usually go around looking dour, as far as I know, anyway.'

'What were you thinking about when you went into her room?'

'Thinking about?' Tricia wrinkled her forehead. 'I don't know – oh, yes I do. I'd just been helping with Mrs Kester. And something Nurse Jensen said – anyway, I remembered a patient I've been nursing on Men's Surg. Three – a Mr Suckling. A nice man. He's got an inoperable carcinoma of the pancreas and – '

'So you were thinking about death.' His voice was flat and impersonal.

'I suppose so. Yes. That could have made me look a bit – '

'A bit dour. All right. Then what happened?'

And so it went on. Step by step, he took her through the whole episode, making her tell him in every detail just what happened between herself and Sandra, and as she told him, gradually the sick feeling left her, and she found herself relaxing. And at the end of it all he stood up, and looked down at her and said, 'Well it could have been worse. The whole business was in part my fault. I suspected there was more depth to this girl's psychiatric problem than I discussed with the nursing staff, but I didn't want to – well, never mind. What do you know about her, anyway?'

'Nothing very much. Just that she had a termination of pregnancy.'

'Have you any moral views about abortions?'

She reddened. 'Moral views?'

'Do you approve? Disapprove? Think girls should bear the burden of their sexual mistakes?' he said impatiently.

'I hadn't thought about it much,' she said after a pause. 'I suppose I should have. But it's not something I've had to think about much, so – '

'You should.' He stood up, and moved towards the door. 'Only well informed thoughtful women can make well informed thoughtful nurses. There are some things we all ought to think about and abortion is one of them.'

He turned and looked back at her, and then, abruptly, smiled, and it changed his face quite remarkably, lifting it so that he looked much younger. 'Anyway, you look as though you feel a good deal better. You had a very unpleasant experience in there, didn't you?'

She smiled herself then, a small shaky smile. 'It was horrible, I didn't know what was the right thing to do, really – I could only stand there and talk and talk like some great idiot – '

'Well, that was the right thing to do. You saved her life, you know. But don't go getting too good an opinion of yourself on that score. For one thing, it's what you're here for, and for another, if you hadn't walked in there looking so grim it's an evens chance she wouldn't have created such a performance. However, that's beside the point.' He went out into the corridor towards the lift, and then turned back. 'And you'd better go and wash your face and tidy your hair. You look a mess. Off you go!'

And when he was gone, leaving her furious at his blame for the start of the Sandra episode, rather flattered at his commendation of the way she had handled it, but above all, enraged by his parting shot. How *dare* he make any comments on the way she looked? And the dislike she had felt for him last night began to harden itself into positive loathing.

5

She came off duty at seven thirty that evening, feeling as dejected as she could ever remember being. The only good thing that had come out of the morning's episode had been a certain warming towards her on the part of the other nurses on the floor.

Bridie Cavanaugh had said to her, quietly, when she took Tricia with her to do the afternoon drug round, 'There's nothing makes a person easier to like than havin' to forgive them for something. We all know now that it was you upset young Sandra enough to make her blow off like that and you've had the grace to admit it and show you're sorry. So the girls won't be seein' you as quite as big-headed a little madam as you seemed. And you did, you know! And then, you handled it all very nicely, considering. I'll tell you one thing, young Oxford. I'll not be sayin' anything to Sister Cleland about how the flap started. She'll know what happened, of course – she'll have to – but she won't know your part in it except that you helped avoid Sandra goin' out of the window altogether, do y'see. And nor will the others say anything. So there's nothin' for you to fret about there.'

And for that Tricia was indeed very grateful, for the thought of what would happen when Sister Cleland came on duty next day had been nagging away in the corner of her mind like a sore tooth. Which, added to the other simmering irritation she felt at Dr Kidd and his attitude, combined to create a very uncomfortable feeling indeed.

So, when she came hurrying off duty and saw David sitting in one of the big armchairs in the reception area of the Nurses' Home, his legs neatly crossed, and reading a tidily folded copy of *The Times*, her immediate reaction was to feel a wave of relieved comfort. He could be irritating, sometimes, Heaven knew, and she had a guilty conscience about the way she had behaved towards him over dinner the previous evening but he was *there*; he cared for her, approved of her, wanted her company, and that was balm to her very sore soul. She greeted him with a wide smile, and an impulsive hug that seemd to startle him.

'I thought I'd save you the price of a phone call,' he said, 'and on a nurse's pay every penny helps, hmm? Feeling better than you did yesterday?'

'Better? Oh, not so tired, you mean? Well, I slept last night, which makes a pleasant enough change. But I've had a beast of a day – it is lovely to see you, David.'

'I thought there was more to it than my blue eyes,' he said shrewdly. 'What happened?'

'Oh, no need to bore you with it.' She wished now that she hadn't admitted to being miserable. She had felt for a long time now that it was very necessary to make David always believe she was enjoying every single moment of her working day; any hint that all in her chosen career was not ideal would be enough to make him launch again into his demands for an early marriage. And looking up at him now, at the square, handsome face, feeling the strong security of him so near to her, she knew how little it would take to yield, to say 'the hell with the Private Wing – yes, yes, yes. Let's get married. Soon – tomorrow – now – ' But behind that lay the broad streak of stubbornness that kept reminding her, over and over – you've started something. Finish it, properly.

'But I'm interested!' he said. 'Look, I'll tell you what. Go get yourself into something pretty – that trouser suit, you know, the one with all the colours – '

'The Pucci print thing?'

'Yes. Wear that, put on your face, and we'll go out, and you can tell me all about it. Somewhere really fun. Somewhere expensive and outrageous – '

'David, honestly, it doesn't have to be somewhere expensive, truly it doesn't. And I'm not sure I want to go out on the swinging scene bit, to be honest. Maybe I am a bit tired at that – '

'Oh, not a bit of it. Miserable and depressed, maybe, but not tired. You're too young to talk like that – crawling into bed as soon as you go off duty is no way to live. We're going out. Now hurry up and change, sweetheart. You'll feel twice the girl when you get out of that blue sacking.'

'It's a very nice uniform!' Tricia protested, looking down at the pale blue checked dress with the small puffed sleeves and the tightly belted starched white apron. 'I've seen much worse.'

'It's still blue sacking, and you look better in real clothes. Now are you going to change, or must I come up and dress you?'

'Masterful tonight, Mr Talbot! Well, all right. But I truly don't want to go anywhere special – '

He put his hand on her shoulder and walked her towards the stairs. 'I am indeed very masterful tonight. Very. So we'll go where I think is good for you – now *scoot* – ' and he leaned over and kissed her very firmly and then gently slapped her behind, and she shrugged in a resigned way and obediently went upstairs. And sang softly as she bathed, and changed and put on her makeup, because although there were times when David's proprietorial ways irritated her, tonight she needed to feel cherished and looked after, and David was extremely good at doing that.

She came down the stairs a bare half hour later, and he looked up and smiled and said softly. 'Now you look like my girl. *My* girl, instead of an anonymous angel of mercy – come here and be kissed.'

She felt suddenly shy and gauche, and shook her head awkwardly. 'David, love – not here! The world and his wife go by – I – er – where are you parked?'

'In the usual place. Now, I've phoned for a table at the Trat. You like it there, and Friday's usually a great evening. You really *will* see the world and his wife there. So, let's go, hmm?'

The thought of the very fashionable Trattoria Terrazza and its gay swinging atmosphere, and the gorgeous looking people who used it certainly had an attraction, so she nodded, and together they made towards the door. And as they reached it, it swung open, and Ngaire, looking delectable in a heavy crocheted brilliant yellow dress came bursting in, followed by a tall untidy looking young man in a vivid flowered green shirt with a matching tie, and a very tight pair of scarlet trousers.

'Trish! I've been looking for you! I thought you might be over in the dining room having first supper, and I wanted to catch you before you ate – hi, David! Super to see you!' She stood on tiptoe, for she was very much smaller than the tall David, and kissed his cheek resoundingly. 'You know Skip, don't you?' she pulled the young man forward by one hand. 'He's our newest surgical houseman – isn't he beautiful?'

The young man laughed, and nodded at David who was looking with some distaste at the other's clothes. 'Cantor – Stephen Cantor. Nice to meet you. Hello, Trish. How's life on the half-crown side? Better than pigging it with the hoi polloi on the general side, I'll bet.'

'Hello, Skip. Not really, I'd rather pig it any day. How are you? Haven't seen you for ages – '

'Oh, not so bad, considering. At least I've got a few hours off for once!' He stretched luxuriously. 'First time I've been out of a white coat for a month, I swear. I'm on call tonight, mind you, but technically I've an evening off.'

'So listen, Trish, that's why we were looking for you – and it's great David's here,' Ngaire bubbled. 'Because it's the greatest thing. You know the show they have at the Pigsty on Fridays, sort of local talent and all that? Well, there's this bunch of friends of Skip, and my dear, they've got a little group going – guitars, bass, and that – and they're working at the show tonight! And Skip and me, we're going to cheer them on, and you must come – both of you. Won't you? It'll be a great gig, truly, and you'll love the group. They're really good – '

'The Pigsty?' David looked startled.

'I've told you, David, haven't I? It's the local pub. The Blue Boar, just across the road, backing on to the Docks road,' Tricia said. 'It's a sort of extension to the Royal! Everyone goes there – like a club, really. If you can't find a houseman – phone the Pigsty! It's a great place. The landlord's been there donkey's years – knows everyone who's been at the Royal since the year dot. He knew all the most senior consultants when they were mad medical students, and when he starts on some of his reminiscences – it's hilarious, really. And they have an entertainment set-up at weekends. Professionals on Saturday and Sunday, but amateurs on Fridays – So come on. The show starts at nine, and we'd better be early or we won't get anywhere near the stage – if you can call it that, David. It's about two by four, that's all. But big enough! Let's go, huh?'

'I'm sorry, Ngaire. Nice of you to ask us, but we already have arrangements. Another time, maybe – ' David said, and began to move towards the door again.

But Ngaire seized his arm, and looked up at him appealingly. 'Oh, don't be like that, David! Can't you change your plan? What were you going to do?'

'David's booked a table at the Trat,' Tricia said.

'Oh, well! You can go there any time, can't you? Do, please, David, won't you? Trish'd love to come with us, wouldn't you Trish?'

Tricia laughed. 'Well, it's usually fun at the Pigsty. Why not, David? Honestly, I didn't really want to live it up tonight – shall we?'

'Well, if you really want to,' David said a little stiffly. 'I suppose I could ring the Trat, and cancel the booking. Though – '

'No thoughts!' Ngaire said gaily. 'It's settled. And you can still eat at the Pigsty, David. Old Chalky does the best jellied eels in London. Don't look like that – they're delicious! You ought to try. But there're other things too. Great ham sandwiches and sausage rolls and hot pasties. Ooh, do hurry and phone! I'm famished.'

His lips a little thinner, David turned and went to the phone in the far corner. While they waited for him Ngaire chattered on in her usual fashion, and when he came back to them and Skip held the door open, went on chattering as they crossed the nurses' garden, ducking under the big copper beech tree in the middle (traditionally known as the 'Kissing Tree' so kindly did the great old branches sweep down almost to the ground to create a deeply shadowed private place against its great trunk), while David walked silently a little way behind her, alongside Tricia.

Under cover of Ngaire's talk to Skip, Tricia said in a low voice, 'You don't really mind this, do you, David? It's not as though you'd made plans a long time in advance, after all. I mean, you only decided on the Trat a few minutes or so ago.'

'If this pub thing is what you want, then I suppose that's that. Though I do feel Ngaire is a bit high handed at times, if you'll forgive me saying so. I know she's your best friend but really, it is a little annoying – '

'Oh don't be stuffy, David! She really means awfully well. And she's great fun – we always do enjoy ourselves when we're in a crowd with Ny, you know that.'

'Yes,' David said noncommittally. 'I suppose so. But how much chance we'll get to talk – and I really want to know what it is that's bothering you.'

She squeezed his arm affectionately. 'Dear old David – you are nice to worry so. But really, it's nothing. And I'll be much better off giggling with you and old Ny and Skip than telling you tales of woe. Forget it, and then I will.'

And she reached up and kissed his cheek, and he shrugged a little and then smiled at her. 'Oh, well. If it's what *you* want. But we'll settle a real date for tomorrow or Sunday. Just us. Right?'

'Right,' she said, and they crossed the pathway that led past the Pathological Laboratories to the side gate, and ducked through it to cross the noisy road towards the red brick Victorian building on the far side.

The place was still only half full, with a fairly noisy group of third year medical students and nurses in one corner, and a rather quieter one of dockers in another. One or two couples were sitting at the small marble topped tables, and several people waved at Skip and Tricia and Ngaire as they came in, and after a cheerful greeting from the very fat heavily sweating man behind the bar, settled themselves at a table fairly near the tiny stage at the far side of the big, heavily decorated room with the engraved glass mirrors, and red plush, and gleaming brasswork.

Amid much changing of mind on Ngaire's part and a certain amount of fastidious rejection of food ideas from David, they settled on a supper, and Chalky brought over a tray on which plump, hot sausages, slabs of red Leicester cheese, pungent pickled onions and delicately gleaming dishes of jellied eels (Ngaire having demanded two servings all to herself) jostled large chunks of crusty hot bread and steaming Cornish pasties and glasses of beer and cider and bags of potato crisps. The food was delectable, and they ate very busily indeed, even David admitting that he'd tasted much worse.

By the time they had finished and were leaning back in repletion, they were relaxed and happy, even David seeming to have overcome his chagrin at the way Ngaire had manipulated his evening's plans. And she had undoubtedly made a considerable effort to beguile and please him, rather to Tricia's amusement. The pub had filled up a good deal, for it was now almost nine o'clock, and time and again people stopped by the foursome's table to natter and tease Ngaire a little – for everyone knew and liked Ngaire – before finding tables and corners of their own.

The pop group – a very noisy one indeed – started the show at nine sharp, and the busy pub laughed, whistled and cheered them on, Ngaire and Skip providing the greatest amount of such encouragement.

It was during one of the noisier of the group's offerings that Chalky came pushing through the crowd to shout in Skip's ear, and he swore and stood up.

'Got to go,' he bawled at the other three. 'Some blasted idiot has spread himself all over the road under his motorbike, and I'm wanted. My only night off for a month. I'll try to get back, Ny, but if I can't David'll see you back to the Home. Won't you David?'

David looked sideways at Tricia, and opened his mouth to speak, and then closed it again. And nodded in resigned acceptance. Tricia, very accurately reading his mind, couldn't help being a little amused. As though he had said it, she knew that he had fully intended to whisk her off somewhere in the car as soon as the pub closed, for the time alone with her that he wanted. And much as she enjoyed the hours they spent in each other's arms in the car, parked somewhere quiet and reasonably romantic, much as she enjoyed his kisses, tonight she wouldn't really mind missing them.

Ngaire seemed to accept the loss of her escort with equanimity, applauding the remainder of the group's show with evident pleasure, but when they had departed to a renewed chorus of whistles and shouts, and David had gone to fight his way through to the bar for a last round of drinks, she propped her elbows on the table and began to look around, peering past Tricia, who was sitting opposite her, towards the main part of the big room.

'Now, let's see who's here with who,' she said wickedly. 'It's always interesting to see the way the couples make up and break up and change partners – isn't that Cora James over there? With that red-headed Laurence boy from the lab.? It is, you know. I thought he and Mary whatsit – the radiotherapy girl, you know? were a steady pair. Well, who'd have thought quiet little Cora'd manage that? Good for her. Ooh, and Trish – look, there's your Sister Cleland!'

'Oh, no!' Tricia said. 'Don't tell me that. Bad enough I'll see her on duty tomorrow – where is she?'

'Talking to Mr Carteret, the tutor to the PTS, over by the window. She's not a bad looking woman, you know, out of uniform, I wonder how old she is? I'd give her about thirty, that's all.'

'Old as sin, that's her,' Tricia said maliciously and grinned. 'It's something to know she's human enough to come here with the crowd, I suppose. Tell me if she comes this way, and I'll dodge into the loo or something – '

'I will,' Ngaire said. 'And there's Danny just coming in – he is fun, isn't he? I don't know what sort of a doctor he'll make, but he's a great giggle when he's in Theatre – I say, Trish – '

She squinted through the now very smoky atmosphere towards the door. 'There's a chap just come in I've sort of seen around, but I'm not sure who – what does your Dr Kidd look like?'

'He's not *my* Dr Kidd!' Tricia said promptly. 'And if it is him, and he comes this way, I – I'll – '

'Never mind what you'll do – is it him? Have a quick peek – he's talking to Chalky so he'll not notice – '

Moving gingerly, Tricia looked over her shoulder, and immediately turned back. 'That's him. Disagreeable old – '

'Oh, I don't know. He looks rather fun,' Ngaire said, and then produced a smile of pure wickedness. 'Tell you what, Trish, if you're going to be working on his floor for the next three months, you ought to get to know him better. I'm going to chat him up and bring him over – '

'You dare do any such thing, and I'll scrag you alive!' Trish cried. 'Ngaire Taylor – sit *down* at once!' and she leaned forward and seized Ngaire's hands as she half stood up.

'What's the matter?' David had come back, and put three full glasses on the table. 'You going, Ngaire?' and he couldn't disguise the hopeful note in his voice.

'No – not going,' Ngaire said. 'I just saw someone I thought might like to join us – Tricia knows him better than I do, though. He's the medico on her floor of the Wing – '

'Why not?' David said heartily. 'If he's a friend of yours, Trish – '

'He's not a friend of mine!' Trish said furiously. 'And I don't want to – '

'Oh, Trish!' Ngaire said. 'Don't be so stuffy! So you had a row with him! All the more reason to get to know him properly. It's horrid to be on bad terms with people you're working with. Do let me do the conciliatory bit. I'm not being naughty about this, honestly. I was at first, but now – truly, let me see if I can't patch it up for you.'

'What sort of a row?' David said, looking closely at Tricia. 'Anything to do with what you haven't had the chance to tell me yet, about today?'

'Oh, it's nothing, nothing at all!' Tricia said angrily. 'Really, I can't think what all the fuss is about. Ngaire, sit down and drink your cider, and stop meddling. Is that mine, David? Thanks. And I'll have a cigarette too, if you don't mind.'

'Go ahead, Ngaire,' David said cordially. 'Never mind Tricia –she's just being silly. If you want to bring this chap over, do. Go on now.'

And after a quick glance at Tricia, Ngaire went. And after a pause David said softly, 'Oh, come on drling! You can't blame me for wanting to get Ngaire settled with another of her many friends, can you? I so want to be alone with you for a while, and with Ngaire tagging along, it's awfully difficult.'

He looked more closely at Tricia's face. 'Are you sure this row was just nothing? If it really matters to you, I'll – '

'It's not important, David! Do stop fussing. You're as bad as Ngaire. Anyway, he'll probably refuse to join us, since he's a very ill-mannered – '

'Hi, there!' Ngaire tapped Tricia on the shoulder. 'Look who's joining us! You know Dr Kidd, don't you Trish? And this is David Talbot – Trish's boy friend. So silly, Trish! I thought Dr Kidd was someone I knew, and then of course it turns out I didn't, though he looks ever so much like that man who used to be in the Path. labs, do you remember? And seeing I'd made such a fool of myself, I thought the least I could do was to get him to join us, as he's on his own – do sit down, won't you, Dr Kidd? Or can we call you Adam? It's an awfully nice name – '

He sat down after politely holding Ngaire's chair for her. 'Oh, you know my name then? Perhaps after all you didn't mix me up with an – er – old friend from the Path. lab. – '

Ngaire went a rose pink, and giggled. 'Well, maybe I heard Tricia mention it some time,' she said airly. 'Anyway, it suits you. All rugged and that – '

'Earthy, actually,' Adam said. 'That's what it means. Red earth. Well – Nurse – er – Tricia, did you say? How are you? Quite fit again?'

'Quite, thank you,' Tricia said stiffly, and rather savagely stubbed out her half-smoked cigarette.

'What's that? Have you been ill, Trish?' David said sharply. 'Is that what you meant when you said – '

'I meant *nothing*.' She spoke rather more loudly than she had meant to. 'And Dr Kidd is joking. I am perfectly fit.'

'Adam. Red earth, remember?' he said, and leaned back in his chair. 'You must forgive me if I've spoken out of turn.'

'Not at all,' she said icily.

'For Heaven's sake!' David said. 'Will someone tell me what all this is about? I have a deeply rooted dislike of sitting in on conversations that I don't understand. Tricia, what is all this about your not being fit? I've a right to know, for Heaven's sake!'

'A right? How interesting,' Adam said, and his eyes left Tricia's closed and angry face to sweep a glance over David.

'Oh, they're practically engaged, you know!' Ngaire said happily. 'Isn't that nice? It's super to see people you care about all happy and settled. And Tricia's just about the nicest person I know – and the cleverest. Always tops the list in our exams, you know that, Adam?'

'Ngaire, you talk a damned sight too much,' Tricia snapped.

'Oh, I know. But it's true all the same. You'll see Adam, now she's on the third floor.'

'I'm still waiting to know what it is that – ' David began.

'Ah, yes. You have a right to know. Of course,' Adam said. 'It was foolish of me to mention it, perhaps. But there was an episode on the floor this morning. A neurotic girl did the all-too-common stunt of climbing out on a window sill and threatening to jump. And Nurse – er – Tricia – prevented her from doing so. But it left her a little shocked. It would upset anyone, of course.'

'Was that on the third floor?' Ngaire was agog. 'I'd heard that something happened on the Wing this morning, but I'd no idea! Trish, do tell!'

'There is nothing to tell. Dr Kidd has told it all,' Tricia said, her voice filled with a controlled anger. 'And *I* have a deeply rooted dislike of talking shop in my free time, so, if you don't mind, all of you, we'll shut up about it. David, a cigarette, please?'

'You must have been upset,' he said in a low voice as he lit one for her. 'You don't usually smoke so much.'

'Oh, for God's sake!' Tricia flared and dropped the cigarette in an ashtray and jumped to her feet. I'm beginning to feel like – like a baby! Whatever I do or say, there's one of you – oh, forget it. Look, I'm tired. Do you mind if I call it a day? Don't bother to see me back to the Home. I can find my own way.'

'I'm going back that way myself, actually,' Adam Kidd said, and stood up easily. 'So I'll be glad to – '

'That's all right, thanks, Kidd. I'll see my own girl back to her door.' David was on his feet too, while Ngaire sat still, her face a picture of distress, her lower lip between her teeth, staring from one to the other.

'No one need bother, thank you!' Tricia snapped, and took a deep breath. 'Goodnight!'

She turned to go, thrusting her chair angrily away from her, and a woman who was passing the table cried out, as the sharp leg of the chair hit her ankle, and Tricia said immediately, 'Oh, Lord, I'm so sorry!' and looked up at the woman's face.

'Not at all, Nurse Oxford,' Sister Cleland said, and bent to rub her ankle. 'Not at all.'

And as she straightened up, her eyes moved slowly over the group and stopped as she came to Dr Kidd's face.

'Good evening,' she said, and smiled thinly, and slid her eyes sideways again to look at Tricia's mortified red face. 'How pleasant to see you all enjoying yourselves. Very pleasant.'

6

'My dear old Trish,' the letter began. 'No, please, *please, please* don't tear this up, but read it. Honestly, who'd have ever thought I'd have to write a letter to my best friend in all the world to get her to listen to me? Well, read me, at any rate. Look, Trish, I'm sorrier than I can say about what happened last week, but you won't give me a chance to apologise. I honestly thought it'd help to get you and Kidd on speaking terms, after what you'd said had happened your first day in the Wing. I didn't know about the other thing, whatever it was, that happened that day – the Friday, I mean, when we all went to the old Pigsty. I still don't know much! Only that you clearly hate old Red Earth Kidd like poison, and if you do, then so do I. I mean, what are friends for if not to hate each other's enemies? I just don't know what to do. Every time I see you you stare right through me, and poor old David's kept on phoning me because he says you're mad at him too, and it isn't fair, really it isn't. I mean, what harm has *he* done? I reckon you're just so miserable on the Wing that no one can do anything right. And it was no one's fault you accidentally bashed the Cleland! Anyway, she deserved it. I'd rather bash her with a pub chair than anyone I know! Anyway, me old love, do please, forgive me. Believe me, I meant to do the right thing, and though I know I acted like an ass, I always do somehow, and I'm *lonely*. I mean, I know all the other girls in our set, but you're my best friend. Aren't you? Do come and have a natter in my room when you come off duty this evening. Please? I'll be waiting. Love. Ny.'

Tricia read the scribbled letter again, and then put it in her pocket, and stood for a moment leaning against the nurses' mail board before climbing wearily upstairs.

I suppose I am being a bit juvenile, she told herself. Sulking like this. But she really deserves it, the silly – ijjut. She smiled a little as Nurse Cavanaugh's favourite word slid into her mind. If it hadn't been for dear old Cavanaugh this past week, she'd have gone right out of her mind, one way and another. Sister Cleland being as icy as Greenland, and nagging her and going on at her for every minor misdemeanour until she thought she'd hit her if she said another word; Adam Kidd being remote and extremely punctilious, yet somehow making her feel as though he were constantly weighing her in a balance and finding her very wanting. Altogether, without Cavanaugh's cheerfulness and support, life would have been intolerable.

And I'm lonely too. I miss having Ny to natter to, and I miss David. Only how can I just pick up where I left off? It really wasn't his fault at all, any of it, but I was so mad I swept out of there like – like some demented duchess, and left him standing like a ninny. I owe him an apology, really –

She stood at the top of the stairs for a moment, in the quiet corridor crossed now with bars of late evening sunshine, and sniffed the familiar smells of polish and bath salts and coffee and toast; there was always someone making a snack of that sort in the little kitchen at the far end of the corridor. The doors marched away from her in serried rows, each of them with their little square of white pasteboard that carried the name of the occupant.

For a moment, she could have wept at the familiarity of it all, the comfortable feeling it gave her of belonging. This had been her home for almost three years now, the only home she had really, for she could hardly count her father's home as her's, not since his marriage. And her mother had gone to live in Italy after her remarriage, so that was that. Ngaire had been so marvellous all during that horrible winter, at the end of her first year, when the divorce had happened, making her see how important it was to live her own life her own way, and not to let her parents' private disasters spoil things for her. She and David; between them they had hoisted her over a very difficult patch, and now she was treating them like this, sulking like a great spoiled baby, all because of people as disagreeable and unimportant to her as Cleland and Kidd.

She moved then, to the window at the end of the corridor, to lean out and stare across the garden at the beech tree, at the two or three girls lying out in the sun, greedily absorbing all they could of the warmth that struggled through the smoky London sky. The beech tree. That was where David had kissed her the very first time. It had been a very sweet kiss, she remembered now. Gentle, and kind, and so – reassuring. That was it. Reassuring. And I'm being hateful to him now because of –

But he isn't all that disagreeable and unimportant, is he? a tiny voice in the deeper recesses of her mind whispered. That's really what's bothering you. There's something about that man that affects you. He makes you feel – what? Silly and stupid, and ineffectual. This is very different to the way David makes you feel. When you let him, David makes you feel cherished, and loved and protected.

Too protected. Isn't that why you get so irritable with him? Isn't that why you keep on and on about this business of having a career before you settle down to marriage? Your way of refusing to be looked after? And anyway, why are you thinking about Kidd and David in the same breath, as it were? One's the man who loves you, the other just – nobody really. Just a disagreeable man you have to work with. Disagreeable – but fascinating. Admit it. There's something about the man, the way he moves, the very square look of him, the way the crisp hair grows on the nape of his neck, the way his big hands move when he's working on a drip, or writing up charts, or examining a patient. Strong, and delicate and impersonal and very exciting.

And isn't that really why you and Cleland hate each other so? Never mind the fact that she apparently always is pretty rough on her staff – there's more to it than that. She knows you find Adam Kidd as – interesting – as you do. And she shares the same fascination. You've seen her, watching him walk down the corridor, seen her face when she answers the phone and it's him. And that's why she hates you.

Though she needn't worry about me, for Heaven's sake, Tricia told herself firmly, still standing staring out of the window. Because I am already very thoroughly established with my super David, thank you very much, and anyway Adam Kidd obviously thinks I'm so low I could crawl under a worm with my hat on –

'Trish?'

She turned, and there was Ngaire, wrapped in a towelling robe, her hair standing up in damp spikes on her head, her face flushed with the rosiness that comes with a hot bath. 'Hi Trish,' she said again a little uncertainly. 'Did you get my – '

'Oh, yes, you nut!' Tricia grinned at her. 'And yes. I have been sulking and yes I'm sorry, and yes I accept your apology, and yes let's forget it. OK?'

'Oh, thank God for that!' Ngaire cried, and threw her arms around Tricia so violently that she nearly shoved her backwards against the window, and Tricia laughed and cried out in protest, and fended her off. And a door along the corridor opened and someone shouted, 'Shut up, will you? I'm trying to get some sleep – ' and then slammed, and they both giggled softly, and went quietly along the corridor to Ngaire's room, to sit and drink strong very sweet tea and gobble great doorsteps of hot buttered toast and jam, and talk until it was almost dark.

And long before the hospital slid into the uneasy sleep that carried it from midnight to dawn, Tricia had, with Ngaire's pleading to encourage her, telephoned David and talked for a long time. They were talking still, rather later than midnight, but then sitting in the cool dimness under the 'Kissing Tree' with Tricia wrapped in David's heavy cardigan and warm arms and the marvellous feeling of being loved that he always brought with him to comfort her.

She went to bed that night feeling a good deal happier than she had when she had come off duty. The last thought she carried into sleep was the fact that the next morning Sister Cleland was off for the day and Dr Kidd had booked a lumbar puncture on one of the patients in Cavanaugh's caseload, with which Tricia would have to assist while Bridie carried out Sister's duties. And in spite of herself, it was a rather more pleasant thought than she felt it should be. Remembering the things David had whispered, out there in the shadow of the great beech tree.

'Ah, come on, Trish! be a real old pal, won't you? What harm can it do you, anyway?' Ngaire's voice softened to a familiar wheedling note. 'It's not as though it'd make all that much difference to you, now would it? You said yourself you've decided not to go out at all this next couple of weeks so that you can swot for Finals – though I still think you're mad, at that – so why not?'

'Because I'd have to be out of my mind to get involved again with one of your crazy schemes. I've had enough experience in the past of what happens, and I'm not about to get myself into any more trouble than I am already.' Tricia rolled over on to her back, and closed her eyes against the brilliance of the sun. 'What time is it?'

'Almost twelve,' Ngaire sighed deeply. 'It's not as though it was likely there'd be any problems, anyway – '

'I'll have to go and get into uniform in half an hour. Hell, it's the first real sunbathing day we've had this Spring, and I've got to be on duty all afternoon and evening.' Tricia yawned widely. 'There's no justice in this world.'

'Nor friendship,' Ngaire said mournfully.

'Now just you listen to me, Ngaire Taylor!' Tricia sat up so sharply that the shoulder strap of her swimsuit slipped, and a couple of medical students lazing on the other side of the small swimming pool, that had been built for the staff out of a legacy left by a grateful patient, whistled and called at her. She waved back a little irritably and turned again to Ngaire.

'What you're asking me to do is out of the question on any number of counts. First, I'm in enough trouble with the powers-that-be as it is. As far as I can tell, Cleland sends a bad report on me to the office if I so much as break a thermometer. Twice since I've been on the floor I've had to go to the office and listen to Matron lecture me on the right way to behave. Twice in a month! I haven't had so many bad reports in the whole time I've been here, I swear it. If I risk doing anything as daft as this so near to Finals, I'd probably get myself scuppered for good and all. Damn it all, suppose a case came in? Then what? I'll have been on duty all afternoon and evening anyway, so I'll be half asleep long before midnight – and I wouldn't have a clue what to do – '

'Yes, you would. You're a natural on theatres, you know you are. You've always said so yourself – '

'Liking theatre work and being able to cover for someone are two quite different things,' Tricia said firmly. And then when she saw the miserable expression on Ngaire's face, added uncertainly, 'Besides, I've got a date.'

'Oh, you liar!'

'Not at all!' Tricia looked away, squinting across at the group of boys on the far side of the pool. 'I've got a date with one of the senior students – '

'Trish this is me, Ngaire, remember? You told me what you'd arranged with David about studying, and knowing you, you'd never do anything so sneaky.'

Tricia looked sideways at her, and then sighed. 'Oh, all right, I haven't got a date. I could have, I suppose – '

'Of course you could!' Ngaire put her hand out and pinched Tricia's arm affectionately. 'I've always said you're a cracker, and that if old David hadn't turned up so early I'd be hard put to it to compete with you – '

'Flattery will get you everywhere – ' and then, seeing the way hope flared in the small freckled face, Tricia finished hastily, ' – except on theatres to cover for you tonight.'

'Oh, all right,' Ngaire said, and dropped her head. 'I suppose you really mean it, so that's that.'

'Why can't one of the others cover for you? Surely one of them'd change?' Tricia said. 'You have to take turns at being on call like this, don't you?'

'No joy there – I've tried it. Mary's off sick, and young whatsit's on holiday, and Sister's away too because she's got a lot of extra time off due to her, because of the closure of minor ops and the extra work they had in general theatres last month because of it – that's why I was sent to Private Wing Theatres to help out. I like it better than the General side, and it's nice being able to see you around.' Ngaire looked up and smiled a little shyly. 'Honestly, Trish. I do miss you when we aren't working near each other, you're so good for me.'

'Mmm. Like castor oil,' Tricia said sardonically.

'No, honestly. Except when you're being so beastly like now. I keep saying, no cases *can* come in! I've checked. Private maternity is full, and they've no booked cases due for the rest of this month, so there can't be any Caesars – and the forceps deliveries they do on the Floor. Every bed in the Wing is full – '

'And don't I know it,' Tricia said. 'We're run ragged this week – '

'So how can there be anything to do but cover the phone, and sit there till midnight? People on call don't have to stay after that – they can go to bed. So it's only for an hour and a half. But if you won't you won't,' and again she bent her head, and began tugging at the grass, picking succulent stems to chew on and then spit out.

There was a long pause, and then Tricia said, 'Why is it so important, Ny? You haven't said, you know! I mean, I know that as far as you're concerned a date with a good looking man is the most important thing in the world, but just to see someone for about half an hour – even for you, that's a bit over the top isn't it?'

'Maybe,' Ngaire mumbled, and startled, Tricia rolled over on her front again to peer more closely at Ngaire's face, bent industriously over her grass picking. 'Good God, Ny, you're crying! I've never – what on earth is it? Why is it so important?'

'Oh, it's – it doesn't matter, just a date. Forget it,' Ngaire said with a confusion that was so unusual in her that Tricia worriedly pulled at her shoulder and made her sit up.

'Now, tell me. Why is it so important? I didn't listen to you properly before. To be candid, I hardly ever do when you start on about the men in your life. But I've never seen you *cry* over one of them before.'

Ngaire looked up at her, and sniffed unappetisingly, her eyes red and wet.

'It's Pete, you see,' she said simply, as though that explained everything.

'Who is Pete? And what's so special about him?' Tricia said impatiently. 'And put a move on, Ny, I've got to change in a minute.'

'He's from home. The merchant seaman, remember?' Ngaire quite suddenly went very red and looked away. 'I – I've known him so long, you see, and he – I – we went out together in Christchurch when we were both at school, and – well, he'll be at Tilbury docks tonight for just half an hour. They're only in port three days, and he's not supposed to have any shore leave – he's second officer, and he's needed aboard or something – but he could meet me for half an hour tonight, and I thought – well, Hell, he's only a guy after all. Forget it. I – we'd both better change, hadn't we? I'm not too hungry, but there'll be trouble if we're late – ' and she jumped to her feet, and tugged her bikini briefs more respectably around her bottom before walking across the grass towards the changing huts.

'You're in love, Ny!' Tricia said a little breathlessly, as she hurried after her. 'I do believe – aren't you?'

'Well, what if I am?' Ngaire turned and said it almost savagely. 'I don't exactly enjoy being in love with a bloody sailor I don't get the chance to see from one year's end to the next. And the dear Lord knows I've tried hard enough to find someone else to fall in love with all these years here.' She shrugged then. 'But there it is. I get a cable from Pete, and I'm all of a tiz, and floating on pink clouds six inches off the ground, and can't get away for a couple of hours to meet him. And don't tell me to ask the office for special permission. They know as well as everyone else here the flibberty Ngaire Taylor falls in and out of love with every guy she meets, ha ha isn't it funny, and they aren't going to fall over backwards to arrange for me to meet another guy, are they?' she smiled her crooked smile again. 'Even if this is the only one that's for real or is ever likely to be. Oh, hell, forget it. We'd better get dressed.'

Tricia sat on the edge of one of the anaesthetist's tall stools, both palms flat on the red sorbo rubber of the operating table pads, and looked slowly around. Above her the big shadowless lamp glowed its deceptive softness, deceptive because of the brilliance with which the light picked out every detail of the area it illuminated. Every fine golden hair in the network of tiny lines on the back of her hands shone clearly in it. Beyond the brightness of the centre in which she sat she could see the gleaming tiles on the walls, the rows of chrome-bright shelves, empty now, but which bore rows of equipment and packs of dressings and all the other trappings of modern surgery when a case was in progress. The tall swab rack and the board beside it on which the pack and swab counts were made for each case, the big glass-fronted cabinets, filled with rows of beautiful, elegant shining instruments. They had a tremendously satisfying effect on the eye, with their patterns of loops and slender blades, curved forceps, wickedly sharp scissors, dumpy little hammers and small bone chisels. Lovely, she thought. So *right*, in this setting. If only they'd sent me here –

She sighed sharply then and peered up at the far wall where the big clock whispered the minutes away and creased her forehead in irritation. Ngaire had gone off in a great flurry of excitement – and Tricia had to admit she had never seen her look quite so starry eyed and lovely even though she was dressed only in her uniform, promising solemnly to be back at midnight, in time to take over. And now it was almost a quarter past twelve, and no sign of her. How typical!

She slid her feet to the floor and began another prowl of the theatres, walking softly from the anaesthetic rooms, with their silent patient trolleys and science-fiction-designed anaesthetic machines to the sterilising rooms with their gently hissing banks of chrome sterilising tanks, to Sister's office with its comfortable clutter of surgeon's armchairs and ricketty old coffee table loaded with assorted flower patterned cups and an electric percolator and a biscuit tin; the only human place in the unit, really she thought, though I like the clean perfection. And she took a chocolate biscuit from the tin; being alone in the thick silence like this somehow made her hungry.

She nearly choked on the crumbs as the shrill peal of the telephone shattered the silence, and she whirled to stare at the instrument on the desk with eyes wide with horror. Oh, no! To have been sitting here for an hour and a half, with no call, or anyone knowing Ngaire and she had committed this almost unforgivable sin of switching on-call duties without permission, only to have the phone ring, now, was too dreadful. And where the hell was Ngaire? She should have been here long ago, Tricia thought wildly, staring agitatedly at the door as though expecting the small cheeky figure to come bouncing through it immediately. But the phone rang insistently on, and still there was no Ngaire and something had to be done –

Her throat was dry and, considerably hampered by the remains of the chocolate biscuit, she picked up the hand set and said huskily, 'P – Private Wing Theatres.'

'My God, were you asleep?' a thin voice clacked. 'This is Dr Kidd. Look, I've got to use the theatres quickly. The excision of cerebral tumour from the First Floor that was done this morning – I think he's slipped a vein tie. The intracranial pressure is building up fast, and I've got to release it. I'll want to trephine – burr holes, right? The neuro team are all heavily involved with a major traffic accident on the general side, so I'll have to do it. I hope to God you know your neurosurgical routines well, because I can't pretend I know my way round your neuro theatre all that well. OK? In half an hour, no longer – '

'Oh, no – ' Tricia almost yelped it. 'No, no you can't – it's – not yet. She'll be back soon, you'll have to wait, really you will – '

'What did you say?' There was a sharp crackle as the voice on the other end of the phone was raised. 'Who the hell *is* that? I am talking to the Theatres, aren't I?'

'Yes – yes, you are. But I can't – oh, my God, I should have known this would happen – '

'Who *is* that? Oh, hell, I've no time to waste like this. I'm coming up – ' and the phone crackled and the dialling tone hiccupped and burred loudly in her ear and Tricia stood lumpishly staring at it in horror.

'Oh, no,' she said again, but the phone burred on, and then she heard a distant rattle and clanging, and knew that the lift had opened outside the Theatres door, and any moment Dr Kidd would come storming in –

She put the phone down, and closed her eyes and stood there, absolutely rigid. It wouldn't do any good, but there was nothing else she could think of doing.

'What in the name of all that's – what the bloody hell are *you* doing here?'

She opened her eyes and stood staring at him, taking in the fact that he was uncharacteristically dressed in a polo necked sweater over creased old slacks, and his usually sleek hair was rumpled. They must have called him out specially, she thought confusedly. That sweater suits him. Yellow's his colour.

'You're not on Theatres, are you?' his voice was rough with impatience.

'I'm covering for Ngaire. She's supposed to be on call, but – well, something came up and she asked me to, so I – I must have been mad. She swore she'd be back by midnight, and – oh, I could *kill* her – '

'Well, you'll just have to get on with it,' he said sharply, and turned away towards the central preparation area of the Theatres. 'Where're the neuro packs?'

'I don't know,' she hurried after him. 'I've done Theatres, as a junior, on the general side, but I've never worked these Theatres and – '

'You don't *know!*' he shouted. 'Christ Almighty! What sort of a – how the hell did you think you'd manage when you said you'd cover if you don't know where anything is?'

'Ngaire said she'd checked. The Wing's full, no maternity cases due – she swore nothing could happen – ' Tricia said miserably.

'Not much! Look, this just isn't on! I'll have to call Night Sister and get someone over from the general side, or else they'll have to call out one of the day staff. I can't risk – '

'Oh, *no!* you can't do that! They'll throw Ngaire out on her ear – both of us – if they find out! You can't – '

'Listen, you young idiot, when it comes to a patient's welfare I don't care if they hang you up by your feet and behead you – the patient comes first. I'll phone – '

'But it won't do any good!' Tricia cried desperately, running after him as he loped back into the office. 'There *isn't* anyone else to cover! That's why we did this stupid thing – there just isn't anyone, what with people being off sick and – and – you said yourself there's a major flap over on general theatres, so even if you do call, they won't be able to send anyone.'

He stopped, and turned and stared at her, and then closed his eyes and took a deep breath. 'What have I done to deserve – ' he murmured, and then shook his head, much as a dog shakes water from his pelt when he comes out of a river.

'OK. OK. We'll have to cope. Now, come on. Let's look round this place – instruments? Do you know where *they* are?'

She nodded eagerly. 'Here – ' and almost slid in her haste as she ran over the terrazzo floor towards the second of the three operating theatres that together made up the Private Wing Unit.

He followed her, as she fumbled against the wall for the bank of switches, and then the lights sprang on, vividly, bringing into life the tidy quiet theatre, making it look for all the world like a stage set, as though it were cut out of cardboard and cleverly painted.

He pushed past her, and made for the big instrument cabinets on the far side, and hurried past each one, peering in.

'General surgery – ENT – eyes – skin – ' he murmured. 'Ah – here we are! Trephines, brain suckers – here's the neuro lot.'

He tugged the door open. 'Right. Do the lot – every bloody instrument in the cabinet. Boil 'em and set up on the biggest trolley you can find in the sterilising room. Go and change first, for God's sake – you'll have to get that hair covered, and get gowned up – now *hurry*! And I'll start setting in here as soon as I've changed.'

He came back towards her, to where she stood in the doorway, still numb with the shock of trying to take in what was happening, and he stopped for a moment and looked at her very directly – and his eyes were exactly on a level with her own – and said with a little less roughness in his voice, 'Well, come on! Don't stand there looking like a scalded cat. You said you'd cover for your nutty friend, and cover you will. You've got some sense, somewhere, so use it. Acting the paralysed with fright bit isn't going to do much to help a patient with a bleeding point inside his skull, is it? Think what you're doing, start at the beginning, think out each step logically, and we'll manage. After all, I'm doing the surgery, so all you've got to do is what I tell you. And I'll be telling you every step of the way. So let's get on, shall we?'

7

She realised, quite suddenly, that she was actually enjoying herself. The past twenty minutes had been quite extraordinarily hectic, as together they boiled instruments, broke out the neuro packs – which Adam found in the bottom of the big neuro instrument cupboard ('Be logical, girl,' he'd snapped. 'Where the hell else are they likely to be?') and set gowns, gloves, masks and the rest of the paraphernalia of surgery ready.

In fact, she remembered far more than she realised from her previous Theatre experience, and her hands seemed to take over from her mind, as smoothly she made the pattern of a prepared Theatre build up around her busyness. When she asked Adam what he wanted in the way of ties and sutures, and showed him the big tray of atraumatic needles, tubes of assorted catguts and nylon and silk ties she had found on the lowest shelf of the neuro cupboard, he grunted approvingly and said, 'Lay out the lot – two of each, to be on the safe side. The most important thing is to be sure the sucker's going well. That skull isn't going to be easy to find my way around, I suspect. Right, now. All set? How long have the instruments had?'

She peered up over her mask at the big clock. 'Twenty minutes.'

'Right.' He made for the door. 'I'll call the ward to send the patient up, and then I'll scrub. Then you can dish up the stuff after the patient's on the table, and I'll help set the trolley while you scrub – '

'While I scrub?' she yelped, terrified again. 'But wouldn't it be better if I stayed as dirty nurse? Someone'll have to run – '

He shook his head. 'No. The ward girl'll have to do that for us. I've got to have someone to assist me, and there's no one else but you.' He looked back at her from the floor, and smiled fleetingly, his eyes crinkling over his mask. 'Don't worry. You've managed very well so far. You can do it.'

I wish I could be so damned sure, she thought frantically, as she made a last check that all was ready. It's been a hell of a long time since I scrubbed for a theatre case – and even then it was only an appendix, and not a brain – oh, Ngaire, where the hell *are* you? It's getting near to one o'clock, and you promised you'd be back at midnight. I feel like Cinderella in reverse or something –

Far away, she heard the rattle and clang of the lift again, and then the big doors swung open, and the trolley came in, pushed by a ward nurse, carrying high in one hand a blood transfusion bottle, and guided by Adam himself. Together, the three of them lifted the heavy patient on to the table under the cruelly revealing bright light and she looked down at the waxen face under the almost as white bandage that covered the skull, and thought confusedly 'he looks very young – twenty or so, no more – '

And then, the ward nurse clipped the blood bottle to the stand at the foot of the table, and checked that the tube that ran into the patient's ankle was smooth and the blood dripping steadily, and Adam rapidly fastened the broad rubber straps across the flaccid arms and legs.

'There's no need for an anaesthetic, of course,' he told the ward nurse, who was hovering anxiously beside him. 'He's deeply unconscious, and I don't want to mask any responses we may get as we relieve the pressure on the brain – but if he gets restless – starts to move – during the operation, watch that drip, OK? No, don't worry – ' he caught the look of horror in the girl's eyes. 'I know it sounds odd, but this is necessary and it's normal procedure. He'll feel no pain, of course. Right, keep a check on his pulse and blood pressure, then, and we'll be ready to go in – ten minutes,' he looked again at the big clock, then at Tricia. 'Very well, Nurse, dish up. I'll be ready when you are.' And he went swiftly to the scrubbing-up area at the far end of the theatre.

Tricia, sweating a little in the heat and manipulating the big bowl and instrument tray forceps a little stiffly at first, but then with increased assurance, carried the great trays of instruments from the sterilisers to the trolley, then brought out the stacks of bowls and kidney dishes and little gallipots, and distributed the instruments along the towelled surface of the trolley. Drills, hammers, small bone chisels, burr heads. Check. Suction heads, artery clips, retractors. Check. Sponge holders, needle holders, scissors, scalpels. Check. Swabs, packs, lotions, handbowls. Check –

And then Adam called her, and quickly she tied his gown behind his broad back, and flipped an envelope of gloves out of the drum towards him, thinking absurdly – size eight and a half. I knew he had big hands – and then he was sleeking the smooth, soft, brown rubber over his fingers, twisting his gown cuffs deftly under the wrists of the gloves as he moved over to the table.

'Scrub fast, Nurse,' he said over his shoulder as he went. 'Nurse Thingy here from the ward will tie your gown – ' and Tricia nodded, and kicked the tap control under the basin with her right foot, and as the warm water gushed over her shaking hands, started the methodical scrubbing of fingers, palms, backs of hands, wrists –

Behind her she could hear the heavy breathing of the man on the table, the click and rattle of instruments as Adam set out the instruments in the order he wanted them, the quiet burr of his voice above the rush of water as he told the ward nurse how to connect up the sucker. Then, the sucker hissed and bubbled, faltered and then hissed again steadily, and she looked up at the clock, and thought – three more minutes to scrub –

As the ward nurse tied her gown strings behind her, she hissed into Tricia's ear, 'What's going on here? Why only you? Where's the usual theatre girl?' but Tricia pretended not to hear, to be too busy putting on her golves. It was crazy to think there wouldn't be trouble over this; someone in authority was sure to find out that the wrong nurse had been on Theatres tonight, and then, oh boy, would she and Ngairc be in trouble –

But there was no time to think of that now. The important thing was to get the operation over. Safely. And she found herself praying, somewhere deep inside herself, please, let it all be all right, let him get well, don't let him die – though she knew just how desperately ill the man was, just how slender were his chances. Adam had to find the bleeding point, and find it fast, she realised as she heard again, above the sound of the hissing sucker, the heavy thick breathing, saw the sickly colour of the man's face as, expertly, Adam picked up forceps with which to take off the bandage that covered the skull.

At least we don't have to shave the head, she thought, as she clipped a green towel around the forehead, mercifully covering the blank pallid face and rim of white which showed under the relaxed lash-fringed lids. The stitches that had been put in the scalp only this morning were revealed as the last dressing came off, and she picked up a pair of sponge holders and a swab of cotton wool, and dipping it into the gallipot of prepared skin lotion, began to paint the scalp in long smooth strokes.

Beside her, Adam picked up scissors and forceps and his big square fingers moving with deceptive slowness, began to snip out the stitches, and then the pearly gleam of bone appeared, and she closed her eyes for one sick moment; she had forgotten how momentarily distressing it was, this first assault on a human creature, lying still and helpless on the table. It had always made her feel a stab of pity, made her feel as though it were her own body that was being probed at, and touched with those impersonal cold metal instruments.

But the moment passed, and she was too busy to feel anything for the patient, watching those hands, trying to anticipate each move, trying to decide what instrument he'd need next, feeling a surge of triumph when she guessed right, and then the angry self-blame that came when she guessed wrong, and he waved away one of her proffered instruments and clicked his fingers irritably towards another.

There was a long agonising pause for her then, as he fitted a fine burr to the small hand drill, and after a moment of apparent indecision, set the delicate curved tip of the instrument against the pinkish grey bone, and began, at first slowly, and then more rapidly, to turn the drill, one hand following the other in perfect rotary movements. And the burr head slid gently inwards, and she could only stand and watch, feeling as though the drill were in her own hands, as though she had to make the hairsbreadth judgement, had to decide when the shell of bone had been just penetrated, to stop before the vulnerable brain tissue was touched.

But the judgement was made for him, for suddenly bright red blood welled up, and he said with a suddenness that made her jump, so loudly did his voice ring out in the hissing silence, 'Sucker!'

And she put the long curved sucker end into the hand he held out without looking up, and nodded at the ward nurse, who immediately kicked the switch on the machine on the floor.

The machine bubbled, and the redness slowly shifted from the operation area to the bottle that was clipped to the machine, making its watery contents a rosy translucent and gradually deepening pink.

He reached out his hand again, and automatically, her own picked up the fine Gigli saw – the length of delicate steel wire that was needed to cut the bone connecting the new burr hole to one of those that had been made during the morning's operation, and again his hands moved in a balletic smoothness as the protective shell of skull gave up its defences, and revealed the beautiful convoluted surface of the brain. And she felt that long forgotten surge of satisfaction that she had been used to knowing, in the days when she had been a junior theatre nurse, seeing the very real loveliness of a section of the human body that was usually so secretly hidden opened to her watching eyes. There was nothing to fear, nothing to regard as nasty or ugly in any aspect of the body, and she looked and felt humble at what she saw.

The sucker, probing deeper as his smooth, brown-gloved hand guided it on, bubbled faster, and the pink water in the bottle deepened to a glow that threw a dancing ruby reflection on the grey terrazzo of the floor, and he said urgently, 'I think I've found it – quick. An atraumatic needle – medium size – '

Again her hands seemed to act of their own volition, selecting from the sutures tray the one he wanted, wrapping the glass tube in a gauze swab, cracking it with a sharp twist of her wrists, pulling out the tiny hank of catgut twisted round the filament of gleaming steel needle, and fastening it to the needle holder with a click of the handles as the ratchets met and held.

As she put it into his waiting hand, the sucker sang and bubbled less loudly, and there was a movement beneath the green sheeting that covered the man on the table, and the ward nurse cried shrilly, 'He's moving – Dr Kidd – his legs moved!'

'Good – good – then I have got it – ' Adam said, and there was jubilation in his voice. 'Watch that bloody drip – he'll move more yet – '

Across the big theatre she felt rather than saw the door open, but she didn't look up, too busy preparing another atraumatic needle, knowing he'd need it. When she was ready, and holding it out towards him, she saw the ward nurse scuttle to one side with alacrity, saw her place taken by another, small figure. And looked at the face of the newcomer, and saw above the line of the mask across the nose the wide eyes of Ngaire, and she grinned in sheer relief.

But Ngaire just looked back at her, her eyes showing no response, but Tricia forgot her as Adam put his hand out again, and she took the spent needle from him, and gave him the new one, and he grunted, and jerked his head towards the sucker which he was holding in his other hand.

'Here – keep the suction going – just there. No deeper, or God help you. I've got to get a retractor in – '

As they worked on, the movements of the man on the table increased, and Ngaire called softly to the ward nurse. 'Here! Hold his legs. I'll take the arms – ' and together the two gowned figures held desperately on as Adam, his hands now moving so swiftly Tricia could hardly keep up with his demands, completed his manoeuvres with the needle and catgut, tied the ends, snipped away the needle with the scissors, and very gently, pulled the sucker head from Tricia's hand, and eased it slowly out of the wound.

Then, they all stood still, only the patient moving with an occasional spasmodic heave, watching the operation area. But no more frightening redness welled up, no more did the bottle deepen its ruby glow, and the reflection on the floor stopped moving as no more liquid from the skull came down the tube to join the bottle's contents.

'Right.' Adam's voice sounded very matter of fact, and again Tricia jumped slightly at the sound. 'I'd say we've got it. Nurse – er – Thingy.'

He looked up, and for the first time became aware of the fact that there were two figures beside the patient, and his eyebrows lifted, and he said, 'Oh – Nurse Taylor? Good. You've finished that case in general theatres? Everything all right?'

Ngaire stared at him, and her brows too moved under the edge of her cap, and Adam went on smoothly, 'Well, we're almost through here. Check his blood pressure, will you? And then I want you to give him the drugs he needs – you'll find them ready on the side by the gloves. I put them there before we started – hurry along, now. You can inject straight into the drip tube.'

Tricia could have wept with gratitude as she realised just what he had done. To have covered up for them both, in front of another nurse, was incredibly good natured of him, she told herself as she prepared the skin sutures, and put the needle holder into his waiting hand. He could have raised merry hell in the office for this evening's escapade, but instead – really, a generous bloke. How could she have thought him so disagreeable all these weeks?

And then, suddenly, it was all over. The skin sutures were in the scalp, a row of tidy little knots, and together she and Adam managed to get a firm dressing on, although it wasn't easy, for now the man, albeit still unconscious, was moving considerably, thrashing about heavily so that it took all the muscle power they had between them to hold him still. But they managed it, and then Ngaire was there beside the table with the trolley ready to take him back to the ward, and Tricia hadn't even realised she'd gone out to get it.

The four of them heaved the man on to the trolley and wrapped the red blankets carefully across him, strapping it in place with the wide leather trolley straps, and then the ward nurse, again holding the blood bottle high in the air, was moving backwards out of the theatre, while Adam was at the head holding the man's chin up firmly with one hand, the other on the brilliant white bandage and looking hugely protective there.

The double doors swung behind them, and once again there came from the distance the crash of the lift gates, the faint whining hum as it moved away towards the First Floor, and the two girls stood silent in the shambles that the theatre had become. Looking down at her gown. Tricia realised for the first time that it was heavily bloodstained, that even the floor was spattered, that the trolley of instruments was an incredible mess of discarded towels and swabs and used instruments.

She looked up, and shakily pulled the gloves from her fingers, to drop them into the bowl of water that stood in a rack beside the table, and then she pulled her mask down till it dangled below her chin, and said sardonically to Ngaire, 'Well, hello there. So what kept you? I suppose you realise what you've done, you bloody *idiot*? And that he covered up for you in front of that girl from the ward? Where *were* you, for God's sake? Do you realise what the time is?'

Ngaire too had pulled her mask down, and stood looking at Tricia with her face suffused with misery. 'Oh, Trish – I – you can't – if I tried to tell you, I'd – ' and then her eyes filled with tears, till they spilled over and ran down her face, and she was gulping and sobbing, holding her hands one on each side of her face as though she knew no other way to hold her shaking head still.

But Tricia was in too towering a rage to respond as she would normally have done to so pitiful a sight. 'So I should think, you fool! God alone knows whether we're going to get away with this. If we don't, it'll be your fault and no one else's – do you think that – '

'Well, I hardly see that shouting at her like a fishwife is going to do much good. It would be a little more to the point to use some of the excess energy you seem to be blessed with in clearing this place, wouldn't you say?'

Adam Kidd was standing by the door, both hands behind his neck as he fiddled with the ties on his gown, and then impatiently he tugged until the narrow tapes broke and he pulled off the gown to throw it over the operating table.

'If anyone has cause to be angry, it's me, I would say. More by luck than anything else, it's gone all right. The man should make it because I found the slipped tie easily. What would have happened if I hadn't I don't like to think of. Now, Nurse Taylor – stop that ridiculous noise at once, and blow your nose. And then you can get this place organised and go off duty – '

'I – I'm sorry, Dr Kidd,' Ngaire managed to say, and then took a deep breath, and digging into her pocket for a handkerchief, blew her nose violently. 'I appreciate very much the way you – I mean, that about being on general theatres. You didn't have to cover up for me, and I truly – '

'Cover up for you?' He raised his eyebrows at that. 'You don't think I gave a damn about you, do you?' he flicked his eyes towards Tricia then. 'About either of you for that matter, though you did very well, Nurse Oxford, under the circumstances – better than I'd suspected you could, but only as well as you should have done, since you agreed to get yourself into such a situation that the ability to cope was demanded of you. No, my dear young ladies – ' and the sneer in his voice was very apparent, 'My covering up for you, as you put it, was sheer enlightened self-interest. If you think, either of you, that I have the time or the inclination to get myself involved in a great boring argument involving the nursing discipline of this hospital, that I'm prepared to waste my energy talking about this evening to your Matron and the rest of them, you have another think coming. I couldn't care less about what rules you've broken, or what would happen to you if your breaking of them was discovered. The operation went reasonably well, and that's all

I'm concerned about. And if you've any sense at all, you'll both keep your mouths shut about it. Now, goodnight. You'd better get to bed, Nurse Oxford, and leave your colleague to clean up, since you will be on duty on my floor first thing in the morning, and I want to be sure you're in a fit state to work. And Nurse Taylor will have the excuse of having dealt with a night case, so she'll be allowed to catch up on her rest, I imagine.'

And he turned and went, leaving them both staring after him. And then Ngaire said in a heavily weary voice that was totally unlike her usual one, 'Well, be grateful for small mercies. I'm sorry you had to put up with that, Trish. You didn't deserve it – I should have copped all of it – but – but – ' she swallowed with a noisy gulp. 'Oh, God, I don't think I can take much more tonight – I really don't – ' and again she put her hands up to her face and began to cry with a bitter lost helplessness that twisted her face into a caricature of its usual pert prettiness.

Tricia had been standing very still, staring after Adam Kidd, feeling numb with fatigue and the sort of breathless shock that comes with having a quantity of ice cold water thrown over one. She turned her head slowly, now, and looked at Ngaire, and as the awareness of her misery penetrated, said quickly, 'Oh, don't cry like that, please! It's over now, and even though he – well, whatever he said, he isn't going to shop us, and the girl from the first floor seemed to accept his word happily enough, so she won't shop us either. There's nothing to be so desperate about – '

But Ngaire just shook her head and wept on, and moving stiffly, for now her tiredness was filling her muscles with pain, Tricia went over to her, and put an arm about her shoulders, and led her, shaking as she was, to the sterilising room, to bathe the small face with swabs dipped in cold running water.

'Come on, now, it isn't that bad,' she murmured. 'You don't usually make such a fuss when you get out of a scrape, you daft thing! Now calm down, and give *me* a chance to flip my lid, eh?'

Ngaire turned her head, and buried her damp face in Tricia's shoulder, and slowly the storm of tears subsided until she was breathing more evenly again, only hiccuping slightly from time to time.

'I'm sorry,' she managed at last. 'Truly sorry. I wouldn't have had it happen for the world, Trish, you know that – ' and she looked up with her drowned violet blue eyes looking red-rimmed and anxious. 'It – it wasn't on purpose, you know that, don't

you, Trish? I – truly, I couldn't help it, and I – I don't – I can't – '
again her eyes filled with tears, but this time, she scrubbed at
them with her fists, and shook her head violently. 'No, it's no
good. Look, Trish – do as he said. Go to bed and I'll clear up, and
God bless you for what you did for me tonight. I only wish that –
no, I – tomorrow – ' and she put her arms round Tricia and
hugged her, and then pushed her away. 'Go on now. I'll – there's
things to tell you. In the morning, maybe. But right now, you get
going – '

Tricia was too exhausted to argue, and moved away to the
changing room, and wearily took off the theatre gear into which
she had changed so hurriedly so many aeons ago – was it only an
hour that had passed? It didn't seem possible; and holding her
cap and apron in one hand, bundled herself into her cape, ready
to go away out into the darkness of the garden, and across to the
long since shuttered and sleeping nurses' home.

At the theatre door she looked back, and saw Ngaire moving
about with a sort of desperate effortfulness that made Tricia's
own eyes start with tears suddenly. Clearly, there was something
very wrong with Ngaire, clearly something more than the way
she had let Tricia down was upsetting her. She could never
remember seeing the ebullient Ngaire behave so strangely; it was
as though she had aged ten years since they had last seen each
other.

But she was too tired, now, to think about it, to think about
Ngaire, or Kidd, or what had happened this evening. Every fibre
in her was crying out for rest, and she went out of the door and
down the dim staircase, leaving Ngaire in the vividly lit theatres,
cleaning up and scrubbing instruments. Tomorrow, we'll talk
about it, and I'll find out what's the matter with her, tomorrow.
Not now.

8

The next morning should have been a rather pleasanter one than Tricia had ever spent on the third floor since, for the first time, she was allotted her own patients, though clearly somewhat against Sister Cleland's will.

'I have no choice, since the pressure of work on the floor is so high,' she said sourly. 'But I am warning you, Nurse, you will be under my eye very closely indeed. There are two new admissions you are to take – Mr Philip Bartlett, coming in this afternoon for investigations – he'll have room 306 – and in 305, a Mrs Joan Slattery, coming in for cosmetic surgery to the face. Now, get the rooms ready in good time, and make sure all the charts are correctly prepared.'

But despite the mild satisfaction of at last being treated as one of the floor's nursing staff rather than a barely tolerated errand runner, her anxiety about Ngaire kept coming between her and her work. She hadn't been in her room early in the morning when Tricia went to call for her at breakfast time, and she had been surprised not to find her in the dining room when she got there. And the same thing happened at lunchtime; the junior theatre nurse told Tricia, when she put her head round the door to ask if Ngaire were on duty, 'She's off for the rest of the day – had a case last night'; but she wasn't at lunch – nor at tea or supper.

It really was very odd, considering how rarely a day passed without the two meeting somewhere in the big hospital, and particularly so after the events of the night before.

And remembering those events, Tricia had found her face had suddenly flamed when, while she was in the office with Sister Cleland having the notes of her two new patients checked, Adam Kidd had come in. She realised immediately that Sister Cleland had noticed her embarrassment, felt the resentment in the other woman, but couldn't control the response.

But clearly he was going to be as good as his word, and made no mention of the operation of the night before, presenting Tricia with his usual chilly attitude. Which should have pleased her, but somehow made her feel obscurely hurt. During that hour last night, there had been a sort of rapport between them, and her gratitude for his statement that he would make no report of what had happened had made her feel a definite warmth towards him. But he had quenched that very effectively, now.

She had to accompany him when he went to examine the two new patients in her care, and she couldn't resist feeling a moment of malicious pleasure because he did not arrive to make this round until after Sister Cleland had gone off duty. 'If she wants to think I like Kidd, let her,' she thought. 'I know how much I dislike him, and that's good enough for me – '

And yet, dislike him or not, there was still that infuriating fascination to be found in him. She watched him as he greeted Mrs Slattery, stood by quietly as he examined her heart and lungs and made a general assessment of her condition, and told herself 'it's because he's a good doctor. You can dislike someone, and still admit they're good at their job – and he is. He's got this silly creature eating out of his hand – '

She had taken one of her immediate dislikes to Mrs Slattery. She was a little woman with a superb figure which she knew how to show to its best advantage; she had arrived wearing a very well fitted trouser and sweater outfit that revealed every curve, and was now sitting up in bed in a demure white cotton pyjama suit that made her look very young and appealing until one looked at her face.

A small pointed face, with a heavily made up complexion that couldn't disguise the lined forehead, the sagging flesh under the eyes, the crêpiness of the neck. She was forty-five and looked it – but wouldn't look it much longer, as she told Adam Kidd with a brittle gaiety that made Tricia's lip curl.

'Do show me, Doctor,' she said in her high girlish voice. 'I'm dying to see – can't you give me some idea of the effect?'

'Well, I'll try,' he said good naturedly. 'Nurse, bring a mirror from the dressing table, will you – that's it, hold it so – '

He sat down on the bed, behind Mrs Slattery, so that she had to lean against him – and she did so with a kittenish wriggle that hardened Tricia's dislike of her – and then put his finger tips to each side of her face.

'Now, there'll be two incisions here, just in front of the ears – ' he slid his fingers over her cheeks from the turned-up nose towards the ears, and the lines disappeared, giving the little face a taut young look. 'Then, a gentle lifting here, to the hairline – ' His fingers moved up her brow, smoothing out the lines again, 'and finally a tightening here – ' he stroked her neck, and again the skin tautened, 'with the incisions just here at the hairline behind the ears. You'll have to be shaved at these points, of course, but it will grow again very quickly, and there'll be no scars to be seen.'

He grinned at her as he stood up, and she settled back against her pillows. 'So you should appear to shed a good ten years or more. Will that have the effect you want?'

Her eyes shadowed for a moment, and then the girlish smile came back and she said, 'My dear, it's got to! But you know that, don't you?'

'I know,' he said. 'Now, tonight, I'll order a sedative for you – you need plenty of sleep to prepare you – and tomorrow nothing to eat or drink after six a.m. You'll be going to theatre about three in the afternoon. Any problems, let me know. Your surgeon will be here to see you tonight, and maybe the anaesthetist, though as I've examined you now he'll only have to order your premedication drugs. Enjoy it all, now! You'll be getting a good rest thrown in with the operation, after all!'

Tricia looked back for a moment at Mrs Slattery – who was again peering in the mirror – and as she followed Adam Kidd from the room, and could have snorted her disgust. Trust Sister Cleland to give her a stupid woman having a face lift as one of her first special patients, she thought. She did it on purpose, because of what I said about private patients in general. Anyway, I was certainly justified in my opinion as far as this one's concerned.

But the patient in room 306 was a very different sort. He was sitting up in bed, very erect and still against the pillows piled up behind him, his face thin and white above the scarlet of his silk pyjamas. He was a man of about forty, and quite remarkably handsome, with a strong square chin with a small cleft in it, and very dark eyes with incredibly long sooty black lashes, and curly dark hair. But his cheeks were hollow and his hands pathetically bony, lying idly on the counterpane.

'Well, hello there,' he said with a sudden brilliant smile that was aimed at both of them as they came to stand beside his bed.

'Nice to see you! I was getting tired of the view from the window. Half a tatty roof and an expanse of dingy London sky isn't exactly exciting, is it? Not like you, now, Nurse. You'd brighten any patient's day! Am I going to see more of you in here? I hope so, I must say I liked the look of you as soon as I saw you this afternoon – '

He looked up at Adam Kidd then and and said wickedly, 'Lucky fellows, you doctors! Now if we had such decorative creatures around working with us, I swear we'd never get a building up – but architects don't enjoy your sort of privileges. Well, Doc, what are we going to do here? Are you going to find out at last what it is that's wasting so much of my time? I'm getting very bored with all this you know – ' he grimaced. 'Weak as a cat most of the time, and no one can tell me why! It's really too ridiculous – '

'We'll do our best, Mr Bartlett. I know it's very tedious for you but we'll hurry as much as we can. And since you approve of your nurse, you must let her spoil you – don't do a thing for yourself she can't do for you.'

'A pleasure to follow such eminently sensible medical advice,' Mr Bartlett said promptly, and put out one hand to pinch Tricia's arm playfully.

Pink faced, Tricia extricated her arm gently, very aware of Adam's sardonic gaze, and then there was a tap on the door, and gratefully she hurried across the room to open it.

Outside, a woman muffled in a very expensive looking fur coat and clutching a huge bunch of flowers in one hand, and a big gold-topped green bottle in the other, peered at her; a very pretty woman, Tricia realised at first glance, as well as a very elegantly dressed one.

'I'm so sorry,' she said. 'But I'm afraid Mr Bartlett can't have any visitors at the moment – the doctor is with him – ' but already the woman had moved forwards, and slipped past her into the room.

'Maxine, my dear girl! You made it very quickly!' the man in the bed said.

'I know – aren't I a marvel?' she cried gaily. 'I thought I'd never be able to park, but there was this absolute poppet of a man – a real dish, I promise you, who helped me – too darling for words –how are you, Philip, my angel?' She leaned over the bed and kissed him. 'Comfortable and all that? I say, this is a luscious room!'

'As comfortable as can be expected,' Philip Bartlett said with mock solemnity. 'Doctor, this is my wife, Maxine.'

'How do you do, Mrs Bartlett,' Adam Kidd said. 'I want to talk to you later, but right now, if you don't mind . . .'

'I know, I know – I'm in the way!' she dimpled at him, holding her head to one side. 'But you have a delightful way of saying so. Really, Philip, if I'd known they had such charming doctors here, I'd have insisted on your coming in weeks ago!'

'If I'd known about the nurses, I'd have needed no insistence,' he said, but his voice sounded less cheerful than it had. He's tiring very quickly, Tricia thought. All this social chitchat – it's out of place in a hospital room. ' – so we're both happy,' he finished. 'Anyway, away with you, and leave me to my medico. There's some sort of waiting room I imagine – '

'We'll really have to get to know each other better, all of us,' Maxine Bartlett went on, her eyes still on Adam. 'Little parties, Philip, darling, yes? I'll bring more champagne and lots of delicious goodies, and we'll have ourselves a ball.'

Tricia opened the door. 'I'll show you the waiting room, Mrs Bartlett,' she said a little frostily. 'If you'll follow me, please – '

'I know when I'm beaten!' Maxine said, and laughed a high tinkling laugh. 'I'll be waiting for you Doctor. With eager pleasure, I assure you. See you later, Philip, angel,' and putting the flowers and the champagne bottle on his locker, she blew him a kiss and went out.

Tricia took her to the small visitors' waiting room, and turned to return to room 306, but Mrs Bartlett put her hand out to stop her.

'He looks awful lying there, doesn't he?' she said abruptly. 'Worse than at home, somehow. Do you know – ' she stopped and bit her lip, staring at Tricia. 'No, I don't suppose you know anything yet, do you?'

Tricia shook her head. 'I'm sorry. Dr Kidd will tell you all he can when he has examined the patient. If you'll just wait here –'

'Kidd – is that his name? He looks rather nice. Is he?'

'I really couldn't say,' Tricia said, and now there was more frost in her voice. 'If you'll wait here he'll be along very soon. Excuse me, please,' and she left the woman standing there and hurried back to room 306, irritated and uncomfortable. Ye gods, but what a collection of people you meet in a Private Wing, she thought. Either playing at being patients or treating an illness like – like a fashionable cocktail party.

When she got there, Adam was writing a list of test requests. 'Nurse Oxford, will you call the laboratory about this lot?' he said, and gave her a sheaf of them. 'And I'll want a blood tray now to take some specimens. As soon as possible, please – '

She helped him as he collected specimens of blood from Mr Bartlett and then made the bed and washed and settled the weary man to have a short rest before dinner, while Adam went along the corridor to talk to Maxine Bartlett. And remembering the interest the woman had shown in her husband's doctor, she felt a stab of angry pity as she looked down at the man in the bed, now lying with his eyes closed in exhaustion. Whatever was wrong with him – and it would be a while before the test results came back with that information – he was clearly a very sick man, yet his wife could twitter and giggle at another man like some – some silly chorus girl.

I wish I was back on nights she thought bleakly. Or in theatres. Anything rather than this horrible place – and that thought reminded her of Ngaire and her odd behaviour, and resurrected her worry about the way she was keeping out of sight. Altogether, being Tricia Oxford wasn't very comfortable at that moment.

It was perhaps her distress about Mr Bartlett that made her speak as she did to Adam Kidd, when she found him sitting at the desk in the office, scribbling a last note into one of the charts.

'Perhaps you'll see what I meant, now, when I said what I did about private patients on my first day here,' she said tartly, putting the chart she had brought from Mr Bartlett's room in front of him.

'What?' he looked up, abstracted. 'What was that?'

'I said – oh, never mind. It isn't important,' she wished now she hadn't started.

But he put his pen down. 'What was it you said about private patients that day? You must forgive me if I don't remember every word that falls from you. You say quite a few of them.'

'That they aren't really patients at all,' she snapped. 'Or that some of them aren't. And even those that are, well, it isn't easy to take their problems all that seriously, is it? That woman!'

'Which woman?' he said with a slightly exaggerated patience.

'Mrs Bartlett! Her husband's obviously ill, and she couldn't care less, that's pretty clear – and as for Mrs Slattery!'

The phone began to ring, and he turned his chair towards it, but she went on raising her voice a little above its noisiness,' – a face lift! It's all wrong, wasting beds on such things, when there's so many people on the general waiting lists needing real care – '

She stopped then as he spoke into the phone, and turned away, but then she froze, for standing just outside the office door, her frilly pink housecoat clutched around her, was Mrs Slattery, her face bleak as she stared at Tricia.

Filled with compunction – for whatever her opinion of a patient she certainly didn't intend the patient to hear it – Tricia opened her mouth to speak, but Mrs Slattery just shook her head almost imperceptibly, and walked on, her head held high. Clearly, she had been on her way from her room to the lavatory, and had passed the door just in time to hear Tricia's remarks. Tricia stared after her, her lower lip caught between her teeth, and could have bitten her own tongue off, so upset with herself did she feel.

Behind her, the phone clattered, and Adam's voice said sharply, 'Now, where was I? Ah yes, you were about to repeat your well known views on the patients here – '

'I'm sorry,' she said quickly. 'I – shouldn't have. I was just a bit – '

'A bit half-cocked as usual,' he said wearily. 'If you'd waited, I'd have told you a little more about these patients of yours. Making judgements on the basis of minimal information is a pretty juvenile thing to do, don't you think? The essence of good medical care – and that means nursing too – is to collect all the facts, and then act on them. Not to jump to ridiculous conclusions in that immature fashion.'

'Immature!' she said, stung. 'I'm not exactly a child, you know! I'm twenty-two – and you can hardly call someone who's had three years of nursing experience immature!'

'Some people can be nursing for thirty years and at the end of it all they've done is had the same year thirty times over. They're still juvenile in their attitudes. You need to watch yourself. You've got a lot more to learn about life as well as about nursing. I seem to remember saying that to you before – when the Sandra contretemps occurred. You'd never thought about the problems implicit in abortion, as I recall. Nor about any other such important aspects of life as the effects of illness in a patient on relatives – '

'That's not fair! I've often had to deal with relatives of patients – '

'No doubt! But you haven't learnt much, have you? You're assuming Mrs Bartlett doesn't care about her husband's illness because she seemed so – flighty. Isn't that what you were saying, in effect?'

'Well, isn't she? It was more like – like a party in there, when she came in!'

'What do you expect her to do? Come in tears? Of course her husband is ill. Very ill, and well she knows it. All I can say is that if you think she doesn't care, you've got a lot to learn about people. There's more to maturity than mere age, I assure you. It's a matter of understanding people, and how they tick. If you could learn to look outside yourself and at other's needs with the same anxiety you show for your own you'd be surprised how much better a nurse you could be. And how much more successful a person.'

He stopped then, and rubbed his face a little wearily. 'Oh, for heaven's sake – why do I bother? I've lectured more nurses about nursing than I care to count. And much good it does them or me, as far as I can tell. Get these specimens to the lab., will you? That'd be more to the point right now than listening to me pontificating.'

He stood up and handed her the last of the specimen forms, and the small bottles of blood he had collected from Mr Bartlett. 'And by the way – Mr Bartlett is likely to be a very difficult patient. He doesn't know how ill he is, and he mustn't know because I have it on excellent authority that his isn't a personality that can cope with stress well at the best of times. And his illness is a very severe one. He's in a very active phase of acute leukaemia. You'll need all the tact you have.'

There was a long pause, and then she said softly. 'I'm sorry. Very sorry,' and looking more closely at him, added without thinking, 'It's upset you a lot, hasn't it? Seeing him?'

He raised his eyebrows at that. 'Well, well! So you can be perceptive after all! Yes. It's upset me. I hate to see a young man, someone with the gifts he's got, wasted to a disease we haven't the answer to yet. It's a wicked, cruel thing – ' He shook his head irritably. 'However, the way I feel – or you feel, come to that – is beside the point. It's his feelings that matter. And he isn't to know, not by any sign from anyone, just how bad his outlook is. Remember what happened with Sandra, and learn to control your thoughts and therefore your expression when you're with a patient. You have a remarkably expressive face, you know. Everything you think is written all over it. So remember that.'

Immediately she went scarlet with embarrassment, and looked down at the floor. 'I'll remember,' she said stiffly.

He moved to the floor, and then turned back, and suddenly, put his hand on her shoulder. Startled, she looked up.

'I seem to have done nothing but bully you, one way and another, since you came to this floor. Look, I'm sorry. I don't know why I should let you annoy me so – but there it is, you did, very much and I indulged myself by showing temper. Just – remember what I try to teach you and we'll get on much better. All right?'

She stared at him, and opened her mouth to speak, and then, feeling like a stupid fish, closed it again, and shook her head, bewildered, only to stop, and then nod. And he laughed, his face crinkling at her, and after a split second, she laughed too, and he squeezed her shoulder, and went, leaving the doors swinging behind him, and Tricia a good deal shaken. So shaken and bemused she went off duty shortly afterwards, and quite forgot to go and see Mrs Slattery to apologise. Indeed, for all she was aware of her at that moment, Mrs Slattery might not have existed at all.

9

She found a note waiting for her in the nurses' home when she came off duty, asking her to call David. 'Urgent' the receptionist had written across the top, but after a moment's thought, Tricia decided to go up to her room and bath and change before calling him. She really needed time to collect herself, and anyway, he'd promised to leave her a full week for study, since finals were looming so closely, and he was cheating to ring her like this. But in case it was really urgent, she would phone a little later on in the evening but too late to be coaxed out for a date.

She stopped outside Ngaire's door and tapped loudly, but there was no reply, and vaguely uneasy, she turned away. Where the hell was she? And on an impulse, turned back and put her hand on the knob. Ngaire never locked her door, and if Tricia left a note on her pillow maybe she'd have a better chance of getting her as soon as she did come in.

She was fumbling in her pocket for her notebook as she walked into the room, so it was a couple of moments before she realised that Ngaire was there, curled up on her bed, lying with her face to the wall.

Tricia stared, and then crept towards her. Sleeping maybe — perhaps that was why she had ignored the tap on her door. Ngaire's eyes were indeed closed, and Tricia was about to straighten up and creep out again, remorseful because she had forgotten Ngaire might be sleeping, when she noticed that her lids weren't really relaxed, that they were trembling a little like those of a child pretending to nap.

She sat down on the bed beside the small curled figure and looked at her, thoughtfully. And then said gently, 'You'd better tell me, Ny. You can't go on like this. I know it isn't the business of theatre last night that's upset you like this because that's all settled anyway – and you're not one to fret unduly about such things. This is something quite other, isn't it? You'd really better tell me.'

There was a long silence, and then Ngaire rolled over to lie on her back and stare up at the ceiling, her hands behind her head.

'I've been – it's been so strange. All day. I've been like a sort of robot. Not feeling anything much. But I ought to. I ought to feel a lot.'

'Why? What happened with – Pete, wasn't it?'

'Pete,' she said it softly. 'Yes, Pete. That's who it was.'

She laughed then, and turned her head and looked at Tricia, but there was no amusement in her laugh, only a brittleness that made Tricia shiver slightly.

'It's funny, Trish – how long have you known me?'

'Almost three years.'

'And what do you know of me?'

Tricia frowned. 'Know of you? I know – well, that you're fun. A bit of a nut, often, but fun. That you're a great friend. Fond of men – '

'Fond of men. Yes. That's it, isn't it? Ngaire the man-eater, that's what people think I am. Including you?'

'That's not fair! I've just always accepted that you like men, that's all,' Tricia protested. 'But I know there's no harm in it. It's like playing games with you. That's all it is.'

'Really? And what about my morals? Have you ever thought about that?' Ngaire was looking at her very directly, and Tricia hesitated, and reddened, and then spoke a little shyly.

'Look, Ny, you're my best friend. You've been absolutely marvellous to me, all this time. Without you I'd have gone spare when my parents had their flap, really. And when a person is a friend – damn it, you don't think about morals! I mean, as regards men, which is what you mean, isn't it? It's none of my business.'

Ngaire smiled then, a little wryly. 'Well, bless you for that. But I suppose if it came right down to it, you'd have to admit you thought me a pretty experienced person, as far as sex is concerned, anyway.'

There was a pause, then Tricia said unwillingly. 'Well, I suppose so. If I'd ever thought about it – which I haven't.'

'I believe you. Well, Trish, let me tell you something. I am without any doubt as stupid, and naïve, and – and idiotic as any kid of fifteen getting ready for her first date with a fella who's barely old enough to have started to shave. I knew from nothing – nothing – '

She lay staring upwards, in a brooding silence and then Tricia said gently, 'Knew?'

Ngaire slid her eyes sideways, and produced that brittle mirthless laugh again.

'Got it in one. Past tense. Yes. Knew.'

The silence came down again, and then Tricia stirred and said with an attempt at briskness, 'Well, you've gone this far, so you might as well finish. I think you'll feel better if you do.'

Ngaire sighed sharply, and then sat up, to fold her arms round her hunched knees, and she began to speak in a flat sort of voice, never once looking at Tricia, but staring in front of her in a blind way that made her seem like a little old woman rather than the bouncy half-child Tricia had always known.

'I've been head over ears in love with Pete as long as I can remember. Ever since school. And then he went and joined the Navy and I died a little, I think. I couldn't imagine staying in Christchurch without him. I couldn't imagine living from one trip to the next, seeing him once a year if I was lucky. So I cut my losses. It must have half killed my folks, but I took off. Came to England to train as a nurse, and fill my life with guys and find someone to cure the Pete infection. And it worked fine for a while, in a way. I mean, I found I could get any guy I fancied – but then as soon as one of them showed an interest in me, boy, did I shy off! Talk about the affronted virgin act! But they were nice fellas, most of them. Took it well, treated me like a silly little girl who didn't know any better than to be a tease, and were – very kind. And there were letters from Pete to keep me going. Every time I thought I was over the – disease – God damn it, he'd write again from Timbuctu or Granada or somewhere romantic, and there I was, crying into my pillow for him again. But I wasn't going to let him know it, not clever Ngaire. Oh, no! I wrote him great reams about the life I was having. Box of birds, that was me. Box of birds. And now they're all dead – '

She took a deep breath, and then went on.

'Anyway, that's how it was up to yesterday. And he called me. First time ever he made Tilbury – he's done British runs before, to Southampton, to Hull, to Liverpool – but this time, Tilbury.

Could I meet him? Could I! I would have moved heaven and earth to meet him – well, God damn it, I did, didn't I? And copped you with it.' She turned her head briefly and looked at Tricia. 'Forgive me for that. But it had to be done. Anyway, I met him – there on the docks – '

She stopped, and then went on painfully, 'He looked great. Bigger somehow, more of a man than I remembered. I think I could have died when I saw him. He was – there he *was*, you see, the one man in the world. Mine. My Pete. Oh, *hell* and damn and – '

She put her head down to rest on her knees, and took a couple of deep breaths and then lifted her face again.

'He took me aboard. He was on standby watch or something – most of the crew were ashore, and apart from a couple of blokes up on the bridge, there was just the two of us, in his little cabin. We had a drink – '

Again she turned and looked at Tricia, and her eyes were flat with misery, as opaque as pebbles. 'Oh, do I have to spell it out? I loved him, he was there, he was all I'd been waiting for all these years, so there it was. We made love. It hurt and I cried like hell, but it was all right – all marvellous. I loved him, you see. You can't talk about morals when it's love. Can you? I never stopped to think. I loved him, and I wanted him, and he loved me – it was all beautiful – beautiful.'

Tears had begun to trickle down her face now, spilling over as though she had no awareness of them. 'It would still be beautiful. It isn't that I'm mourning my lost innocence or anything of that sort. I've more – sense than that. It's more than that.'

She put a hand out and touched Tricia's shoulder, as though she needed the comfort of human contact, and then dropped her hand again.

'It was only me, you see. Only me who saw it that way – beautiful. Not him. He's been married more than a year now, got a baby on the way. A girl I knew at home. Great girl, she was. Quiet, but nice. Great. And Pete said – a fella gets lonely. Needs a girl – being a sailor, it's a tough life for a man. And here I was, old friend, living it up like mad, one of the new swinging set – I mean, New Zealand girls aren't like your usual swinging London girls, but I'd been here a whole three years, and there were my letters, all about the guys and the parties here – I can't blame him. He saw it as I suppose I used to with all those guys I went out with. A bit of fun. A way to forget the girl he really loves, just for a while. Only the difference between us was that I – I never had gone so far before. He's a man, so it's different. But for me – well, I don't feel very marvellous any more. So there it is. Now you know. And where the bloody hell I go from here, I don't know. I just don't know.'

And she leaned back against her pillows, and then miserably turned her face to the wall and wept, and for a long time Tricia sat beside her in the dwindling light of the early evening, until at last the sobbing stopped, and Ngaire lay asleep, looking as flushed and helpless as an abandoned baby.

Stiffly, Tricia got to her feet, moving awkwardly for fear of disturbing the sleeping Ngaire, and stood looking down at her feeling a bewilderment and unhappiness for her friend that held a lot of shame in it.

To have known this girl so long, to have leaned on her and relied on her as she knew she often had, and yet to have known so little of her. It was shaming, deeply so, and suddenly she heard, as vividly as though he were beside her, Adam Kidd's voice. 'There's more to maturity than mere age – ' And there's more to friendship than just knowing someone, she thought bleakly, and then slipped silently from the room, closing the door carefully behind her.

'Oh, there you are, Nurse Oxford!' the suddenness of the voice made her jump. 'Really, it is too bad of you to disappear so thoroughly! Your boy friend has been down the hall waiting for you this past half hour.'

Home Sister, a middle-aged and exceedingly fussy little woman, peered at her in the dim light of the corridor. 'Really, Nurse, you must speak to him, you know. I've seen him here many times, of course I have, but he's never been so discourteous as he has this evening. He suggested the receptionist staff hadn't given you his message! And really, I would prefer it if these young men did not come here smelling of drink. I'm as broad-minded as the next person, I assure you, but really – you must speak to him. I'll tell him I found you – '

She bustled away down the stairs in a clatter of heels, and Tricia stood still, outside Ngaire's door, and closed her eyes for a moment. David. He'd phoned and said it was urgent, and then she hadn't called. And remembering Ngaire's misery and the look in her face when she had told her sorry little tale of being unloved, Tricia felt a great lift of gratitude for David, for his unswerving reliability, for the way he made her feel, always, loved as well as very much desired. And moving swiftly, she followed Home Sister down the stairs to the hall where David was waiting.

He was sitting in the big armchair, his chin sunk on his chest, his eyes apparently fixed on the toes of his shoes, which were slowly swinging from side to side as he rocked his crossed ankles.

He saw her as she came down the stairs towards him, and stood up with an awkward heave, and as she came up to him and opened her mouth to speak, he shook his head, and taking her arm in a tight grip, propelled her towards the door. And not until he had ducked with her under the overhanging branches of the big beech tree and they were both hidden in the dimness against the trunk did he say a word.

And then all he said was 'Tricia – ' and put his arms round her and kissed her so hard and so hungrily that her head was forced back against the tree, and her lips felt bruised under his onslaught.

She managed to pull back her face after a moment, but he kissed her throat instead, and his hands were hard against her back, and caressing her with a barely controlled violence.

'David – stop it – stop it!' she managed to say breathlessly, and wrenched her head sideways as his face came up and he tried to reach her mouth again. 'No, damn it – you smell foul – stop it, do you hear me? – stop it at once – '

And then, as his hands moved down her body, she managed to pull one arm free of the combined shackles of his grip and the folds of her heavy cape, and pulled her arm back and struck out.

Her hand hit his face fair and square, so hard that her palm stung, and there was a moment's horrified silence as they both stood perfectly still. And then he pulled away, and said thickly, 'I'm sorry. I don't know what – I'm sorry.'

'David! Are you all right? Did I hurt you? Oh, God, I'm sorry! But you've never been so – you've never been like that before! And what's the matter with you? You've never drunk whisky as long as I've known you! And you reek of it. What's the matter?'

She could just see him in the half light, one hand held to his cheek, and she put her arm round his shoulders, and led him round to the far side of the tree to the little wooden bench that curled round the trunk, and sat him down and then sat next to him, looking up into his face.

'David?'

'I'm sorry, Trish,' he said after a moment. 'I don't know what hit me. No, that's not true. I do. But – well, I've been thinking about it for hours – what I'd say, how it would be, and then – well I thought you were keeping away from me, because they couldn't find you in your room they said, and – well, then there you were, and I couldn't help it. And I'm sorry.'

'I wasn't hiding. I – there was a problem. I'm sorry. I really meant to call you. I just went up to change first, and then – I got held up,' she finished lamely. Well as David knew Ngaire, she couldn't say any more about her to him. 'But David – whisky! Why?'

'I told you. I was planning – thinking about what I'd say. Needed some Dutch courage, I suppose.'

'Well?'

'Well what?'

'What were you going to say that needed so much courage?' That you're tired of waiting for me, the little secret voice deep inside her whispered. That you aren't going to sit about any longer while I finish what I started. And a little bleak chill rose in her. But she said again. 'What were you going to say?'

He sat silent beside her for a moment, and then sighed heavily. 'Oh, I don't know. It sounds so – when I first thought about it, it made sense. But now – '

'If it made sense before, it will now. You'd better say it, whatever it is,' she said in a low voice. Put me out of my misery now, and let's get over with it, whispered the little voice.

'You're a very innocent girl, aren't you, my darling?' his voice had softened now, sounding more familiar to her. 'So naïve. So young.'

She was nettled. This was the second time today a man had suggested she was silly and young and lacked understanding. Even Ngaire had implied it when she told her story. Now she let her annoyance thin her voice to a sharp edge.

'How do you mean, naïve? I don't imagine I'm any more starry eyed than the next girl of my age. I'm not exactly a baby – it's some time since I grew up, in case you hadn't noticed.'

'Oh, I've noticed. My God, I've noticed. You're very much a woman in some ways. You've certainly got the body of a – very much the body of a woman. It's not that I mean. It's just that – well, you don't really know what makes me tick, do you, even after all the time we've been going out together?'

Again the accusation of a lack of understanding; now she was thoroughly angry. 'Look, David, I don't know what the hell it is you're trying to say. And I'm not about to sit here in the freezing dark until you get round to it. Either say it and get it over with, or shut up – '

'I'll say it.' He said and his voice was hard again. 'I'll say it – right now. I've told you. I'm a one girl man. I want you – *you* and no one else. And I want you so much sometimes I could – I could – ' he put his hand out towards her, and then seemed to shrink back inside himself, away from contact with her. 'But you don't seem to understand that, do you? You just talk about getting married, sometime, when you've got your bloody nursing out of your system. And I'm supposed to sit about and wait with *my* system shot to hell because of it. Well, I can't. Not any longer. And – ' he swallowed noisily, 'I think I know the answer to both our problems. A way to – to make it possible for me to wait a while to get married, and a way for you to go on with your nursing until you've had enough.'

'Well?'

'It's not that unusual, damn it, not these days. Once, I'd have been horrified. But not now. I'm not a prude, and I know what we both need. So – '

She sat very still and felt the cold moving into her bones. And said softly, 'Spell it out, David. I'm naïve, remember? I don't know what makes you tick. So spell it out. In easy words.'

'Get yourself fixed up with the Pill or something,' his voice sounded sulky in the darkness, but gradually became more eager, developed a note of pleading. 'Damn it all, why not? I must be mad to go on in this – this half dead and half alive fashion! I love you and I want you, and I don't see any sense in suffering much more of the – the hell of seeing you and almost not daring to touch you for fear of the way it makes me feel. Why not? Then I'd be able to let you go on as you are, with no more of those awful arguments about when, when – *when* we'll get married. Doesn't it make sense to you? It must, if you care for me – '

She didn't speak for a long time, and when she did her voice was genuinely puzzled.

'I don't understand you, David, indeed I don't. You're – you're suggesting we start sleeping together now, as though we were married, and say that you wouldn't mind waiting till I had finished my nursing career – but you won't get married and then let me finish it! For God's sake, what is this? Why would it be all right to have the girl friend you sleep with working at a career, but not your wife? I don't understand.'

'There's a hell of a difference,' he said roughly. 'A hell of a difference. I can be stubborn too, just as you can. And I've sworn no wife of mine will go out to a job. I mean that. What we do while we're engaged – well, that's our affair. No one else's. But I'm going to hold my head up in the world when I marry. My wife won't have to have a job.'

'I don't understand,' she said again, and stopped. Her mind was a maelstrom of feelings, memories, words. Ngaire's anguished misery of making love with a man who didn't love her as she loved him. Adam Kidd's face as he had looked when he told her she was immature – and the change in him when he had apologised and left her in the office. His voice saying, 'There's more to maturity than age – ' And then Ngaire's face again, so full of misery, but also, so full of – what? Understanding, wisdom. It might be painful to acquire such understanding, it might demand sacrifices, but surely it had to be done? Somehow?

Tentatively, she put out her hand and touched him, and then shrank back as he turned on her and seized her in that terrifyingly violent grip again.

'No, please – David, I can't think properly if you – if you bully me. Stop, please – '

At once he let go, and stood up, and moved away from her, and she could see him standing silhouetted against the branches of the tree, his height bulking against the stippled greyness of the night sky. It must be getting awfully late, she thought inconsequentially. I hope Ngaire's all right. And then mentally shook herself and opened her mouth to speak. But he was already talking.

'Look, Tricia, I've said it. I had to, and I hope to God you can understand why. I'm not trying to pull a fast one on you. I do love you, and I do what to marry you, but it's got to be on my terms if I'm ever to keep my own self respect as a man. If you can't understand that, then God help me. But I'm hoping you will. Think about it, my darling. Please, think carefully and – I'll call you. Or better still, I'll wait till you phone me. I don't want to feel, ever, that I bullied you into this. Or that I cheated in any way. I've got to, because if I don't I – oh, my God, I wish to hell I didn't want you so much!' and he plunged away through the overhanging branches, making them creak in protest as he thrust them aside, and she could hear his heavy footsteps as he went rushing away across the garden.

She sat there for a long time, watching the lights of the windows in the ward blocks towering up above the garden winking unevenly through the moving branches as they creaked and cracked slightly in the evening wind. Sat and thought, decided and changed her mind, over and over again. Until the sound of the remote clanging of the Path. Lab. gate, which was locked up for the night at ten o'clock, brought her an awareness of the passage of time.

Moving wearily, she went into the Home and up the stairs, to find Ngaire. In their separate ways, each needed the comfort of the other tonight. Perhaps, in talking to Ngaire about her distress, Tricia would find an answer to her own dilemma.

10

'Ah, there you are, Nurse Oxford!'
She looked up, startled. She had come on duty straight from the Home, not bothering with breakfast, and had walked through the double doors leading on to the third floor with her head down, staring at the ground as she walked, and totally wrapped up in brooding over the happenings of the previous evening.

Adam Kidd was sitting in the office, and he got swiftly to his feet as soon as he saw her, and came out to stand in front of her, his hands thrust into his pockets, and with an expression on his face that was frightening. He looked furiously angry, his lips pinched and his jaws clenched.

'What the hell did you say to Mrs Slattery yesterday?'

'Mrs Slattery?' she said, momentarily bewildered. 'Say? What about?'

'Morning, Dr Kidd! You're bright and early today! Or have you been here all night?' Bridie Cavanaugh came through the doors behind Tricia, and she stepped aside to let her pass.

'Bloody nearly,' Adam snapped. 'And all because of – look, I have to talk to this – this *nurse* somewhere in peace. I'll use the linen cupboard. Come on – ' and he turned on his heel, and marched away.

'What have you been after doin' *now*?' Bridie murmured, staring after him.

'I don't know – at least – oh, hell,' Tricia said miserably, 'I think I know, look, cover up for me if Cleland comes hunting me, there's a lamb,' and she followed Adam to the linen cupboard, and closed the door behind her with cold fingers. He was standing with his back to the window, his hands still in his pockets, and glowering, and without any preamble she said, 'I know – or I think I do – what you mean.'

'Oh, you do? You can tell me why a patient due for operation this morning got so agitated last night that she packed up her things and decided to march out? Why it took every ounce of tact I had to persuade her not to? Why she needed heavy sedation to get a night's sleep? Why she is right now heavily sedated so that we can get her to the theatre at all this afternoon? You know why?'

'Oh, surely she didn't – I mean, I didn't mean her to hear me, but even though she did, there was no need to – '

'Hear *what*, God damn it?'

She closed her eyes for a moment, wearily. 'Last night, when I was talking to you in the office. I – I said something about people having face lifts when there was such a long waiting list on the general side. And the phone rang and you answered it and then I saw her – she was walking past the office door, and I think she heard me. I meant to go and apologise. I didn't mean to upset her, of course I didn't! It was you I was talking to. But – I forgot – ' and with a sudden memory of why she forgot she found herself filled with embarrassment, and couldn't look at him.

'I see! You said – ye Gods, girl, how can any one person be so bloody *stupid*? I thought, last night, I'd got some sense into you, but – '

'This happened before – before you started to talk to me. Properly, I mean. And – well, it was the first time you'd ever been anything but hateful, and – and that was why I forgot, I think.' To her horror she felt her eyes become hot and sandy, and knew that any second now she would cry. And swallowed hard and blinked, and looked down at the floor again.

'Oh, for pity's sake! Don't go weeping all over me. You can save that sort of little girl trick for your boyfriend. It cuts no ice with me.'

'It's not a trick! Damn it, I don't – I've never – oh, *damn* – ' and then she was crying in good earnest and furiously she rooted in her pocket for a handkerchief and, not finding one, scrubbed at her face with a corner of her apron.

There was a silence for a moment, and then he moved and came towards the door, and she stepped aside to let him pass. But he stopped in front of her, and held out a handkerchief taken from his white coat pocket.

'Here, you'd better use this. And let me tell you a little about Mrs Slattery, will you? Then perhaps you'll see just how much harm you almost did.'

'Almost?' she managed to say, her voice husky.

'As usual, I picked up the pieces. I seem to do it all the time on this floor. Mrs Slattery makes her living as an actress. She's not at all a well known actress, but she gets by, or always has up to now. She has a son of seventeen, the only person in her life she has to care about. The child's father dumped her long ago – never married her, never even knew about the child. So she's had to keep the pair of them by her own efforts, but she managed to send the boy to a good but expensive school. Silly of her perhaps to land herself with a commitment like that, but as she sees it she has a responsibility to the boy. She had him, and apart from any feeling she may have for him, she feels she owes him a debt for the start she gave him. Being a bastard, even in this day and age, isn't easy. Anyway, he's bright – very. Due to sit his A levels shortly. But over the past couple of years things have been getting very difficult for Mrs Slattery. She gets very little work, very little indeed. Her face – it's paying the price of all these years of heavy make up and hot stage and studio lights – and she believes that's why she can't get work. She believes that if her face can be made to look more as it used to she'll be back in employment. Maybe she will, maybe she won't. The important thing is *she* believes it. Without improvement to her face she's scared to even *try* to get work. Understand?'

'But she can't be all that – I mean, it costs a bomb to be a patient on this floor, doesn't it? About eighty pounds a week? And there are the surgeon's fees – '

'I'm coming to that. Indeed, I am. And then you'll see why I was so furious with you. Mr Chatterton, her plastic surgeon, has know Julia Slattery for years. He came to us here at the St Cuthbert's Wing and asked us to help what he regards as a very deserving case. He couldn't get her a bed on the general side –there just isn't any provision there for this sort of cosmetic surgery, however psychologically important we may think it is that a particular patient have such treatment. But we managed to get her a bed on this floor without charging for it. It wasn't easy, but we managed it because there are one or two small funds available. Mr Chatterton is operating for no fee. So we were pleased with ourselves. We were in a position to help, but Mr Chatterton had a considerable job in persuading Mrs Slattery she should accept the offer. She's a proud woman, however desperate her situation may be. And though *you* may not think the problems of an ageing actress with one son to support are very important, I happen to feel that everyone is entitled to respect for their needs. And what happened? On her first evening here, a silly girl who has more tongue than sense says something that makes her think that she is depriving another person of treatment they urgently need. This just isn't true – I know that, and Mr Chatterton knows that, and if you thought about it, you'd know it, too, because the only people being deprived in this situation are Mr Chatterton of a fee, and this wing of some money it can well spare. But Mrs Slattery believed what she heard *you* say – and wanted to go because of it. And if she had, it's my guess she'd never have been able to get another professional job again – not because of the lack of the operation, but because of the lack of the psychological security the operation will give her. She'd have been forced to take her son away from his expensive school just at a stage when it would very likely ruin his entire educational future. Now do you see what you almost did?'

She nodded bleakly. 'Yes. I'm sorry. I was sorry last night, but now I'm even more sorry. I'll go and apologise to her right away – '

'You won't! You'll keep right out of her way. Whatever you do, you'll keep out of her way, because you've done enough damage. No apologies will help. I've persuaded her, she'll have her operation, and that's that – '

'But she's on my case load!'

'She won't be – not after I've spoken to Sister Cleland.'

'Oh, no! Must you do that? I mean, she loathes me so much already that she'll – '

'That's your problem,' he said curtly. 'Have you finished with that handkerchief? Thank you.'

And he went, leaving the door swinging behind him and Tricia with her head aching miserably, and filled with apprehension at the thought of the inevitable confrontation with Sister Cleland.

But when it came later in the afternoon (and it was typical of her to keep Tricia waiting for the summons, on tenterhooks, as long as she could) she was surprised at the tone Sister Cleland took. She leaned back in her office chair, and looked at Tricia, standing there with her hands very correctly clasped on her apron front, and there was a look of sardonic pleasure on her face.

'Well, you *have* blotted your copybook with Dr Kidd, haven't you? Very thoroughly indeed, going by what he said to me this morning. Really, Nurse, if you had been within his reach last night I have a distinct impression he'd have almost killed you – and although he is impatient in many ways, I've never known him to be so violently angry! You'd better keep out of his way as much as you can from now on. I've taken you off Mrs Slattery of course – he was adamant about that – but you can keep Mr Bartlett, and run for the rest of the staff, especially Nurse Cavanaugh. And for your own sake, remember what I said – keep out of Dr Kidd's way!'

And that was all. And talking about it to Bridie Cavanaugh later, as they made the rounds with the evening drugs, she expressed her surprise at the mildness of the rebuke.

'I thought she'd – I don't know. Get me thrown off the floor or something! But she was – it was odd. Almost *amused*! I don't understand it.'

'You can be daft as a brush, sometimes, young Oxford, indeed you can! The best thing Adam Kidd ever did for you as far as she's concerned was complain about you – she's feelin' *much* better! I told you right at the start, she's a strong fancy for the lad. And she's been worried about you horning in.'

'She's the daft one, then. He loathes me, has done ever since I came on the floor, you know that. As if he'd ever be interested in me, any more than I would in him!'

'I can't speak for you, seein' I don't remember ever discussing the matter with you – though I've wondered, I must say, seein' how much you keep sayin' you hate the man, and I always think that's a very interestin' thing to say about anyone – but I'll tell you this. If you think he isn't interested in you, you're daft as *two* brushes.'

She grinned a little wickedly at Tricia as she shook a bottle of medicine and then, with an expert twist of her little finger, drew the cork and poured a carefully measured dose.

'Oh, I've seen him. Watchin' you walk down the corridor. That's a very beguilin' walk you've got, do you know that? Ah, sure you do – you'll have been told often enough, I dare say. And it's remarkable, really, how much more time he seems to spend on this floor lately. He used to keep away as much as he could, I always reckoned he found the Cleland a bit more than he could cope with. She's a determined lady, and she really – ' she shook her head admiringly,' – goes after what she wants, does La Cleland. Here, give this to room 319, will you – '

Red-faced, Tricia obeyed, and came back to Bridie as fast as she could.

'You're making it up as you go along,' she said hotly. 'And it's not funny! Adam Kidd thinks I'm stupid, immature, useless – '

Bridie raised her eyebrows at that. 'Oh, he's told you all that has he? You *are* getting on! You'll have him on his knees next.'

'Bridie, will you stop talking such utter rubbish? You may be right about Cleland – I wouldn't know – but you couldn't be more wrong about Kidd and you're crazy if you think you're right about *me*. I – I'm engaged, anyway – ' Her voice trailed away then, and Bridie said shrewdly, 'Really? Ah well. Many a slip and all that – it's a good thing bein' engaged, isn't like it was way back when my mother was a girl. Now, then a betrothal *was* something! Now it's all different, and maybe it's as well in some ways. I wouldn't be makin' any weddin' plans yet, me old love. Not with yourself in such a twist and a turmoil.'

'Who says I am?' Tricia said quickly. 'I'm nothing of the sort! Just hating Private Wing, that's all.'

'Yes, of course, to be sure,' Bridie said soothingly. 'Anyway, it's none o' my business. But you asked me why Cleland was so easy on you, so I told you. Let me tell you somethin' else. She's a devious old piece, and she wants that Adam in the worst way. And now you've discredited yourself in front of him – or so she thinks, silly old twit – she'll do her best to get you shifted. I promise you. There'd be no point in doin' that if she thought Adam Kidd had any sort of lingerin' fancy for you. But now she reckons he hasn't – well, I'd watch my step that's all. Now, look, here's Mr Bartlett's medication. Do your best to make him take it all – he tried to persuade me to drop it in the sink this morning, poor devil. It's pretty foul stuff – ' she sniffed the bottle of medicine and grimaced, ' – and the Lord knows what good it might do him, but there, it's worth trying, I suppose.'

'He's pretty grim, isn't he, Bridie?' Tricia was grateful for a chance to change the subject but also she genuinely wanted an answer. She couldn't even think about Philip Bartlett without feeling that sharp stab of angry pity.

'Yes,' Bridie said soberly. 'He is. His blood picture – ' She shook her head. 'Shockin' results to the tests, shockin'. And this stuff – ' she held out the bottle. 'When I see someone is on this, I could almost throw up my hands. It's one of these new experimental drugs – developed at Dr Travis' Research Unit at the University, and they try it out here. I've never seen 'em give it to anyone who isn't pretty hopeless – it has some pretty nasty side effects on the nervous system, from all accounts, but a bit of sensory loss is better than dyin', I suppose.'

'Does it ever do any good?'

'Not often, though I've seen a couple of pretty incredible results, I must say. There was that child we had here last summer, now – gorgeous wee thing she was. Only about seven or so. And she was bad – very bad. Acute Hodgkins. I wouldn't have given her a month to live, and that's a fact. But she bloomed on this stuff, though we had to fight to get it into her, she hated it so. She's not been back since and she walked out of here lookin' like a normal child after six weeks on it. So maybe – I hope it'll do as much for Mr B. Anyway, go and give it him, there's a good lass,' and Bridie trundled the drug trolley away, humming softly beneath her breath.

Philip Bartlett was sitting in an armchair beside the window, looking out at the garden below with a lacklustre expression on his face. But he turned his head as she came in, and produced one of his brilliant smiles.

'Well, it's my delicious nurse! How are you this evening? I don't seem to have seen much of you today, and I thought you were my special girl. Hell, do I have to take that stuff? It tastes like – well, I'm too much of a gentleman to tell you.'

'And too much of a gentleman to have ever actually tasted whatever-it-is, so how do you know? You've got to swallow it, so the sooner the easier.' Tricia held out the medicine glass, and he took it unwillingly, and she turned away to bring a glass of fruit juice from his bedside table.

'I'm sorry if you feel I've been neglecting you. I looked in after we'd settled you at lunch time, and you were asleep, and then later, you had visitors, so – '

'So you spent the time canoodling with some delectable doctor in a quiet corner.'

'Not at all! I spent it folding sheets and scrubbing the sluice, actually. You've a funny idea of hospital work if you think there's time for such – nonsense. Go on – swallow it! Good! This should help it down.'

She tried to move away after giving him the fruit juice, but he held on to her with his other hand, watching her with eyes bright over the rim of the glass, and then put the glass down on the table beside him and reached for her other hand, so that she was pinned to his side.

'No nonsense?' he said softly, looking up at her through his incredibly long lashes. 'None at all? That sounds very dull. With delicious creatures like you around, and all these single rooms with bored men like me in them – bless us, child, I'd have thought – '

She had to move then, and got her hands away with a sharp tug. 'You'd have thought all wrong Mr Bartlett. Now, are you ready to go back to bed yet? I imagine your visitors will be here soon and – '

'Oh, Maxine's here already. Talking to Doctor Kidd, I believe. She's been with him for heaven knows how long – but there, I thought. Why not? Then when my splendid nurse comes in, I'll be able to talk to her, and enjoy her company in peace – ' and he laughed up at her and again tried to reach her hands.

'Mr Bartlett!' she began hotly, and then stopped, looking at the thin face with the too-bright eyes. 'You're not serious at all, are you?' she said slowly. 'Isn't this – oh, a sort of game you play all the time? With all the girls at your office, girls you meet at parties, every nurse who comes in here?'

He raised one eyebrow a little. 'Well, well! Such a noticing child as it is, then! Well, you could be right. Damn it, life's too short not to enjoy every moment of it, and grab every opportunity of a little amusement. Isn't it?'

He sighed sharply then, and his brightness faltered for a second, and then the smile came back, more brilliant than ever. 'So, watch your step, my love! One false move and – voom! I pounce!'

'I'll watch!' she said, with a gaiety that was difficult to produce, for she could have wept for him. But if this was the way he wanted to play his game of living, then play it he should, and she'd join in according to his own rules. It was little enough that anyone could do for him; at least let him be amused. 'In future, I'll have to bring a chaperone in with me, to keep me safe! Nurse Cavanaugh, now!'

'Splendid!' he sounded a little abstracted suddenly. 'Then I'll have two to pounce on. Look, Sweetie, do something for me, will you? I'd like to say goodnight to Maxine before I go back to bed. I'm a bit – oh, tired, I suppose, though I've done sweet damn all but sit here all day – and once I'm in bed I'll be fast asleep. Which would be a shade depressing, not to say boring, for Maxine. So detach her from the fascinating Dr Kidd for me, will you?'

'Of course!' she said at once. 'Anything else before I go off duty?'

'Just a kiss – ' he murmured, with a smile on his face, but it had lost some of its sparkle now.

'Some other time!' she said, and smiled back, and with a friendly tap on his shoulder went to look for Maxine. As she went along the corridor towards the visitors' room, she thought angrily 'Hateful woman! How can she be so cruel? To have to be sent for like this, when she ought to be with him – poor devil – '

The floor was peaceful as she hurried along past the subdued buzz of sound coming from each door, as visitors chattered, and the individual television and radio sets that the rooms boasted pouring out their programmes. She could hear the clatter of glass as Bridie, down at the far end by the medicine cupboard, put away bottles and drug charts, and in the office Sister Cleland was sitting, head down over the report book, as Tricia passed the door. 'Only another five minutes!' she thought, 'and then I can go off duty, and that means I'll have to make up my mind one way or the other, and phone David. And there's Ngaire, too. She was a lot better by the time we both went to bed last night, but even so, she'll need to talk more. Maybe we should go out for a meal, just the two of us, and I'll phone David tomorrow – '

But, as she had all day, she pushed the thought of David and his demands to the back of her mind. When she got off duty, then she'd think about it. Not now.

The visitor's waiting room door was closed, with the light gleaming softly through the frosted pane, and she tapped on it and without waiting for an answer walked in. And then stood very still.

Adam Kidd was standing beside the small armchair in the corner, and close to him, her hands gripping his shoulders, and her face buried in the front of his white coat, was Maxine Bartlett. One of his arms was round her shoulders, and his head was bent as with the other hand he stroked her glinting fair hair. He seemed to be murmuring in her ear, and looked up sharply as the door opened.

'I'm sorry to disturb you,' Tricia heard her own voice coming very clearly, but somehow from a long way away. 'Mr Bartlett is asking for you, Mrs Bartlett. I told him I would tell you.

Goodnight.' And moving very stiffly, she stepped backwards, and closed the door, and turned, feeling as though she were made of wood, to walk back along the corridor towards the office.

'May I report off duty, please, Sister?' Again, her voice sounded in her own ears like a stranger's, remote, unreal. And at Sister Cleland's dismissive nod, she turned and went to the changing room to get her cape, and finding Bridie and Ingrid Jensen there, also preparing to go off duty, said a mechanical 'Goodnight – '

'Hey, you're in a rare hurry to rush off tonight,' Ingrid said with a rallying note in her voice. 'Who's a clock watcher now, young Oxford?'

Tricia stopped by the door for a moment, and then hugged her cape closely round her shoulders. 'I've got to go,' she said, not looking at them. 'I've – I've got to make a phone call. Right away.'

11

But when she came off duty, Ngaire was sitting in Tricia's room, and turned to her a face that held an expression that was a heart-rending amalgam of misery and pretended gaiety and a sort of woebegone courage that made Tricia's icy numbness melt quite suddenly, made her stand in her doorway, her cape still clutched about her, with tears streaming down her face. And then Ngaire came and put her arms about her and wept too, so that they clung to each other like lost children.

It was Ngaire who recovered first, and pulled back, and sniffed loudly, and then managed a watery laugh. 'Oh, Trish, honestly! Aren't we the most – here, look at your face. Your nose is like a cherry! Crying's supposed to be pretty in a girl, but you look lousy.'

'You don't look exactly marvellous yourself,' Tricia said huskily, and wiped her eyes on a corner of her apron. 'You've got mascara all over the place – '

Ngaire turned and went to peer in Tricia's dressing table mirror. 'So much for dauntless bravery and all that,' she said, and began to mop away the traces of her tears. 'I thought – it's bloody silly, sitting mourning over what can't be undone. I spent ages putting my face on, and I needn't have bothered – ' she turned to look at Tricia then. 'Why did *you* cry, Trish? I mean – just sympathy and that?'

'I – yes. Sort of.' Tricia moved heavily towards her bed and sat down. 'Well – ' she struggled for a moment. 'Not entirely. I mean, everything's so – oh, what the hell. It isn't important.'

Ngaire came and sat beside her. 'Yes it is,' she said softly. 'You were so – great last night. To me, I mean. Just being able to talk to you about it all made it better. Honestly. I'm not nearly so miserable now.' It was her turn then to try to be honest. 'Well, that isn't entirely true. I'm bloody *bloody* miserable. And I will be for a long time, I'm thinking. But – well, talking to you about it all made it – gave it shape, you know? I mean, right now it's like sitting at the bottom of an enormous black pit and it's all cold and drear – ' she shivered suddenly. 'But I can sort of see a bit of light at the top. I'll get out of it one of these days. I know that much. Last night it was – I felt buried alive, you know? But now I know it'll take time, but I'll get out – What's the matter, Trish? With you, I mean? What's upset you?'

'Really, it isn't important,' Tricia said. 'Not to worry – '

'Oh, sure! You say not to worry, so I say, great, here's old Trish, says she's a box of birds, looks like death warmed up and gone cold again, but she says not to worry! So I won't! I mean, is it likely, I ask you?'

'I – I've got to phone David,' Tricia said abruptly.

'What's so bad about that?' Ngaire peered more closely at her. 'You two having problems?'

'Yes. Problems.' Tricia stood up. 'And I'd better go and – I'd better phone him before I – I'd better get it done.'

'Get what done?' Ngaire frowned suddenly. 'Trish – what is it? You look like – doom or something. What have you got to get done?'

'Oh, it'll take too long to explain,' Tricia said wearily. 'And anyway, what the hell? It doesn't really matter as much as it did, so I might as well let him be glad – I suppose he will.'

'Look, you're talking in riddles. And I demand the right to be the confidante tonight. You held my hand when I needed it, so I'm going to hold yours now. No – no arguments. Whatever it is you want to talk to David about, something tells me it can wait, that it *ought* to wait. Never do important things on an impulse. Lesson one, learned by me the hard way.' Ngaire grimaced sharply. 'You learn it the easy way from Aunty Ny. How are you off for lolly?'

'Lolly?'

'I'm as skint as usual. But if you can manage to pay your own way, I can stretch to a couple of sausage rolls and a bag of crisps with some of Nobby's coffee over at the Pigsty. We'll natter, find out what's what. It's better to talk in public about important things. You can't get all emotional, can't go over the top when you're in a crowd.' Again her face darkened, and then, with deliberate gaiety, she pulled Tricia to her feet. 'Get yourself out of uniform, Trish, and we'll go over. No – no arguments. We'll go. Put a move on.'

The Pigsty was quiet when they got there, for at this stage of the month money was tight among the students, both medical and nursing. A few dockers were having a quick beer on their way home from their overtime shifts and talking loudly to Nobby at the bar, and the girls found a quiet table in the corner in the shadow of the little stage.

Nobby served them quickly, not in the least minding that they wanted coffee rather than any of his more expensive liquid stock, and shoved a Cornish pasty in front of each of them when he brought their order.

'Compliments of the 'ouse, an' that. You look 'ungry – nah, shut up. You can treat me to a splint and a sticky plaster next time I need one – ' and he lumbered back to the bar and left them in their quiet corner.

They ate in silence, and not until each had pushed their plates away and were sitting, elbows on the table and their hands curled round the big white mugs of thick black coffee, did Ngaire start to speak.

'Now, me old cobber. Give out. What is your problem? Tricia Oxford, here is your friend. Talk away.'

Tricia smiled thinly. 'Ha, ha. Very funny.'

'No – I suppose it was pretty weak. E for effort? No? Okay, try again. What's the matter, Trish? What's up with David?'

Tricia looked at Ngaire for a long moment, and then said abruptly, 'He wants me – he wants us to start sleeping together. Not to wait till we're married. He's adamant about my not going on nursing after we're married, so this is the only answer for him. And for me, if I'm to hang on to my own ideas about working and all that.'

There was a pause. Then Ngaire said carefully, 'I've got to think about this. After – after what happened with Pete, my first reaction is as long as a man's talking about marriage you've no problem. I mean, it isn't that you – any girl – should use sex like – like bait or something. You know, promise to make an honest woman of me and you can have your way with me. It's more – knowing it's right between you both, you know? I mean, if you love him, he loves you, where's the problem, really? You do love him, don't you, Trish? I know how he is about you – '

'Of course I do – ' Tricia started. And then buried her face in her coffee cup again. 'Yes, of course I do.'

Ngaire leaned back and gave her a long considering look. 'Then what is it? Morals and that? I mean, do you feel that *marriage* is what matters when it comes to sex? I'm a bit – oh, I suppose lots of people'd disagree with me. I think what matters is the feeling between people. That and a sense of responsibility about babies, of course. But that's no problem these days, not really.'

'I don't *know*,' Tricia said, suddenly irritable. 'I've never thought about it much. And don't *you* start on me about being immature – '

Ngaire raised her eyebrows. 'Who said anything about immature?'

'It doesn't matter. No, it isn't that – moral scruples, I mean. It's – oh hell, I don't know. Maybe I'm just not particularly interested in sex. That's why I – why I found it so difficult to – to just say yes last night.'

'Last night? After you were with me?'

'Yes.'

'Hell, you poor old thing. For bad timing that takes some beating.' Ngaire frowned and thought for a moment.

'Listen, Trish – are you trying to say you don't – you're not interested in sleeping with David *at all*? Or just have doubts about jumping the wedding bells? Because I've known you a long time, and I'd have thought – well, I don't see you as a chilly type lady, not one bit. Never did. You've never struck me as being anything but a warm giving emotional sort of person. I mean, you hit the roof like – like a bomb at all sorts of things. That's always been your problem, to be honest. You're not all that controlled a person – and the way you move and all – hell, Trish, I don't, I couldn't believe you in the Ice Maiden role.'

She stopped, and then said a little shyly, 'Let me ask leading questions, huh? All this time with David – haven't you ever got – I mean, what do you do about the love life bit? You haven't been just holding hands all these years, have you?'

Tricia smiled a little 'No, of course not. We – get together a bit, of course. Neck a little. But – well, this hasn't come up before. I – I suppose I've known always David wanted more than I – I wanted, but I've always known, too, that he'd never try to push me too far. He's a very conventional bod, you know. That's why he – why we argue so much about my working. In his book, wives don't go out to work.'

'So he's a sweet old fashioned thing. Not such a bad thing at that. It – it must be great to know someone cares enough about you as a person not to – well, not to just take what he wants. But look, Trish – when you do neck a little, as you say – doesn't that make *you* feel – hell, you know what I mean! Do I have to spell it out? I may be living in the swinging London scene and all that, but I'm still a nice New Zealander. And we don't talk that easy about sex. You know what I mean.'

Tricia nodded. 'I know. Well, David makes me feel – loved. Important. Sometimes, after a while, when we're alone, I've got pretty – involved. Had to hold on to my hat, you know? But I can't pretend I think about it a lot. I mean, I don't find myself – ' she shrugged. 'Eager. Wanting him. Except for being comfortable and loved and – so I guess I'm just a chilly type lady at that.'

'No. That isn't on.' There was a long pause, then Ngaire went on softly. 'And is that all? No one else you do – who does make you think about being eager? No one else who makes you shiver when you see him?'

'Shut up!' Tricia put her coffee mug down with a clatter. 'Look, don't you start! I've had enough from Bridie Cavanaugh already – I do not – I am *not* interested in Adam Kidd, and I won't as long as I've a head on my shoulders. All right? So shut up! My problems with David concern David and me, and no one else. Get that clear – '

'All right – all right,' Ngaire said, and her voice held no expression. 'I've got the message very clear. Loud and clear. Not another word. Just a big piece of advice. And for God's sake, Trish, take it, because I know all the way through to my middle that it's the best advice you can have. Don't call David tonight. *Don't call him.* Think a bit longer, take your time, and *think*. Will you do that? To please me?'

Tricia stood up, and fumbled in her bag for money for the bill. 'Yes. I'll take it. It makes sense at that I suppose. But it's not because of – '

'I know – I know, it's not because of what I said about someone else. I know. But wait. Look, let's – '

'Let's nothing, Ny. Do you mind? I've had the lousiest of days, and all I want now is to sleep. I'm going to bed. Forgive me, but I want to do the I-want-to-be-alone bit. Okay? Bless you for listening, bless you for advising, and – I'll see you.'

And she went, leaving Ngaire staring into her coffee cup, a twisted little smile on her face.

Tricia tried to accept all of Ngaire's advice. Certainly she didn't phone David, but that was the easiest of things to do. Doing nothing, she reminded herself wryly, is no problem. But thinking clearly and calmly about what she should say when she did, that wasn't so simple.

As she went about the third floor all the following day, and the day after that, her thoughts chased each other from one side of her head to the other, like a hamster in a cage. And time and again, a sharp visual memory came welling up above her attempts to create careful thoughts. The picture of Adam Kidd holding Maxine Bartlett so very close. The sight of herself standing at the door, staring at them. The feeling of sick furious hate that surged in her when she had seen Adam's big hand on Maxine's glinting hair. It was as though, each time, she was a little separate creature, sitting in a corner of the room, staring down at the scene below, watching it acted out, over and over again –

I don't care for him. I don't. I don't. I don't. She told herself that over and over again. I don't. I don't. It's just Bridie, with her great Irish imagination putting notions into my head. She flattered me. It doesn't matter if a man's a boor, looks like the back of a bus; tell a girl he likes her, and she goes to a jelly. That's all it is. No more –

And so it went on. And on and on, until she was moving about her work like an automaton, not really aware of what she was doing, though she managed to do all she had to, relying on the years of training behind her to take her through the mechanical jobs of bedmaking, and treatment giving, and all the rest of it.

But her abstraction was apparent. It was Philip Bartlett who made her realise the fact when she went to make his bed and settle him for the afternoon of the second day after her conversation with Ngaire.

She had finished the bed, leaving the covers invitingly folded back, and then moved over towards Philip Bartlett in his chair by the window. Her nursing eye noted, almost automatically, that he looked less well, now. He seemed to be dissolving a little each day, getting thinner, his pallor getting a little more marked. But his eyes under their absurd lashes were as bright as ever, almost too bright.

He looked up at her now, as she leaned over to unwrap the blanket about his knees, and said softly, 'Come out, come out, wherever you are!'

'I – what's that?'

'Well, you're not here, are you? Bad for a man's morale that, being in the same room with a girl who is so obviously somewhere else. What is it, pretty delectable Nurse Oxford? Tell your old friend Philip all about it.'

'Oh, I'm sorry if I've been a bit – remote.' Skilfully, she slid one arm behind his back, putting the other hand under his thin elbow, and eased him to his feet. 'We've – er – we've got finals coming up. I haven't done as much revision as I should, and that's a fact. I guess I'm thinking about the signs and symptoms and treatment of heart diseases all the time. They're sure to put that in this year's paper – I'll try to forget hearts and think about you whenever I'm in here, I really will.'

He was on his feet now, and she led him, one arm firmly round his shoulders towards his bed, and felt the weakness in him as he reached it, to stand with his legs braced against it. He moved then, putting his hands on her shoulder, and she let him make her face him, almost instinctively. He was so weak, so thin, that any determined effort on her part to stop him would probably have made him fall.

He was taller than herself, and she looked up at him, and smiled, trying to produce the coquettish look she knew pleased him, and feeling the sadness about his illness deep behind her eyes and hoping it didn't show. He knew, she knew, just how ill he was, but the fiction had to be kept up between them, somehow, the fiction that he was going to be well, that he was really quite well now.

He smiled down at her, and said softly, 'My, but it's a nice face. I've always had a fancy for eyes like yours. I had a cat like your eyes, once. A marmalade cat with marmalade eyes. Very naughty cat, was my marmalade cat. Not to put too fine a point on it, a very randy little cat. Out and about all hours of the night, when any other self-respecting feline would be curled up on the boss's lap. But my marmalade cat only curled up on my lap when she was too tired to seek her outrageous friends on the garden fence. She'd lie there and look at me with that wicked little look in her marmalade eyes, and – well, there they are again, looking up at me from your face. Such naughty eyes – '

And, then, he bent his head, and very gently kissed her, his lips hot and dry on hers. And the movement made his weak frame sway, made him cling to her, not in any sudden access of passion, but in a desperate need to hold on to her support. And again acting instinctively, she put up her own arms to hold on to him.

For a long moment they stood there, not really kissing at all. Just clinging together, their lips touching but not really meaning anything much, and all the pity she had welled up in her, pity for him, for herself, for all the unhappiness there was.

And then, the sound came, and she realised dimly that the door had opened, and tried to extricate herself, slowly and gently, so as not to topple him from his precarious pose, and it was as though it took a year. She knew there was someone there at the open door, knew she was being watched, but she could only move gently, as though she was a character in a jerky old silent film being run at half speed –

'Well!' The sound cracked across the room like a whip, and then at last Tricia and Philip were apart, he leaning a little breathlessly against the bed, half sitting on it, she standing beside him, one hand still protectively on his shoulder.

Sister Cleland was standing at the door, her face white with a sort of triumphant rage that Tricia recognised with a sense of weary inevitability. Something like this had to happen. It had been waiting to happen ever since she had come to work on the floor. And somehow, she just didn't care. But then her eyes moved, and she saw, standing behind Cleland's straight back, Maxine Bartlett and Adam Kidd.

Kidd's face said nothing to her, nothing at all. He just stood there, silent, looking over Sister Cleland's shoulder at Philip Bartlett. And Maxine Bartlett – she stood very still too, but her expression was – what? Tricia felt remote, uninvolved as she looked at the beautiful face and tried to assess the thoughts going on behind it. And saw not the surprise or outrage, which she would have expected, but a curious amusement, mixed with a sort of relief. But couldn't understand why and didn't really care much anyway. She looked instead at Philip Bartlett, and said softly, 'Shall we get you back to bed, Mr Bartlett?'

He looked at her, and his lips quirked into a grin. 'Well, that's the way the old cookie crumbles, hmm? *In flagrante delicto* is the phrase, I think. Pity they came so soon, isn't it? Just think what beautiful music we'd have made if they'd waited a little longer – '

'I will put Mr Bartlett back to bed, Nurse.' Cleland's voice spat across the room. '*You* go to my office immediately. I'll deal with you later.'

'Oh, Sister, nothing to fuss over, is there?' Philip Bartlett said, and there was a sharp note in his voice which Tricia recognised as a return of weariness, held back until now by the excitement of the confrontation. 'Nothing to throw a fit about, surely – '

'I am not throwing a fit, Mr Bartlett, I assure you. But such behaviour is – well, that is something between myself and my staff. You are not involved – ' Briskly, she came towards him and as Tricia fell back, began to help him out of his dressing gown and into bed.

'Not involved?' he murmured as he lay back gratefully against his pillows. 'Damme, *I* thought I was involved – didn't you, Maxine?' and he turned his head to shoot a wicked glance at his wife.

'As ever, you wretch, as ever,' she said, and then looked at Sister Cleland. 'Really, Sister, if – '

'If you don't mind, Mrs Bartlett, this is *my* concern. Nurse – go at *once*, do you hear? And on second thoughts, do not go to my office, I have nothing further to say to you. You are to go to your room, and wait there until Matron sends for you. She will do so very soon, I assure you. Now *go!*'

At the door, Tricia stopped, because Adam Kidd was still standing there, blocking the way. He looked down at her, and opened his mouth to speak, and then looked across at Sister Cleland, who was now tucking in Philip Bartlett's counterpane with a controlled anger, and he closed his mouth, and stood to one side.

And Tricia, her head held high, walked out, and collectedly went along the corridor to pick up her cape, and go to her room in the Nurses' Home.

12

She sat there, on the edge of the bed, for a very long time. She watched the sun move fitfully across the room, creeping from her dressing table stool, to the wardrobe, to the washbasin in the corner, and knew time was passing, but didn't really feel it.

For much of the time that she sat there, she didn't think at all. She just let words and pictures move idly across her mind. Words she had shared with David. Pictures of herself working happily on the general wards. Words Adam Kidd had thrown at her. Pictures of Adam Kidd and Maxine Bartlett, and then of herself and Philip Bartlett —

And then, quite abruptly, the whole of it shifted, slid into focus. It was like looking at the maddening blur of three dimensional pictures, and then changing the viewer slightly and seeing it all clear and vivid. The background, and standing out against it in sharp relief the knowledge of what had to be done.

It was all so easy, really. So short a time ago, it had all been so right. So neat. So comfortably neat in a world that had once threatened to disintegrate around her, back in that winter when her parents had shattered her world by parting from each other. She had painfully built up that security, with David standing as a bulwark on one side, and the hospital and nursing and all that it promised on the other.

But now, and she had to admit it honestly, she had lost the comfort that was David. He would have to be told. Somehow. But there it was — he had in these past weeks lost all his value as a comforter, as a source of love and security, because of a stocky man with streaked hair and glasses, who had square hands and a biting tongue and little but scorn for her. She couldn't dodge it any longer, the truth about him, and God knew, she'd tried.

Adam Kidd did matter to her, far too much. The fascination she found in him was more than mere physical attraction. For good or ill, he would always be a part of her, in her memories of these last hateful weeks, inextricably bound up, now, with all her life at the Royal.

But that was all he could ever be. There was never to be any relationship there. Never to be any peace and comfort to be found with him. It would have to be found away from him – and that meant away from the Royal.

She stood up, abruptly, and went to sit at her dressing table to stare sombrely at her reflection in the mirror.

Finish what you start. Finish it even if you hate it, hasn't that always been what you've said? But you've been wrong, all this time. There's no sense in pushing through to a conclusion if it isn't going to give any satisfaction, is there? Her reflection stared back. Well, is there? the secret buried voice asked again.

No. No sense at all. There's more than one way to finish what you start, but you've never had the sense to see that. The way to finish what you've started here is to cut your losses. Cut them, clean and sharp and painfully – but then, afterwards, you'll at least be clear of your misery. Eventually.

How? Sit here and wait for Matron to send for you? One thing's sure, she told herself with a sudden savage humour. *She'll* cut my losses for me, very thoroughly. Necking with private patients – and getting caught doing it by the patient's wife as well as the Floor Sister and Registrar – is no way to make friends and influence Matrons. Is it?

'No!' She said it aloud, and the sound of her own voice bounced back at her from the mirror. I'll do this myself. I'm sick of letting things just happen to me. This, I'll do myself. I'll go, right now. I'll take some gear, just what I need, and I'll go. I've a little money in the bank – enough to see me through till I get a job somewhere. There's always the YWCA hostel or something. I'll go, now, and when they send for me, boy, oh boy. Surprise, surprise, Tricia Oxford didn't wait. For once she had the sense to really finish what she started.

She felt almost elated as she started to prepare. Dropping her soiled uniform in the linen box – I'll never wear *that* again – changing into a dress and coat, throwing as much as she could cram into her suitcase, and leaving without a qualm her lecture notes, her text books, all the paraphernalia of the student nurse, in the bookshelves. To be doing, to be busy, that was the thing.

She left her room, the room she had called home for so long, with never a backward glance, not even taking out the little pasteboard square that read 'Student Nurse P. Oxford. Third Year' from the door. It just didn't matter any more.

She went swiftly down the stairs and then on past the reception desk in the main hall, and the fussy little middle-aged part-time helper who sat there busily taking messages each day up until five p.m. looked up as she put down the telephone and called out, 'Nurse Oxford, is that you? Oh, I am glad – that saves me traipsing up the stairs to find you, and I can't deny I'm more than a little tired at this end of the day – now, what was it? – oh, yes. You're to go to Matron's office right away, they said. Can you go now, and not waste *any* time because Matron is waiting for you – you can leave that here, if you like.'

She peered curiously at the big suitcase Tricia was carrying. 'Going on holiday, are you? Lucky girl! Anyway, you can leave that here behind the desk and I'll watch it and tell Home Sister when I go off before you return, so that you needn't drag it over to the hospital – it *was* lucky I caught you before you left, wasn't it? Another couple of minutes and you wouldn't have got the message. I hope everything's all right? Or perhaps Matron just wants to see you before you go – '

'Perhaps,' Tricia said, and then couldn't resist adding, 'And she'll just have to want, won't she?' and found a childish pleasure in the shocked look on the little woman's face. No one ever spoke to her about Matron like *that*, you could almost hear her thinking; what *had* this naughty nurse done? But the pleasure to be found in the other's curiosity and disapproval was short-lived, and she pushed her way through the big doors, and holding her head as high as she could, marched purposefully towards the back path by the Path. Lab. and the way out. Tricia Oxford, leaving, finishing what she started. Let 'em all look!

'I'll take that.'

The voice startled her and she dropped the case and whirled, to see Adam Kidd ducking out from beneath the branches of the big beech tree.

'I was about to come and get you, quite honestly. I thought that for once I'd been wrong. But I wasn't. I knew you'd do this.' He picked up her case, and turned and went back under the tree and she stood stupefied for a moment before following him into its shaded protection.

'What the hell do you mean? Give me my case at once!' she cried furiously, and reached to grab it from him.

'Oh, do sit down and stop being a bore,' he said, and shoved the case under the seat that curled round the tree, and then sat himself firmly above it, stretching out his legs in front so that she would have had to physically shove him away to get at her property. And for one mad moment she contemplated doing just that, but then looked again at his squared shoulders, and the way his white coat stretched across his chest, and hesitated.

'That's better,' he said, 'Good sense prevails. At the moment. Are you going to sit down? There're a number of things to be said, and I'll get a crick in my neck if I have to sit and look up at you all the time. Sit down. I won't bite.'

'Would you kindly tell me what the hell you think you're doing? Would you kindly return to me my case, and let me go? There is nothing I have to say to you or anyone else here, and *I* can think of nothing more boring than conversation with you now or ever!'

'Really? How limited your imagination must be.' He smiled then. 'Oh, cool down, will you? You really are being remarkably obtuse. But then, you have been all the time. But you'll learn, if you'll give yourself half a chance. Come and sit down. Tricia, won't you? Please?'

And almost before she realised she had moved she found herself sitting beside him, her hands gripped on her lap, and staring at her own outstretched feet crossed on the grass before her. And there was a pause, and then he said in an unusually soft voice, 'Well?'

'Well what?'

'Are you going to tell me where you're going, what your plans are, or do I have to tell you? Choose which ever will take the least time, there's a good girl. I've been sitting here waiting for hours, I assure you, and there's work to be done, even among those despised private patients. Which shall it be?'

'You don't need to waste a moment of your precious time on me,' she snapped, childishly. 'As far as I'm concerned, you're sticking your nose in where it isn't wanted – '

'Yah, yah, yah, I'll tell teacher – ' he murmured in a soft chant and put a hand under her chin, and pulled her face round so that she had to look at him. 'Come on, you can do better than that – '

'Oh, go to hell,' she said again and pulled her head back.

'Eventually, no doubt,' he said equably. 'Oh, very well, I'll tell you then. You've been sitting there, in your little cell of a room in that – that pile of red bricks, and you've been thinking. Or trying to. Hating yourself, hating me, hating everything. And, I hope, hating that stuffed shirt boy friend of yours – '

'How *dare* you – you, you – I could – ' She almost spluttered in her rage, and he laughed at her, his eyes glinting behind his glasses.

'Oh, my dear Tricia, you're going to find out a lot about what I dare and what I don't dare. I'm a law unto myself, do you know that? If I think a thing needs saying, I say it. Hadn't you noticed? I rather thought you had. That's why I'm here now. I've got something to say, in a moment. But first things first. Where was I? Hoping you'd at last seen that your – fiancé – it suits him, that label, doesn't it? – your fiancé is not for you. Some girl somewhere is going to think the sun rises and sets in him, but not you. You never did, did you?'

'I don't know what you're talking about,' she said mulishly, but she slid her eyes sideways to look at him. And finding him looking at her with a sardonic gaze, immediately switched her eyes back to looking at her own feet.

'Oh, yes, you do. You'd be surprised how much I know about you. Know how you think, how you feel. I know how desperately frightened you are – '

She looked at him very directly at that. 'Frightened? Me? What of? Of course I'm not – '

'Yes, you are,' he said gently. 'Very frightened. Frightened of being lonely. Frightened of insecurity. Of making decisions. Of leaving one way of life behind you so that you can take up the next load and enjoy it as it should be enjoyed.'

'Look, you can go trying your – your parlour psychology on someone else. I don't know where the hell you think you got your knowledge of me from, but it's all surmise – pure surmise.'

He laughed then. 'But it isn't wrong surmise, is it? That's why you're still here. If I weren't on the right track, you'd have shrieked blue murder long since and got your case back and gone marching off. Of course I'm right. I've got to be. I've been watching you and learning about you for some time now – '

'Only a few weeks!'

'Yes. Only a few weeks. Long enough.'

'Anyway, I don't see – '

' – what it has to do with me. We'll come to that. Now, let me complete my – analysis. You sat there this afternoon, and you decided that since all is so hateful, you'd just quit. Just like that. You wouldn't wait about to be nagged and bullied – you'd had enough, that hateful Private Wing, that hateful Sister Cleland, that hateful man Kidd – '

'You have a point there!'

'I reckoned it'd take you about an hour to get to the stage of actually doing it. Well, I was wrong. It took you almost – ' he glanced at his watch. 'Dear me. Three hours. There's even more character to you than I guessed. That's nice to know – '

'You – I – you are the most *impossible* – ' she started to say, but he laughed, and said, 'I know. Maddening, isn't it? Someone else being so right? Now, I've told you – and you've got to tell me something. Why? Why in the name of good sense did you choose to behave like that with Philip Bartlett when you must have *known* someone'd march in as it happens we did? Were you just being stupid? Or what?'

'It's no concern of yours,' she snapped.

'I don't agree – but you can say so if you choose, so now tell me. He *is* my patient, you know. Isn't that a legitimate reason for me to show interest?'

There was a long silence, and then she said flatly, 'I was sorry for him. So sorry for him. Poor wretched – it was a game he played. It made him feel better. Dying men don't flirt with girls, only healthy men do that. So he had to pretend to have this whole thing going with me' she shrugged. 'And I played the game with him. That was why.'

He leaned back against the seat then, and she was startled at the way he suddenly sighed sharply, and she turned and looked at him. He had his eyes closed, and his lower lip caught between his teeth, and a half smile on his face. And then he opened his eyes and caught her gaze and said softly, 'Now, that I didn't know. That I thought was something you'd not learn for a long time yet.'

'Learn? What?'

'The – dynamics of the dying state. That sounds pompous, I know, but it describes what I mean. How people react to such desperate facts of life as love and birth and death and partings, they are the dynamics of human experience and they matter very much. And you've learned, somewhere, how to help a dying man come to some sort of terms with the fact of his own death. I did you an injustice. For a horrible while back there – I was afraid. I was afraid it was for real – that you were involved with him on a personal level. Or that you were perhaps quite different to the way I had assessed you, and were just behaving – ' he shrugged. 'Stupidly. Unthinking. I'm glad you weren't – '

'You're *glad*? You were? Horrible? What are you talking about?' She couldn't look at him, but she was very aware of his bulk on the seat beside her, and grasped her gloved hands together even more tightly, knowing that they would shake if she relaxed for one moment. 'What do you care about my involvements, either with Mr Bartlett or my – my fiancé? As far as I can see you've got plenty of personal involvements of your own. Including Sister Cleland – ' she added spitefully, and then could have bitten her own tongue.

He chuckled softly. 'Well, well. That gets under your skin, does it, the Cleland thing? Interesting. And what about Maxine Bartlett?'

She shrugged, still not looking at him. 'None of my concern.'

'Really? You should have seen the expression on your face the other evening, when you came into the visitor's waiting room – '

'I was *disgusted*.' She snapped it out, furiously. 'Disgusted with her, with you – '

'And with your own reaction. You were so eaten with – jealousy, for want of a better word, that you – '

'Jealous! How dare you suggest such a thing! You can go necking with every blasted patient and visitor that the third floor gets for all I care, you – you – '

'Oh, let's not fence, Tricia, for God's sake. You love me. You have done this past month or more, and you don't know what the hell to do about it. Can't even face up to it. Unless, this afternoon, you found out? Sitting there, all that time? Is that why you took so long to make your decision to go?'

His voice was very soft now, and she sat frozen into immobility, but her pulse thumped in her ears so loudly she felt the whole world must be able to hear it, and there was a deep cramping pain in her chest that hampered her breathing and made her feel almost ill. But somewhere, deep inside her, under the thumping pulse and the breathlessness the little voice that inhabited the most secret corner of her mind was singing, and shouting, and crying out in a great pæan of joy.

But she kept her eyes resolutely on her feet, and managed to say, 'I saw you – of course I did. And I – wondered – '

'Do you think you have a monopoly on understanding, you silly, silly creature? Do you think that only nurses develop an instinctive way of helping people – patients and their relatives – over the hurdles of living? Those two, Maxine and Philip Bartlett – they have a very special relationship. Based on love and care and habit, and companionship and friendship, and garnished with games, all the years they've been together, garnished with games. She knows he's dying, and she's mourning in desperate grief already. But she's playing the game his way, too. Pretending to flirt with me, when I'm in the room with them, because that's how it's always been when they've met interesting people. And by going on with her flirting game, she's trying to convince her Philip that all is well, that he's going to get better, because if he were dying, she wouldn't play the game any more, would she? And he – seeing what she was doing, and loving her as he does, he played the same game for her benefit. Both of them desperately acting for each other, doing all they can to get each other through their private hell. As for me – that evening, she needed someone to let her stop acting, someone to let her cry out her grief and her terror and her knowledge of loss. That's what I gave her. A shoulder to cry on, a person against whom she could spit her rage at what was being done to her, a person who'd let her come creeping into his arms for comfort afterwards. A father, if you like. That's what you saw. And were jealous. You were, weren't you?'

She said nothing for a moment, her mind twisting and whirling with confusion, and then she heard his voice sharpen as he again took her chin in his hand and made her turn her head towards him.

'I've got to be right, Tricia. Got to be. Because God help me, I couldn't be less personally involved with Maxine Bartlett or poor yearning Sister Cleland, on account of I'm involved, up to my ears, with a silly, gangling, long-legged, immature, incredibly sexy, student nurse.' He looked at her for another long moment, and then said, his voice infinitely tender. 'You silly, stupid, idiot. Life with you is going to drive me mad – but what can I do about it?'

And then he was kissing her, and she felt herself drowning in a wash of feeling she had never before known, and was almost shocked at the intensity of it, frightened by it, and tried to pull back, but he held her closer and enveloped her in his own strength and she lost her fear, and clung to him, and let the voice inside her sing its wild joy in her ears.

They sat there for a long time after that, saying nothing, and holding on to each other's hands, and he let one finger tip trace the pattern of their interlocked hands, and smiled at her, and she smiled tremulously back.

'You'll have a lousy life with me, you know that?' he said at length. 'I'm a selfish bastard in many ways. It's got to be my way. Not yours. Can you take it?'

'I know. I can take it.'

'I'll make you want to kill me sometimes, we'll probably fight like cats.'

She smiled secretly to herself, contemplating the joys of a life spent fighting like cats with Adam. 'I know.'

'You'll hate me often.'

'I know. I often have already.'

'Your friends will say you're mad.'

'One won't.'

'The funny little New Zealander? No, perhaps not. That's a girl of parts. I like her.'

'I'm glad. She needs liking.'

'We all do. Tricia – ' he let go of her hand, and stood up, and pulled her to her feet, and stood very close to her, looking at her face, inch by inch, as though he were taking an inventory. 'I love you. Try to remember that, will you? I didn't want to. I tried not to, but there – '

She smiled at him, very serenely, suddenly feeling very old, very wise. 'Poor Adam. I know. I know just what you mean. I've tried not to, as well. Very hard. Loving you is going to be painful. Being loved by you is going to be worse, in some ways. I know. But that's the way it's got to be, isn't it?'

He stood back from her, still holding her hands, and peered at her in the deepening afternoon light. And then nodded.

'Yes. You understand. All right. No more problems. All you've got to do now is go and see Matron. Tell her the why's and wherefore's of this afternoon's episode with Bartlett, just as you told me. She's – quite a wise old bird, that one. It'll be all right. Go on – '

'No – please, Adam. No, I can't – I've got to leave, you must see that – '

'And later, tonight, you're to contact David and tell him. It will hurt like hell, and he'll be very difficult, but you'll do it.'

'No – '

'Tricia! Let's not start the fighting yet, for God's sake! It's been a long day, damn it. Do as you're told, will you? You know you'll have to eventually, so let's save all our energies and do it now, all right?'

'But – '

'Because that's the way it's got to be, isn't it? Now and always?'

She took a deep breath then, and put her head back, and stood, her eyes tight closed, feeling the cool evening air against her hot cheeks. And then nodded submissively.

'Very well, Adam. If that's the way it's got to be.'